C.H.I.P.S. IN CHINA

JIM WILLIAMS

Vancouver, BC

C.H.I.P.S. in China

First published in Canada in 2011
Published by Bing Long Books

This is a work of fiction. Names, characters, places, and incidents are the products of the author's imagination or are used fictitiously. Any resemblance to actual events, locales, or persons, living or dead, is entirely coincidental.

info@binglongbooks.com

ISBN: 978-0986776113

Library and Archives Canada Cataloguing in Publication

Williams, Jim, 1962-

C.H.I.P.S. in China / Jim Williams.

ISBN 978-0-9867761-1-3

I. Title.

PS8623.O53455C55 2011 C813'.6 C2011-903407-7

Printed in the People's Republic of China

C.H.I.P.S. IN CHINA

CHAPTER CONTENTS

For Carric Williams,

you are the love of my life.

You are my dearest jo.

One
Flight to the Future

The plane's acceleration pushed Hudson Smith back into his seat. He loved this moment when the g-forces took over, and he knew that the pilot was committed to getting airborne. Jo didn't. She knew that this was the moment of most crashes, and she gripped his arm accordingly.

"Hudson, please hold my hand," she gasped.

Her palms were sweaty, Smith realized, and he caressed her forearm to reassure her. Outside in the distance he saw the two distinctive red stripes bookending a large maple leaf on a solitary pole on the edge of YVR—Vancouver International Airport. The oasis of nationalism was a reminder to foreign travellers that though it may seem like they were in the United States, they were in Canada. Behind the flag was a pair of mallards showing the way as they headed out west across the water to Vancouver Island. The Strait of Georgia was in the process of being renamed The Salish Sea, and Smith knew it wouldn't matter to the wildfowl, whales, or the sockeye what the waterway was called. It would still remain the favoured transportation route along this rugged coast for men and animals alike. West was his direction as well. C.H.I.P.S. in China was their destination. When his daughter found out he was going to teach English at the Canadian Harmonious International Peace School, she had said, "Dad isn't it amazing that you have to fly west to go to the Far East?" Yes, he thought, here I go west to go east.

Smith rejoiced at the prospect of flying. He often recited "High Flight," a sonnet by John Gillespie Magee Jr., at this moment of take-off. He had learned it as a grade nine student in his guidance class many years ago. The US President, Ronald Reagan, had quoted from it when the Challenger disaster occurred, and he wondered if David Frum, Reagan's Canadian-born and educated speech writer had been taught it and remembered it for the soberest moment in US space history. There were many times when he had thought about pursuing his pilot's licence, but finances were an obstacle too difficult to overcome. Today he would lose a day of his life, but next year coming back to Canada he would get to live the same day twice.

Lift off. Ah, it was a miracle that man could fly. Icarus came to mind. Foolish boy. What would the ancient Greeks say of men and their marvellous flying machines? He stared at the mountain-capped city as it shrunk below him with its waters hemming it in on three sides. The blue Pacific (though here it was often gray as it reflected the moisture laden clouds), the green forested mountains (though the North Shore was decidedly less green than it was when he first flew to Toronto at the age of fifteen as the city slowly conquered the hemlocks and firs), and the city of glass (as architects had nicknamed Vancouver), was truly beautiful. Young and clean, its vigorous people were smug and looked to the Orient, not to Europe as the rest of the country did. A cosmopolitan place. Fusion cuisine. East meets West. Hongcouver. The Port City. The Terminus. The Pacific Rim City. Northern Cascadia. The gateway to a country with a future, a country with resources the rest of the world dreamed of, a dream that was giving rise to a metropolis that would be in the same category as London, Paris, Tokyo, and Beijing. This was the desire of Vancouverites, and Smith admired its politicians' moxy, its citizens' pizzazz, and their outlook for the future.

"Goodbye, Canada. Goodbye, Vancouver. I'll miss you. Let the adventure begin."

"Remember the green Hudson. China is not green like Canada."

Inside the Boeing jet he recounted the colleagues he had just met. There was Tony Vander Kwaak and his wife Debbie and their kids Ruthie and Josh, Randy and Suzie McMann, Relic–Hudson wasn't sure of Relic's real name, he had said, "Call me Relic. Everyone does."

"Jo, who is that couple in the seats two rows in front of us?"

Jo craned her neck, and said, "That's Matt and June Peterson. They're freshly graduated from UBC-O."

In the row across from the Peterson's were Eric Peterson, his new boss, and Sarah Whippet, one of the vee-pees. Jo took out a staff list and they read down the column: Rich Bannerman.

"Who's he?" Hudson asked.

"The old guy."

"Ah, I see. Who's Dan Best?"

"He was the Math Department Head with the cutie on his arm. Amanda Johnson. She had the neon pink blouse and the petite nose."

Jo's finger dropped over Kaitlin Coyote. "She's a good friend. She had the goalie stick at the check-in counter when we arrived."

"Oh, her. I pictured her to be shorter from what you told me."

She continued, "You met the other couple: Craig and Katie Dickens? He's your Department Head. Katie and Craig have the three kids."

Hudson nodded his head vaguely recalling his superior. He scanned the seats nearby to spot the Dickens' family, but they must have been in the rear of the fuselage.

They read the list with the skill that teachers have after having taken attendance for years. Cathy Friesen, had been wearing blue, and Jasminder Gill was wearing red. Don and Connie Hawk, Amanda Johnson–Dan Best's partner. There was the athletic Gerri LeMaire, and Heather LeRoy, who could be fun, while Terri Patrick came from a long line of hockey royalty. Jo's catechism continued as she went through the others on the flight: Jill Redbourne–a spunky Brit, and Tom Spence, Karen Song–a Korean-Canadian, and Bobby Wilson who was a bit heavier than the other men. These people would be his new friends, confidants, and co-workers during his time in China.

China was a mysterious giant. Trudeau had gone there in the early 1970's...was it before Nixon, or after? he pondered. He decided to look it up on Google when they landed. Panda bears, the Great Wall, Mao, Communism, ping pong, dragons, chopsticks, factories, *The Last Emperor,* and Kung Fu. Did he know anything else about the Middle Kingdom?

"Jo, what do you love most about China?"

Without a hesitation Jo replied, "The people."

Smith unconsciously touched the Canadian flag pin that his daughter had given him, as he considered where he would put the Canadian flag that his oldest son had given him and the British Columbian flag that his younger son gave him. "Make sure people know you're not American, Dad."

The stewardess offered him water, and he asked for a second bottle, as he knew that air travel frequently dehydrated him. His children had meant well, but in his journeys he hadn't met an American he didn't like. Urban legends abounded about wearing the maple leaf in Europe, but was wearing the red leaf necessary in Asia? His backpack had a large maple leaf on it–a gift from Jo's mother. Perhaps he would put the flags in his classroom at the Canadian Harmonious International Peace School in Baishantan near Shanwan in Northeast China. A bit of the homeland in his workplace might be good; after all, he would probably spend more time in the classroom than in any other. How would his Chinese students receive that? The overt nationalism that China had demonstrated to the world during the Beijing Olympics had surprised him. Would it be an insult? Would it offend? He would ask Relic who had been there since the inception of the school. He would know. Relic was the unofficial school historian.

In the waiting room at Gate B22 there had been two types of travellers: teachers, and Chinese nationals. Smith introduced himself to many of his compatriots and others sought him out. They were a lively, tanned group as summer neared its end, and, with a few exceptions amongst the contingent, very young. Why, they look younger than my own children, he thought.

Relic was an exception. "Probably in his early 40's," Jo had whispered to him. Hudson had given her a puzzled look. "Laugh lines, crow's feet, that's how I know," she had answered his unasked question. Relic gathered a crowd the way slick salesman would've in the 19th century. He was living history. Smith hadn't wanted to leave his luggage, so sometimes he could only hear one side of the conversation between rookies and the undisputed veteran.

"Yep, I've been there since the beginning. Served under ten different principals."

June Peterson had asked, "Do you like it there?"

"I love it there."

A woman in blue had quickly asked, "Why?" almost as if she had been challenging him.

Relic had taken the attitude in stride. The new teachers were always a bit nervous, and usually it was their first trip abroad. "Why? Good kids, cheap living, hockey in winter, safe. You'll love the people."

The oldest man there, Rich Bannerman, had asked, "Are the apartments suitable?"

"The teacher's apartments are fine, but I live off campus now with my family."

Another question had come quickly from June Peterson, "Do they like it there?"

Nonplussed, Relic had reassured her, "Yep, they love it too."

A heavier set fellow wearing a Saskatchewan Roughriders jersey had asked, "Is there any problem with the food?"

"No, the food is good. The water is not; although, there was a family a couple of years back that found out their kids had been drinking the water from the bathroom taps because the kids thought only the kitchen taps had the bad water. They survived."

A British accent, louder than a normal speaking tone had queried Relic. "What is the climate like at present?" The twinkle in her eye showed her spunk.

Hudson had asked Jo, "Who's she?"

"I think that is Jill Redbourne. She's from the Queen Charlotte Islands, but originally she was from Devonshire, England. I think she's going deaf. She's travelled everywhere.

Relic had answered the question for the tenth consecutive year, "It'll be hot when we get there, but let me assure you, you won't remember Baishantan as a warm, green place."

Hudson had glanced at Jo, and she had leaned in and whispered to him, "I warned you it would be cold."

The woman in the blue pants and top had then asked if there had been any surprises for Relic's kids.

"My kids? Yeah, there were some surprises when they were very little. There still weren't very many 'wai guo ren'—Foreign people—in Shawan at the time so strangers were constantly touching my daughter's platinum blonde hair. People would come up and take a photo of her, but the staring bothered her the most."

"Is it still like that?"

"No, not anymore. She just stares back. Most people realise they've crossed a line."

The teachers gathered in closer, and Don Hawk had asked about transportation.

"We bought a car, but I used to ride a motorbike. They're cheap. About $400 Canadian. No, no licence or insurance needed, or helmets either. The driving habits take some getting used to. Drivers will turn left even though traffic is coming. Don't be surprised to see cars veer into the other lane. Speed is not the issue. Lines are. Red lights are only suggestions."

Hudson had not heard the next questions tossed Relic's way, but Relic shook his head, "No...no...no. The police are different. Attitudes are a little bit more relaxed. Bribes? I wouldn't."

The Saskatchewan football fan had asked, "Where's the best place to go for a night on the town?"

"There was a time when I knew, but I don't party like that anymore. I'm a family man."

"Don't tell me you're a whipped man," the Saskatchewan fan had moaned.

Yeah, but there are benefits too."

Stretching his legs out underneath the seat in front of him, Smith took an instant liking to the people around him. Weren't they all on the same journey? Weren't they all his countrymen? Maybe the group didn't realise it yet, but he did. They would need each other this year. The group divided into those starting their careers and those ending theirs. Smith was an oddball. He was in the midst of his career. After twenty-three years of teaching, Hudson Smith was pursuing a long-term dream of teaching in a foreign setting. His ex-wife had left him just days before a three-week Maui vacation to celebrate their twenty-fifth anniversary, and only a day after he had secretly bought her a new ring that he planned to use as they renewed their vows. Little did he know that she was planning vows with someone else. Suicide had crossed his mind, and the depression of rejection and the greedy demands during the divorce negotiations soured him; however, he realised that now would be a good time to rebuild his life. He had lost forty pounds, had recently started sleeping through the night again, and wanted to live life to the fullest. China promised a new beginning. His new burgeoning relationship with Jo was blossoming into a long-term commitment, and he was thinking of asking her to marry him.

McLean's had reported that China's amazing progress from backward nation to progressive modern superpower was due to economics. Years ago, but not that far back, all the produce belonged to the community. However, in the 1980s some cooperatives figured out that they could meet the quota and sell the extra food produced to other communities, once their own needs had been met. The farmers had led the way by figuring out ways to go around the controlled economy and sell off surplus crops for profit. Profits led to investments, investments led to jobs, jobs led to competition, which led to better production methods, and finally to disposable income. Where once bicycles and donkey carts ruled the roads, now luxury cars and cube trucks moved China's people and goods. Movement created the money as the surplus food found new markets in the cities. The Communist Party called it socialism with Chinese Characteristics. What it really was was capitalism.

Smith had read everything he could about the awakening

Dragon, and still he knew he was in for a shock. Helpless in daily commerce, he would be an illiterate, and he would have to rely on survival strategies he had seen in the English as a Second Language students in his classes. Ask, sometimes nod your head, pretend you understand, point, and smile. These methods disguised the anxiety and helped kids to cope in the new cultural setting. Now it was his turn. He smiled. Good teachers learn from their students too.

China's meteoric rise wasn't really all that meteoric. It had taken twenty years since Deng Xiao Peng had reformed the economy. In one article Hudson had read the premise was that Deng hadn't had any choice because the peasants were already doing what the reforms changed in law. The regime merely recognized the de facto situation. Pictures he had seen showed a China that was urban. Bullet and Maglev trains speeding across the landscape at speeds of over 400 kilometres an hour were being built in a variety of locations. Chic brand name stores like Versace, Gucci, and Rolex were in Beijing, Shanghai, Guangzhou, Harbin, Wuhan, and Shanwan. The cyber world of Apple with its various "iProducts" were replacing the markets with their hundreds of stalls, and the fried burgers and fries of McDonalds were seen as foods to enhance your status because the cost of these western foods was substantial compared to local foods. Visionaries created an architectural legacy with tall skyscrapers, and uniquely shaped buildings. Essentially, the functional art helped China to emerge onto the world stage.

Relic's voice had carried over the waiting room chairs. "Weird stuff happens every day. Take pictures early because after a while you don't notice it anymore. Things like the women with their pink scarves over their head as they wear masks, or how the women wear pyjamas in town while they shop, or the fireworks."

June's husband, Matt Peterson had asked him simultaneously, "Why?"

"Why? Well, Chinese women don't like to have dark skin–so they cover up. The pyjamas? Comfort, I guess."

"I know that the Chinese invented fireworks, but what's different about Chinese fireworks?"

"The fireworks?" The veteran had thought a moment, "There are so many reasons, but they are usually just white shots straight up, but not very high. The first time I heard them, I thought someone was shooting a gun."

Jasminder Gill had been silent up to this point, but the word gun reminded her of the stories her grandfather had told her about the war in the Kashmir between India and Pakistan in the 1970s. "Is there any racism, trouble, or violence at C.H.I.P.S.?"

"Last year there was trouble on campus as some Chinese boys picked on and then beat up a Korean boy. To resolve the issue, the Chinese boys had to pay for doves that would be released at the next flag ceremony. They were not kicked out. We're a business first–school second."

Matt and June had asked again at the same time, "Is it true that flag ceremony happens every week?"

Everyone had smiled at the young couple as Relic scratched his ear, "Yes, flag happens every Monday 10:25 sharp."

"What were the doves for?" asked Bannerman who had sat down to rest. He was wiping his face with a clean white, starched handkerchief.

"The doves were a symbol of the new peace."

"The boxes of birds they brought in were not doves–they were common Hill Pigeons," Tony Vander Kwaak, an enthusiastic birder, had interrupted. His wife, Debbie, had held their son Josh on her hip while he had twisted her hair as though he was learning to tie shoe laces. Ruthie, their oldest, at five, held Tony's right hand and tried to swing from it while he adjusted his Vancouver Canucks baseball cap with his left hand.

"Yep, they weren't doves," Relic had agreed, and he had continued. "First off the emcee couldn't pronounce doves. He kept saying doe–ves. The other students brought the boxes forward. I think there were at least five boxes each containing twenty birds. The birds had been purchased three days earlier and had been kept in the boxes until the great moment arrived. Well, the plan was to open the lids at the same time, and like you see at the Olympics, the birds would fly free. A great picture really," Relic had paused here in the story to take a sip of his Coke. "Imagine all those birds flying off into the morning sun, but they didn't. When the emcee said, 'Release the doe–ves', the lids were opened, the birds flew out and flew right at the kids. They were like World War II kamikazes except they dropped three days of pent up crap all over the students and staff. You should have seen everyone try to take cover. There was one casualty as Chairman Meow, the school cat, caught one of the pigeons as the crate was opened and had a light snack." The newcomers roared their approval of the tale, and several second-year teachers agreed that it had been quite a spectacle.

Jo had smiled at the memory and reached up to massage Hudson's neck. Relic had blurted, "Oh, hey, there was one more thing about that flag ceremony. The school often unveils huge signs to encourage the students and staff. That day the new sign said, "PEACE, CHERISHING YOUR FUTURE."

The stewardess had announced that their flight was now boarding, and the Canadians had picked up their carry-ons and lined up for their flight to the future–a future at C.H.I.P.S. in China.

Two
My Mind's Been on the Blink

The jet lag had not yet worn off. Hudson Smith was searching his dress pants' pockets for the daily agenda that he had used for the last week. The adjustment from Pacific Daylight to Beijing time was not complete for this Canadian teacher at his new gig at the Canadian Harmonious International Peace School in China. Sweat ran down his forehead, behind his ears, and through his goatee as he left the classroom on the fourth floor of C.H.I.P.S.. Military marching music blasted out of the tinny speakers.

Tom Simon came out of his class and said, "It's flag ceremony, Hudson."

"Right, I forgot."

The sunlight streaked the dim halls, the humid air was thick with the aromas of teenage boys, dingy metal lockers opened and shut, and the Chinese boys' faces were glowing with the sweat that they also felt as no breeze blessed the entire region. Since the Narita Airport in Tokyo, he had been suffering from the heat, and had been profusely dripping as his internal cooling system tried to keep him alive. His shirt stuck to his back, and he mopped his brow with a hand towel while he moved with the herd down the hallway, straining to hear a familiar word amongst the babble trying to compete with the military marching music.

He dropped his laptop off in the office and joined the mob of boys and harried staff pouring themselves down the stairwell. There were other glistening faces, and Smith realized that the heat had a toll on his students as well. He hoped this break outside would refresh them all. Mondays were special because after the first period there was the flag ceremony. Flag symbolically opened the week at the school, and served as another technique to instil the masses with Chinese propaganda. Smith smirked as he thought of how he was glad he did not have to be part of such patriotic silliness back in Canada. Here he felt the Chinese and the Americans shared the same nationalistic flaw. Pledges of allegiance, inspiring speeches, national anthems–he was glad he was above all that. He was Canadian.

Hudson Smith smiled as he saw the boys, who now had distinctive faces, greeting him as he walked along with them. His short-sleeved shirt clung to his back as the sweat tried in vain to cool him off. Some of the boys had rolled up their shirt so their belly protruded as a way to cool down. Several were fanning themselves. The buildings surrounding the compound trapped the heat and the basketball courts became like an oven.

Really Hudson was part of a human migration that was every bit as cyclical as the great salmon spawning which occurred in his home province of British Columbia. "Every Monday?" he had asked Dickens, and he remembered the shudder in his core when he was told–"Every Monday." It was something that his girlfriend, Jo Loch, a four-year veteran of C.H.I.P.S. and with six-years' experience in China, had not told him during their many Skype conversations. However, she had told him so much that when he arrived, he felt familiar with the place and with the people.

The third flight of stairs down students bumped him into the wall, and the new white wash thinned to water during the summer repainting transferred to his new dress shirt. Not again, he thought, but the crowds of boys pushed and jostled their way past him without a glance, just like the crowds of adults on the local light rail system affectionately known as the "*Qing Gui*" pronounced Ching Gway. Each floor added to the flow of bodies like each stream in central British Columbia added to the Fraser River. The uniforms cascaded past him on the stairwell built to handle two bodies wide, but now it was bulging with four. As he stepped outside, yellow Gobi Desert dust blasted his eyes and stuck to his sweaty neck and hands.

He strolled through the homeroom lines, and stopped at Jack's side. All the Chinese boys took on English names at C.H.I.P.S.. The thought was that this was one way to help the boys adjust when they studied in North America. Secretly, Smith thought it was because the Chinese didn't think that the Canadians could wrap their tongues around their names. One boy had told him that Canadians were so dumb they didn't understand that family names should come first to show honour to one's ancestors. Truly the first few weeks had been trying as he had tried to say the boys' Chinese names, but now, despite the continued mispronunciations, he was having some success. Rote repetition helped. Jack had a necklace on. This was taboo according to the school. Uniforms were to be uniform. How could one learn if one was worried about fashion? The school policy had to be enforced. Smith knew that. He asked Jack to step to the side where counsellors would escort him back to the dorm and get him properly dressed, and he continued up the line greeting each boy by name as he made his way to the back where the Canadian teachers stood. The lines stretched on and on. Over 1,800 of China's best now stood waiting, and their bored faces glistened while they patiently endured both the temperature and the messages.

Hudson took his place beside The Birdman, and he took a drink from his water bottle. Tony Vander Kwaak, The Birdman, was a fanatical ornithologist. He had been in China for half a dozen years and was about to publish a guidebook on birds in the Baishantan area. Smith liked him. Birds had long been an interest for Smith, and back in Canada he had had a birdbath that on a day like today would be a haven for many varieties. Hudson could name some fifty different species, but his new friend was an expert. Birdman, the staff called him, spoke with the passion of a boy collecting hockey cards, and he was enthusiastic about the new Chinese initiatives to save habitat.

As he wiped the sweat from his brows with the back of his hands, and scanned the sea of black hair in front of him, Smith noticed a common magpie on its usual roost above the old building housing the library to their left. The newcomer considered pointing it out to Tony, but then he remembered how Tony dismissed such common avian sightings. Truly the magpies were everywhere, and once the autumn leaves had fallen, it seemed like their unruly large stick nests were in every tenth tree. The bird's alcove shaded it from the pitiless sun, and provided it with a spot to scout out food dropped by the boys. Directly beneath the bird he saw old Chairman Meow, the school's rat-catching cat, looking up and wistfully hoping the bird would come down for a meal while a swirl of gritty dust and plastic wrappers blew past him.

On the other side of Tony were Relic and Dickens. Relic, Hudson found, continued to be the source of answers for all questions about expats living in China. Each year Relic thought about going back to Canada, and each year he discovered new reasons to stay. His Mandarin was impeccable; although, it had the heavy slurring which was characteristic of the *Dong Bei ren*, or North

East people, and students from Beijing smiled a polite smile and told him that they had trouble understanding such Baishantan words. Bai Shan Tan, or White Mountain Beach, was the small farming village which in the time Relic had been here had become a thriving small city of twenty-five thousand with the plan to make it a city of half a million in a decade. Yes, Relic had seen change, and in personal ways as well. He had added a wife, who graciously indulged his desire to live here, though her heart was pining for Kits Beach in their native Vancouver, a daughter and son, the Canadian ideal of the perfect family (although, it was double the size of a Chinese family), and enough wisdom to keep Confucius happy as he pursued truth and understanding in this land across the sea.

Dickens, too, had changed in his stint here. He was a man who loved community, and he brought this concept to his classes. By the end of each school year, his students knew they were part of a family. Dickens's warmth, and genuine care brought the students into a relationship that he and they would never forget. Former students made trips to see him, they filled his inbox with messages, and there were some who would Skype him from across the globe. His former students knew he was a busy man, but Dickens always had time for them. Here at C.H.I.P.S. he had worked hard to create a vibrant community in and out of his classrooms with the students and staff who typically left after one or two years. Despite the turnover, Dickens continued to make life in China interesting for the Canadian teachers by instituting various events, hosting parties, and running sports clubs. The Chinese Crokinole Championships, the Shanwan International Short Film Festival, the Shanwan Expat Fashion Show, and the Baishantan Snow Tigers—an expat hockey team all owed their genesis to Dickens.

Together, Relic and Dickens were the heart and lungs of the school. Hudson realized this by the time the Japan Airlines flight had landed in Shanwan. Every newcomer had their eyes looking out the windows as the Boeing 747 had taxied up to the cold Stalinesque building. Relic said, "Welcome to China." Hudson Smith, taking another swig from his bottle, noted that these two men would become important to him, and he wanted to get to know them better.

Reverting his gaze back towards the school and the centrepiece three flagpoles, Smith saw the six students wearing white gloves in addition to their thin blazers. They must be cooking, he thought. One of two boys who came forward took the microphone from Mr. Ge, the Chinese sponsor of the Zhou En Lai class, the school's honour class named after the long-time communist leader, and spoke, "Welcome to flag raising ceremony of Canadian Harmonious International Peace School." Two new boys left the group and brought out the red flag of China. "Raising flag of People's Republic of China, and sing national anthem together" the host of the ritual shrilled.

Smith winced. "Use the pronoun," he muttered under his breath. The two boys connected the flag to the centre pole and one of them with a flourish unfurled the red cloth with a sweep of his arm except as the other started to raise the patriotic banner the free corner got stuck in the ring holding the attached corner. As the Chinese national anthem blared from speakers that crackled and hissed, each eye focussed on the flag that looked like a wounded bird spiralling to its death. The 1,800 teenage boys sang the militaristic words as the flag continued its flight. Each pull of the cord bound the flag more tightly to the pole, but no one moved to correct the problem as it would bring dishonour to the boys.

Hudson looked to Relic and Dickens to question them, but they were distracted–Man Meow was swatting at a fly. Smith's head swung back to the podium, and realized that now the boys were looking almost everywhere but at the front.

The second group of boys then moved to the flagpole, and Smith could see, brought out a Canadian flag. "Raising flag of Canada, and sing national anthem of Canada," instructed the voice while Smith again winced.

"Should we sing?" Hudson asked the vets.

"If you want," Relic's voice trailed away.

The boy threw out the red maple leaf, and as the anthem's prelude completed, Smith joined the singing with a few other teachers. No boys sang. The humid air was heavy in his lungs. This flag with its two vertical red stripes looked like a starched sheet as a gust of wind above them that offered no respite from the heat on the ground, held it perfectly taut. The maple leaf looked powerful as it slid up the pole beside the wounded red duck in the centre. The pride in his heart swelled as he thought, you may be the 'workshop of the world,' but Canada looks like the tiger right now.

He took his water bottle and drained the remaining liquid. Relic whispered to him, "You'll need to buy more of those. Your shirt is drenched. Come to my office after. I'll give you a dry shirt. I keep a couple of extra around for days like this."

The same process was repeated. The school flag and anthem had their turn, and once again the wind, just a few meters above them, bedevilled the boys' efforts as the flag folded on itself and limped up the pole. The host introduced the final two boys who had remained to the right of the flagpoles, and they came forward to deliver two speeches–one in English, and the other in Mandarin. These were brief didactic inspirational secular homilies that spoke about duty, harmony, and obedience. The speeches were like the motherhood speeches of politicians back home, Smith thought feeling the sweat now actually dripping down his chin, as the boy opened with how each student should make his country, his parents, and his teachers proud by studying hard and doing the best work possible. As the lilting English continued and the r's and l's found new places to reside, the dignitaries on the left hand side caught his attention. There were seven adults who watched the proceedings from up front, and they were the face of the company.

Closest to the flagpoles was the Headmaster–Mr. Wang (it rhymed with gong). Mr. Wang, whose head was beneath the tall Chinese woman and the Canadians to his left, had developed the school from one class and had a vision to bring C.H.I.P.S. schools to every province in China. It was an ambitious goal, but his Memorandums of Understandings with the BC government had given him great credibility with Chinese parents looking for ways to obtain entrance at prestigious North American universities for their sons. The University of Toronto, the University of Waterloo, and the University of British Columbia headed the list. They were the goal. Studying abroad was a huge status symbol, and though expensive, was worth the sacrifices that both parents and grandparents would make. The prestige of a son studying abroad was good for business, as it would let the customer know that the family was intelligent and rich. Wang surveyed this portion of his empire with a Confucian stoicism, while his reddish cheeks betrayed his drinking habits.

"Who's the woman beside Wang? She's cute."

"She's dangerous. Stay away from her. Lots of power and she strikes quickly."

Beside Wang was the lithe and pretty assistant Miss Xiaoqing Chen. Though she looked like a model, she was a cutthroat when it came to personnel decisions. Last spring, she had chastised a Chinese teacher for using too much toilet paper, and lowered her salary due to the waste. How she discovered such waste Smith did not want to know.

Even Canadian teachers could not escape her wrath as Karen Song, an English teacher, found out when she had hosted a book sale. Tearfully she had told Smith about Chen's scolding, "No money is to be used on campus! All transactions must use the school debit cards. Why, how do we know that teachers won't just fly to Bali with all that cash?" That was rich, Smith thought. The few hundred *kuai* brought in was all sent to the book company. The school actually benefitted by receiving book credits for sales generated. Control. Control was what mattered to her.

The high-necked sweater, worn despite the heat, accentuated her thin figure. Her soft pink tongue darted between her thin lips, and her cold eyes matched the upcoming winter's frozen weather, but once spring arrived she would remain icy. Xiaoqing's shiny leather boots almost touched her knees and oozed power. The hard heels echoed and sounded like a machine gun rattling its fire through the halls wherever she went, and to the teachers and other staff, they were just as menacing.

Further down the pecking order was the Canadian principal, Eric Peterson. Peterson had been a long-time successful administrator who at the end of his career was looking for an adventure, a new challenge, and something unique. He found all these in China. The only problem he felt was that he was quite powerless. Every decision had to be run past the Head who owned the company. This was usually first filtered through Miss Chen whose only mission was saving the business money. Business. Yes, the word galled him as he squinted into the sun and thought of how the education of teens had become subservient to making a profit.

Quality education, mixing the East and the West, a new way of educating the future leaders of China were the slogans used as bait to entice him across the Pacific, but soon after arriving Eric had realized that he was a puppet, and he was depressed with how the job description had failed to match reality.

"Eric's the guy we all feel pity for," Dickens told Smith. He has signing authority, but it's limited to pens and other small supplies. "Anything over a hundred *kuai*, and he has to ask Chen."

Beside Eric Peterson was the Chinese principal who ran the Chinese portion of the school as students graduated not only with a BC Dogwood diploma, but also a Liaoning Provincial High School Certificate. Mr. Zhou was a dedicated company man who had risen through the ranks of C.H.I.P.S. schools in other provinces first as a math instructor, then academic advisor, vice-principal, and now here he was some ten years later as principal of the flagship school. He was publicly grateful to Wang, but privately irked at how these Wai gou ren (as foreigners were known) were paid so much more for doing the same work. He smiled and behind the smile looked for ways to apply Sun Tzu's *The Art of War* against his Canadian counterparts.

At the end of the line beyond Principal Zhou were the two Canadian vice-principals, Sarah Whippet and John McAdams. They stood close together which wouldn't do anything to dispel the rumours on campus. Both were efficient bureaucrats who smoothed the many bumps along the road of working with 1,800 teenage boys who were living away from home. Whippet especially would charm the young men with both her alluring physicality and her motherly wisdom while McAdams, playing tough cop, was the disciplinarian that the boys dreaded and respected. His thinning hair was providing no protection from the sun, and soon he tried to shield his scalp with the agenda for his next meeting.

Smith regarded the admin group up front with some displeasure and some pity. He was an experienced teacher, and after the last few weeks of observing the team, he disliked the parsimony of Wang and Chen, felt pity for Eric Peterson and Zhou, and genuinely liked McAdams and Whippet who provided much of the face-to-face encounters he had with the administration as a whole.

The speech's platitudes were finishing with a polite applause given, and the moment the entire restless crowd was waiting for began as the ceremony's host intoned, "And now I declare Canadian Harmonious International Peace School Flag ceremony over. Teachers may go first." Some boys bolted from their lines. If they were quick, they could avoid the sweaty crush on the stairs and have a few minutes to play a video game before their teacher arrived. Others remained chatting indifferently as they waited obediently for their teachers to go first.

The Canadian flag was still as straight as a prairie road above them. Smith wiped his face with the back of his hand again and found there was a slight film of dust on his moustache and goatee. Then he pulled out his new cell phone and checked the time. He was numb with boredom, and he could hardly feel his legs from standing on the hard cement. Vander Kwaak, Relic and Dickens all moved quickly towards the building, and he tried to keep up to them.

"Relic, I do need a shirt." Stupid nationalistic rituals, he thought. With his head tucked down he walked the tiled area past some of the wilting lads while the tune of "The Maple Leaf Forever" jingled in his head.

Three

WELCOME! BOCK!

Hudson Smith sat in his rocking chair and reflected on the previous week. The final day of preparation before classes began was filled with meetings. Teachers worked together to decide what units of study would be covered, in what order the prescribed curriculum should be taught, and what items would be evaluated. Such discussions would lead to greater continuity and coherence in this large school. Administrivia such as attendance lists, signing out texts, and filling in government mandated forms were on the day's menu.

He sipped a sweet iced tea as he considered the odd highlight of the first week. It was something that would be hard to convey to his children who had never been a part of anything military. Perhaps his father would understand best as he had been a sea cadet and then a reservist when the Cuban Missile Crisis had occurred just before Hudson's birth.

Eric Peterson had decided that the Canadian teachers would show respect and support for their Chinese hosts by attending the student military exercises the day before school started. It was a generous offer, but generosity is easy when it doesn't impact oneself. The staff left their meeting in the muggy confines of the theatre to go to the soccer pitch to watch the spectacle of grade ten boys marching. Smith was a pacifist and such military displays didn't interest him. He wasn't alone in the interest department. Very few of the teachers were, and the ones who were truly viewed the event as an anthropological study.

From the front of the stands Smith could see the boys already lined up on the field in rows of eight with two leaders per row. From the far end a short man in a sparkling tuxedo replete with tails and top hat came in front of the columns. "Who is that?" Amanda Johnson asked.

"Apparently, a local magician," mused Randy McMann. A pair of camouflaged porters carried a small three-step podium for him. When they placed it down, he mounted it in three crisp steps and took out a wand, and tapped it three times. Eyes barely over the podium, the maestro looked from left to right, then he tapped the wand another three times. The loudspeakers boomed forth the Chinese national anthem, and the boys sang it loudly. The sparkling tuxedo's arms waved furiously as though they were beating off dozens of mosquitoes. Slicing the air as though the wand was a sword, the little man ended the music and the song with the same stroke. The maestro magician spun around, descended quickly, and left the same way he came. Like clockwork, the porters returned and carried the podium away. Precision was the important element of the ceremony.

There was a murmur amongst his colleagues over the performance they witnessed. Their chatter eased off as their eyes were drawn back to the field.

At the front of each of the groups were two leaders who gave the rhythm for the rest of the 'soldiers'. A military man came out of nowhere and stood in front of the microphone and barked out a command. The boys began marching in place with their arms moving straight out. Sixty plus lines moved in perfect unison. The captain turned around and saluted Mr. Wang and the other school dignitaries. Wang arose, and looking positively embalmed, joined the Chinese army captain for a review of his 'troops'. The two strode past the Canadians, who were starting to feel the heat and humidity of the mid-day sun, across the track to the squads of young lads. There were ten groups who had begun the long march to nowhere, and Wang and the captain saluted each group as they walked past.

McMann provided dialogue and commentary in a Monty Pythonesque style, "Men, you look great."

"Thank you Master Wang. You look dead."

"Yes, but I am feeling alive though I don't look it. I shall give a roll call. Only respond if you are not here."

"Nero, Stalin, Chamberlain, Churchill, Napoleon, Eisenhower, Attila, George Bush. I see we are bookended with villains."

The Canadians smirked and chuckled at his banter. There was some truth in the names as Hudson Smith had looked over his class lists and noticed a number of the students had chosen names from the leaders of the past and present. Smith enjoyed the mocking comments of his colleague, and yet he was disturbed at the thought that the military played a role in the education of these boys. In fact he was disgusted that the school was allowed by the BC Ministry of Education to use the blatant nationalistic act as part of their physical education program.

Earlier at breakfast the kitchen crew had been bringing in a vat of fish to be part of that day's lunch offering, but the vat cracked and the fish slid across the cafeteria's floor just as the doors opened to the 1,800 hungry boys. Without looking down the boys walked through the slimy mess, and the grade ten boys splashed the briny waste onto their pants and their shoes. The staff tried to clean up the fish, but to no avail. The mobs slogged their way to the food. The fish and its odours became part of their attire for the day.

The uniformity was key. It was reinforcing the idea of conformity, obedience, and grooming the young men's acceptance of the military. The school uniforms were the same; the haircuts were the same. The grimace on each face–the same. The chant of, "*Yi, er, san, si*" was the same. Six hundred boys from all over China were immersing themselves into the river of the Chinese military that Chairman Mao had once boasted had over two hundred million men in its ranks. This river would eventually end up in the Holy Land as predicted in John's Revelation two millennia ago.

While the boys marched on the spot, Hudson noticed that Chairman Meow was moving through the squads and rubbing his head against many of the legs during the split second they were in contact with the ground. The chubby cat Chairman meowed loudly as though calling other cats to the aromatic smell of the fish he had found on the young troops. Calls he made. Responses he got. Cats from the teachers' apartments, cats from the restaurant across the street, cats from the homes by the beach all arrived soon. Beckoned as they were by the Chairman, they arrived with purpose in mind: find the fish, and lick the flavour up. Dozens of cats were mixed in with the hundreds of marchers; marchers that had walked through the fish slop that morn. The cats were going crazy meowing, rubbing, and pacing around the boys.

As Smith watched the mass march, his eye was drawn to a boy

who flopped onto his rump to tie his shoelaces. While every boy wore white running shoes, this boy's shoes were bright pink. A camouflaged soldier ran up to the lad, and yanked him to his feet. McMann, sitting beside Smith, leaned in and said, "Take a good look at that kid because it's the last time we'll ever see him."

Smith smiled and focussed on the lad. As Wang and the captain passed by the pink shoes they hesitated, but decided not to lose face by stopping. Immediately after they passed by, with the salute still lingering in the air, the pink shoed boy pulled out a pair of blue sunglasses and put them on.

"The kid's got guts," McMann stated. "Is he Canadian?"

The review continued and Wang and his military escort made their way back to the rest of the elite watchers under the shelter of the grandstand. Students came to the mike and gave a staccato speech. Hudson, unused to the accented English, heard the first one say something about "White Mounting Beach" while the next spoke of the "razing sun," but the final orator stated that the "C.H.I.P.S. vision encompasses wentire world," and he ended with the students who would soon be "sullying into the world." Then the first group, led by the school flag with the industrious beaver gnawing away at the tree of life and the red flag of the People's Republic, marched around the track.

Smith chuckled as he thought of Orwell's character Julia in *1984,* a novel he loved to teach, who had said that marching was, "sex gone sour."

"George, I wish you could see this," Smith muttered under his breath.

Fish smells accompanied the boys and soon the aroma found its way to the stands. "What is that?" Amanda complained as she pinched her nose.

The marching continued with each squad joining in as soon as the previous group had left its place. Finally, it was pink shoes' turn. Individuality reared its head again as pink shoes moved out of sync with his line. His arms also were out of sync with the group. The polite applause for each passing squad from the dignitaries' section dwindled as more people noticed the pink shoed wonder and his blue sunglasses. In front of the stand the cats following the squad made up a rag-tag group. The felines reminded Smith of the guerrilla fighters of the American Revolution. Disorderly imps they were.

When the final group passed, fireworks shocked the teachers as large cannons had been rolled in behind the unsuspecting Canadians. They all jumped. "My heart hit my ribs," blurted one of the new teachers. The cats had scattered.

Relic smiled, "Pretty good sound, eh? Get used to it. There are always fireworks going off around here."

"It reminded me of my days in cadets," piped up old Rich Bannerman as he mopped his brow with a meaty hand. "You know, marching, pageantry, cannons, flags, and inspections."

"I hope the smell is something that we don't have to put up with," Amanda stated.

"That wasn't too bad," stated Relic. "It was only fish. Wait until the sewage pipes back up."

Amanda's face dropped at the prospect.

As they walked back to the steamy meeting room where the walls were sweating as profusely as the Canadian teachers, workers unfurled a large banner from the mezzanine of the library building. A magpie flew off as they did so, but the bird let them know it wasn't happy with an interruption in its routine. In large gold lettering on a red background it read: WELCOME! BOCK! STUD! NUTS!

Four
A Morning in the Life of Eric Peterson

Flag again...Eric thought as he considered his speech to the 1,800 boys at his school, and Mr. Wang's announcement that he would be coming to flag today. He looked at the beautiful flowering plant in the corner. It seemed to thrive in the stifling September heat that spoke of a long summer, but Peterson knew better. By October, the chill of the early Siberian breeze would bring a frost that would last until mid-April. However, before this wicked zephyr arrived, his suit would cook him while he basted in his own juices up front in full view of the slender teens.

"Miss Hu, would you bring me some cold, cold water please?" Peterson felt he had to repeat the reminder as Hu would normally bring in hot water as the Chinese believed that cold water was bad for one's health.

His weight had been a constant battle ever since he had broken his ankle in his final year at university. That injury coupled with his new marriage saw him gain twenty-five pounds, which he had never lost, as family and friends fed the newlyweds over the Christmas season, and the inactivity allowed his waist to bulge. He unconsciously pulled at his belt loops.

Hu entered the room and placed the water on his desk. “Thank you, Miss Hu.” She smiled and left as she closed the door behind her.

Checking C.H.I.P.S. CHATTER, the internal messaging system, was often the first thing he did in his daily routines. The discussion forums on the online messaging system gave him a quick pulse of staff morale, humour, and chagrin. This morning there were the usual Monday bulletins, but he opened them anyways to keep abreast of the staff.

On Mon 7:11 am, Craig Dickens said:
Jiaozi. Get your red hot *jiaozi.*
You like-ah the shrimp-ah? The beef-ah? Try the pork-ah lady.
Very Delicious.
You heard it here first thing Monday morning. Order your *jiaozi* on the CHATTER today by noon, and my *ayi* will have them ready for delivery for Tuesday. The price is ten *kuai* for twenty *jiaozi.*
Very Cheap.
CD

Eric thought about ordering some more of the tasty dumplings stuffed with various types of meats or vegetables for supper on Tuesday.

On Mon 7:13 am, Don Hawk said:
Ball hockey on Tuesday? Who’s in? Can we get two guys to volunteer for goal? McMann and Dickens are both out. Are any of the Koreans available?
Don

Peterson wished he could play, but there was always a meeting with Mr. Wang and Mr. Zhou on Tuesdays after school. Why, he’d even play goalie to get out of the meeting where he felt every bit as pelted as the goalie when Relic released his legendary cannon slap shot at the net.

On Mon 7:18 am, Janie Brown said:
Tired? Hung over? Join us for yoga on Wednesday after school in the gym. Guys are definitely welcome.
JB

Yoga after work, he considered, would help the stiffness he was feeling. Would he have to wear tights? he wondered. He couldn't imagine doing those stretches with tights on. He scrolled to the next staff announcement.

On Mon 7:21 am, Tony Vander Kwaak said:
Attachments: kestrel12.JPG (685 KB); littleegret38.JPG (692 KB); mandarinduck8.JPG (612 KB); WhooperSwan4.JPG (711 KB).
The birds are starting to move. Here are pictures of my latest foray to the Bo Hai.
Tony

The Bo Hai, Peterson thought as he looked up instinctively to gaze out the window at the Yellow Sea, was the body of water on the opposite side, the west side of the peninsula, and he realized he hadn't been there yet. He opened the JPGs, and the pictures of kestrels, egrets, and ducks Peterson saw were beautiful. He made a note to ask about Tony's book when he saw him next.

On Mon 7:28 am, Rich Bannerman said:
Just to let you all know I made it up the stairs again. I'm 64, you know. It's 130 stairs. Would someone change rooms with me? Please? They won't kill you young bucks. There's a lovely view of the Sea. There's a breeze usually.
The Old Guy

Old Rich Bannerman had complained to Eric about his classroom being on the fifth floor and there being no elevator. This complaint was the first time that Bannerman moaned about the location on The CHATTER. Peterson had hoped to give the most senior member of the staff a room on the first floor, but then on the first day the Chinese staff took it over as an office. By then, all the other classes were spoken for, and so Bannerman had to go to the fifth. I'll see what I can do for the old whiner, thought Eric.

Sarah Whippet popped her head through the door. "Don't forget to ask Wang about the bus." A new bus to replace the old rusting hulk was high on Sarah's list of important items, but not on his. She was right. The old beast needed major work, and it was a terrible travelling billboard for the school with its cracked windows, peeling paint, and belching oil exhaust. "A new bus is sure to attract new parents," Sarah insisted.

"Thanks Sarah. I'll be sure to mention it to Mr. Wang."

It would certainly improve the school's image Peterson thought, but his main goal right now was to get textbooks for the Advanced Placement classes. It was fine to offer classes, but Heaven forbid that one purchase books. So much for the permanent sign on the old building that read "Building Excellent Education on Tradition of China and Canada", he mused.

His office door opened, and McAdams stepped in before Eric could read the next message. "There are two students I dealt with yesterday, and I will be recommending expulsion. Mr. Liang, their counsellor, has been convinced this is the best route for the boys. I know Mr. Wang will not like that so I thought I would give you a heads up."

"Who are they?"

"Lionel Li and Ottawa Cai."

"Ottawa Cai?" Peterson remembered meeting the boy for the first time last week, and how the Canadian capital, Ottawa, made him sigh as it taxed his overseas earnings while providing him with nothing in return–unless he counted his passport.

"Yes."

"What did they do?"

"They haven't been to class yet."

"Oh." Three weeks had passed since opening day.

McAdams left the room as quickly as he had entered. John McAdams was not one to wait around, nor was he given to reflection. Snap decisions often left Peterson cleaning up the mess or soothing relations between the concerned parties. Of course Wang wouldn't like it. Students were money. Money drove this place. Happy students' parents whispered, but unhappy students' parents shouted. Keep the students happy, and keep the parents happy was Wang's mantra. The school's reputation was essential.

Wang wanted C.H.I.P.S. to become the Chinese Eton with a generation of the nouveau riche graduating from its program. The new China had to have new leadership who were familiar with Western ways, and this meant an education overseas. Therefore, discipline was a non-issue. Confucianism's emphasis on rigorous self-control kept the students in control, but when one had tasted the forbidden fruit, offered by the West, of a non-conformist culture, of ways to express oneself as an individual, and of the joys of illicit relationships, well, that student's rebellion, though simple in Canada, was major in China. He thought of how Lionel Li, for instance, had come back to school with longer hair. This was against school policy, and a counsellor had basically put him under house arrest until he had agreed to get it cut. The issue was off the radar in Canada, but here it constituted a major infraction.

Peterson thought of the innocence he saw in Chinese kids. They were sincere when they sang Michael Jackson on stage in front of their peers. They were in earnest as boys held their friends' hands as they walked down the school's halls. They were being completely honest when they said that Hitler was a great leader. They had been taught that Tibet and Taiwan had always been Chinese, and that the Dali Lama was a corrupt insurrectionist. This naivety he attributed to a lack of irony in their society or to their poor knowledge of the outside world.

Picking one's nose in public or spitting in public buildings were cultural taboos in Canada but not here.

The racism was different. It was a result of education. Their social studies text book told students that Japan and America were their enemies. Hence, students openly complained about the Japanese. They praised light complexions and teased their darker classmates, but they criticised how the Americans treated the black minority. Their own xenophobia was apparent as they wouldn't include Korean students in group work

They didn't understand how multicultural Canada was, nor how Canadians would ostracize them for such attitudes, nor did they understand the opportunities that awaited them in the West. The student body was a different clientele than the one Eric was used to dealing with back in Port Coquitlam.

Peterson had been enticed from POCO to China by Wang's vision, credentials, and offer of a huge salary. Since then, he was disillusioned. Wang's mission of "Melding East and West" became increasingly difficult to see as resources were limited. The Head's credentials of an English degree from Peuing University, an MBA from Oxford, and a doctoral candidacy from Shanwan University were purported to be fictitious as it was said Wang had paid some scholars to write his papers and take his exams in many courses. This academic fraud was rampant in China, and shrugged off by university and government officials alike. The salary was very generous when one considered the lower Chinese taxation. Peterson mulled over the loss of his idealism as he neared the end of his career.

Suddenly, he spotted Wang walking out of his huge office–the one across the hall from his own. It was time to go to the meeting. The All-School-Committee-for-the-Greater-Good met in spacious quarters across from the main campus buildings in an annex of the gymnasium. Peterson put a smile on his face, and pushed away from his desk ready to hear the decrees of the Headmaster.

Wang sat at the head of the long table that filled the room. The table's gorgeous iconic cherry wood gleamed, and the sun's reflection on the polished surface often blinded the lower management's eyes even though they formed a second circle in the room. The dark mahogany panelling and large chairs seemed to belong to another era. The lighting at Wang's end was unusual because it worked and because the back lighting was stronger so it seemed to surround him with an aureole. Wang was a gravitational field unto himself as the entire room felt tilted towards him, and since his chair was larger than any other with an enormously carved back, it would fit in at Buckingham Palace.

Peterson sat at his spot and started to put on the translator headphones, and he looked up to Wang at the end of the table.

He stopped adjusting the headphones. The light behind Wang's head, the powerful chair, the Head's staring down at him. A shiver ran down his spine, and he reached for his glass of water. Wang's seat was raised on a foot high platform so that Wang sat higher than every other person around the ten-meter table. Each person waited patiently while instructions were given at the All-School-Committee-for-the-Greater-Good. Mr. Zhou, the principal, Mr. Ge, the counsellor, and Mr. Li, an old crony as far as Peterson could tell, entered the rooms, briefly nodded their heads, but never made eye contact with Wang. Peterson thought of how alpha dogs were greeted by the powerless. Each Chinese staff member would nod their head in deference and keep their eyes lowered as they moved to their assigned places. The Chinese staff was on one side. The Canadians sat on the other. Each spot was equipped with a translation headset and a microphone with a button to summon, and the translator sat in the back corner in a room that had a white curtain so she was unseen. It reminded Peterson of the Wizard of Oz. The unseen voice that was sonorous and sometimes accurate belonged to a doctoral candidate at a nearby university.

The entire meeting would be conducted in Mandarin except when the Canadians spoke. The translation began. "Dear good morning my employees. The All-School-Committee-for-the-Greater-Good are begins. Are there any reports?"

Silence was his response.

"Last meeting Mr. Peterson asked about flag ceremony changes. I have decided to hold flag ceremony in the auditorium when weather is too hot or too cold. This change will happen today."

Peterson looked at McAdams who had grabbed his arm. Their eyes met and they wondered how they would arrange the seating of

1,800 in a room with a capacity of 1,200. This was not the change they had asked for.

"Library has been donated books by C.H.I.P.S. school. C.H.I.P.S. will no longer buy a magazines–they are made from poor paper, and they must be replaced often. Online is better. I have decided to close library on evening to save power and wearing out of students' eyes."

Sarah whispered to Eric, "Miss Chen asked me about the life span of a book, and when I told her three years, she suggested that this could be extended if fewer boys read them. C.H.I.P.S. would save money by not replacing the books as frequently."

"Mr. Wang," Peterson waited as the Headmaster looked up and several of the Chinese staff scrambled to put on their headsets, "Mr. Wang, may I suggest a cost savings to the school regarding the flag ceremony?"

Wang was leaning forward in the monstrous chair.

"If we hold the flag ceremony indoors, there will be greater cleaning costs for the auditorium, and the seats may wear out sooner than C.H.I.P.S. has planned."

Wang sat back in his chair and folded his hands into each other, "Mr. Peterson makes good point. Flag ceremony will please continue outside."

Peterson smiled, and Wang redirected his gaze onto McAdams as a fly landed on the Canadian's hand. McAdams tried to flick the fly off, but it flew around his head and buzzed at his neck before coming to rest on the top of his left ear. Instinctively, he brushed it away.

"Mr. McAdams, I have read your note about your recommendation to expel two students. Lionel Li and..." here he shuffled through some papers, "and Ottawa Cai. I have decided to give boys a second chance. Their fathers promised me boys would behave. Also, unfortunately, Mr. Liang, boys' counsellor, is no longer with us. He could not handle counsellor position as it was too difficult. We wish him a peace and harmony."

Peterson gave McAdams a quick look. John's recommendation had cost Mr. Liang his job. The remainder of the meeting was uncomfortable. Another decree, another reversal, another decapitation–another meeting of the All-School-Committee-for-the-Greater-Good.

The short walk across the road from the gym to the campus proper allowed Eric to ponder his future. The vision that he had brought with him had withered like grapes in a drought when he realized his true position. Costs, financial restraints, budgets were words he was used to, but the randomness of the pronouncements continued to catch him off-guard. An AP economics course obviously needed textbooks, and the approval had been given, but the next day Peterson was told to photocopy the books. Then the copier broke down before it was done, and the message arrived–the copier would not be replaced. Ho, ho, ho, Peterson thought, a school of 1,800 and no copier–maybe I should order some slates next. It was late September, and the AP Economics 12 teacher had said he could not teach the course without texts. Perhaps the web had made this less true than it had been. Couldn't more up-to-date material be found online? Couldn't guest speakers be contacted through Skype? Such an approach would be unconventional, especially for an Advanced Placement course, but not impossible. The reliance on the content-laden, American-based curriculum was a concern for Peterson, but students perceived it to be more academically challenging than the normal fare. Shouldn't our normal BC courses be challenging too? he wondered.

In PE classes each of the sports had a single item to work with. One basketball, one Frisbee, one football, one soccer ball. The Chinese teachers were accustomed to limited supplies, but the Canadians were not. The 'wasteful' Canadians tried to implement a program designed with students having access to materials, but here they improvised every day. Every item used by teachers had to be signed out. Every pen, every felt, every roll of tape. All must be accounted for. This was a holdover from the Cultural Revolution and the Great Leap Forward. Such thrift had been common during the Great Depression, Peterson thought, but this parsimonious frugality was ridiculous. China was wealthy. The students' parents paid huge tuition. There was money for supplies, but why was it so hard to obtain any?

Peterson had been told that each Chinese middle manager was held responsible for the use of supplies. If a department increased its use of paper for example, the manager was called in to explain. If electrical bills went up, then the manager responsible would go to the classroom and twist the fluorescent tubes so that only one of the two in each fixture would work. No wonder so many students wore glasses, reflected Peterson. If he could not control costs, he was gone. Someone would replace him, and since China's greatest asset was its huge population, there was always someone ready to replace another. Alternatively, if supplies use decreased, that manager was publically acknowledged, and others were told to perform like him or be dismissed. These public 'beheadings' frustrated Peterson. There was no logical pattern to follow it seemed, and this tension didn't create frustration amongst the Chinese staff; it created competition.

Toilet paper was one battlefield. The custodian was constantly hiding it on the Canadian staff. The Chinese staff did not expect C.H.I.P.S. to supply TP, as very few places in China did, but the Canadian staff did not consider it a luxury. Friction rose between the two camps over such a meaningless item. "We are a school." Eric told Wang one time, "I want to focus on education in the classroom. I shouldn't have to fight for TP in the staff washroom."

He remembered as Wang listened impassively and quietly replied, "Then, do not."

Eric was jolted from his thoughts by the raucous magpie above the old building. The noisy creature often looked down on the proceedings like a European gargoyle. Many a time Eric's eye had caught the bird's movements during a flag ceremony. At least I can allow my eyes to ponder its beauty Eric thought. First period ended right then, and the rush of testosterone out of the building was impressive. Boys, who moments before struggled to keep their eyes open in math, now were wary like hunted rabbits as they moved to the homeroom lines. Eric spoke to Sarah and to Miss Chen. Sarah mentioned something about the up-coming October break, and Miss Chen, whose tongue darted out and back several times licking her dry lips, stated there would be a new plan to help C.H.I.P.S. become more environmentally friendly.

The four guards strode past Eric in perfect unison to their place near the old building. Their crisply pressed navy blue uniforms were sharp, and the military-style brimmed hats gave them an air of authority that erased their youth. They would stand to attention and tap their heels together. Hands saluted while the Chinese flag was raised, and the anthem was sung enthusiastically. Their zeal was evident to Eric from across the courtyard, and he usually looked over the boys' heads to see the guards' performance.

Wang stiffly took his spot nearest the flagpoles. Each of the administrators fell into their place. Chen, Peterson, Zhou, Whippet, and McAdams stood admiring the flag ceremony emcees stepping up to the microphone. The ceremony began as it usually did with the student taking the mic from Mr. Ge, and the songs and the raising went smoothly. Peterson noticed the magpie was looking on from his usual roost. The long tail feathers made it look nearly twice as big as it actually was. Without any sense of irony the boys delivered the speeches both in English and Mandarin. They implored the boys to study harder, to give glory to C.H.I.P.S., their teachers, their parents, their province, their hometown, to their country meanwhile behind them a new red banner was unfurled over the building's entry, which stated in gold block lettering "WOK HARDER, MELDING BEAST AND WEST."

Five
Extracurricular

An expat community is tight. The relationships in the community tend to last for a lifetime, as people have learned to rely on each other in the foreign land. Banding together, the interlopers give each other cultural support and teach one another the ins and outs of the new land. Thus it was unfortunate on the new teachers' first day in China that one of those relationships got off to a bad start. The first misspoken words of the year occurred. When the freshly recruited teachers got off the bus, they were brought to a meeting room, where they were given an orientation package, an apartment assignment, and a general greeting. As Eric Peterson, their principal and soon-to-be mentor, quietly entered the room from behind, the excited group continued their chatter describing their first impressions to each other. Janie Brown said as Eric passed unnoticed behind her, "I'm just here to 'Par-tay!'"

Stopped dead, Eric asked her from behind, "Really?"

"Oh yeah, I've been told this is a great place to party," she said to the unseen person behind her. The school did have that reputation in the early years as all of the staff had been young adventure seekers, but now as the school aged, so did the personnel, and there were a dozen or so families amongst the

C.H.I.P.S. staff. The place had changed dramatically. The teacher apartments had become a quiet refuge, and those wanting nightlife went to Kai Fa Qu.

Eric spun the chair around to face the young lady who still didn't know who had asked the question, but now it was dawning on her that this was someone important. Internally, Eric was angry, but he knew that he couldn't show it and keep the respect of his new staff. "If you want to party, I can ship you back to Canada today." The internal volume increased, but the external remained calm and measured. "You're here to work, to teach some of the finest minds in China, and to be professional." Now the woofers in his brain were blowing out as he maintained his outward professional demeanour and finished, "If you are here just to party, please consider teaching somewhere else."

The room was silent. Most had been involved with their own conversation when Eric's quiet lecture began, but now there was no question that all eyes were on him and the new teacher withering before him. Eric lifted his head and scanned the room. His impromptu scolding sent a chill through the room, and now he would have to regain these rookie teachers' confidence. "Welcome to C.H.I.P.S. and to the greatest career one can have. You will be teaching the minds of China's future leaders. We expect you to be thoroughly professional teachers and excellent ambassadors of Canada."

* * *

Wednesday night at The Ever Rising Club in Kai Fa Qu was a bit slower than the weekends, but the lights and the throbbing music encouraged the young to dance. Janie Brown, her desire fuelled by vodka shooters, scouted the dance floor for a partner. Her friends had already gone home. She was tired, but she wanted to be held; she needed human contact as after a month in China she was feeling isolated and homesick. A tall blond man caught her eye, and she smiled at him, twirled her luxurious hair with her index finger, and invited him to sit at her table by glancing and nodding her head at the empty chairs. “Hi. I’m Janie,” she seductively said.

In the morning she realized that she felt like a partially devoured loaf of bread. I can’t believe I did that, she thought. She couldn’t remember his name, or much of the evening, but she had to get to work. Why do I keep doing this to myself? she pondered.

* * *

Jo Loch and Hudson Smith had known each other for seventeen years, but their love was a recent phenomenon. Their story showed once again how small the world was and how rich relationships are meant to be. They had taught together for several years and had been friends, but Hudson, who had been married, had moved schools and Jo eventually went overseas to teach at C.H.I.P.S. in China. When Hudson’s ex-wife had left him and the kids for another man, he decided to pursue his dream of teaching abroad. His successive applications to Abu Dhabi, England, and Cambodia fell through as there was no position at his friends’ school in the Emirates state for the first time in years, he was too old by a year for the English government grant given to schools hiring foreigners, and the volunteer position at the Phnom Phen School angered his ex-wife as she thought he was trying to shirk support payments. Hudson wanted peace, so he continued to look and found the C.H.I.P.S. ad in *The Vancouver Sun.* He applied and started to do his homework by asking a former colleague about his experience there. “Why don’t you contact Jo? She’s still there, you know." So he did. First he sent a tentative email, and received a response three weeks later as Jo had been in Thailand and Bali on her Spring Festival break. She answered his questions thoroughly, was sorry for his marital breakdown, and encouraged him to come to China for the adventure of his life. He sent an email each week to ask Jo about China–how he should prepare, what clothes to buy, what accommodations were like–and she generously answered his questions with honesty and wit. After a couple of months of these missives, Hudson received a Facebook request from Jo so he could look at the pictures she had posted of her life in China. Intriguing, thought Hudson. He began to look forward to the occasional chat they had. Jo was open with her feelings and honest, and Hudson found that refreshing.

Jo had felt the same way apparently, and she asked some of their mutual friends how Hudson was coping in Canada. They told her he had been shocked and hurt by his situation and was taking care of Carson and Lillian, but really they were adults at university. His children encouraged him to go overseas, as they too loved travelling. Carson would live with Hudson's parents, and Lillian was already preparing to live with a friend. Jo's interest in Hudson was growing, and so she invited him to Skype her. Technologically incompetent, but willing to learn, Hudson had his daughter set up the program, and she showed him the basic functions. So the former Pong player began a Skype relationship that had blossomed into romance and by the early fall he proposed to Jo at the point overlooking the Baishantan Beach.

Jo, thinking back on the first Skype call, said, "When I first saw you, I was shocked at the beard. You had said you were growing one, but I never imagined it to be over a foot long."

"I just thought you would realize it was long since I was playing

Father Christmas in the play."

"I hadn't thought about how Father Christmas looked. I've never read or seen The Lion, *The Witch and the Wardrobe."*

"I'm glad it didn't scare you off," he said holding her hand as they walked along the shoreline.

"You know, I used to think how all the great guys on our staff were already married, and wondered when God would send someone my way." She gazed out onto the bay following a gull. "Later, I became comfortable with being single, and I was fine with that. At my age I knew that if a man came my way, it would probably mean that he had been divorced." Jo wiped a few wind-blown strands of blond hair from her green eyes, "Then out of the blue God brings you back into my life." She smiled, "I couldn't resist your heart or your voice."

Hudson smiled, "Thanks. I do have a voice and a face for radio, don't I?"

Jo laughed and gave him a small playful punch to the shoulder. She took his hand and squeezed it three times while the sky was ablaze with reds, oranges, and pinks.

* * *

Students rarely know the undercurrents of a teacher's life. Hudson's own son had once pointed at the portable classrooms and had asked with all the innocence that grade ones possess, "When do the teachers go to their houses?" Even though his dad was a teacher, he hadn't logically understood that teachers didn't live at the school. They had a life away from the class. Janie Brown's life would have shocked the Chinese students as she partied at least four times a week. The Focus Bar served two for one daiquiris on Tuesdays, and the music was always loud. A Chinese man came up to her at the bar and asked her to dance. Janie shook her head. The young man asked again. "Go away."

When he asked a third time, an engineer from a local German auto parts manufacturer came over from the other end of the bar and said, "Honey, I'm sorry I'm late. It's good to see you." He gave her a peck on the cheek. Janie was startled, but played along.

Backing away, the polite Chinese youth–does he even shave yet? Janie asked herself–apologized and left.

"Thanks for saving me. I really appreciate that."

The engineer, at least ten years her elder, sat down and ordered two drinks.

* * *

There were healthy relationships in the school community, and the Vander Kwaak's seemed to be the model family. Debbie and Tony's kids were inquisitive, articulate, curious, healthy, and kind. Reading time was around 7:00pm, bedtime at 7:30. Routines like the Saturday morning pancakes at Peter's Restaurant, the daily walk to the beach with Debbie, and bird watching on the motorbike with Tony brought order and security to the two foreign tots. Their blonde hair often made them the centre of attention when they were in public, and they preferred time at home with their family. A weekly Skype call with both sets of grandparents allowed the family to see each other grow older. "Life overseas would have been so much harder before technology," Debbie said to Tony one night while they did the dishes together.

"Yeah. Our children wouldn't know who their grandparents were."

"Thanks for helping with the dishes."

"Anytime. Anything else?"

"No. What have you planned for 'date night?'"

"I thought we'd go to Kai Fa Qu and eat Indian at the Victoria Hotel, then your favourite: the Blind Massage place. I've already booked number seven for you. She's the one you like, right?"

"Yeah. Honey, that'll be great. I can hardly wait. I haven't had a massage for a while."

"I know. Is there anything else you want me to do tonight?"

"Ayi is coming tomorrow so there's no laundry to do. I downloaded a movie, but let's go to bed."

* * *

The downward spiral of Ms. Brown continued. Janie was late. She was very late. Who was the father? She'd been with a dozen guys at least. None of them was Father-material. She held her pounding head. "I need a drink." It was nearing Christmas, and this worry on top of schoolwork, a slight flu, and homesickness was stressful. In the pit of her stomach she wondered what to do. Her parents would be upset. She was upset. Choices needed to be made. She ran to the bathroom and retched. "What should I do?" she moaned over the toilet. "I'll ask Jo. She's older and wise. She'll give good advice. Oh, why me?" Janie made her way across the apartment to her cell phone and started calling Jo.

* * *

Scheduling the courses for students and teachers for a school of 1,800 is like a giant sudoku puzzle, and Eric Peterson assigned the task to Sarah Whippet and John McAdams. Stressful situations often bring people into a closer relationship, and Sarah and John, over the week of fifteen-hour days creating the timetable, found themselves secretly admiring the other's work, intelligence, and determination. Whippet's high cheekbones and auburn hair made her the vice-principal of choice amongst the boys. If they had a problem, they would see Whippet. As the week in the office struggling with the schedule neared its end, McAdams started to notice her physical attractions as well. He caught himself staring at her, and realized that he needed to maintain a professional distance from his colleague. McAdams played bad cop, and he relished the role. The boys feared his presence like the Grim Reaper–he never brought good news. He kept his distance from Whippet, but she started to find excuses to come to his office to discuss mundane things. When she invited him to come to her house to watch a movie with friends, and no one else came, (She said that she had forgotten to invite the others.), he realized that she might also be interested in him. Chinese subtitles came on the screen, and Sarah asked him to fix it. When he turned around, she softly said, "Come sit by me."

* * *

Each year several BC universities sent student teachers to China for their final practicum. One of the benefits to C.H.I.P.S. was a trial run of these new teachers. Since the school was always hiring, the principal could offer positions to some of the best ones. For the older staff, the benefit was new ideas from the young, enthusiastic teachers, but for the younger staff freshly minted by the institutions and in their first or second year in the classroom, the student teachers were potential dates, boy or girl friends, and mates.

Ali Javaherian, or Java as his very best friends called him, was an excellent math teacher. Raised in North Vancouver, he was part of a tight Iranian community, and he still practised the traditional Persian festivals like "Leaping over the Fire." He had enjoyed his first year at C.H.I.P.S. making new friends like Bobby Wilson, the physics teacher. Java was polite, clean cut, and handsome, but he was waiting on a serious relationship until he got home. At least that was the plan until Zarrin Kayani, a gorgeous English student-teacher, showed up from Simon Fraser University. Despite the university advisor warning the student teachers not to become involved with anyone during the practicum as they would already be busy, Zarrin was attracted to Java, and he was smitten by her. Since Java had been assigned a math student teacher to sponsor, he was at the introduction meeting when he laid eyes on Zarrin. After the meeting, Zarrin came up to him and said, "I have been told about you, Ali Javaherian. You are almost as handsome as your cousin, Noor, said you were."

His smile betrayed him, and he invited her out to dinner.

* * *

Janie Brown stood near the check-in counter at Shanwan International looking at the departure times for Tokyo. Jo stood by her. Jo had worked with Whippet on the situation to allow Janie to go home with her classroom reputation intact. It was up to Janie now to mend her reputation at home. Her parents had overcome their initial shock and invited her to come home when Janie told them she would keep the baby. She told Jo that she didn't want to compound one mistake on top of another. She would love this child though she was scared and felt trapped.

Jo gave the broken young woman a red silk scarf to remember China. Gently, Jo took her hand and wished her all the best. She promised to stay in touch using Skype and to visit that summer. Both women were in tears as Janie left.

Six

The Communist Liberator

It seemed like a regular flag. The counsellor, Mr. Ge, barked out in Mandarin at the boys to get into their lines, to stand straight and tall, to move forward, and to be quiet. The admonishment had its desired effect as the boys straggled into place.

In sharp contrast the first emcee's crisp movements efficiently took the microphone from Mr. Ge with his white gloves gleaming in the sunshine. There were large white puffy clouds hanging over the Yellow Sea like anvils ready for the strike of the hammer on the hot iron. The six flag raisers stood ready behind the podium, letting the grade ten boys admire their height, their pressed uniform blazers, and their gloves.

Ah, the mystique of the gloves. The hidden imperfections of the hands, the focus they drew, the power imbued.

"Ironic isn't it, eh?" Dickens said to Smith at the back of the lines of boys facing the podium. "The gloves, I mean. They're not very revolutionary, are they? Can you think of a more bourgeois piece of clothing?"

"A tux?"

"I'll give you that, but often gloves are part of the tux outfit. Bare hands bring revolutions. Gloves, well, these kids eat that stuff up. They love to dress up. I've often seen girls wearing those long gloves like Audrey Hepburn in *Breakfast at Tiffany's.*"

"I love that movie."

"You can download it if you want from Youku.com. You can get any old classic film there."

"I would like to see The *Hunchback of Notre Dame* and *The Passion of St. Joan* again. Thanks for the tip."

A quick survey of the school yard showed Smith what he was expecting: the administrators stood to the left of the flags, the boys in their semi-straight lines in the C.H.I.P.S. uniforms, the teachers disinterested at the back, and then (one could not forget), the guards, who seemed indispensible at the gate, but whose presence was mandatory at the left of the boys during the ritual. In front of the uniformed men the secretaries provided a feminine oasis. The magpie was on his perch and his black and white tail feathers pointed down to the ground like a dowser's rod. Chairman Meow, tail swooshing back and forth, and teeth chattering with the excitement of the hunt, kept his back to the entire event as he stalked a grasshopper. "All's right with the world," Smith quoted one of his favourite Victorian poets–Robert Browning. Meanwhile he wiped away the sweat that beaded on his large forehead, a witness of the thirty-five plus Celsius heat.

"Craig, do you think I could wear a hat to flag? What would the admin say?"

"It's not the admin that would mind. The Chinese staff would think you are being rude."

"Even if my head burns?"

"Yeah, it's cultural."

Visibly deflated, Hudson turned his focus back on the ceremony unfolding before him.

The flags were raised: Red Stars–China, Red Maple Leaf–Canada, Red Beaver–C.H.I.P.S., and the music from the national anthems echoed in each listener's ears. Today it seemed louder than usual. The gloves moved efficiently as they hoisted the flags into their commanding position. Stiff movements. Crisp movements.

It was now time for the sentimental speeches. Sappy, cliché, mundane. These words came to Smith's mind as he analysed the past speeches delivered on the podium while unconsciously cleaning his left ear. The anticipation of an error made him feel like a ghoulish NASCAR fan looking for the ultimate ten-car crash, but it was the only thing that kept this routine vaguely interesting.

This week the Mandarin speech would come first. Smith caught some words: *hao* was good, *ying wen* was English, and *lao shi* was teacher. Otherwise, the message flew above his head like the clouds that eclipsed the sun briefly before moving on to the Korean Peninsula just across the sea. How did the international students cope with the speech when he found that he couldn't?

Checking up on his thoughts, he slowly turned his head towards the mostly Korean group. The boys were poking at each other, and moving restlessly, kicking backpacks and whispering. Attention was such a rare commodity, but who could blame them? They, too, couldn't understand the droning.

The speaker system had cut out once last week, and the technical difficulties continued this week as the student emcees spoke into the mic and no sound emerged. The awkward giggles of the front rows revealed a relief that at least it wasn't them in the bind. A Chinese counsellor, his black hair slick with some kind of gel, rushed forward, alert to the error this week, jerked the sound cable and reconnected the loose wire inside.

A student came out of the black-haired sea. He walked forward to the hosts who seemed relieved to see a fellow student coming to their aid. Their rescuer extended a bare hand to take the faulty mic from their gloved ones. All eyes were on him. This wasn't unusual, as the speech giver often came out of the homeroom lines. Facing his peers, he started to deliver an extraordinary speech.

"Friends, counsellors, teachers, countrymen 'lend me your ears.' I was scheduled to speak, but last night a counsellor, an honourable man who loves me, said that I would not be allowed to do so since I had disagreed with him over the cleanliness of the classroom. Furthermore, for my own good, he grabbed my ear, and pulled me to a chair. This was not the first time, comrades, that this had happened to me. Nor to you."

"Another time, for my own good, I was made to carry heavy bags of laundry until I was too exhausted to stand. This also was not the first time comrades that this happened to me. Nor to you."

"Pushed, slapped, pinched. All for my own good. Many of you have suffered from such abuse from the counsellors who are honourable men. We should not. We are communists. We are revolutionaries. We are the sons of China. We must 'Rise Up.' 'Under the enemy's fire,' we must be proud to move forward. I love the revolution that our beloved Chairman Mao brought, that Deng Xiao Peng reformed, and that Hu Jiantao has perfected.

We are communists. We are revolutionaries. We are the sons of China. Some of our counsellors are our oppressors. We must stand tall and move forward."

The reference at the beginning was a well-chosen allusion, Smith thought. Marc Antony's speech at Julius Caesar's funeral was a cunning oration that manipulated the crowd into agreeing with him and slowly led them to the irony of the conspirators' actions. Quoting the Chinese national anthem, in English, so the counsellors would have trouble interpreting what was being said, was also a clever use of rhetoric. Patriotism here ran high. Invoking the leaders of the Communist Party fed that patriotism. There was much discussion in the dorms about the twenty-first century as China's century, and most often Smith agreed. Dabbing the moisture from his face and neck, he pondered, how could it not become the most powerful nation on earth? A counsellor at this point started to move towards the brilliant orator whom Smith could not recognize. The boy noticed Counsellor Ge moving like a train, and he knew his time was short.

"Do not be bullied. The counsellors are honourable men. We are communists. We are revolutionaries. We are the sons of China. We must stand tall and move forward."

Ge reached the podium and stretched out his hand to take the mic, and the liberator moved it so the attempt was fruitless. Ge continued his quest. The exterior calm hid the raging dragon beneath. The communist liberator had potential, Smith thought. Why is he not in my advanced English class? I must speak to him afterwards and arrange for that to happen.

Standing tall was precisely what each boy was doing. Each student was erect, shoulders were back, head up. All extraneous chat was finished. Moving forward was precisely what each boy was not doing. The stillness was odd as though the group were members of Xian's famed terra cotta army and not flesh and blood.

In August each year the grade ten boys came two weeks earlier than the older students to take part in the nationwide military training. Eric Peterson had brought the Canadian staff to watch the drill inspection this year for the first time. Marching, standing straight, and repeating slogans seemed to be the focus of that time, and maybe for the first time in C.H.I.P.S.' history the training was bearing fruit during the school year.

Before Counsellor Ge finally grabbed the microphone away, the audacious lad shouted, "Long live China! I love China!"

In unison 1,800 boys responded, "I love China! I love China! I love China!"

The air was electric when Mr. Ge said, "I now declare the C.H.I.P.S. flag ceremony finished. Students, let teachers go first." The teachers started the trek back to the classes, and for the first time in memory, they noticed that the boys did not move.

When Smith got up to the fourth floor office, sweat now pouring from his chin, ears, and nose, and with a new burn on the top of his exposed scalp, he looked out and surveyed the court beneath him. The boys were still standing tall. They were still motionless. The Chinese counsellors moved about them haranguing the Sons of China to go back to class. A half hour later the same strange scene greeted him; the revolutionaries were still and determined warriors, and Smith said aloud, though he was alone in the room, "That kid has got to be in my class."

Seven
The Battles

Tony Vander Kwaak was not easily flustered, but when he walked into the English Department office that Monday morning, his ashen face told Hudson that not all was well with the Birdman. "Mr. Wang just yelled at me for not wearing a tie to flag." He wiped the sweat off his forehead that was a result of the thirty-six degree Celsius heat and the tongue-lashing he had received.

Hudson considered his reply then said, "He's probably upset after the workman ruined the ceremony today. He's angry and wants to lash out at someone." It was true that Wang wanted things to run smoothly at the school, but at today's flag when a Liaoning Provincial Education Bureau official came to present Mr. Wang a plaque for his advancement of Chinese education, a worker from the on-going renovation of the cafeteria building lifted his wheelbarrow and started moving towards the gate. Undeterred by the flag ceremony, the man dressed in high white gumboots and wearing a blue C.H.I.P.S coat stopped in front of the podium and the official, took out a rag and wiped the sweat from his brow before he cleared his nasal passages one at a time. The boys squirmed with delight like they were tasting an orange for the first time, and the Canadian teachers, who were still permitted to wear shorts, craned their necks to watch the events unfold. Chinese counsellors came to assist the man, but he refused. He slowly picked up the cart loaded with a steamy mound of soil and walked the rest of the way.

The human ox was gone, but the damage had been done. The official said to Wang, "A former student, is he?"

Wang was furious. He had been upstaged by a peasant. The education official had belittled his school. Once the ceremony was over he politely saw the official to his waiting black Lexus that was taking him back to the capital in Shenyang. Wang stalked back to his office, and it was then that Tony had stepped out of the staff washroom looking for toilet paper. "Where's your tie? Why are you not wearing your tie?" Vander Kwaak automatically reached to check, thought of retreating to the safety of the washroom, but the Headmaster was not a man to trifle with.

"I forgot it this morning," he softly stated.

"Forgot it? Forgot it? What else do you forget? Are the students served well by a man who forgets a tie? Maybe you forget your lessons also? You are Vander Cluck? If it happens again, you will be back in Canada." The Head walked down the dimly lit hallway while Tony tried to collect himself.

This morning had been rushed as his daughter Ruthie was sick. She had fallen into Tadpole Creek the day before. The wind, as they rode the motorcycle through what Ruthie aptly called Plastic Bag Forest, had chilled her and now she had a runny nose. Tony had taken more time with her than usual that morning. She didn't want to get dressed or eat any pineapple he had cut up for her breakfast. Feeling the clock ticking, he then rushed off to class before donning the tie. The cool ride of yesterday was forgotten as a warm southern airflow from the tropics continued to fend off its Siberian relative. Summer would continue for another day.

The heat had claimed a victim in the back row at flag. Mrs. Peterson, one of the newbies, had fallen over. The sun had beat down on her in the first two classes, and now the humidity and heat caused her to pass out. Her husband, Mattie, had said that he was ready to cook tonight when June fell forward landing hard on the ground in a crumpled heap.

As Mattie cradled her head, Relic asked, "What happened, Mattie?"

"I don't know. She fell."

Sarah Whippet saw it from the front row, and moved through the homeroom lines to the stricken woman. She ordered the men to carry her into the building. "Into my office," she said.

While the men were getting her a drink of water, the Chinese nurse came in at the request of Mr. Zhou. She started to move her hands over the young teacher's torso without actually touching her. The Canadians looked at each other and back at her as the nurse started to push down hard on June's shoulders. Was this Chinese medicine? "What is she doing?" Whippet asked. "Get her out of here," and Smith herded the woman out of the crowded office. McAdams came in, and he offered his office fan to help cool the young woman. Grabbing it without acknowledging him, Whippet plugged it in, pointed it directly at Peterson, and turned it on high. The compassion continued, but Whippet closed the door after pushing two well-meaning teachers out. "Give her some space," she commanded. The sweat was dripping down Smith's forehead, and despite the fan, he felt the heat even more in the office. "Get some water ready," the vice-principal continued. The bell went at that moment, and as the room cleared of the teachers who headed out for the third period class, and Miss Chen entered.

When June came to her senses, the only ones left were Whippet and Chen. "I trust you are feeling better," Chen stated.

"What happened?"

"You fainted. Fell like a limp doll," said Whippet.

"Oh." She rose to her feet and shook her head to clear the cobwebs.

"Here's some water for you," the vice principal offered.

"Thanks." June took the offered cup, drank it, and set it down.

"Well? I think you should be going back to class, shouldn't you?" asked Chen as she trailed her finger back and forth over Whippet's desk.

"Oh, um, yes. Yes, I do have a class."

"Yes. That's why you get paid."

June was reaching for the doorknob when Sarah said, "Teach them well."

John McAdams ran his hand through his thinning hair and then rubbed his eyes. This morning he had received a text message at 2:13am from one of the new teachers asking for a sub. Ridiculous, he thought, don't they think how the phone rings? He had specified at a staff meeting that he should be called between 6:00am and 7:00am. What irked him the most is that this miscreant had not left a name, and the number wasn't on his cell phone list.

Several times now his sleep had been interrupted. A phone call at night is never good news, he thought, never good news. He started to compose a CHATTER message.

Later during his spare block just before lunch Smith made his way to the Dayun 125, the cheaply made Chinese motorcycle that he rode like he was Dennis Hopper in Easy Rider. He had purchased it second-hand from Disco Ping in Baishantan. With the hot summer air chilling at night it would soon be time to put the bike into storage. He parked it across from the upper entry gate where he had always done so. Recently the youngest guard, no more than twelve thought Smith, had told him through various signs and gestures that he wanted him to park it two hundred meters down the road. His response was to ignore him. The next day there was a more senior guard there who gestured the same way. Again Smith ignored him; however, when he got on to go home, the tires were flat. This is how wars begin, thought Smith steaming over the incident. He walked the bike the two kilometres into Baishantan to the repair shop where they fixed it quickly for eight *kuai*. The third day he parked it at the gate again, and other teachers had started to ride their bikes as well, and the collection grew. After a lovely break, and eating a Snickers bar, he opened his C.H.I.P.S. CHATTER.

On Mon 10:22 am, Sunflower Hu said:
Hello teachers :

REMINDER: Please park your motorcycle at the lower gate .
Thanks for your cooperation,
School Office

He immediately sent back a brief response to Sunflower:

On Mon 10:30 am, Hudson Smith said:
Why?
Hudson

Within the minute the red flashing radio wave was on his lap top screen signalling a new message.

On Mon 10:31 am, Sunflower Hu said:
Hi Hudson,
This is the decision made by Eric and Mr. Zhou at beginning of this semester.

Sunflower
Hudson scoffed at the suggestion that Eric Peterson was in on this decision. He decided to contact Eric to see if what he was told was true. He forwarded Sunflower's message and added his question.

On Mon 10:43 am, Hudson Smith said:

Hi Eric:
I'm wondering why the decision was made about having to park motorcycles at the lower gate and cars can park alongside the "upper parking" area by the upper gate. Could you clarify please?

Thanks,
Hudson

On Mon 10:44 am, Eric Peterson said:

Hudson,
Wrong, wrong, wrong. The decision was made by Mr. Zhou. I accepted it after unsuccessfully trying to convince him otherwise. I do not know why they want the bikes at the lower end other than they might feel they look unsightly. I will talk to him again.

Eric

On Mon 10:48 am, Hudson Smith said:

Greetings Eric:
I sent the message back to you as I know we had discussed the motorbike problem before, and I knew where you stood. When Sunflower said that you had made the decision, I thought I would call her on it. Perhaps she misunderstood the directive's source. I appreciate you reopening the discussion; after all, it can't be a safety concern since other vehicles are also parked there. Aesthetics may be the answer, but they shouldn't be when one considers the unsightly bus the school has parked there (a real testimony to the community).

Hudson
On Mon 10:50 am, Eric Peterson said:

Don't worry. Continue to park the bike there. This is my school.

Eric looked at the computer screen. Person to person worked so much better he thought. Quickly looking in the bottom right of the laptop he realised that it was 11:00. Lunch would be good to order now. He leaned out of the office door, bumping the indoor rubber tree, which was losing its lustre, and he spoke to the secretaries who were typing, talking, and filing on behalf of the school, "Lunch is on me today ladies. I am calling Peter's, and I'll pass you the phone to give your order." After each of the women stated their choice, Eric asked for the Greek salad, a clubhouse, and a bottle of ice tea. He had briefly considered the apple pop which he had tried the previous week, but he went with his favourite instead. This was a service the Canadian teachers used frequently from Peter's. Delivery was always quick. Within twenty minutes the cheap and nutritious food, like a bacon cheeseburger, would arrive right to his office. Once he had paid the pittance for the meal that had no delivery charge and no tip (as gratuities were not given in China), he would continue with the day's agenda. The afternoon promised some excitement with a guaranteed discussion with Mr. Zhou over the motorcycles.

When Eric's stomach growled, and the women behind their desks like sentinels kept looking his way, Eric realised something was wrong. The quaint Chinese ringtone beckoned him from his work. "What's that Peter? The guard won't let you through the gate? What? Why not? Let me speak to him please." Eric's temperature and pulse were rising. "This is Mr. Peterson, the Canadian Principal, and I would like you to let Peter on to the campus to deliver my lunch." The principal listened carefully to the broken English on the other end of the call, and the secretaries leaned towards his office to hear the discussion.

"What do you mean that you cannot let him on? Peter has been on campus every day since I got here. The secretaries want their lunch. I want my lunch. Who said he could not come in anymore?"

Peterson felt his temperature increasing when he understood that perhaps this was not his school as he heard the guard say, "Mr. Zhou." Sunflower smiled despite her hunger.

On Mon 11:04 am, John McAdams said:

This is to remind you of the protocols to use when calling for a substitute teacher. Please call me between 6 and 7 am, or until 10 the night before. I have now received calls at 2:13am, 3:30am, and 4:04am. Please be more considerate and use your common sense. I cannot book a sub at such an early hour as the subs are sleeping.

Your lesson plans should be left in your mailbox in the office before 7:15 for the sub.

John McAdams

In two minutes Don Hawk responded to McAdams.

On Mon 11:09 am, Don Hawk said:

Dear John,
(I've always wanted to say that)

If I am ever sick, I would love to bring my lesson plans to the office at 7:15; however, the secretaries don't unlock the doors until 7:35. I want to follow the dictum, but I can't.

Sorry you lost your sleep,

Don

On the third floor, with each boys' stomach full of delicacies like *nu rou mian, ma la tang,* and *xin la mian,* Tony Vander Kwaak, still bothered by the morning encounter with Wang, was teaching his students. "China is making some of the same environmental mistakes that the Western societies made. Why, all the birding spots I have are under threat of development. The developers are filling in watercourses and marshes. Taking down entire mountains and filling in the sea. What will birds eat? Where will they go?" he asked his thirty Social Studies 11 students.

Robert Xiao, who was pulling at the threads of the school crest and trying to pull out the beaver's teeth threads, without looking said under his breath, "Who cares?"

Vander Kwaak wheeled around. "Who said that?" No one

moved. All eyes were down. “Who said that?” Silence greeted him. It may have been the stillest room in all of China. “Don’t you know what happens to people who have that attitude?” He walked over to his console. No room had a teacher’s desk. He quickly brought up the search engine and looked for a quotation. This was a teachable moment. They didn’t come every day. Once he found the gem, he put it on the screen:

“First they came for the communists
and I did not speak out–because I was not a communist.

Then they came for the Jews
and I did not speak out–because I was not a Jew.

Then they came for the trade unionists
and I did not speak out–because I was not a trade unionist.

Then they came for me–
and by then there was no one left to speak out for me.”

Pastor Martin Niemöller

The boys read the piece in continued silence. While they read, Tony thought of the Black-Winged Stilts he had seen that morning. The long twiggy pink legs accentuated by the stubby little body with its needle-like black bill had been foraging the Baishantan beach. These migrating birds were going south from Siberia to winter in Borneo. Their instinct pulled them hard right into this zone that was developing so quickly it was already upsetting the delicate natural balance. Thousands of birds were lost as the Chinese development changed the very landscape that for millennia the birds had used as a flyway. Mountains disappeared, lakes were filled, marshes were made into moonscapes ready for factories and housing. As a foreigner he had done his best to draw to the government's attention the variety and size of the local species by publishing a guidebook, taking dignitaries on tours, and appearing on a local television show a number of times. The silence continued. The blue suited lads looked at each other. They looked down. They looked out the window. The banner rippled with the slight breeze. OUR GLORIOUS ETERNAL FUTURE IS NOW it stated. The sun was going down already in the hazy air. They did not look at Vander Kwaak. "WHO WILL SPEAK OUT FOR THE BIRDS?" The tension was growing. Chinese people did not raise their voice–it showed a lack of self-control.

Xiao was feeling brave and cocky. "Maybe the birds are communists."

The laughter filled the room. Tony Vander Kwaak smiled. "Maybe they are," he said once the din stopped. "Maybe they are, and some day there may be none left." The silence returned as the boys considered the enormity of the statement.

Eight
The Chinese Church

A long and rocky history had accompanied the Great Commission in China. Britain's Opium War had done a great deal to harm the trust of the Chinese, but Niccolo Ricco, the Italian priest, and Hudson Taylor, the English Methodist, after whom Hudson had been named, both left legacies of love, and a foundation of believers that had lasted hundreds of years. "It only takes a spark to get a fire burning" though, and the spiritual descendants of these men numbered in the tens of millions. China was officially atheist. However, the government realized it couldn't ignore religion, so it tried to control it.

The officially recognized church in China–The Three Self Movement–played by the government's rules. It submitted sermons for scrutiny, never preached about Christ's resurrection, and registered their existence and all foreigners when they walked through the doors. The underground church, or house churches, remained unrecognized and unacknowledged. House churches were cosy, warm places where the members were like a close family. They did not advertise their existence as they wanted to operate without government approval as they held that a church without discussion of Christ's resurrection wasn't much of a church since that was the crux of the faith.

Baishantan, to Hudson's surprise, had a church, but he couldn't figure out which of the two camps it belonged to. It was open about being a church. There were two crosses on the building's front, and there was no doubt that over one hundred local residents attended weekly. The confusion for Hudson was that this open church met in a renovated house, and as westerners, he and Jo had never been asked to register. Even a new resident who had moved from a house church in Beijing wasn't sure about the Baishantan Church's status. He explained to Hudson, "China is best thought of as an empire. Local sentiments and local government officials can either enforce the law vigorously, or they can tolerate practices if they seem respectful. I suspect that this is what is happening here. It is my understanding that several of the Shanwan Municipal Government are Christians, and they accept Christianity's existence."

Smith walked through the gate and up the crumbling sidewalk. Decay was all around. The fence sagged and was missing sections, the woodpile looked depleted, wood chips surrounded the well-chewed chopping block, and the windows were all covered with plastic that created a dingy appearance. Before he started up the steps a balding woman wearing a multi-coloured coat opened the door and her beaming smile and welcoming arms eased his spirit. "*Ni hao. Shangdi zhu fu.* (Hello. May God bless you)," Jo said, and the greeter was stunned that this white woman spoke to her with such fluency as she greeted and blessed her. Unfortunately, the colourfully clad woman thought this was a green light, and a torrent of Mandarin burst forth drowning Jo and Hudson in its flow.

"*Ting bu dong.*" Hudson remembered to say the words which

translated literally meant, “I hear, but I don’t understand.”

The woman chuckled, and said to a second woman at the entry door, “*Ting bu dong*,” and the other woman also appreciated the situation with a giggle.

The woman in Joseph’s coat grabbed Jo’s forearm and led her down the church’s one aisle to the front wooden pew. Before the bewildered Canadians was a full choir wearing white gowns with a salmon coloured vee sash. Music filled the sanctuary from a stand-up piano that had seen better days, and the voices of the congregation and choir vibrated in Hudson’s bones. An old man, sitting at the end of the otherwise empty pew, slid over to the new couple and gave them a copy of a Chinese hymnal. “*Ting bu dong*,” Hudson whispered to him, and apparently that was all the old fellow needed to take the book back. Another hymn rose up, but this time Jo and Hudson recognized the tune and joined in with the singing as a Chinese version of “Amazing Grace” filled everyone’s ears. Tears of passion filled some of the choir members’ eyes as the words penned by the ex-slave runner, John Newton, impacted their souls. To the left of the choir was a podium and behind it was a short, darker faced man wearing a light blue woollen suit with a bright purple tie who had been bouncing up and down during the music. Evidently, this was the pastor. When the song was done, every one sat down, and the pastor stopped his swaying. Behind him was a unique combination of miniature flashing Christmas lights, a Jewish menorah, bright Chinese characters, and plastic neon orange flowers. From the ceiling plastic grape leaves and plastic grapes rounded out the decorations. Hudson whispered to Jo of the eclectic display, “They are offering up everything they have. Would my church back home?”

Ratty old cushions were on the pews trying to soften the seats. Dim lights were overhead. The flooring itself was a patchwork of linoleum. There was one luxury item. The sound system was modern and the soundman utilized it to its fullest potential. Hudson recalled a Chinese-Canadian friend of his telling him when he was seeking as much information about China as possible that people liked to talk loudly in China. Truer words...thought Hudson.

Pastor Wu was a character. Though Hudson spoke little Mandarin, he could tell the impish pastor spoke vibrantly and every once in a while he squeaked out his words to the congregation's amusement, used pauses to emphasize certain ideas, and joked as the congregation burst into laughter. The twinkle in his eye showed his interior life was alive. Smith could feel himself sitting down on the inside. The pastor must have asked for the people to pray, because unlike the prim and proper North American mainstream churches where the pastor led prayers for the people, and occasionally a person was selected to pray and was probably worried more about how they sounded than what they said and whom they said it to, the entire body of believers broke into audible prayer at the same time. It was as noisy as a Christmas family gathering at the Loch's. The delightful cacophony was lost when Smith also entered into prayer with his Master. Jo tugged on his sleeve to bring him back from his prayerful reverie, and when he opened his eyes he saw that he was the last one left standing.

Apparently, now the dynamic pastor directed them to open their Bibles. The hiss of the turning rice paper pages sounded like the tide coming in. Dog-eared and highlighted, these were not the display Bibles he often saw in North American homes. These were well used. While this text search was going on a cell phone went off and the person getting the call hastily got up and walked over to the side where an addition had been built to connect with the sanctuary. A woman behind him tapped his shoulder, and showed him where they were to turn to. "*Ting bu dong, xie xie*," he quietly responded trying not to draw attention.

Then Jo got an idea. She pointed to the woman's Bible and turned her own to the table of contents at the front. She counted the number of books down the column, "*Yi-ma*? *Er-ma*? *San-ma*? *Si-ma*?"

The woman was puzzled for a second then understood the meaning. She quickly pointed at the left column and said, "*Liu.*" Today's sermon was from Romans the sixth book of the New Testament.

A week later Hudson and Jo came in through a side door to avoid the spectacle of being dragged to the front of the church. This addition to the house allowed more people to attend, and was on two levels. Jo led Hudson through the kitchen where the largest wok he had ever seen was ready for action. The next room had shelving for Bibles and hymnals, and there were two wood burning stoves right in the middle of the aisle. The stovepipes were connected and vented the smoke outside. Hudson considered that he would have to remember to duck his head otherwise he would break the flimsy set up. They turned right and moved up three concrete steps of varying heights and settled down on what seemed to be old recliners covered in a burlap cloth in the third row. Again the balding woman with the multi-coloured dream coat greeted them as they sat down, and the pastor waved them forward. Jo and Hudson wanted to be part of the Chinese Church. They wanted to show that the Church wasn't just for white people, and that Westerners would meet with their Chinese brethren and not stay in isolated compounds. Church after all was a place for brothers and sisters to meet. They appreciated the offer, but did not want to take a special spot, or be 'shown off' by the Church. They wanted to be treated like everyone else so they stayed put. Cell phones interrupted the service again, but no one seemed to notice the ring tones and discussions. Ironically wearing an olive green Mao cap that looked like a souvenir from The Long March, an old saint with shaking hands came beside them. He took some wax out of his coat pocket and set it down on the seats. An old Chinese musical instrument stood in the corner. Jo whispered to him, "That's an *erhu*. It's called that because it has two strings '*er*.' Get it?" Hudson nodded and stared at the man as he waxed the bow. "Hudson, it would be great to hear him play it," Jo whispered again as the old man stood up, hands shaking, and walked into the main sanctuary; however, instead of turning left to the front, he went right and walked out of the building, bow in his right hand and erhu in his left. Puzzled, the Canadians refocused on the pastor.

Partway through the sermon Hudson needed to answer nature's call. He borrowed some tissue from Jo as he always forgot to carry some, and made his way to the section that was obviously a toilet. When he opened the door, he was surprised to see a hallway with two signs. This was a dilemma. Which one should he choose? Out of courtesy for those nearest the door, Hudson chose the farthest sign. The squattie was all cement with a hole in the floor and a waste basket for tissue. When he emerged from the stall, a wide-eyed woman stared at the man coming from the woman's section. She giggled as he passed by, and when he re-entered the sanctuary, his face was as red as the Chinese flag. The clearest lesson for Hudson was not the sermon, but the meaning of the Chinese characters he had just seen and would never forget.

Three couples surrounded Jo and Hudson once the sermon was done. Jo's Mandarin now was a real asset. Leaning against a wall, Hudson listened closely as he tried to understand the gist of the conversation, and occasionally he heard a word that he understood, but the words came too quickly. They were even giving Jo some difficulty, but the Chinese couples were laughing with Jo, and showed an inclusiveness that he appreciated. Hudson wondered how often he had missed out on similar opportunities in Canada. True, the multi-ethnicity of Canada made it more difficult to distinguish newcomers from long-time residents, but he resolved that when they returned to home, he would try to be more inclusive. Later, as they drove home on the Dayun 125 he noticed a road sign which beckoned tourists, "White Mountain Beach–a Place for Families."

Nine
To Market

Grilling mutton on the street, the Uyghur man in his skullcap grinned at Smith and offered him a sample of his *chuanrs.* The aroma of the Halal meat filled his nostrils. Who could resist? He bought a couple of the meat sticks for Jo and himself. Beside the *chuanrs* was another Uyghur man making naan bread. The Uyghurs were a Muslim minority group from the far western province, and they had more in common with the "stan" nations than they did with the Chinese. It was Saturday—market day, and like his ancient Anglo-Saxon forbearers, the local farming population brought their produce to town to sell. Twice a week the spectacle organized itself at 5:30am, and it stayed open until 6:00pm when the vendors packed up their stalls and went home to a well-deserved rest from the constant bartering. Centred one street off of the main road, the market would go unnoticed by those passing through the growing village; indeed, Smith considered, it was late September and some of the staff did not know it existed. Today he was on a mission with Jo: find food for the week.

He decided a good plan would be to scout out the booths and stalls first, and then like a general, plot his attack so that he could move effectively. Since everything had to fit on his motorcycle with

Jo and himself, careful planning was needed. Backpacks ready—they moved.

They looked at the riotous mass in front of them. Women, men, children, dogs, and cats moved in the market's narrow passage. Some chickens pecked at the grains near what they called 'The Rice Store.' Weaving and honking, there were several motorbikes slowly driving among the shoppers adding to the chaos. Shoppers walked, slaves to their cell phones. Others pulled their child along. Old men were playing *xiangqi*, or Chinese Chess, on a wooden box while a crowd of supporters were watching and bantering. Permanent fruit stands were on the right, vegetables on the left. Seaweed merchants with the salty scent wafting up from bowls of dampish green and purple stringy goo were next. Then came the seafood: scallops, shrimp, oysters, clams, fishes with long noses, flat fish, whelks, hairy crabs, and sea cucumbers. This assortment was displayed in tanks, in buckets, or on a quickly placed cloth. Then came the seed roasters, some baked goods, vegetables and temporary fruit stands. Reds, greens, purples, yellows and oranges filled his eyes. This would be a hard jig-saw puzzle, he mused. Smith glanced at Jo, and she indicated they should continue their mission inside the covered market where the meats and other permanent stands were. Granville Island had nothing on this, thought Smith. Here the real China presented itself. Buildings, people, public squares, and now food—everything was on a grand scale.

Chicken Lady was always a good first stop. Her crazy bouffant stuck out everywhere, and in the market she was a lighthouse that beckoned all. "*Ni hao,*" Jo greeted her as an old friend might greet another at the farmers' market in Deer Lake Park. The smile said it all. Regular customers. Not lookers—buyers. The Chicken Lady put her left hand on her table where various chicken heads and feet were kept in plastic tubs, and reached underneath with her right hand to find the right Styrofoam cooler. She knew her customers. Unlike the local people, these foreigners always bought the breasts. She had pondered this before. Why white meat? she wondered. It was not as tasty as the dark meat of the thigh for instance, nor was it as nourishing as the chicken heads. It was not as delicate as the chicken feet; yet, time and again the foreigners came for the cheapest cut she offered–the breast. Her white rubber boots splashed in the chicken juices spilling from the table as she jostled the breast bag into place. Flies landed on the spindly feet, and she swooshed them away even as she wrapped up the bag and weighed it. Stopping to answer her cell phone, she picked up a thigh and tossed it on the scale as well. One thing which was guaranteed at the market was that the vendors always made sure the customers had the right amount. Never undersell the customer was the prevailing attitude, and Smith had tried a variety of new foods from this "topping up" policy. The phone conversation continued as he put the heavy purchase into his backpack, and she showed Jo and Hudson the price on the electronic scale. Twenty *jin*, so seventy-five *kuai*. Amazing. They looked at each other and laughed. Over ten kilos of chicken breasts for about twelve Canadian dollars was a great bargain. Exchanging money and receiving change, both the Chicken Lady and the Canadian couple had smiles on their faces.

Vegetables were next. Surprisingly potatoes were plentiful. They bought some large ones after they bumped the excess dirt off. "Two meals worth, and some for a soup," Jo said as she started to touch the eggplant. Broccoli, carrots, and onions were tossed onto a scale, and after payment, tumbled into Hudson's pack. "*Bu yao*," which sounded like boo and yao (rhyming with Mao), meant 'don't want', and it was the phrase she used to discourage the pushy vendors' pleas to buy from them. Salad greens, for under three dollars, and now the pack was filled. Weekly groceries equalled fifteen bucks. While Jo bartered with a fruit stand owner, Hudson went down the row and turned right and arrived at the toothless sweet potato seller where he bought a roasted sweet potato to snack on for lunch. The old rusting barrel oven had a few on top, but the old man, his skin tanned from sun and smoke, lifted the lid and with his bare hand pulled out two better looking treats from the inside grill. His baseball cap proclaimed allegiance to the New York Yankees–a team and sport he had never heard of before–and he replaced the lid without even looking. One *kuai* and a *wu jiao* were forked over, and the warmth from the snack felt great in his jacket pocket as the first hint of winter air appeared.

This warm feeling evaporated quickly as he changed directions to get back to Jo, and he was confronted by a man with no legs. Smith took stock of this man's situation. Tin cup in hand, the man had arrived just moments before, Smith thought, because he had just passed through this way to get the sweet potatoes. Chinese people stepped over him and around him, but no one stopped. Smith was moving to give the man a sweet potato and some *yuan* when the sweet potato vender grabbed his shoulder from behind. He said something unintelligible to Smith, but his pointing finger showed Smith the reason for this unexpected intrusion. At the corner of the nearest building was a man wearing a leather jacket, mirrored sunglasses, and several gold necklaces. The meaning was clear. This man was 'pimping' the legless man, and the sympathy aroused by his situation only fed the younger man's lifestyle. A beggar-master in Baishantan, who knew? The age-old exploitation of people discussed in Rohinton Mistry's contemporary novel *A Fine Balance,* and made famous with Fagan from *Oliver Twist* still existed. "*Xie xie*," he said to the vender who waved his left hand and muttered something he didn't quite make out.

Hudson turned, but his loaded pack bumped a short man who

had a number of gourds he was selling. "Oops. Sorry." The rural musical instruments were unlike any he had seen before, and the man gave a quick demo of how to play. "*Bu yao.*" Undeterred, the music man walked beside the Canadian showing him shakers and how they sounded. "*Bu yao.*" Where did this guy learn his technique? Did he sell encyclopaedias too? Emerging from a tent stall, Jo helped him by offering a honey sesame bun to him and the vendor. The travelling salesman shook his head, and continued on his way as the pair bit into the baked treasure. These buns were as close to cinnamon buns as they could find in China, unless you counted the dry, stale ones Ikea sold. The bakery also offered cream puffs. For a recent gathering Hudson had gone to the shop and asked for six dozen, and the baker was puzzled. Then it dawned on him, and he understood. Everything here was sold by weight not by item, and he had asked using imperial standards. Why a dozen? Ten made more sense, and food sold by weight made even more sense. Many aspects of his own culture that he had never questioned were challenged in this gentle, ancient land.

The prize of the day, and there were always prize finds of the day, was fresh-pressed sesame oil. Jo showed Hudson where she had found the aromatic oil. The mill press looked ancient as the woman with the pink, checkered scarf over her head shovelled in more seeds into a rusty hopper, and her husband turned the wheel's handle to grind the tiny seeds and press out their nourishment. Out of a spout at the front of the contraption came the slow, but steady, ooze of brownish liquid. It dripped down a tin funnel into the waiting bottles. "How much?"

"Only fifteen *kuai,*" Jo whispered not wanting to interrupt the focus of the couple.

"Can we take some back to Canada?"

"I don't know."

"My sisters would love it."

"Our mothers too."

"Are you willing to have it spill inside your check-in?"

"Sure, I would double bag it, but would Customs confiscate it?"

"I don't know. We should look it up online before we buy it for gifts."

"It would be a great gift, but I would hate to lose it at Customs."

"Yeah. We'll check about importing it."

"The clothing people are back."

Hudson had noticed how this Chinese concept of 'people' had crept into Jo's language. *Ren* was the Mandarin word for people, and it was used as a base with hundreds of adjectives to describe exactly what kind of people they were. Foreigners were *Wei gou ren* or out of country people.

They wove through the crowd and waved at Relic and his wife from a distance. They had originally told Jo about the market while at a flag ceremony. Four young men were playing cards. *Pu Ke* was the most popular game in Baishantan, and it was characterised by a player literally throwing down his card with a shout. The spectators were laughing as a card slammed down.

After a two-week absence, the clothing area seemed to be further away than it usually was. Each stall offered a good variety of clothing from traditional Dong Bei scarves to name brand knockoffs. Hudson had seen Nikee shoes, Marco Poolo shirts, and Celvin Kleane pants. Still there were legitimate articles to be bought here. Some winter gloves might be handy, he punned to himself as he stopped at the first table. Jo moved on and a sweater caught her eye. The vendor's words drew her in closer, but it was the soft velvety touch of the silk that sold her. When Hudson came back to her she held up the purchase for him to scrutinize, "Only six *kuai*. Only a buck!" she reported to her fiancé. "Such a deal."

"You should buy those for your sisters. Guaranteed to get through Customs," he teased.

"I already did," she smiled. Clothing was a passion for all the Loch women.

There in the midst of the lane was the flower girl. She was from the country, and she had a wide assortment of Gerbera Daisies to go with her wide smile. The tall, colourful flowers caught Smith's attention. He loved cut flowers. In the past he had bought flowers weekly, and he wanted to continue this good habit. Interestingly, Chinese people rarely bought cut flowers as they thought they were a waste of money since they only lasted a short time. Live plants are better, he had been told, but Smith was tired of the colourless landscape. I'll liven up the house with these red, yellow, pink, and orange petals. "*Duo shao qian*?" he asked her.

"*Wu jiao.*" Five jiao was equivalent to seven and a half cents.

"*Wu jiao*?"

"*Dui.*" Yes.

"*Wo yao er-shi—ge.*" I want twenty. The young country girl, the trusting kind of Miss that the Scottish poet, Robbie Burns, would have wooed and won, seemed pleased at the sudden windfall. Smith was buying half her stock.

Satisfied with the mission accomplished, they started back to the motorbike with a full backpack. Hudson was fussing for his keys when Jo said, "Look." His attention was directed to the spot where he had left the legless man. A woman who had been selling *baozi*–steamed buns–was giving the man a small plastic bag of the delicious stuffed balls. The man quickly popped one into his mouth, and started to reach for a second when the beggar-master who was yelling at him to stop was cut off by several shoppers. This human wall allowed the man to finish off the entire bag uninterrupted. It was the first complete meal he had had in months.

Ten
A Day in the Life of Hudson Smith

Smith walked into the office, sweating from his four-story hike, and removed his deerskin gloves and Cowichan toque. The frosty room forbade him to remove his navy blue down jacket. A space heater was trying in vain to dispel the icy air, but Smith's breath was still visible. The crokinole board on the centre table was primed and ready to play. Tom Simon and Craig Dickens were masters, and both were practicing daily for the up-coming Chinese National Crokinole Championship in Shanwan. The study carrel that served as Smith's desk was piled with papers. He greeted Steph, his colleague who was right out of Simon Fraser University, and Tom, and opened the satchel to get his laptop. First thing to do was check the messages. Tuesday was a busy day it seemed. He opened the systems' message board, C.H.I.P.S. CHATTER, and dove into the messages.

On Tue 7:21 am, Sarah Whippet said:
Danny Li is suspended beginning this afternoon until further notice
Sarah

Shoot. Now I have to get material ready for him, thought Smith.

On Tue 7:21 am, Karen Song said:

Hello Everyone,

I'm just wondering, who has tutorial in 408? Yesterday I have lost my Winnie-the Pooh pencil case which has my computer remote and adapter for the projector unit inside and I know for certain I had it in that classroom for Block F as I spilled my almonds from my purse into the case. Just wondering if the person who has tutorial in 408 saw it during the Tutorial block. Any information would be helpful since those two objects are my "best friends" in the classroom! Thank you.

Karen

Oh Karen, your best friends–ouch. The next entry had been sent yesterday after he had left and it led to a series of chats on the department head restructuring initiated by Miss Chen. The old teacher's union mentality quickly rose to the surface.

On Mon 3:21 pm, Dan Best said:
As "The Teacher Formerly Known as Math Teacher" I thought I'd share the breakdown of some numbers:

If you are a 4th year teacher, you make $40,000/year here.

Teaching 8 blocks, that's $5,000/block

In past years department heads received one block off to compensate for their work, though many claim they use more than that block to keep on top of their duties.

Next year, with 4-5 dept heads on campus, I expect that the dept head workload will double (though I could be wrong if the job description changes and work gets shunted off to the Chinese secretaries).

In the final analysis, the $1,500 offered to each department head is:

A. Less than before.

B. More than before.

C. Equal to before.

D. A joke, and an insult.

On Tue 7:24 am, Don Hawk said:
We've heard a lot about how being a department head has no weight when applying for other jobs (not the same weight as IB training or AP teaching). The logical conclusion? It seems there is absolutely no reason on God's green earth for anybody to be a department head at this school next year.

On Tue 7:28 am, Eric Peterson said:
Greetings all: I think that this misrepresents the importance of department head experience. I agree that it might not give one an advantage in applying for a teaching position, however it gives evidence of leadership interest and experience if you ever decide to seek administrative positions in the future.

Eric

This discussion had been raging for several days, and Smith was tired of it. Next Hudson opened a new forum and read a message from the day before.

On Mon 4:28pm, Bobby Wilson said:
Hi Most illustrious Colleagues of this or Any Other Galaxy,

I am wondering if anyone knows of a quality picture framing company in Shanwan or kai fa qu?

I have a large painting that would like framed. It told me so, and I agree. The companies in the market (kai fa que), say it is way too big, but I have seen even bigger ones in all the bars and hotels around here.

Thanks

Bobby

On Tue 7:28 am, Don Hawk said:

You can get things framed everywhere (Pulandian market, Hong Mei, even Baishan). But don't expect any real quality. Bigger ones?

On Tue, 7:32 am, Heather LeRoy said:

There are quality framers at the Traditional Arts and Crafts Market in Shanwan... well there were last year, anyways.

On Tue 7:33 am, Janie Brown said:

that building has been torn down - not there anymore. There is a pet market there in the parking lot before the lot is rebuilt

On Tue 7:34 am, Heather LeRoy said:

It's moved...now it's on one of the corners of the traffic circle that has the big metal ship sculpture in the middle...sorry, that's the only way i can give directions...landmarks only, haha and there is another one which is by the circle with the huge soccer ball.

Smith thought of the water colour painting he had picked up at a local artisan's market, and the beautiful frame that he had picked up in Kai Fa Qu, but he decided not to contribute to the discussion. The comment of 'don't expect any real quality' showed a lack of investigation. Good quality also meant good prices, just like home, and most of the teachers were fresh out of university, and wanted everything cheap.

The final comment was a great truth. Here, in China, he was illiterate. He found himself saying things like, "Near the IKEA, or to the left of the 'Chicken Lady.'" Great empathy had been aroused for his grandparents from Holland who gave up the comforts and security of their homeland to go to Canada in the late '40s. The veteran teacher understood his students being tired after a full day of trying to comprehend English when he was tired after a brief conversation. Mandarin's four tones, the various dialects, and little time to study all conspired against his progress. Street signs, store signs, food product labels all baffled him. Frustration was daily. It was humbling to go from a highly articulate position in society to one where the native speakers giggled, or mocked one over the pronunciation. Hudson had found that he had started to frequent the restaurants that he found with picture menus. The entire Canadian staff re-named restaurants and streets in a way that harkened back to Chaucer's day and the signs outside of the pubs that gave them their name. Hence the "Big Fish" or "Blue Dolphin" restaurants in Baishantan, as the Canucks knew them, were seafood places with a large flounder painted above the door, and a blue neon dolphin sign announcing the delicacies therein. None of the teachers, save Relic, knew what their real names were, and ethnocentrically no one cared.

On Tue 9:12 am, Hudson Smith said:

I just started reading a book that Dickens loaned me called *Making Marriage Work* by Henry VIII....
I hope your meeting went well.

Love,
Hudson

On Tue 9:27 am, Jo Loch said:

This made me lol. You know that I am related to Ann Boleyn (sp?) don't you?
Love you,
J

On Tue 9:29 am, Hudson Smith said:
Yep...

On Tue 9:30 am, Jo Loch said:
Should I be worried? :)

On Tue 9:31 am, Hudson Smith said:
No.

On Tue 9:28 am, Relic said:

Does anyone know why the Great Blue Wall was erected today at the main driveway? I know there is a building going in the vacant field, but seriously...a wall already?

On Tue 9:30 am, Don Hawk said:
Perhaps we should picket the site until the Wall comes down. It worked in Berlin.

On Tue 9:32 am, Janie Brown said:
But it didn't in Tiananmen Square...perhaps we should have a contest to name the wall...I'll put up a prize for the best and most creative name.

On Tue 9:40 am, Craig Dickens said:

How about painting a mural on it? My name offering is Pink Floyd's or Wall Street East.

On Tue 9:45 am, Randy McMann said:
Here is your winner: The Grand Eternal Project Dividing the East and West.

On Tue 9:48 am, Pete Holland said:
LOL Perhaps we should use it as a 'Word Wall.'

The last one Smith laughed at and wished it was his. The 'Word Wall' project had been implemented as a way to optimize the use of English in the classes. It consisted of students choosing a vocabulary word, creating a picture of it, defining it, and giving an example of it in a sentence. Jill Redbourne, the new English Curriculum Coordinator, had designed the project for every teacher in every grade. She was a spunky Brit who, despite living nearly thirty years in BC, had not lost her Yorkshire accent. The thrill of the adventure had taken her first across the pond, to the arctic, and to the Queen Charlottes. She had lived two life spans, and her sense of adventure in the twilight of her career had not dimmed. She lit up a room when she entered, and (due to her declining hearing), she was heard by all as well. The 'Word Wall' was just another way to expose students to more English, but it became a symbol of top-down authority, and the teachers despised it. Littering the walls and the halls were words, a definition, and the corresponding Chinese character. The science and math teachers had scoffed, but begrudgingly gave in and completed the task.

On Tue 9:30 am, Eric Peterson said:

Hi Everyone,

I just met with Miss Chen to inquire about the chalk line going across the driveway and I was informed that on the weekend the blue wall will be extended to block access to the school from this route. As of today, Monday, to access dorms, teaching buildings, and apartments on campus it will be necessary to proceed around the outside of the main building. Since the project manager has complete control on how the work is done, he controls the access to the campus. It is unfortunate since I don't see the project getting underway for at least another month.

EP

On Wednesday Eric ate crow as the road was dug up, and the piping installed. On Thursday footings were in, poured and the first signs of rebar sticking up for support pillars appeared. "China moves fast," he noted to Janie Brown as he passed her in the hallway nodding towards the project outside.

Each teacher was left in awe of the project's speed until Relic said, "What is built fast, simply won't last." The crane is China's 'national bird' the joke went, and from the number of projects and the rate of construction, one had to agree. There was, however, a dark side to the on-going building. Poor quality materials had led to a disaster in the Sichuan province when the earthquake killed thousands. Charges were laid, and convictions were reached quickly. The thirst for retribution ran high in the region as hundreds of children were killed in poorly constructed schools. Bribery was rampant in the inspectors. Money laundering, stealing peasant land, and government corruption all were issues in the torrid economic climate. An entire ghost town existed in the southern city of Ordos where there was a city built to accommodate a million people, but no one had every dwelt there. It was a ghost town with no ghosts.

The flag ceremony this week had in a way also been one where Smith learned of the ghosts of the C.H.I.P.S. past. Tom Simon had stood near him, and asked him what his previous principal had been like and Smith described him in glowing terms; however, when Hudson returned the favour and inquired about the last principal to lead the good ship C.H.I.P.S., Simon became agitated.

"Well for starters, Sutherland couldn't remember your name. He called all the women 'Sweetie' or 'Doll,' and he gave nicknames to the men. He knew I'm a Liberal Party supporter so he called me 'Trudeau.' Craig became 'Poet-boy' even though the old famous Dickens was a novelist. He walked like a rooster strutting in his barnyard. It was probably because he was so short. Little Man's Syndrome. You know the type. Smaller, so they try to be tougher. Full of bravado, but he gave up last year in the final term. When Peterson came in to job shadow, he deflected every question to him, saying, 'Don't ask me, mate. There's your man.' It's funny though, that last term he seemed really happy. Believe me, we are so happy to have Eric Peterson here."

Smith remembered to check for the magpie, and like Old Faithful, it was there in the sky with a long stick in its beak. It tucked to pick up speed like a Crazy Canuck skier and then opened its wings to slow down as it landed on the library building. The magpie started to rip up the latest banner with its sharp talons and black bill. Its bright blue tail feathers as long as the rest of the body contrasted with the white breast. The golden threads would make a nice lining for the large nests they built. The infamous block lettering already was starting to split where the magpie did his mischief; this week's misspelled message might not last long: ETERNAL OPTIMIZATION OUR HEALTY GOAL.

Eleven
Upside-down

Tony Vander Kwaak turned off his cell phone. He shook his head, and the surreal conversation replayed in his mind. "I would like to know what your room rates are please? Do you have a room available for next Friday and Saturday night?" He wanted to surprise Debbie with a weekend getaway, and he had already arranged for friends as a ruse to invite them over for dinner and bridge afterwards, but in reality they would take care of Ruthie and Josh. Then he would whisk her to Shanwan for a weekend where she wouldn't have to lift a finger. Massage, reading, dining out, sleeping in, and leisurely mornings with tea and an actual newspaper would be the order of the day. He would pack her suitcase for her, and even include 1,000 *yuan* with a note saying– 'Go Crazy!'

"So you do have a room available for Friday and Saturday? Good. Can you give me the room rates? What? No. No! I want the room rates–I do not want roommates. Room rates. Roooooom rates. Raaates. As in the price of the room. No. I do not want to book a roommate, thank you. I want the price, the cost, of the room. No, I don't care if they are short or tall. I do not want a roommate." Eventually, he got the price. It was reasonable. A five star hotel for under $100 Canadian per night, but Tony was still unsure if a 'roommate' would show up or not. The nonchalant attitude of the hotel staff towards prostitution shocked him.

As Hudson Smith stepped outside of the New Building, his face turned up. The sky was blue, and though the chill of October warned of things to come, there was no heat to turn on. The central government decided when the heat started, and the general rule of thumb was that that would happen on November 15th. Hudson had already added a duvet to his bed, but soon it wouldn't be enough. He hoped that Jo had an extra one in her upstairs apartment that he could borrow.

The magpie flew through the courtyard and announced its presence as it alit on the building. The banner flapped in the breeze. MAKE HONEST AND TRUTH YOUR FRIEND it read. My, how a sentence can be so changed by missing a single letter, Smith pondered, but was it really missing, or was it another command lost in translation? He adjusted his toque on top and then reached for his gloves that he had stuffed into his coat pocket the previous evening. Flag ceremony had become part of his weekly routine so quickly it both amazed and bothered him that he could adapt to the communistic indoctrination.

The clear sky last night allowed him to rejoice in the stars. Cloudy skies over BC's Lower Mainland did not permit such viewing very often, and here, though it wouldn't happen much longer due to the cold, the light pollution was less obstructive as well.

He was glad he brought his sunglasses as today's flag would be bright. Putting them on, he perused the gathering masses. One of his own students would be speaking today. He made a note to congratulate Thomas before class. It was an honour for the boys to be chosen to speak at flag, and the boy had bounced into Smith's office before the hotel conversation to tell him. "Of course I'll be at flag," Smith assured him.

Hudson took his place at the back of the row, and his mind slipped back to Canada. Now he did the time zone math in his head 12+3=15. China was 15 hours ahead. A half-day behind plus three. Ten-thirty am here, seven-thirty pm there. Smith wondered what his children were doing. Such calculations were often performed– he missed them. Did they miss him? China was a long way from home. When he was a child, his great-grandmother had often said, "Like digging to China." It represented something distant or something ridiculous. A world they couldn't comprehend, and now here he was. University ate up his children's lives right now. He recalled how that had happened for him as well. Weeks would go by where he didn't think of home, it seemed. There were new ideas to grapple with, new friends to chat with, and new possibilities to dream of. Finally, he understood now why his own parents were joyous when he called. Life had a strange way of repeating itself. Hudson thought, I'm seeing my father in me, and I see myself in my own children. Wasn't that an upside down world? What's old is new.

The Chinese anthem began, and its military message filled the hearts of the boys with patriotic love as it encouraged them to "Rise up! For the ones who are not willing to be slaves! Take our flesh and blood to build our new Great Wall...." Sad, he thought, how the same ideas of boys 'desperate for some ardent glory' that Wilfred Owen ripped into in his famous poem, "Dulce et Decorum," could ring true in such a distant land, in such a distant time. The song continued, "Rise up! Rise up! Rise up! We are united and we charge forward under the enemy's fire...." Then again, the literature teacher in him thought, the idea wasn't new to Owen either. The sixteenth century Anabaptists of Europe had turned the concept of war and a Christian's support of it topsy-turvy too. Pacifism was an issue he dealt with in his Literature 12 class as he compared the ideas of the late-coming Donne's Anglicans, Milton's Puritans, and the dissenters of John Bunyan to the Anabaptists of Menno Simons and John Zwingli.

Theological questions were pushed aside as Canada's anthem with its Ti, Ti, Ti, Ta beginning entered his ears. He thought of how patriotism in Canada was said to be non-existent, and how Canadian commentators both mocked and envied the patriotism of the Americans. The great diversity of his land with three seacoasts, prairies, mountains, rich farmlands, and two deserts made it impossible to say the terrain is why he loved Canada. The great diversity of its people, the First Nations and their understanding of working with not against nature, the two founding nations, the Euro-immigrants willing to till the soil, the hard-working peoples of the Orient, and the refugees of the Underground Railroad all made a mosaic that was unique and beautiful in the world and made it difficult to pin down a cultural reason for loving Canada. Its stable government with original mottos of 'Law, Order, and Good Government,' its social welfare demonstrating values of compassion and concern, its ability to provide citizens with clean water, great healthcare, and justice in the courts were all reasons to love Canada, but not one of them alone was the reason he did. There was no doubt that he loved Canada–perhaps more than ever. A warm glow grew in his heart, touching his soul. He actually felt a little taller. The smile grew steadily as the warmth reached his fingertips. Smith realised that you are not really Canadian until you leave Canada.

A rising commotion suddenly disturbed his thoughts. The teachers, then the boys had that under current that exists in classrooms at times when a secret was passed around. He asked Tony Vander Kwaak, “What’s up?”

“That is,” was Tony’s laconic reply. Smith’s attention was directed to the flagpoles. There, rising to its pinnacle, was the proud symbol of Canada. The red stripes on the right and left side were in place as usual, but the red maple leaf in the centre of the flag was not reaching to the sky–it was pointing straight down.

Twelve
Holding Court

The boys were at lunch. *Jiaozi* (dumplings) and *nu rou mian* (beef noodle soup) fed the lads as they chatted. Stuffed after spending $2 Canadian, they chatted, ranted, and laughed. Several other customers looked their way because of their raucous ways, which was quite unusual in a land where loud speaking is the norm.

The room was typical of Chinese village restaurants. The decor was non-existent. Black fuzzy mould spread up the walls from the base. A golden frog with coins decorating it like warts was on the counter beside a large jar of clear liquor containing a deer's penis and testicles for virility. A poster of Chairman Mao was partially covered by a stack of beer cases. There were cracks in the walls, peeling paint, the flooring needed sweeping and mopping, the windows were smudged with oil and smoke, there was pinky-orange mould in the corners, the table a smear of past meals, and yet the food was plentiful and delicious. Moreover, it was cheap.

After a few times out, Canadian teachers knew that this could never be replicated at home. Health inspectors would shut it down, landlords would charge much more rent, food was more expensive, and wages here were so low one would be accused of slavery in British Columbia. It had been in a transplanted place like this in

Vancouver's Chinatown that Smith's step-great-grandfather, Wang Kee, had worked for six years. The first three years he paid back the head tax that his uncle had paid for him to emigrate to Canada, which the Chinese called "Gold Mountain," and the subsequent three years allowed him to gather up a stake and set out on his own to run a small Chinese restaurant in a brick building on Thurlow Street.

Relic was holding court in the loud and crowded restaurant, and both veterans and rookies were in rapt attention. "There was one time I felt afraid at the school. It was the year Beijing hosted the Olympics. Some French minister criticized the preparations, and the next day was Sunday. In Shanwan, a mob attacked the French department store chain Carrefour and looted it while the police looked the other way. For many days everything foreign was suspect or attacked. Nationalism is a powerful catalyst in controlling people. The counsellors at the school met with the boys and the next morning each locker had a Chinese flag on it. Two of my favourite students came to me that morning before school began and told me that some students had labelled me a 'Capitalist Roader.' That was the term Chairman Mao used to incite fear in the peasantry. The basic idea was that the person so charged was leading people astray through capitalist ideas. It meant being ostracized, and in many cases–death. Several other teachers were also warned in this way, and tensions were high. Though these boys were born well after the Cultural Revolution, they had all heard stories from their parents and grandparents. In the courtyard, the flags of the other nations were torn down, some Korean boys were beaten up, and then came the weirdest thing of all. At flag the boys, maybe for the first-time in C.H.I.P.S. history, were all in uniform, many had painted the Chinese flag on their cheeks, and sang the Chinese anthem loudly. At the top of their lungs. Loudly. An 1,800 voice choir is electric. Sound penetrates your very flesh. The teachers all looked at each other, and I know we all felt the same way. I was glad that this wasn't a military academy. Then, the boys did not raise the Canadian flag, or sing "O Canada." It was a slap to our faces. I've seen film clips of Hitler addressing people in the great Berlin stadium and the masses' response. I felt the same way during that flag. It was freaky."

"What about the Biblical darkness?"

"Oh, yeah, I had forgotten about that...three years ago when Sutherland was principal there was a flag ceremony that was freaky too. There was an electrical storm that blew across the Bo Hai, and the sky became very dark. It was actually so dark in my class a few minutes before flag that I turned on all the lights. Seriously, it could've been midnight–that dark. The air became cold–very cold as the cloud neared. The pressure dropped. Anyway, as the cloud grew in intensity, the boys grew more antsy. So did I. The basketball courts have metal supports and hoops. They are higher than anything else outside, and once the first lightning strike hit nearby, all the teachers fled for buildings. The students did not know what to do, but instincts took over when the first rain drops hit. The rain was so powerful and so heavy that it bounced off the ground and flooded Mrs. Li's sewing room. I was afraid then too, and like Dickens said, it felt Biblical. Other than those two times at flag, I've always felt safe."

"Come to think of it, there was a third time when I nearly shit myself. I was in a black cab going out to the reservoir to play some shinny."

"What's a black cab?" Pete Holland and Mattie Petersen asked simultaneously.

"They are the unofficial cabs. No licence, but without them we'd be stuck so often without rides. Anyways, every once in a while the regular cabs get upset over the black cabs taking their business even though they won't take us to out-of-the-way places, and they take actions to warn the black cabbies to get lost." He paused to take a drink from the green Tsingdao bottle, replaced it, wiped his mouth and continued.

"So there I was in the cab, and I was looking left to see if Vander Kwaak had finished putting our gear in the trunk. When I turned around, there was this huge muscular guy in a uniform in the front passenger seat, and he was pushing our cabbie in the ribs with a shovel handle telling him to get out. Well, the cabbie wouldn't get out, and as I looked out his side, I could see why. There were four other guys all dressed in uniform, and they looked ready for a fight."

"Like the cabbie, I decided I was staying put, but Vander Kwaak– he's yelling at these guys that the cabbie is his friend who is taking us out to the reservoir to play hockey."

"Those thugs reminded me of the old New Westminster Bruins in the '70s," Dickens added.

"Yeah, they probably would have fit in with those guys, because they eventually grab the cabbie out of the cab, and then they yank me out too. When I saw them swing the shovel handle at the cabbie and topple him like a tree, I thought I was next, but then the leader shook his fist in my face, kicked the cabbie's front grill, pulled off the VW ornament, and signalled his boys to leave. I was shaking from the adrenalin, let me tell you."

* * *

Meanwhile back at the school another meeting, this one sombre, was taking place. Eric Peterson reviewed the memo from John McAdams, his bad cop vice principal. He placed the paper down, and rubbed his temples with his fingers to calm himself. He looked into the office at the surly looking lad, but his gaze came panning back into his office on the large rubber plant his predecessor had left. The plant seemed to have acquired a layer of dust, and did not gleam like it had when he arrived. Peterson thought over his decision of last night. He disliked being placed in the position of judge and executioner by these boys, but he felt he had exhausted the ways to bring this boy into line.

"Miss Hu. Please send in Jeff."

The secretary caught the student's eyes. "You can go in now." The boy's adrenalin was pumping through his veins as he entered the foreign principal's office.

"Come in Jeff. Please have a seat. Mr. McAdams has told me that you have continued to miss detentions. The detentions were given to you because you were skipping classes. In fact you have missed a total of 35 classes in the last three weeks your counsellor tells me. You have been suspended twice, and yet this pattern continues for a third term. Why? Why have you hurt yourself this way? You have been warned. You have people who have given you extra chances. You have teachers who want you to succeed. You have parents who pay your tuition, and you have shamed each one of them. You have left me no choice but to expel you. I have discussed this with your parents, and your father will be picking you up within the hour as his plane landed in Shanwan twenty minutes ago. I wish you every success in life, but right now you are on a road to failure. I hope you can straighten out your life. Your counsellor will take you to the dorms. You will not need to attend flag. Good day."

* * *

Headmaster Wang was also holding court with his assistant, and the pretty woman licked her lips as she listened to Wang, "Miss Chen, I have a plan that will save the business money, and I want you to implement it, but it may not be popular."

"Mr. Wang, I will do my best to serve you and to bring efficiency to the company."

"I think if we use less electricity, the business will benefit and prosper. Classroom lights, hallway lights, use of the auditorium and gymnasium must be minimized. The school public address system also uses electrical power unnecessary to our task."

"I agree. I know how I will approach this idea. I will tell the teachers that the business wants to be more environmentally friendly. This can be very positive. I will send a C.H.I.P.S. CHATTER memorandum today."

"Very good, Miss Chen. That will be all. It is time for flag."

Thirteen
Money Matters

The school had an ATM right beside the library for the resident students and teachers to access cash. Mr. Wang had arranged for it, and for each transaction made, he received a *jiao*. Now a *jiao* wasn't worth much, but Wang knew that this cash flow would grow as his school grew. The small coin with the rice stalks on it reminded Smith of the old reverse side of the American penny and its two ears of wheat. There were about six and a half *yuan* or *kuai* to a Canadian dollar, and there were ten *jiaos* to a *yuan* so the coin was worth a penny and a half Canadian. Hundreds of transactions each day led to easy money for Wang.

Smith walked to the Bank of China ATM located at the far end of the main entry of the original school. The foyer was large and spacious. The Chinese built big to accommodate large numbers, Smith realized. The public buildings were important, and the architects designing them treated them accordingly. He avoided a gob of spit on the tiles and got to the machine. While a student greeted him, he inserted his card and the machine gave him the language choices of Chinese, English, Korean, and Japanese. Password? He punched in the six digits to enter the system. How he hated the number of passwords this new society needed. Passwords for his bank card in China, his account at home, his credit card, his online accounts, his driver's license, photocopy machine, school phone, medical card, Facebook, VPN, Gmail, various online reading journals, College of Teachers membership and others all required he remember some type of "Open Sesame" like Ali Baba. The worst offenders were those cyber minions who required numbers and letters. Smith was a word man. His password had always been the names of favourite authors, but when a web-based system refused to allow him to use his favourite, he was ticked off at the presumption that the machine and organization knew better than he did. One place asked him to verify his identity by asking what type of car did he first own. He entered VW Bug, and was refused, so he re-entered VW Beetle, then he tried Bug, and since the system refused this third attempt, it shut down and forced him to get a new password. Rats, he thought, it must have been Beetle. O the tyranny of technology.

The Bank of China assigned him the number he had punched in. Smith didn't want the hassle of going to a branch to pick his own password and the barrage of questions he would be unable to answer coupled with the ridiculous mimes he and the bank teller would be forced to use, so he went to the ATM each day to check on his balance. It was clumsy, but he didn't want to forget his assigned password. Savings...enter...balance inquiry...enter. The number came up, and then so did some Chinglish. The machine asked, "Would you like an advice?" Despite seeing this week after week, it brought a smile to his face. Whoa boy would he like some advice? Of course. Some people don't seek advice, but others do, and they listen and weigh the ideas before decisions are made. Smith liked to seek out advice. He thought back to the last time when he turned his back on advice. His lawyer told him not to give his house to his ex-wife, and Smith naively believed she would realize if he surrendered to her the one real possession they had, she would understand his sacrificial love for her. Smith didn't know about the other man, but when he found out, he was horrified at how he had probably given his children's inheritance to another man and his family. Seldom was ignored advice so costly.

Now that Jo and he were building a life together, he remembered some of the advice offered to him at DivorceCare about communication. They had open and frank discussions every day. He loved it. He loved her. He stepped away from the machine so Mattie Peterson could use it, and as he looked up he noticed for the first time the beaten sign over the Physical Education Office that said, "Devote to Health for Human." As he walked back on the tiles to the front doors, he braced himself for the blast of wind he would have to endure for the fifty meters before he entered the other cold building. The bills were still crumpled in his wallet, and he tried to smooth them out to make it thinner. As he stepped out, Miss Chen was coming in and her tight leather boots clicked along the tiles. Her large calf-length coat swallowed her petite frame the same way she swallowed subordinates and spit them out. Relic had advised him to avoid her if he could, and Smith had done a good job on that front. Their paths had not crossed since he had arrived. She stopped and greeted him, "Hello Mr. Smith. I have been wanting to speak with you and Mr. Dickens about paper usage in English Department-ah." She was nervous to speak to one of the English teachers, and as Xiaoqing Chen waited for Smith's reply, her tongue moistened her lips.

"Oh?"

"It seems you use a great-ah deal of paper."

"We use some for tests and some for stories."

"Yes. We will cut-ah back-ah."

"I'm sorry?"

"Paper is unnecessary for tests. Please to use classroom console for all-ah tests in future. You will read-ah new policy on my C.H.I.P.S. Chatter this afternoon-ah. Good for enwiroment."

Smith shrugged and left before he let her have it. Good for the bottom line, he cynically thought. Head down he trudged the fifty meters across the compound thinking about the ramifications of such a policy. Students would have to wait until the slowest reader in the class finished each page before he could scroll down. Boys weren't the most patient of creatures to begin with. Paperless tests sounded fine, but he would have to then have his students send them to him, and if they arrived, he would have to wait while each one downloaded. He would have to open it. He would have to mark it with a program he was still learning how to use. Save it, and send it.

That afternoon, as promised, the policy letter arrived. "Smith, Song, Simon, Steph, did you read the Chatter?" Dickens inquired.

"No, what's up? Steph asked as she focussed on her marking.

"Read it. It's a beauty."

Smith, Song, and Steph opened their Chatter, and got the same red radio waves announcing a missive. Smith opened it and read:

On Tue 2:21 pm, Sunflower Hu said:

Hello Dear Teachers:
Please open and read attachment from Miss Chen which will optimize our implementation at C.H.I.P.S..
Yours truly,

Sunflower Hu

Smith opened the attachment at the same time as the others. He could hear Dickens pounding his keyboard at his side. Once it opened he read the scanned letter:

Canadian Harmonious International Peace School

13888 Baishantan Lu,

Shanwan, Liaoning

People's Republic of China

116688

Staff Announcement:

At Canadian Harmonious International Peace School we believe in values that will help our students optimize their implementation. One of our values is that we will do everything possible to keep our skin green. This sustainness will make C.H.I.P.S. a leader in environment protection in China. As such there are several changes to policy that are effective immediately now.

There will be no paper used for tests by teachers.

All teachers will turn off lights in the classroom if it is daytime.

There will be no hallway lights used.

The school gymnasium and school auditorium only if there are groups of thirty or more, and permission must be obtain from Miss Chen by writing a lotter explaining the purpose of the usage. The principal and the school's General Affairs Department must have first signed the request letter.

Computers shut off must be once the teacher is done with them.

Hand dryers in all washrooms will no longer available.

Staff washrooms will no longer have toilet paper supplied.

These economic measures will be good for C.H.I.P.S.. Thank you for helping C.H.I.P.S. become a sustainable. Teachers found not comply with new measures will be docked 500 *yuan* from their paycheque and may be dismissed.

Sincerly,

Miss Xiaoqing Chen

Turning to Dickens, Smith tried to read his face. What would the veteran say? The Department Head waited for the others to read the letter. "This is brash. No wonder every student in my classes wears glasses. It's a good thing that the doors are kept wide open to let in the sub-zero air, and to let out the warmth. The coal-burning furnace will really help the environment, won't it? Global warming be damned. Does anyone have some toilet paper I can borrow?"

Smith tossed him his emergency roll, and as Dickens walked into the hall and before the door shut Smith heard him say, "Boy, it's dark out here."

All across the campus the ripples of the announcement washed over the staff. Mr. Wang sat behind his dark mahogany desk and reviewed his letters going to various departments within the school system. Miss Chen lightly knocked at the Headmaster's door. "Come in. Ah, Miss Chen. Please have a seat." She sat down in the chair that her employer had nodded towards. "Miss Chen, I read your e-mail to the staff. I fully support your efforts to reign in our costs." He brought his hands together and flexed his fingers. His eyes fluttered, and he stared at Xiaoqing. "Is there any way to rein in our employee costs?"

Xiaoqing Chen considered this new direction. She knew the Chinese staff would support the effort, but the Canadians, she knew, were unlike Chinese people. They asked questions, would upset societal harmony, and were blunt in their criticism. Was it their own education system that created them? Hard to control, but everyone had a price. Sun Tzu had been quite clear on leading people into uncomfortable areas. "Mr. Wang, I do have some thoughts on issue."

Wang's focus broke. He raised his head and looked down his nose. "I am ready to hear them. Yes, I am most interested to hear them."

It wasn't only the staff that was feeling the constricting power of Xiaoqing, the students felt her tightening on their wallets too. Kevin, a strong thinker and fluent speaker who knew the pros and cons of the school's system, sat down in his desk with a plop and his face was contorted with anger that he couldn't freely express. He took out a pen and started to tap it on the desktop. Other students entered the dim room singly and in bunches. When Roy, a usually quiet boy, came in and immediately started speaking Mandarin to Kevin and Leo, Smith knew something was up. The stoicism was breaking down. With as much disinterest as he could feign, Smith asked, "What's up guys?"

"The school announced that everyone has to buy a new C.H.I.P.S. tie, and I looked at the tie, and it has poor quality, and it costs much," Kevin responded. The floodgate opened.

"It's made in Korea," Roy hissed out the words.

"All th-th-th-they wa-wa-wa-want ismmmmmmmmmmmmmmmmon-on-on-on-eeeeeeeey, Leo stated.

Smith smiled. His thoughts rifled through his mind. C.H.I.P.S. was working. The boys were becoming critical thinkers. It was a tribute to the Western education they were receiving that they would even consider a challenge to authority. They were changing. They would change all of China with this new ability.

After the day ended, Dickens pulled out his *xiangqi* board to play Smith. Dickens would play red and started first sliding his cannon in behind his soldier and in front of the general. Smith countered by moving his horse to protect his own soldier. The circular pieces continued to slide and jump around the board as the two neophytes tried to position themselves for victory. The elephants couldn't cross the river; the horses were blocked; the chariots zoomed horizontally and vertically while the two men matched wits. At the end, Smith used a double cannon formation to conquer Dickens's poor general. Both men smiled at the competition.

Hudson went back to his computer, and he opened his CHATTER to find yet another message from the office:

On Tue 4:30 pm, Sunflower Hu said:
Hello Dear Teachers:
Please need to read that Miss Chen asked us to will noticefy you that our C.H.I.P.S. pay deposits will be delayed this month. Your pay deposit will occur on the 19th as the bank is closed for technology upgrade from the 15th to the 18th. Sorry for the

inconvience.

Thankful,
Sunflower Hu

This was the second time in two years this had happened. Last year it set off a near riot, Dickens had told him, as Chen had announced this at a staff meeting. The school had given several reasons why the payments could not be made a day early, and none of them satisfied the Canadian teachers who were all tied into Internet banking and preapproved withdrawals. "Dickens, read the CHATTER."

"I am. I am. Well, give her credit. She learned not to tell us in person. She lost so much face last year."

Already the CHATTER was heating up as teachers vented over this breach of contract. "How can they expect us to trust them when they keep breaking our trust?" One of the first CHATTERS said. It was an irritant of course, but for Hudson and Jo such a problem didn't impact their financial picture; however, they empathized with the younger staff who had student loans and credit card payments to make. They were the ones who would be hurt most by this pronouncement. It perpetuated the mistrust between the two camps, and the poisonous atmosphere would hurt students.

Outside the workers unfurled the banner of the week. The familiar gold block letters exhorted the boys. It read: GLOBAL ECONOMICZING FOR MILLENNIALL RESULTS.

Fourteen

The Great Savings Plan

Seven years before Smith's arrival in China, the Canadian Harmonious International Peace School announced that there would be a new benefits package for its staff who stayed beyond two years. Teacher retention was the package goal. A revolving door was one way to describe the staff at C.H.I.P.S. over its first eight years of providing Western education in an Eastern setting. This was the first change in the contract that had ever favoured the staff, and the one teacher who had served longer than any other, Relic, was a bit skeptical, but even he was won over when the first letter containing his RRSP growth statistics for the previous year arrived. The school would provide one percent per year to a maximum of ten as a bonus for those who stayed longer than the first two-year contract; however, Mr. Wang did not foresee a tightening job market in British Columbia, nor did he envision the dozen or more staff who would marry Chinese nationals and start to call China home. Thus, this pension plan became a cost that was a thorn in the flesh to the payroll department and to Mr. Wang. Miss Chen understood this fact and knew that to gain favour, if she could pull off her new proposal, Wang would be indebted to her.

Xiaoqing waited in the main office for Mr. Wang's secretary, Sunflower, to give her permission to enter his private office. While waiting, she adjusted her new dress. It was the latest Korean fashion, and she knew that the secretaries had all noticed it when she walked into the main office. Her fingers slid across the handles of her computer bag, and she slowly gripped them. The plans she had written inside would change the school forever, but they could wait until summoned. Patient waiting was something she had mastered in working with Wang. Swaying back and forth almost imperceptibly she could see through the glass windows of the spacious room that he was looking at a newspaper and sipping tea. The large high backed reclining chair made with Italian leather was imposing enough as it looked like a throne, but the desk he sat behind was easily a meter wide. A gulf separated any person who had an audience with Wang and left no doubt who was in control. Each office door had a window with frosted glass which had a clear space where the Chinese flag's stars and beneath it the Canadian maple leaf had been embossed. As her soft pink tongue licked her lips, she waited for the secretary's nod for her to enter.

Mr. McAdams left Eric Peterson's office that sandwiched the main school office with Wang's. Secretly Xiaoqing admired the way anyone could walk in and speak with the Canadian principal. It made everyone feel they were on the same level. "Hello, Miss Chen," he called out as he waved at her. Such a happy man, she thought. Either he is oblivious, or an idiot. Xiaoqing nodded slightly, wet her lower lip, and waited.

At the same time two floors above, Relic sent a C.H.I.P.S. Chatter message during his first break in the class.

On Mon 9:21 am, Relic said:

I need some help from you sport fans. The landlord at the barn has increased the rent by five hundred *kuai* per month. The Shanwan Roller Hockey League can't afford the hike as most of our kids are Chinese. I can't increase the fees. Can anyone help us? Feel free to Chatter your ideas to me or drop off your donations to my office.

Relic

Smith thought of how sports had helped Jo and him become the people they were today, and knew he had to contribute to keep kids playing.

Xiaoqing surveyed the main office. Four secretaries were typing letters, reading computer screens, and speaking on the antiquated telephones. Of the four, Xiaoqing liked two: Hu Ying, who used the English word Sunflower as her first name, and Zhang Jing. They gave her proper respect, but the other pair, Guo Luo Jun and Zhuang Fei, had become too close to the foreigners. Their English was excellent. It was even apparent in the office décor as student artwork hung on the walls surrounding the office. Western abstract art is so childish, Chen thought. Straight lines, circles, squares, and triangles of various colours were supposed to bring beauty and peace within? Wang should not allow this. Good Chinese watercolours in the style and form of the masters should be here. Our students should be taught the classical way in the art room. Her thoughts were interrupted as Miss Hu said, "Miss Chen, Mr. Wang will see you now." Hu rose from behind the desk and started to make tea for Wang and his assistant. As Xiaoqing slipped past the massive door with its beaver carving, she thought that the secretary had been well trained.

"Ah Miss Chen, please have seat." He waited for her to settle before he continued, "The tea is very good that Hu Ying makes." Timidly the secretary entered the room with her head bowed down. She placed the tea tray with its two cups and glass press on the small table beside Chen. The steam rose from the delicately painted cups, and the soft scent of jasmine tea danced in her nose. Mr. Wang would discuss many factors in the typical Chinese way before he got down to business.

Peterson called Whippet on the phone. "Sarah, Wang told me today that he has plans for another school in Malaysia. I thought I would let you know so you could approach him about a possible principalship. You are ready for a challenge like this. You have been doing a superb job; you are tactful; you are proactive; you are a leader. Yes, I will give him my recommendation, and you my full support. You'll apply? That's great. You will be an excellent choice." As he hung up, the school bell sounded.

Sarah immediately called John to tell him of the great opportunity. Silence was the first response followed by a timid question, "What about us?"

The bell signalled the end of the class, and the blaring marching music flowed from the speakers in its place as though a lunatic conductor had hijacked the orchestra. Smith bumped into Dickens as they walked out of their rooms on the way to their office and then to flag. "Did you see Relic's Chatter?"

"Yep. I did. The landlord has poor Relic in a spot. There is no other facility that could host roller hockey."

"Need might cut two ways though. I bet the landlord needs him too," Smith slyly said. Craig Dickens's head made a double take to make sure he had heard right, then as they continued into the office putting their books down and grabbing toques and gloves to wear outside, they moved to flag ceremony creating a plan that might work.

"I believe you have a proposal to save the school some money."

"Actually, Mr. Wang, I have several plans and each will save the school large sums.

"What are the main premises of your money saving initiatives, Miss Chen?"

"The first and most important one is that we eliminate the pension plan. Secondly, we make it retroactive to last year. Third, we cut back on luxuries. Fourth, we raise class sizes, and eliminate positions. Furthermore, we under utilize our recruitment possibilities."

"What luxuries are we unwisely offering?"

"The staff bus to Kai Fa Qu for shopping is one such luxury. The morning shuttle bus from the *qing gui* is another. Free paper, water and felt pens for classes is another. We can sell the computer printers and have teachers supply their own."

"What positions do you suggest?"

"We are over-staffed in the English Department, the Physical Education Department, the cleaning staff, the office, and the Canadian administration. The potential savings is nearly a million Canadian dollars."

A smile crept across Wang's face. She had said, "million."

"Student recruitment can increase by a hundred per year by requiring our Chinese staff to enrol at least one student each. If they do not, we cut their pay. Such performance clauses are common in the West."

It was a bold plan he knew. What if teachers balked at the idea? He watched Chen pull out her laptop.

"Most importantly for our profit optimization is eliminating the pension plan. In the computer are projections based on this new way. They are most beneficial to C.H.I.P.S. school. Conservatively, pension plan will save two millions."

Rising from his desk, placing his tea cup on a granite coaster, and indicating the door, Wang said, "Ah, I would like to hear more, but right now it is time to go to flag. After you, Miss Chen." They entered into the office that was alive as a dozen or more teachers and administrators checked their mailboxes before going outside.

"Hello Miss Whippet, Mr. McAdams. It will be icy this morning at flag I believe," and as they left the office, the hallway fulfilled Wang's prophecy.

As they moved through the open front door, Sarah was emboldened to ask, "Mr. Wang, I understand that you are opening a school in Malaysia next year. I would like to apply to be the principal of it. I am ready for the challenge of bringing the C.H.I.P.S.' style of education to Malaysia, and to operate an elite school."

Wang stopped at the top of the steps and considered this sudden request. He could eliminate one of the vice-principals here by sending her there. The savings Miss Chen were speaking of were already coming true. "Your suggestion requires some consideration, but I thank you for offering to advance C.H.I.P.S. in Malaysia. We will speak further on this matter."

Dickens and Smith searched the myriad of faces at flag for signs of Relic. They had a plan of attack to help the Roller Hockey League, and the sooner the better.

As the Chinese flag was rising in the sky, Xiaoqing looked down the row of administrators and considered each one's fate. Meanwhile Sarah Whippet thought that maybe next year she would be seeing the star and stripes of the Malaysian flag rising above her head. McAdams was shivering in his thin pants that were no match for the wind which cut through more efficiently than any tailor's scissors. Peterson was absently mulling his retirement and reading to his grandchildren.

On the dormitory behind the homeroom lines the workers in their trusty grey uniforms unfurled the latest banner. The block letters ended with an exclamation mark. It read: SAVE MONEY FOR YOUR HEALTY!

Fifteen
On Team

The future leaders of Chinese business, university professors, and scientists filled the basketball court. The Siberian wind was punishing, and Smith's long johns tried in vain to protect him. Everyone present wished they were somewhere else, anywhere else, but here they were obediently at flag. The mind can do marvellous things when it wants to disassociate itself from unpleasant situations. Smith's mind drifted back to the previous evening while the secular rituals began.

Hudson sat in Peter's, the local restaurant that catered to the large Canadian population in Baishantan. He thought about the trip to the diner and still couldn't believe that his cabbie had cut off a bus and a dump truck by driving around them on the left (directly into on-coming traffic) and veering in front of them to turn right. The horns were still blaring in his ear. A true multi-tasker, the cabbie had done this while carrying on an animated conversation on his cell phone and listening to Michael Jackson sing, "Beat it." Jackson was big in China.

Now at the restaurant Smith started to relax. The host had opened the door for him on his arrival, escorted him to a table in the empty place, and hovered over him after he had sat down expecting his order immediately. This had happened to him in nearly every restaurant he had gone to in China. The level of service would put every Canadian establishment to shame; however, he wanted a few moments to read the menu without the waitress standing by his side. All he wanted was a few minutes to collect his thoughts. Just a few. There was one thing he loved at Peter's, and that was pumpkin soup. It was creamy, spicy, and delicious. Warm and aromatic, rich and nourishing, it was his usual first choice, and he anticipated it and the comfort the steamy bowl provided. "I'll have the pumpkin soup, please."

"Would you like the large or small?"

"Yes, I'll have the large please." Dressed in three layers of sweaters, the young lady left to report the request, and he admired the decor. Laminate flooring, the tablecloth, the walls–it all reminded him of Vancouver. Typically a Chinese diner was a little more like a one star hotel with no table cloth, no clean floor, and no clean walls. She came back.

"We have no large soup."

"Oh, I'll have the small then."

"Would you like two?"

"If you have enough for two, can't I just have a large?"

"We have no large bowls–only small ones."

"Oh. I'll just have one small, thanks."

"Okay," and away she went.

A few moments later she was back. "We have no small soups."

Ordering was always an experience. Sometimes it was a surreal conversation like the one he just had. At other times it was a language issue. Many places spoke no English and had no English menus. This was expected. This was China. Adventure, he reminded himself, was why he was here. He used a point and hope strategy when all else failed.

Squid on a stick, sold by street vendors, was cooked on a grill with a cement trowel pushing the sea creature flat so all the legs were evenly cooked. Smith thought it might actually be cuttlefish, but he had left his reference books behind in Canada. Sea cucumber, of a different variety than the ones thrown away by fishermen in the Strait of Georgia, was a delicacy here. Hudson hadn't ordered the latter, but there was still time to try this local flavour before he left China for home.

Tu dou ni, a mashed potato dish with pepper, onion, gravy, and cilantro, and *di san xian*–the three vegetables of the earth (green peppers, potatoes and egg plant), and gou ba rou, which was close to sweet and sour pork, were delicious and had become his personal staples in Chinese restaurants. *Tu dou ni's* acrid cilantro smell would waft through the air, and tickle every nose in the room. *Di san xian's* earthy brown colours swam in a lake of oil. A good gou ba rou would shine, but the tongue would rejoice over the sweet twice fried pork. *Jiaozi* were a dumpling dish that not only was familiar, Smith likened it to perogies, but it was superior to the bland Euro fare, as it contained a meat stuffing and not just potatoes or cheese. The prices were great and Jo and Hudson dined out for under $3.00 each a couple of times a week.

Niu rou mian, or beef noodle soup, was often a lunchtime dish Hudson ate at the school cafeteria. He had called the cook, making the noodles in the way which Marco Polo had first witnessed and brought back to Italy, the Noodle Man and had even posted a video on Facebook when he had his Virtual Proxy Network up and running. The noodles were great, the broth tasty, but the beef at the school was often filled with cartilage and veins. He added the hot pepper sauce with the seeds and ground peppers, a bit of soy sauce, green onions and some kind of green vegetable leafy stalk either celery or parsley as far as he could tell.

The Canadians had renamed the restaurant *tu dou ni* as it served a mashed potato dish which was shaped like a volcano and had a raw egg as its lava in the cauldron and a gravy moat with cilantro. In the Dong Bei region potatoes were more common than rice as the harsh climate dictated the crops. A rice farmer here could grow one crop, and a potato farmer could capture a niche market for the earth apples. *Tu dou ni* was a kid's dream. Once the volcanic ingredients were mixed together it was superb; although, Smith always wondered if the raw egg would give him some kind of bellyache. 'China Belly' was fairly common amongst the staff, except among those who would not eat local food. When Smith had heard of this, he shook his head in disbelief–this wasn't Kitsilano, he thought. Of course the food is different. Of course it could cause minor ailments. It also caused joy. He had never tasted cooked cucumbers before, nor apple flavoured potato C.H.I.P.S., nor had he had corn on pizza. The delights of bean ice cream, apple milk, corn yoghurt, and silkworm larvae also were options he had never had in Canada. Jo had convinced him to try chicken head *chuanrs*. These shish-ka-bobs, four heads to a stick, were cooked outside over a charcoal fire, but after they had eaten the gristly-cartilage orbs, they realized they wouldn't ever do that again.

Western food was available, but with shipping costs and limited supply, it was expensive. Some restaurants offered Western cuisine, and Hudson still shook his head over the burritos he had eaten with a side of whipped cream instead of sour cream. Western fast food joints were everywhere, bringing with them the increase of obesity and heart problems; however, these places had a cachet of being Western and therefore conferred status on their eaters as wealthy. It was not uncommon to see young Chinese professionals eating there in their business suits working their iPhones. Status, not food, was the main goal.

While Hudson wasn't too particular about the food he ate, water was one area that he was cautious about. Herbicides and pesticides ran-off from farmer's fields and infected the aquifers and the tap water. Bottled water was his drink of choice, and at one *kuai*–cheap. Best to be safe, Hudson thought. Each hotel he had stayed at also provided bottled water, and he was surprised to learn early in his sojourn that the locals also used bottled water. When he asked his students about the drinking water situation in their hometowns, each stated that they used bottled water. Hudson thought about the clear, clean streams in BC, and realized he had been blessed with an abundance of the precious liquid in his homeland.

Beer was another liquid common and tasty for some. Breweries in Harbin, and Qingdao spoke of the availability of grain and hops. The Germans had a colony in Qingdao in the nineteenth century, and they had set up several large breweries which when the Japanese took over the region, were kept in operation. Ice, Dragon, Keller, Snow, and the eponymous Tsingdao, dominated the Chinese market. Tall green bottles with 620 millitres of brew dwarfed those of home, but the 3.5% alcohol content made a larger bottle necessary to provide the same kick. Smith avoided beer. He was the antithesis of the Canadian male. At university he realised that if he continued to drink it, the methane gas he produced would cause a super nova. He preferred wine, and occasionally found a local red that was palatable, but there was lots of plonk in between. His own palate had grown in tandem with BC's vineyards' quality and reputation over the last decade. Why, he had even brought a treasured ice wine from a winery near Kelowna the largest city in Canada's pocket desert. Sweeter and thicker than an ordinary wine, these vintages were specially created using grapes harvested at eight below zero Celsius that prevented certain enzymes from causing a bitterness to develop. Some years the right conditions never presented themselves, and so the wine was rare and sought after by connoisseurs around the globe. When conditions were perfect, the result was a dessert wine without compare. Only in Canada, Hudson thought, only in Canada–the land of ice and snow.

At that moment he looked up as Canada's flag rose to the pole top. Suddenly, the red five starred flag plummeted to the ground. The cable had snapped. The flag fell. There was an audible gasp. It raced down the cylinder. It looked like an arrow with exceptionally large tail feathers. This will not end well, thought Smith. One of the flag raisers tried to stop it, but the metal grommet hit him in the face, and he fell as though he had been decapitated by Madame Guillotine. The flag finished its decent in a crumpled heap on top of the student, and several Chinese counsellors ran to the assistance of the flag and ignored the boy. While they wrestled with the flag (and how it could get so tangled in an instant Hudson could not figure out), the wounded lad's classmates came to his rescue and lifted the groggy boy up and led him to the school clinic that the boys referred to as a hospital. As they passed through, the lines moved to make way for the group and then slipped back into their places like the sea. The commotion was immediately forgotten because to panic over it would mean that someone would lose face, and the ceremony continued smoothly to its end.

Since the cable had snapped, only the school flag and the "True North strong and free" flag remained, and as soon as the boys heard the directive, "And now I declare the Canadian Harmonious International Peace School flag raising ceremony closed. Students please wait for your teachers," the guards rushed forward to remove the national interloper and to raise the five stars of the Peoples' Republic. To the side of the platform, beneath the preening magpie, a new wooden billboard hung stating: "ON GOAL, ONE SCHOOL." Beneath the slogan were the larger than life images of the Canadian and Chinese administration. Apparently, the photographer hadn't noticed that all the Canadians wore light colours and all the Chinese dark, nor had he noticed that each group stood in its own row.

Chapter Sixteen
The Best-Damned Hockey Team in China–Without Ice!

Another Monday, another flag. Smith ached as he passed by his homeroom. Legs stiff, groin sore, buttocks bruised. Hockey had punished him. The Baishantan Snow Tigers were an outfit that had an eleven-year tradition of playing and carousing through the country. Smith was now part of the brotherhood. He had been convinced to join the team, though he was a weak skater, as they went for a weekend to Jilin City in the northern province of Jilin. Over the years Harbin (China's hockey Mecca), Shenyang, Qingdao, Shanghai, Beijing, and Hong Kong had seen the rag-tag group's skills. The Snow Tigers were a tight knit group led by their founder and most skilled player–Relic. When the school had finally grown to a point that there were enough teachers to put together a team, Relic initiated it. It didn't matter if some of them had never played before. A team needed bodies. Experience would come. Strictly speaking, the team wasn't entirely made up of C.H.I.P.S. teachers. A few American ex-pats from Minnesota, or Massachusetts were welcomed as well as a couple of Chinese players who, for whatever reason, found themselves in the lower end of Liaoning.

The Snow Tigers played on the frozen ponds and the local reservoir. At one point they played daily in a small pond behind the school, and when the developer put a high wall around the property, the Canadians built a large stile like their English ancestors had on the Cotswold meadows. Then the developer started to build and the Canuck ex-pats sought different venues within the area.

Relic bought the pucks, the nets, and ordered in skates and sticks from Beijing. Relic's Mandarin was excellent, though his contacts in Beijing laughed at his Dong Bei accent that slurred each word like a Texan drawls out English. He searched for teams to play against. He encouraged teams to invite the Tigers to play, and to host the team in their homes or in restaurants. He begged. It wasn't just the games he wanted; he wanted the cultural exchange as well. Relic had a great respect for the country and its people, and he had the heart of an evangelist–except his religion was hockey. This fervour to find venues was due to the problem that Baishantan had no hockey rink, and thus the Snow Tigers were like Mennonites of old looking for a place to land. They had a mantra which was "We're the best-damned hockey team in China–without ice!"

While Relic organized games on the ponds, and in other cities, it was Dickens, the English Department Head, who made sure that each Tiger player would have memorabilia from his stint in China. Jerseys, knit sweaters, patches, t-shirts, pins, steins, flasks, hockey cards, and jackets were his province. The school uniform seamstress was always willing to do the extra jobs that Dickens brought her. Her specialty became old woollen jerseys, and new teachers would ogle the 1928 Canadian Olympic team jersey, and the 1919 Vancouver Millionaires uniform that the vets wore. It wasn't unusual to see teachers wearing the 1948 RCAF jersey, a team that had won Olympic gold, or obscure jerseys from teams like the world champion Trail Smoke Eaters, or the Kansas City Scouts. Copyright? What copyright?

Dickens, though a consummate wheeler-dealer, was a pretty good goalie too, and he shared the time between the pipes with Randy McMann who had played in the WHL with the Moose Jaw Warriors and the Medicine Hat Tigers. Goalies often are a different breed, and Dickens loved the history and tradition of the game, and could spin a yarn to match. An avid reader, he also knew details about the game's stars that few others knew like the time when the Right Honourable William Lyon Mackenzie King met with the 1939 Toronto Maple Leafs at a séance during the Stanley Cup finals with Boston, and how Syl Apps spilled his beer on the Prime Minister.

Smith, who was a Habs fan, relished his Rocket Richard replica. When he wore it, he felt like he belonged in Roch Carrier's famous book *The Hockey Sweater.* Today at flag, however, he felt like a busted up Rocket as he stood behind his charges near Dickens. The overnight sleeper train from Shanwan to Jilin had taken fourteen hours one way, and the six bunks in each compartment were designed for people considerably smaller than his 6'4" frame. He had thought when he first took the job in China that he would be huge in comparison to Chinese men, but to his surprise the younger men in Dong Bei were tall strapping lads due to their diet that included milk and wheat. These young men, dressed in their camouflaged pants and long olive green coats with a brown fur trim, also suffered on the train. The silent stares emanating from their large heads while they smiled with tobacco stained teeth were disconcerting to Smith. Legs as thin as saplings hung out of the short bunks. The trains were from an earlier era when nutrition had kept people small. Flag ceremony today would provide a good stretching for his legs and back.

He noticed Relic, standing as far away from the speakers as possible, still had red eyes above his unshaven chin, and his slow movements mimicked every other teacher who had been on the trip. The local moonshine called *baijiu* was the drink of choice by most of the team during the trip. Smith pitied the three Chinese families who shared the car with the thirty Canadians who staggered up and down the narrow aisles challenging each other to down more *baijiu* than the last. At ninety-five proof the *baijiu* was a potent beast unleashed upon the unsuspecting rookies who carried the large thirty-gallon urn throughout the trip. McMann, the team's goalie and sport bets bookie, had bags under his eyes that reminded Smith of potato sacks. The *baijiu* hadn't hindered him from stopping the puck though as he was nearly unbeatable during his games. The potato sacks were understandable, Smith thought. At two-thirty that first night he had met McCann and a rookie named Pete Holland racing each other to the WC. Holland lost, and he opened the rocking train's door to solve his problem.

The train had arrived back in Beiwan, just north of Shanwan, at 5:00 on the Monday morn, and they were all in the class by 7:30. The toll of two nights drinking and two days playing showed. In a short weekend, they had travelled 28 hours by rail, two hours in buses, and played five hockey games and one game of shinny on a pond beside the Songhua River. For many of the BC players, it had been the first time they had ever played a game outdoors, and they were excited at the prospect of taking part in this quintessentially Canadian activity.

"Skating outdoors. I'm going to be skating outdoors tomorrow, Hudson. In China. Finally, I can be called Canadian. It never froze hard enough in Victoria."

The games had been tiring for Smith. His borrowed skates were too narrow, and it still felt like the skate blades were pressing against his soles. He had already decided that he would watch the outdoor game.

After the games, the Tigers went a number of different directions. Some went to a disco, others went shopping. Smith and Matt Peterson went to an Italian restaurant, ate a passable pizza with real pepperoni, and then they went to a hotel that looked like it had a bathhouse. "Have you ever been before, Peterson?" Smith asked.

"No, but I am ready for a soak and massage. I'm sore."

"I'm not surprised." Peterson was fresh out of UBC, and had played more than any other player. He was a good skater, stick-handler, and shooter. Fit too. It took a lot to wind him. Smith could tell by his slow gait that Peterson had done a bit too much after weeks of inactivity. "Let's go there. Tony said it was a good, clean bathhouse."

They trudged down the street. Cabs honked at them, hoping for a fare. The locals stared at them. Here, foreigners were rarely seen. The tall men entered through the large revolving doors, and were immediately greeted, given sandals, and escorted to the front desk. English was not spoken here.

"*Ni hao*."

"*Ni hao*, to you too."

"We would like to use the spa and have a massage...wait, um, *wo yao* bath."

A puzzled grin was the response.

Changing course Smith said, "Mattie, I'll just point."

The clerk gave him a menu of services, and after being shown a variety of price lists all in Chinese characters, Smith went to the wall behind the desk and pointed at the pictures of the large hot tub, and the massage tables. He had hoped this would clearly indicate what they wanted. Nods of heads, smiles, and once a wristband locker key was given to each man, they were shown the way.

The locker room was clean and the attendants were efficient. When the two men went into the pool area, all was clean. They showered on the side, brushed their teeth, and shaved. All the supplies were there–a sign of a good bathhouse. The tub water was clean; the various tubs had a variety of temperatures that soothed the aching bones. Smith rejoiced as he scoped out the other naked men in the pools and realized that no one was smoking. It was a bane in living here that nearly 85% of men smoked. He and Peterson watched a game between Twickenham and Manchester on the large screen over the end pool while they drank a bottle of ice tea.

Following the relaxation of the tubs the men had put on the supplied cotton shorts and top and had gone to get their massage; however, the reputation of foreign men preceded them, and two young ladies wearing red silk robes patterned with dragons and walking in two-inch stilettos led them up the stairs to a private room each. The silk dragons seemed to move with each step. Black, luxurious tresses swayed alluringly. “Hey, are you thinking what I’m thinking?” asked Peterson through the wall.

The room was draped in red silk hangings, and the bed had many red cushions with gold embroidery and tassels.

“Mattie, I don’t think they understood that we just wanted a massage,” Smith responded. The girls were puzzled at the

Canadians yelling to each other through the walls. "Just tell her '*Bu yao*' which means 'Don't want,' Smith called, and Smith, following his own advice, told the smiling buxom girl, "*Bu yao*," then "*BU YAO*!" as she started to take off her silk robe. Smith bolted from the room, and almost crashed into Peterson who was also making a mad dash.

"What will June think?"

"She'll understand. I'll vouch for you. I know Jo will laugh."

In the hallway Smith pantomimed to the young lovelies what they wanted–a muscle massage. No more, no less. Another puzzled look greeted them. The women called out for help, and this time Peterson mimed a massage to the supervisor who came to them. At last they were led to the right room, and a foot and back massage were given to the relieved men.

The anthem for Canada had just finished, and the magpie squawked its approval. The student maestro began conducting the 1,800 voice, male-choir in the school song, and Smith's mind drifted back to the weekend as the beaver gnawing a tree moved up the flagpole.

The team had eaten at the local McDonald's for breakfast. It was quick, cheap, and familiar. Spenser and Munroe asked the guys to be quiet, which of course roused the entire team to sing Tom Connor's "The Hockey Song" at the top of their voices. Even the two hung-over players joined in for the chorus. The coffees were drained, and the team hopped into cabs and made their way to the hotel.

Following the game, a resounding 9-5 victory for the Snow Tigers, the team stopped to eat at a Uyghur restaurant before playing an old-timers' team on the pond. Uyghur's were Muslims. They formed the largest minority group in China and originated from the western region. As Hudson walked from the street through the kitchen alcove, the smiling eyes of a Turkish-looking man wearing a small round white and blue cap was testing a soup. Relic had called ahead and steaming lamb *chuanrs*, soups and naan flat breads were waiting for the team. Tsingdao beer washed the tasty meal down. The family owned business featured the cook, and a pair of hefty women bringing tray after tray of food and beer to the seven tables. Their hips kept bumping into the tables or the players as they wove their way through the narrow aisles between tables. The huge smiles on their faces showed they knew their week had been made.

Presented with a bill for a mere two hundred *kuai* or thirty Canadian dollars, Relic announced, "Men, this is God's Country." Each player left full and contented for little more than a dollar, Smith marvelled. Surprisingly, when the players left, so did the family. Why continue to work when today's windfall could be enjoyed?

Jilin was a beautiful city with parks winding along the Songhua River. The old-timer's team had created an outdoor rink with one-foot high boards by flooding a soccer pitch with a small diversion of Songhua water. The river was famous in China. Smith rolled his eyes in recalling that every note-worthy thing seemed to be 'famous,' as it was the most northern river not to freeze over. Cynically, he wondered if it was due to the hot waste dumped into the river by factories upstream. The Chinese players had created a jury-rigged Zamboni that they used to clean the ice and smooth the surface. Consisting of two oil drums and an old rubber mat attached at the back, a skater would pull on the arms of the home-made Zamboni and skate around the rink while pulling on a rope to release the water. It was simple, and it worked.

The scene greeting the disembarking Canadians could have come from the Rideau Canal in Ottawa, said to be Canada's longest skating rink.

"Cool."

"Very cool."

"Finally, I get to play outdoors. This is awesome."

"Boys, let's enjoy the game. Don't worry about the referee. He'll be biased."

"This is like it's from a painting."

There were people from every age level who were skating, playing *tuo luo*, which was a toy much like a top that was struck with a thin willow stick or a thin leather strap to propel it across the ice, or pushing each other on sleds. The happy communists did not mesh with the portrait the Western media often gives of an oppressed people. There were families obviously playing tag, and children and seniors chasing after the *tuo luo* as it travelled across the frozen sheet.

Smith sat out the shinny game as already his bones ached, and he wanted to take advantage of the great afternoon light. Truly, it was a perfect spot to try out his camera's sport setting. Many locals came up to Smith as if he were a strange exotic creature, and he was. Very few *Jianada ren*, Canada people, came this way. Russians maybe; Canadians? No.

The large rink had two tiny nets of about two feet by six inches. Before the game the Tigers met at centre ice with the Jilin Old-Timers for the obligatory photos, handshakes, and exchange of mementos. A rigorous game of shinny between the teams which saw twenty skaters aside ensued, and the Snow Tigers proved their supremacy as they beat the hometown oldies 4-1 in a half hour game before they raced to the station for the trip home.

A minor crisis occurred at the station as McMann declared, "I'm not getting on that train unless my gear is found."

Apparently, Peterson had picked it up for him and lugged it on the car. After some tense moments, the message about the missing gear went up the chain like a fire brigade of old. Exhausted from the binging and from the games most of the players crawled into their bunk and when the three-o'clock train departed, most of the Tigers were asleep in their lairs.

The weekend had been an enjoyable time of camaraderie, playing, and cultural adventure, thought Smith as the flag ceremony's emcee student broke into his thoughts to invite the teachers to be dismissed first. The magpie flew off the building's edge and angled itself into the sun where Hudson lost sight of it.

Pushing his way past the blue blazers, Smith heard Dickens call, "Hey, Smitty. Are you sold? How did you enjoy it?"

"I loved it. I couldn't play when I was a kid. Growing up on Vancouver Island there was no outdoor skating. My parents couldn't afford the registration or the equipment. Really this weekend was a dream come true, even though I can't skate very well."

"Good to hear, good to hear. We go to Shenyang after the New Year's. Will you go?" Dickens asked as they slowly walked under the new red banner draping the building encouraging the boys to 'OPTIMIZE YOUR IMPLEMENTATION'.

Seventeen

The CHATTER

The C.H.I.P.S. CHATTER was the interoffice system of communication. Broken into a large number of sub-groups or forums, it offered staff a quick and efficient mode of contact. Smith subscribed to English 12 for the Fainthearted, The Not Jane Austen's Book Club, Sports News, Stuff For Sale, The E-Staff Room, Eats, Announcements, UBC-O Cohort, Today's Chinglish, and Chuck Norris.

Upon opening it, the humour subtle, the outrage blunt, the wit sharp, and the decrees weary informed and entertained the reader.

Dickens had shown Smith the system, and the two often enjoyed the cyber-repartees that they not only instigated, but contributed to as only English teachers can–with Wildean charm. Smith opened the Sports News forum and read the latest postings.

On Mon 9:21 am, Don Hawk said:
GO LIONS GO!!! Eat Green Meat
Don

On Mon 9:25 am, Matt Peterson said:
'Riders tame Mustangs on the prairie. Lions? Pussy cats more

likely.

'Rider Nation Member

On Mon 9:32 am, Don Hawk said:
Score at halftime Lions 14 Riders 10

Take that you Prairie Oyster Eater!!!
Don

On Mon 9:38 am, Relic said:
Did you know that the Chinese call testicles: eggs?
Relic

On Mon 9:45 am, Amanda Johnson said:
Are there any volunteers to help me with the reproductive unit for Bi 12?
Amanda

Smith chuckled, and knew there would be a price for Amanda to pay over her sloppy use of language.

On Mon 9:48 am, Don Hawk said:
Amanda I think there are many on staff who would be willing to help you in that department...lol.

Don

Hudson shook his head, and moved to Today's Chinglish where staff would contribute the weird and often delightfully curious ways the Chinese translated English on signs. He hadn't been to the forum in a week, and since the rule was only one post per day, he enjoyed five at one time.

On Mon 8:11 am, Kaitlin Coyote said:

Spotted at the National Geological Park on Saturday on a garbage can:

Other waste

Dust and other living rubbish

"Other living rubbish" brought a smile, and Hudson thought, nice catch Kaitlin.

On Tues 8:08 am, Matt Peterson said:
We saw this beaut in front of the gymnasium: Please avoid stepping on human skin green.
Mattie

On Wed 7:00 am, Craig Dickens said:
The charm of the mechanical translator continues as I saw this on a new school: "Bilingual Education Leading the Future"
CD

On Thurs 10:12 am, Don Hawk said:
Grass blue under the foot is forgiving! I saw this near the roundabout.
Don

On Fri 9:09 am, Don Hawk said:
Two in two days... a new record. For your safe, do not climax on handrail.
Don

Smith thought to himself, I need one more smile, and Hudson clicked on the Chuck Norris forum.

On Mon 8:02 am, Don Hawk said:
When Chuck Norris does push ups he doesn't actually go up, he pushes down the world.

Don

Later that morning at break Smith opened the CHATTER and explored the Stuff For Sale forum.

On Mon 7:30 am, Heather LeRoy said:
For free at my desk:

1. s-video to s-video 1.8m cable
2. RCA (red-yellow-white) TV cable
3. Large package of individually wrapped duck tongues (seriously - from a parent who wouldn't take no for an answer)

Heather

On Mon 8:30 am, Kaitlin Coyote said:
How does one cook a duck tongue?
KC

On Mon 8:41 am, Craig Dickens said:
Actually, you don't cook them. You have them as an hoers d'oevre with quackers.
CD

On Mon 9:33 am, Heather LeRoy said:
KC if I knew, I might attempt it, but I really don't know how to cook them, and frankly I don't care.
Heather

On Mon 10:37 am, Matt Peterson said:
With apologies to Dr. Seuss
Would you have them on a train? Would you try the monkey brain? Try the tongue, try the tongue, and you will see it's lots of fun.

Matt

On Mon 11:02 am, Tony Vander Kwaak said:
I hope it was a domesticated duck. Duck species worldwide are on the decline. I haven't seen any Little Grebes at all this year, and they used to be everywhere. Does the package come from a regular farm?
Birdman

Smith looked out his office window and shook his head as a pink plastic bag tumbled along, lifted into the air, and lodged itself into a tree. In two minutes he would be back in the class teaching the future leaders of China, and today he would continue the poetry unit he was developing with Dickens. He had looked at The War Poets–Owen and Brooke–now the focus would be on tone. Poetry was difficult for the students as they became bogged down in the vocabulary. When he asked them to circle unknown words after reading a selection, one of his better students lamented, "It looks like a bubble sheet."

Vocabulary was a nemesis to the lads. Without a good command of the words of the language, could higher order thinking be achieved? Was thought reliant on words? Orwell had demonstrated in *1984* that if a government controlled the language, it could control its people. Hudson knew his pupils were intelligent, but they relied on translating the ideas from Mandarin. This was a source of their problems. The boys memorized reams of words. Gaps were evident though as they asked what pigeon, boots, and shells meant. They wanted to be fluent now. Hudson told them, "When you dream in English, then you will be fluent."

Cultural literacy was also a problem. White meant goodness, purity, and innocence in the West, but to his students white was used to symbolized death. Allusions such as David and Goliath, Hercules, Scrooge, and Columbine were impotent for the future leaders of China. "I wish I could give my classes a vaccination like Algernon received," Tom Simon moaned to Hudson one quiet afternoon as they played crokinole in the English office while their visible breath curled around them.

"Give them time. That's all they need."

After teaching his class the poem "Siren" by Margaret Atwood, Hudson assigned another poem for homework: "Riddle" by William Heyen. The vocabulary would be simple enough, but the allusions to the concentration camps would have to be explained. It was shocking to him that a number of students at Halloween had dressed up in Nazi uniforms, and several had expressed in a paragraph the desire to meet Stalin, Hitler, and Mussolini. Anger had risen in his Western educated mind and coursed through the distant Jewish blood in his veins. These naïve lads thought about the power, but not the consequences. Hudson had considered this one evening with Jo, and she wisely reminded him that 1930s Europe hadn't considered the consequences either.

The frosty air slashed at him as he came out of the class. Adroitly, he stepped over the fresh spit on the floor and made his way to the office where he would check the CHATTER for the latest announcements.

"Hello, Mr. Smith."

"Hi Nero, are you not going to lunch?"

"No. I have to do my calculus homework. Then I must complete my computer presentation for history."

"What are you doing the presentation on?"

"I call it 'The Great Dictators of the 20th Century.' All the most powerful strong ones will be discussed by me."

"Whom did you choose?"

"Hitler, Stalin, Castro, Bush, Churchill, and Kim Jong Ill."

"What? No Canadians?" Smith playfully mocked.

In all earnestness, Nero replied, "Mr. Smith, you know that Canada is a democracy. Oh, there is my partner. Bye Mr. Smith."

Opening the CHATTER, the librarian (he was the only other Canadian beside Relic who did not use a name on the CHATTER), had posted something about a score.

On Mon 11:41 am, The Librarian Ogre said:
Librarian Ogre 1–Rats 0. You heard it here first folks.
LO

The response was quick and somewhat predictable.

On Mon 11:52 am, Craig Dickens said:
Attaboy.
CD

On Mon 11:52 am, Don Hawk said:
How about bringing your tried and true methods to my room, office, and floor?
Don

On Mon 11:54 am, Tony Vander Kwaak said:
Obliterate them. They are the number one thief of eggs, and they will often kill fledglings too.
Birdman

On Mon 11:55 am, Craig Dickens said:
Don, if you guys cleaned your office once in a while, the rats would have nothing to eat. The boys sneak food in here, and leave a feast each night for the Norwegian wonders.
CD

On Mon 11:57 am, The Librarian Ogre said:
NEWSFLASH!!!!!!!!! Librarian Ogre 2 - Rats 0. In broad daylight...the peanut butter is working wonders. Stay tuned for further updates.
LO

On Mon 11:59 am, Relic said:
One year the supply and demand principle was illustrated by the increase in cats. We no longer had rat feces on our desks. It was great, then Mr. Wang instituted a new policy that only one cat would be allowed on campus–Chairman Meow–and since then the rats have steadily re-established themselves. In fact, Wang would say that this is impossible as the government announced that Shanwan was a rat-free city.
Relic

On Mon 12:01 pm, Amanda Johnson said:
I hope it is being done in a humane way.
Amanda

On Mon 12:05 pm, The Librarian Ogre said:
Never fear. The brilliance of the science department is helping. Bobby Wilson, scientist and Saskatchewan farmer's kid, brought in the hi-tech set up. A pop can with a dowelling through it acts like a wheel and an axle. The can spins, and it is suspended over a bucket of water. Peanut butter is spread on said can. A ramp out to the can assists the little beggars to get to the can, and when the

unfortunate creature leaps on to the can, it spins him off after a moment or two of looking like a lumberjack in a logrolling contest. The creature drowns, which is a gentle quiet death I've been told.
LO

On Mon 12:11 pm, Craig Dickens said:
Drowned? Are any of the rats named Ophelia?
CD

On Mon 12:15 pm, Heather LeRoy said:
Would anyone be interested in helping me set up the first C.H.I.P.S. prom?
Heather

A prom, considered Hudson, would be a wonderful event, but where would the dancing partners come from? He slid his cursor to a different posting and clicked on it.

On Mon 9:02 am, Bobby Wilson said:
Why do we have music coming through the speakers before school and at lunch? My head is aching...
Bobby

On Mon 9:27 am, The Librarian Ogre said:
Sshh everyone. Bobby's tied one on.
LO

On Mon 9:29 am, Bobby Wilson said:
I have not. The music is tinny. I mean really what kid is in charge of this slop!!!!!!! He should be punished by having to listen to accordion music.
Bobby

On Mon 10:02 am, Don Hawk said:

Now you haave hurt my feelings. Don't you like my disco party CD?
Don

On Mon 10:04 am, Terri Patrick said:
I have wire cutters in the lab.
TP

On Mon 10:05 am, Gerri LeMaire said:
The PE Department has the fitness to shimmy up the pole to use those cutters.
Gerri

On Mon 10:09 am, Relic said:
Isn't the whole idea to let the kids have some ownership over the "radio station"?
Relic

A flash came on the computer screen. The waves washed over the entire page to indicate that there was a new posting.

On Mon 12:39 pm, The Librarian Ogre said:
Librarian Ogre 3 Rats 0. This is starting to look like a rout here folks.
LO

On Mon 12:41 pm, Craig Dickens said:
Rout? I'd say a...massacre. Maybe we should rename the library? How 'bout–Little Big Horn?
CD

On Mon 12:45 pm, Tom Simon said:
Drowned, right? I humbly submit: Waterloo.
Tom

On Mon 12:46 pm, Dan Best said:
Trollumbine...
Dan Best

On Mon 12:46 pm, Karen Song said:
The Tower.
Karen

The names catalogue continued: The Titanic from Kaitlin Coyote, Nanking from Janie Brown, Vimy from Vander Kwaak, and Pearl Harbour from Pete Holland. Such silliness, thought Hudson, and such a fun way to entertain each other in such a distant ex-pat community.

While Hudson was teaching his first afternoon class the idea of extended metaphor by assigning his students the task of imitating Carl Sandburg's "The Fog," more CHATTERS followed:

On Mon 1:39: pm, Sunflower Hu said:
Teachers of Zero Li (Jia Zhong) (0776888) in 10-10

She is sick off from now to January 14 because of bipbones' fracture. Please mark him execussed abcess during this period. Thank you.

Sunflower Hu

Hudson smiled as he considered how the gender pronouns gave the Mandarin speakers fits. He appreciated how well the secretaries Sunflower, Jing, Luo Jun, and Fei spoke English especially when he compared their use with his feeble attempts at Mandarin and his struggles with the four tones.

On Mon 1:42: pm, Sunflower Hu said:

Dear teachers,

You must check your chinese account later tonight or tomorrow morning! Maybe money will be deposited then.

Thanks,

Sunflower^^

Oh not again. People are going to go ballistic. The weariness in his mind was interrupted by a student.

"Mr. Smith, you should do this. It's so hard. I think you cannot."

"I agree with Cyprus. This cannot be done."

"Mr. Smith, I think you can do it, but not in the time you have given us."

Complaining to an authority? Challenging an authority? The students were becoming more Canadian each day, Hudson thought.

"Okay. I accept your challenge."

Hudson took out his pen, and he started to work. Dong Bei storms were brutal, powerful, and he must capture that in an image. Sandberg was a superb poet. His extended metaphor of a cat for fog was perfect. A cat is quiet, soft and caressing. What could capture the fury of a Dong Bei storm?

After ten minutes he moved his third draft to the white board, and allowed the students to see the choices he was making. Crossing out train in the first line and inserting the word express, he stood back from the board and moved the word again to the sixth line.

Twenty minutes later, Smith announced, "Gentlemen, please look at the screen. This is the poem that I created in the style of 'The Fog.'"

The boys looked at each other, and they knew their ruse to get the assignment as homework where they could ask friends and search the Internet would not happen. Speedy dropped a pen, and Robert kicked it to the very front of the room. It spun like a maple leaf seed pod, and bounced off Hudson's heel. Hudson scanned the class to see who owned the pen. Robert's head lowered, but every other boy made eye contact with him. In a conspiratorial manner the uniformed lads tried to pretend nothing had happened. Their eyes drilled the board as they read their *lao shi's* work:

The Winter Storm

The 12:12 arrived

on time...

Its white comet tail

stretching back to Siberia.

Rocking, roaring, hissing–

This arctic express

Freezes passengers at Shanwan Station.

Hudson Smith

"Note the use of the spacing to create motion for the eyes. I tried to use lots of 'S' sounding words to duplicate the sound of a train's brakes and the steam. The 'S' sound also is used by poets to help create motion. Any questions?"

"Yes, Robert, the time reminds us of a schedule like a train, also we understand that the storm is expected as the passengers are waiting at the station. In the Dong Bei, the storm arrives as if it were on a schedule."

"Yes, David, I did choose the words deliberately. The words 'express' and 'comet' are powerful like a train–fast. A 'comet' is also a ball of ice, and 'Siberia' has connotations of the cold, lonely isolated region that remind Westerners of the Gulags where the Soviets sent their dissidents. Dissidents means–"

"We know what they are, Mr. Smith."

"Okay, I was just checking. By the way, I changed the poem at least five times before I was satisfied with it. How about you?"

"Yes, Berry. The poem uses an extended metaphor of a train to compare to the winter storm." The bell went, and as the students filed out, Hudson returned to his computer to check for new announcements.

The Ogre's single-handed quest to turn the library into a rat-free zone would continue, and when Hudson checked his CHATTER that night before leaving a final posting said:

On Mon 4:59 pm, The Librarian Ogre said:
LO 4 Rats 1. I'll give the Norwegian fellow credit for scoring the first rat victory of the day, as he jumped off the ramp onto my arm as I was removing rat #4 from the drink. The beggar gave my hand a nip, but fortunately my science lab gloves kept his fangs to himself. I hope he got a good piece of asbestos from the chomp. Maybe I'll update tomorrow if his carcass is lying around.
LO

Eighteen
The Evaluation Team

British Columbia saw an opportunity in the early 1990s to export education. It saw education as a way to make money. This short-sighted view forgot that education is really a savings account that only receives its return by having citizens who try to improve others' lives by their contributions to society. Offshore schools were developed, and wisely the government saw China was a huge market. In fact, since the sleeping tiger had awakened, the economy's growth performance was consistently number one in the world, and BC had a toe-hold in a booming industry: teaching English. The Canadian accent is light, and with its marked absence of a thick lilt or drawl, it is preferred to both the Brit's and Yank's. There is the idiosyncratic 'eh?' which is an endearing, earthy way to ask the listener 'Don't you agree?' Thus, BC made a polite entry into the tiger's den.

These offshore schools sprung up quickly in the world's largest market, and, like the seed in the parable, some fell on rocky soil. The Canadian Harmonious International Peace School was not one of these. It was planted in good soil, and was producing a large bounteous harvest for the Headmaster who was also the owner. Mr. Wang had met with BC officials in 1991, and by feting the Ministry's civil servants, soon gained the Memorandum of Understanding he was seeking. In China it was like a license to print money. In a country of a billion and a half people, competition was plentiful and fierce. Students wishing to enter Chinese universities must write a nation-wide exam and score highly. Entry was not guaranteed. Thus, as Deng Xiao Ping's reforms took place, and a new middle class emerged, parents looked for ways to help their child get into a prestigious post-secondary school. Wang provided this way. Parents would send their son to his school staffed by both Canadian and Chinese teachers where their boy would graduate with a BC Dogwood Diploma as well as a Chinese one. This high school certificate was like a key. It opened doors to every university in Canada and the United States. Asian parents loved the status conferred on them when they told of their son studying abroad; they spent huge quantities of cash to do so. Sometimes grandparents and aunts and uncles took extra jobs just to make it happen. Eager to help their son, parents closely watched the university rankings, and teachers felt the brunt of the frenzy. Students would cry when they couldn't get in to a school like the University of Toronto or Stanford because of their English score. The rote learning method, which dominated Chinese classrooms, served the boys well in Math and the sciences, but it did not work for English. Couple that with the difficulty in learning a language in three short years and expecting to compete with native speakers, well, that was a recipe for disaster. Fluency took longer. All the ESL experts agreed. Such pressure led to rampant cheating. Integrity had no position with some of the boys, and trying to challenge this culture was difficult in the classroom. Smith hated this part of the culture. It stood against everything he believed. One of the conditions the BC Ministry of Education placed on C.H.I.P.S. was that it would have to be monitored for accreditation each year. History repeats itself,

Smith moped. The Red Cross monitored concentration camps in WWII.

Now a team was here. It was a good gig if you could get it. Free travel, a week's work at one school, and go on to the next. The remuneration was excellent, and C.H.I.P.S. made sure that the teams were comfortably ensconced in five star hotels, dined in great restaurants, and driven wherever they wanted to go. Principals were given bonuses based on the reports taken back home, and the blinding effect of currency encouraged them to control the tours of the evaluation teams.

The team leader was Tyler Johnston. He had been a teacher, vice-principal, principal, superintendent, and a university professor. TJ, as his friends called him, loved his work; although, he hadn't been in the classroom for over thirty-five years. When his friend, Dave McKay, called him from Victoria to do a two-week assignment for the Ministry in China, he balked, but when his wife said she had always wanted to see Beijing, he called up Dave and agreed to the offer. Now at seventy, still spry, and still witty, he told Peterson that he would drop in on teachers unannounced to see the quality of instruction at C.H.I.P.S.. He went up a floor to where the ESL students were working on English.

Her Irish lilt always entered the room before she did. Mrs. Robertson, from Dublin mind you dear, had been a principal of several of the McSchools in Richmond, the island city that was home to Metro Vancouver's airport and its largest Chinese population. McNair, McRoberts, McMath, and McNulty (all named by trustees who saw that the future held Wang, Zhao, and Li as the new vanguard) had seen her manning the office as though 'The Troubles' had come across the Atlantic. Her gift of the gab did her in good stead, and because of her placement in Richmond, she had taken Mandarin and Cantonese courses to be able to communicate with her parents. They loved her because very few Canadians took the time and effort to learn the Middle Kingdom's languages. Cantonese was more difficult she found because there were seven tones instead of Mandarin's four, and coupled with her Cork County accent, her Chinese caused numerous furrowed brows and tilted heads. However, her attempts always broke down the barriers.

Frequently, she said to her Chinese parents at her Richmond school, "You and I are the same you know. Oh, I know dear we are from opposite ends of the globe, but we are both immigrants."

Mrs. Robertson knew her math. She had been entered into King's College in Dublin at the age of fourteen, and had graduated at the top of her class at eighteen. Born with gap teeth and like Chaucer's Wife of Bath, a born traveller, Alice had been to all the continents. The Irish lass had fallen for Malcolm Robertson, a poor Scottish teacher, when they were in London at a math conference. By this time Alice was leading teacher education programs, and Malcolm was trying to interest the young hooligans of a rough area of Glasgow that numbers were a way to have power instead of the guns and drugs that drew them like trout to a worm. Their idealism brought them together and bridged the mistrust the two Celtic branches held for each other. Malcolm was back home right now probably asleep, she thought.

Robertson knew her part of the team was merely a figurehead position. Most Chinese students were ready for algebra in grade seven, and for calculus in grade ten. The crux of the matter was that they were better prepared for the higher level math than Canadian students. Foundational math is often rote learning, and the Chinese excelled at this in their educational system. They worked hard and played with numbers like she had in her early days, and like this culture, her Irish parents had disdained the pursuits of pleasure, like movies, which seemed to preoccupy the majority of her Richmond students' time. Mathematics here were a cherished and honoured pursuit, and thus, the teachers in those classes not only had no difficulty with the vocabulary of other subject areas, they had keen pupils ready to push the limits. These teachers could relax–unlike their Canadian counterparts who had many students struggling with basic numeracy. The C.H.I.P.S. provincial exam scores were often 15% higher in math than the provincial average. Universities drooled at the prospect of getting these kids on campus not only as a cash influx, but also many became the university's math whiz kids. This freed Robertson to look at the misfit subjects like Planning, computer science, and the fine arts of dance, drama, and art and design. She had been selected by the team to also address the students at flag ceremony on the Monday they were leaving.

The final evaluation team member was Steven Carter. Carter was young and vibrant. He had been a superintendent at the age of thirty-six, and the BC media loved his out-spoken educational views. The province was politically polarized and Carter was a good looking, up and comer who had been courted by both parties as he was their most treasured type of person–he was electable.

Carter walked down the second floor hallway just before class began. He felt that one could take the pulse of the school, which was a reflection of the community at large back home, by seeing the interactions in the halls not only between students, but between teachers and students and teachers and teachers. Why even the custodian at one school, obviously a much beloved man, made a difference by learning the name of every student in the small school of 650 by studying the yearbook so that he could greet every student by name. When Carter had asked why he took the time to do this, he simply replied, "They are worth it." Going the extra mile was such a rare trait. Carter was so impressed he recommended that the man be given a bonus by the board, but the man's own union blocked the idea as unfair. People were a school's greatest resource; although, the administration at many schools forgot this truth, and were rewarded with disgruntled employees. Carter had made it his mission to empower his employees whom he referred to as colleagues–BCTF be damned. By trusting his staff to take risks and giving them responsibilities that most principals clung to, he created teachers who loved working for him. They were no longer deliverers of a set curriculum, they were decision makers, and they responded to being valued like this.

Upstairs, Tyler Johnston walked into Hudson Smith's English class.

Meanwhile, Alice Robertson went through the library's doors, saw three students with their heads on the tables sleeping, and she knew that she had found her evaluation recommendation. The boys should not be allowed to sleep, she thought. Such disrespect, and the librarian does nothing. Change would be coming.

Miming to the cleaning woman on the fifth floor, Steven Carter smiled, thanked her, and closed the window. The breeze stopped, and the aroma wafted to his nose. He turned around and opened the window again. The cleaning woman smiled.

Later that night, the evaluation team met at the Donkey Dumpling Restaurant. It had a great reputation for authenticity, and several of the staff had recommended it.

TJ picked up his Tsingdao Beer and put it down again. It was warm. "*Ni hao*," he started in Chinese, but having plumbed the depths of his language skills, he asked in English, "Can I get a cold beer, please?" The waitress puzzled over what he wanted, and then she left.

"I saw a lively class this afternoon. He's one of the older guys on staff," TJ continued. Sorting through his papers he found the notes he wanted. "Ah, here it is. Smith. Hudson Smith. English 12 class. He was teaching *Animal Farm* by Orwell. He had the students singing the song 'Beasts of England' which is a parody of the communist anthem 'The International.' The boys were enthusiastic singers, and afterwards they went over the vocabulary, and continued to read the novel. I can see why the class needs to be double blocked. There were so many words that the lads didn't know. I pity the task ahead of the teachers–they're being asked to do the impossible."

"Did he use any technology?" asked Steven Carter.

"Yes. He used the projector unit to run a short clip of Stalin speaking, and a group of labourers singing 'The International.' I spoke to him after class, and he showed me his unit's assessment strategies which included: formative and summative assessments, an oral component, an in-class write, and a self-evaluation. He told me he wanted the students to critically analyse the privileges of the communist party. He may get himself into trouble, but it's good teaching. What did you see Alice?"

"Well, I think the lesson I saw was a bit more interesting to the boys. I went to a Planning 10 class, and there was a young lass there who was teaching the boys about condoms. She had purchased bananas and condoms and was showing them how to put them on correctly. The poor girl. The boys were making it difficult, and so I left earlier than I wanted. It was pretty obvious that she was adhering to kinaesthetic learning. Quite clever actually. I have always thought this type of learning was best."

Carter nodded his head. "I know I loved it the most as a student and a teacher." The cold Tsingdao arrived, and smiling at the waitress, he took the large green bottle and hoisted it to toast his companions. "Cheers."

"Cheers," responded Alice and TJ.

"I also went to the gymnasium to observe the P.E. classes."

"What was that like?"

"Steve the gym is three basketball courts large, but there were six classes in there and no sound board to absorb the noise. I would go batty teaching in that environment. Many students stood against the wall. On the floor there were chicken bones, plastic bags, and spit. There was hardly any equipment. One class of 36 had two badminton racquets and one shuttle. Can you imagine?"

"No. I can't. Imagine a class being asked to share two pencils, or two computers. There would be outrage in a BC community."

"I saw outrage here today."

"What? Where?"

"I watched a socials class where the teacher showed a short clip from YouTube from his computer on the abuses suffered by First Nations in BC. He then asked students to think why this situation arose. The students couldn't believe Canada would do that to its First Nations and they were engaged right from the beginning, but then he turned the issue to China's migrant workers who do not have a *hu kou*, an urban residency permit. In groups, using a recorder, a facilitator, a reporter, and a devil's advocate, the boys realized that their country has some issues as bad as our past treatment of the First Nations, and they wanted justice."

TJ spoke up, "There are many good teachers here. I saw a class where the discussion was great. The young woman tossed her lesson plan out the window. That took some guts with this old coot sitting there watching. Kids had to write down then ask five open-ended questions such as: 'What do you think Chairman Mao would say if he saw what Beijing looked like today?' And 'What would Confucius say if he came into our school?' There is critical thinking happening, and that is a pleasant surprise."

"The teachers at C.H.I.P.S. are excellent, but the facilities and equipment are second-rate. That's going in the report."

Eric Peterson went to the microphone to introduce the various team members to the boys and teachers at Monday's flag after the anthems had been sung. The late autumn weather in Baishantan brought heavy dews from the Yellow Sea, and the tiles outside were slick with the frosty moisture. As Alice Robertson made her way to the poles, her smooth soles on the leather knee high boots couldn't grip the surface. It happened so quickly that Eric, who had just finished saying her name, looked to the audience to gauge their reaction and looked back again. His head snapped down as he saw Mrs. Robertson in a heap thrashing around like one of the turtles he had seen in the restaurant he had eaten in last night. Other delegates rushed to help her up, and it was at that point when Peterson saw, swooping in from above, the magpie. Long a spectator of the proceedings, today the bird became an active participant as it flew straight at the rumpled mass that was Mrs. Robertson. Before she sat up, the bird strafed her, snatched her wig from her head, and flew back to its perch with what it thought was a small helpless creature. The boys oohed. Then when they comprehended what had happened, they tried to stifle their laughter, but could not. Peterson seized the moment and for the first time since flag began at C.H.I.P.S., the principal dismissed the students. Poor Mrs. Robertson's wig hung from the third story ledge of the library building like a pelt of some small creature. The magpie was pulling at it with his talons, but the duped bird realized there was no treat to be had and flew above the students in search of a potential meal. Waving in the breeze, it was retrieved later by order of Mr. Wang himself.

Below the hairy flag was this week's red banner that Smith hadn't noticed as he attended to the delegation's needs. The lucky gold block lettering announced to all: "TWO COUNTRIES FORGE NEW COPULATION."

Nineteen
New Year's Eve in Harbin

In early October as the blue skies and warm air of Shanwan succumbed to the grey Siberian skies and the chilly foreshadowing of winter, Smith stood outside wishing he had worn his long johns while the flag ceremony began. Dickens, his face looking haggard as though each crease remembered the cold onslaught the frosty air would soon bequeath the land, stepped alongside Hudson and invited him and Jo to Harbin for the New Year's Eve weekend. Harbin was renowned for its Ice Palace Hotel, its Borsch, sausage, and its hockey. The ice festival was a major tourist attraction. In fact, Smith had seen a news story in British Columbia on this northern city and its wintery wonderland qualities. "Sounds good, but let me check with Jo," he said.

"We could take a flight or ride the overnight sleeper train," offered the English Department Head.

"I think Jo and I would want to take the train. We'd see a bit of the countryside, and we'd see the people a bit more. It's why we're here–to experience China."

"You won't see any more of the countryside because it's a sleeper train, but you will experience China in the train. The ride is longer."

"No problem. We're never in a rush. I'm sure she'll want to, but first let me check."

"Great, I'll book the train tickets when it's time. Jo will say 'yes'."

Though one of the new bullet speed train lines was due to open on the Shanwan–Harbin route next year shortening the trip to three hours, it hadn't yet, and thus the train line was the pre-revolutionary track that stopped in several bergs along the way. The trip from Shanwan would be an overnight nine-hour ride, leaving Shanwan at 10:00pm and gliding into Harbin at a cool 7:00am. Dickens contacted Smith and said that the tickets for a soft sleeper that consisted of four bunks in a private room would cost around 600 *kuai* a person. Of course, the bunks would barely fit him, but all four of them would have their own, and like all train tickets, they could only get them three days in advance. Hudson asked about the hard sleepers. The hard sleeper would be cheaper, at just over 200 *kuai*. They consisted of six bunks in an open room and were booked by common folk. Jo and Hudson would experience the real China.

"Done," replied Dickens.

December can be a long month for teachers in Canada. Students are longing for the Christmas break, leaving early from classes to go on holidays to get the cheap flights and hotels, and anticipating presents from family and friends. Concerts, cards, shopping, food preparation, and the general rush of the entire season add to that pressure. Inclement weather slows everyone down, and can be quite literally mind numbing. Most of this was avoided at C.H.I.P.S.. The weather continued on this side of the Pacific, but there was no break for Christmas. Food prep in China meant arranging to go to one of the five star hotels' buffets for turkey as nobody owned a western style oven, and shopping for family back home had to be done in November, if the teachers even bothered, as the postage to ship gifts to Canada was usually many times the value of any gift that could be sent–so most did not.

Hudson was chatting to his students while he set up his laptop in the class. "Mr. Smith, you are taking train to Harbin? Crazy. You should fly," Tom opined before class began.

"No, we're going by train, but we are flying back. The train doesn't arrive in time for us to get to school on Monday."

The train station was a riot of sound, colours, and motion. Thousands of people milled about the enormous waiting area. Literally hundreds stared at the *wai gou ren* as they waited in line to board the train. "Will it be on time?" Hudson asked.

"This is China. It is a source of nationalistic pride that the trains run on time," Dickens said.

Once the group were herded in, they found berths five through eight easily. They set their luggage under their beds, and within minutes turned in for the night. A conductor came by to collect tickets and to hand out plastic cards indicating she had done so. Dickens gave the group's tickets to the officious woman who insisted on waking up the rest of the travellers. She would come by again an hour before the train would stop. Snoring mixed with the shrill sounds of steel on steel. A snack cart came by selling *pijiu,* noodles, and spicy peas at three times the normal price. The door between rail cars must have opened an average of ten times a minute all night, Hudson thought in the wee hours as he laid on the top bunk wondering if he should brave the squattie toilet and its incessant rocking. Eventually, instinct won out over reason, and as he entered the inside outhouse, he realized that there could be worse facilities than the ones at C.H.I.P.S.. At least at the school there was seldom the stench of thick, dense smoke. Here in the squattie, every smoker had lit up, adding a blue tinge to the already oppressive atmosphere. As he went back to his bunk, Hudson's hand touched the window, and the beautiful frost pattern was instantly changed.

Arrival was right on schedule, and Harbin's cold air woke them all as they exited the station. "Taxi! Sir, taxi."

"*Dou shao qian*?"

"*Er bai, wu.*"

"What? Ha ha ha ha. Two hundred and fifty? *Zou kai*. Go away." Dickens told Hudson that two hundred and fifty was slang for calling someone stupid. This came from a failing score on the national exam that all high school students took, and it was quite an insult. The cabbie obviously was trying to show his disdain for the westerners while gouging them at the same time. "What a cheeky monkey," Dickens declared.

The driver actually pouted at Dickens's scolding, and the foursome queued up in a taxi line. When they arrived at their hotel, they paid thirteen RMB. RMB was short for 'the People's Money.' "Now that's a savings," marvelled Jo, and they all reflected on the station cabbie's audacity.

At the Everbrightnight Hotel reception counter, their three rooms were ready, and the travelling Canadians laughed at the 'o'clock room rate.' Again, the nonchalance over such nefarious activities was surprising. A turn of the century heritage building, the hotel was just off the pedestrian mall and a short block and a half away from the frozen riverfront. It wasn't five star, but it was fairly tidy.

Later Jo and Hudson strolled arm in arm down the walking street. The snowy cobble stones crunched under their feet. A group of six girls, probably high school students Hudson thought, were taking a photo in front of one of the old heritage buildings. "*Ni hao*," Jo voiced, and with a few gestures indicated her willingness to snap a shot of the entire group.

"*Xie xie*," the group chorused. Then one of the girls offered to take the Canadians' photo as well.

The pair moved in front of the green storefront and one of the candied berries on a stick attached itself to Hudson's jacket. The sign above the door said, "1906."

"I love China," Jo said. "People are so friendly."

"Yes, but remember you made the first photo offer. Then came 'opening up'," quipped Hudson using the Chinese phrase that Deng Xiao Ping had promoted as policy in the late 1980s to change China's direction. There was a twinkle in her eyes.

They thanked the girls and continued on their way, marvelling at the Disney characters carved out of ice. "There seems to be no fear of Westerners here like we've sometimes seen in our travels."

"The Russians were here for a long time." As Hudson was speaking, an older woman came up to the Canadians speaking Russian to them. "I'm sorry. We are Canadian–*wo men shi Jianada ren*."

"Ah, *Jianada...hen hao*," and after giving them a wide grin, and a thumbs up, the woman walked away.

A slender woman, wearing a fur-trimmed jacket, thrusting a pamphlet into their faces, replaced her. A horse sleigh ride was offered. "*Bu yao,*" don't want, Jo countered. They continued their walk towards the Songhua River, which cuts through the Chinese landscape like a long silk scarf when a skinny man came out from behind one of the sculptures and seemed to be flossing his neck with a wide white towel.

"What's that?" Hudson asked Jo, but the wraith answered before she could.

"Fox."

"Ah, you know English. May I see it?" Hudson moved towards the man, glad that he hadn't said something about the man's ridiculous appearance. Jo was always reminding him that many people spoke English a little, and his candid comments may offend some. "It's a beautiful..."

"Fox."

"Yes, that's right. A fox. Now that I see it closely who could mistake it. May I? Ah, that is such a soft..."

"Fox."

Jo was smiling her pearly whites. Her teeth out-gleamed the fresh snow around them, and there was that spark in her eyes that was so endearing. "Hudson, he doesn't know any English. He just knows the word: fox."

"Really?"

"Yes, watch me. Can you tell us where the hockey game is?"

"Fox."

"I've been duped again."

They started to leave the square, but the skinny man cried out, "Fox," but this time he went to his portable kiosk behind the sculpture of a princess and bent over a cardboard box where he pulled out another white fox. He placed the fox on his shoulder. It looked like the stuffed bookend Hudson had always wanted to make out of his faithful dog, and he reached out to check out the fur's quality. As he did so, the taxidermy project moved across the back of the skinny man's neck and sat with a steely gaze on the furthest shoulder.

"Yikes. It's alive," he blurted as he fell back.

"Fox," the skinny man grinned.

"You should have seen your face, Hudson," Jo giggled as they walked on. The minus eight degrees with no wind made the morning a clear, crisp delight like the purest alpine air in Canada's Rockies. It was wholesome. The couple breathed deeply as they moved towards the river where their colleagues had told them many activities were available.

The aggressive hucksters continued to confront the tourists in the square before a large castle made from block ice. Inside were embedded lights which would illuminate the ebony and ivory world of the night. Jo and Hudson made their way to the promenade, and the sight, like the air, delighted them. Horse drawn carriages, troikas, sliding chairs with people either pushing or using metal poles to propel the unit, ATV's, pond hockey, horse races; *tuo lou*, a traditional Chinese top game, and bicycle ice buggies were entertaining the masses. There were several areas cordoned off to allow each activity its own space. The river ice further out had buckled under the pressure, but in these sections obvious care had gone into making it smooth enough to skate, slide, and ride on. The people were living steam engines as they left behind a white vapour in whatever they did.

The castle, Jo discovered, was actually an ice slide reaching far out into the frozen river, and for ten kuai each, the two raced against each other on plastic rice sacks. "That was great," Jo stated, and she hugged Hudson when they got off the ice track. They looked around at the busy place. "I've never seen so many people outside during the winter before."

"Me either." Hudson looked into her intelligent eyes and went to kiss her. The romance was shut down before it began as a sharp electrical current arced between their lips. "Youch."

"Here. Let me show you how." Jo reached her hand up to his face, "Grounding. Grounding." Her smile grew as it neared and her lips puckered. "There. I have an electric personality." Kissing Jo, Hudson realized that she was the best kisser he had ever met. She was a professor–a bona fide doctor. They intertwined their hands and continued back to their rooms at the hotel.

After a brief rest and warming, and agreeing to meet with Dickens and his wife at the Russian Coffee & Food restaurant for supper, the pair went exploring Harbin away from the river. St. Sofia Church appealed to them, and provided an final destination that they would work their way to like the European explorers who tried to find the Northwest Passage to India. Treasures awaited them around every corner, and the prospect, unlike those early adventurers, thrilled them.

The onion-domed buildings of Harbin were magnificent as the

thin snow cleaned up the coal dust, and the sun provided the glory. Ice sculptures were found on every section of the pedestrian street, and people were cheerful. "Would this work in Vancouver or Victoria?" Hudson asked Jo. "Could Canadians give up their cars?"

"I think we could give up the car, but would the frequent rain keep the people away? I'm not sure I would want to risk it as a merchant. Remember, Harbin is huge. Ten million live here."

"It would definitely work in the summer and fall. Hey, check this out. Hudson pointed his camera at the long red sign above a green door: 'Russian Goods and Chopsticks Shop.'

"Ha ha ha. Look over here, honey." Jo nodded to a sign that, like early English, was written without spaces: 'CARDDAMOT HEUTLITYROOMOFTHECREAYIVITYPHOTOGRATH SARTS.' As he framed the shot, he made sure to eliminate the nude pictures below. They continued their stroll. Bronze statues of common people involved in everyday tasks were sentinels to the side streets. An artist, a trio of musicians, a carter with horse, a vendor, and a reader added to the character of the town.

Within minutes they saw St. Sofia's steeples with its ornate crosses. To get there the couple walked towards a giant mall across a busy six-lane thoroughfare using the Chinese buffer system Jo had devised. "Hudson, I always make sure there is a Chinese person between me and the vehicles, and I move when they do. They're the experts." In front of the secular temple to materialism and its huge signs showing skinny western models, there was a pair of giant blue and red dragons. As they neared the iconic symbols of power, they both laughed. The entire display celebrating Chinese New Year was created out of Pepsi cans.

Another street, another heart rate raising incident as an old man with a blue Maoist cap and jacket had fallen in the slush on the street maybe five meters ahead of them. A cab driver slid to a stop centimetres before the man, jumped out, helped him up, held out his hand to stop traffic, and escorted the man to safety. Was St. Sofia influencing behaviours already? Hudson thought.

Cathedrals are always impressive structures. Built to glorify God, the eye is drawn upwards; the immensity strips away an observant man's pretensions; the edifice dominates and calms one's mind and soul. Doves, the symbol of the Holy Spirit, were sitting on ledges all around St. Sofia, and while Hudson went to buy tickets to enter, Jo got out the camera and took shot after shot. Later, she decided her favourite was one of an old woman crouching by her granddaughter with both of them pointing to a dove that had descended and was perched on top of the handrail less than a meter away. The joy in their faces, the body language, the dove framed by a circular window with a Russian Orthodox cross told the story of a spiritual hunger satisfied. Inside the great wooden doors the story was quite different.

"They don't even call this a church, Jo. It is a Museum of Architecture. Orwell says in *1984* that churches would be used for museums, and here it is. The guy was uncanny."

"Look Hudson, they've scraped away the religious icons in the paintings on the walls and ceilings."

"Jo, look at this wall. The pillar has bullet holes. I imagine that there is a history here that has been covered up. The Soviet Red Army and the Chinese Cultural Revolution were vicious when it came to religion."

"Ironic, isn't it? Sad too. I mean the men who built this place wanted to honour God, and the tacky gifts for sale in the front entry would sicken them. Why haven't they kept this place up? Don't they understand that a restored church would have even more impact with tourists?"

"That I am sure is the reason. This place represents something even grander than the Communist Party."

That evening after a fabulous dinner of cabbage rolls, perogies, borsch, peloshikis, and Harbin sausage, Craig, Katie, Hudson and Jo went to the Harbin International Ice Festival on Sun Island across from the downtown core to ring in the New Year. "There'll be fireworks tonight, honey," Katie said to her husband.

"Of course there will be, and we might even see them this year."

"Oh, get out," Katie responded with her face blushing.

Jo and Hudson smiled and squeezed each other's hand three times. It was their secret code to say, "I love you." The Ice Festival was outstanding. Huge blocks of ice from the river were used to construct castles, pagodas, slides, lighthouses, and even a windmill. The three hundred RMB, more than their train tickets had cost, was worth it. It was a magical place filled with happy people. Horse drawn carriages moved through the displays, and Hudson felt pity for the rime covered animals. Even their eyelashes were frosty. As midnight drew near the crowds gathered in front of the largest castle and its twenty-four turrets, some six to eight stories high, for the fireworks. For a full hour the skies were filled with red and white blossoms, spirals of green and yellow, explosions of blue and orange. The barrage was beyond any they had ever seen before. Vancouver's Festival of Lights, the fireworks celebration that lit up English Bay in July each year, was like a warm-up for this display.

Jo pulled out a bottle of Chilean red wine, and Hudson uncorked it and poured it into the glasses he had brought. There the four Canadians toasted in the New Year looking to a future filled with love, joy, peace, and harmony.

In the cab on the way home each of the friends wished that they could have had their family with them in Harbin, but there was no other locale where they wished to be. The four planned to share their revelry with family on Skype back at the hotel, and Jo said, "We are so lucky. We get to celebrate New Year's twice." She gave three squeezes of Hudson's hand, and she nestled into his shoulder.

Twenty
The Empire of Mr. Xu

Nobody had as much power over the Canadian teachers on a day to day basis than Mr. Xu. He was the emperor of the photocopier. Life could be routine as he did his work neatly and efficiently, but woe to those who crossed him. For them the manipulation and the small inconveniences manifested themselves as a speck in one's eye. He was an irritant that was tough to remove, though unnoticed by others. The photocopy office where four machines hummed along diligently reproducing the knowledge of the world was located on the fifth floor of the library building. Dickens had begged the administration for a number of years (after Relic had dropped the issue as unwinnable), to relocate the room to the more amiable first floor to save everyone on staff the arduous trek, but always Mr. Xu vetoed the plan. The top floor had a skylight in it that provided bright sunlight to his plants. His collection included over twenty types of cacti and numerous spider plants. Smith had asked Amanda Johnson if the plants had any significance, and she noted that both were renowned for cleaning the air. That's good, Smith thought, as he considered having to spend any more than a minute in the warm, moist, close quarters with Xu as oppressive, despite the light.

Smith had made the mistake one time of asking the emperor, through a pantomime, if he could get a cutting from one of the plants. Mr. Xu violently shook his head, and when Smith picked up his copies later, he regretted his earlier request as the papers had been copied with the second side upside-down. He had to buy a plant for Xu to try to curry favour with him once again.

Waiting for a rush request, Smith could closely observe the emperor at work. Mr. Xu was a very short man, even by Chinese standards, who could barely look over the collection of machines in the crowded office. Smith guessed by his developing paunch that he was fortyish, and his thinning hair was slicked back like a shiny helmet. The tiny man's eyes were also small and very, very dark. The bags underneath them bore witness to his lack of sleep. He was wide-faced with drooping jowls. Smith noticed for the first time part of his right ear was missing. A thick wool suit jacket covered a proper vest, school sweater, and crisp white starched collar with tie. His pants were primitively hemmed several inches higher than when purchased, and his faux leather shoes were gleaming under the skylight's natural lighting.

The rookie C.H.I.P.S. English teacher's nostril hairs were frozen following flag ceremony. He brushed his goatee with his left hand and shivered again as he entered the old building and started the arduous climb. Boys hustled past him as he trudged up the first floor. He chatted for a moment to Tom coming down, and resumed the climb. Smith paused for a moment to catch his breath on the fourth floor, and still the sea of suits with their beaver crests washed past him. It amazed Smith how a little exertion could bring him to a sweat after the cold outside, but the two pairs of long johns, thermal undershirt, dress shirt and sweater beneath his down jacket ensured that his skin was damp. When the photocopy room was reached, Smith sat on a stool tucked inside the frosted glass door and surveyed the scene. Mr. Xu had his back turned to him. The photocopy emperor rarely acknowledged any teachers in his realm due to the complaints he had received and been chastised for over the last two years.

Twice, the Canadian staff had asked for Xu's removal for sexual harassment, and twice the Canadian administration had taken the request to Mr. Wang. Twice Xu had been exonerated. His defence both times was that the room was small, and getting by people in the narrow path usually necessitated some type of contact. Both of the women, Karen Song and another who had left after her complaint, said that Xu had deliberately touched their breasts by coming close to talk about the photocopying they had brought to him. Since there were no witnesses, it became a 'he said–she said battle', and it was tough to fire a person accused in that situation. The women were outraged; the Canadian teachers were outraged; the Canadian administration were outraged, and when similar stories started to show up from the Chinese side as well, Sarah Whippet went to Wang again. She demanded that Mr. Xu be fired for the pattern that had developed. "How many more women will be fondled? If there are any, it will be your fault. You could do something, but you won't."

"In China, family is very important, and you see Mr. Xu is my sister's son. He used to be a teacher until there were some problems. It is my responsibility to take care of him, and keep him out of trouble. Your tone is not type of tone that I expect from a person who wants to be a principal. Miss Whippet, I think interview is over. Please see yourself out."

The photocopiers hummed away. Lime green light looked like a laser show at a rock concert as it bounced off the botanically clad walls. Pillowy soft white noise, the warmth of the complex machines (how far we have come from slate boards, thought Smith), and the stacks of A3 and A4 paper suffocated the room. Hudson felt drowsy despite the bone-chilling flag he had just endured. Through the window he could see the magpie flying past as though it were a cloud being pushed towards the Yellow Sea. Though the place was busy, Smith knew that the exam rush was soon to be unleashed on Mr. Xu, and then the miscreant would not stop for twelve hours a day.

Mr. Xu was short–that much was evident. He had always been short. Even in his elementary school back in Inner Mongolia, he was the shortest pupil in his classes, and this attribute became a curse for him. Girls mocked him. The boys beat him. His own grandfather called him "The Little One." So he avoided people and found his refuge in books. The Cultural Revolution, crushing the intellectual classes, found an adherent in Xu. He knew Mao's Little Red Book by heart. The pithy sayings of the communist leader became his chief study. His teen years, spent in a rural district outside of Pulandian, were no better. His mother told him that he would grow. His father was rarely at home, and when he was, he ignored his diminutive son. Alone, despised, Xu studied hard so someone would notice him. After universities reopened, good scores on the Chinese National Exams won him a spot at Shanwan University of Foreign Languages. He would be a teacher. Respect would finally be his. It was after this time that Xu felt the testosterone surging, but despite his hormones coursing through his veins, there was no growth. He wanted a girlfriend, but the women he approached scorned him. His eyes were a little higher than most women's waistlines, and women were looking for a provider–a man not a boy. He began to look for outlets for his sexual desires. This was when he started to accidently bump into women. When he finally got a job at his relative's school, he started to ask some of the cleaning ladies to help water his classroom plants.

These women started to complain to the Headmaster, and Wang dismissed him from the classroom, and gave him a Hobson's Choice: take the photocopying job, or leave C.H.I.P.S.. Xu took the job, but his fantasies remained. Now they were directed at the female teachers. He was a real creeper.

Smith gave his original papers to Xu, and left the room coursing his way through the human river, anticipating a game of either crokinole with Tom or *xiangqi* with Dickens. A Canadian teacher ahead of him opened the door, and shut it again as a blast of Siberian wind split the air. Smith didn't know who the bundled figure was, but he knew that it was Canadian as the Chinese staff never shut the doors. Adjusting his toque, Smith exited and hurried across the square.

Inside his office Dickens challenged him to a game of *xiangqi*. "I think I've finally figured out how to use the horses. They're actually the key to the game."

Hudson smiled as he realized that it was a truth, but he preferred to use the cannons, in conjunction with the chariots. The cannons which moved like rooks but had to jump to attack, while the chariots moved exactly like the western version's rooks. Karen Song came through the office door, and her bounce and Cheshire cat smile told the men that an idea was cooking.

"I think I have the way to take my revenge on Xu," she announced to the men.

"How?"

"Well, I've been reading Shakespeare. He's taught me how to have a revengeful revenge."

The men paused their game to listen to her plan.

"It's like Falstaff," Smith stated.

"You mean the old drunken knight?" asked Dickens.

"Exactly," beamed Karen. "*The Merry Wives of Windsor* is the prototype. Xu will feel my wrath just like Falstaff in the play."

"Genius. Sheer genius."

"When?"

"Next week. The moon is full next week."

"Exams are the following week, so the copier is not as busy."

A note was taped to the door when Xu arrived for work on Monday. He dreaded opening the note as it obviously bore bad news, and waited until flag was underway. The national anthem was playing in the background when he opened the folded note.

"I have long admired you. You are like a warrior from the Qing Dynasty, and I want to be your lady."

He slowly closed the note, then opened it again to re-read it. Who was this from? he pondered.

Tuesday saw a second note, and this time he opened it before he unlocked the door.

"Meet me at the flagpole at midnight on Friday. Dress up as a Qing Dynasty warrior. I will be your lady."

"Qing Dynasty? Who is she?"

Wednesday morning Xu opened the third note and read, "I can hardly wait to see you my darling warrior, but I must be wooed with a song. I will reveal myself when you begin to sing at midnight at the flag pole when the moon is full."

"A song? What will I sing? A love song, of course." Xu felt his heart race. "Who is this mystery woman?" He decided to go to the market to have a warriors' uniform made for Friday.

Disappointment scourged him on Thursday morning as he reached his door and no note was present, but on Friday his heart sang as he ripped the perfumed note from the glass door.

"Tonight, my Qing warrior, sing to me at midnight, and I will reveal all."

The day was slow as Xu checked the clock every time he made a photocopy for someone. He went home in a trance as he knew the mystery would be solved that night. He had guessed who it might be. Sunflower Hu was a likely candidate as she had spoken to him at the school's opening ceremony. She was cute and came from a good family. Maybe it was Miss Chen. A powerful woman like Chairman Mao's wife. Their son would be handsome, he thought as he unlocked his door and was greeted by the Qing dynasty costume he had purchased.

Minutes before midnight Xu made his way to the school flagpole. The guards at the gate were asleep in their booth, or they might have turned back the Qing warrior carrying a two-stringed *erhu*. Stealthily, Xu made his way across the square as the clock tower rang out the hour. Now, he thought, I get to see my love.

On Monday morning Song related to her office mates how Mr. Xu had lost face. Singing into the night, dressed in his Qing costume,

Xu was mocked by the boys in their dorms which overlooked the courtyard. They shone their flashlights on him and catcalled. Undeterred, Xu sang on, believing his lady love would come. She never did. The boys laughed at him, and after he had waited for his lady, he had to endure the shame of being stood up and the boys' taunts as he walked home beneath their windows. He was now the talk of the campus, and the boys and the Chinese staff called him 'Romeo' whenever he passed.

No longer would he bother women in his stuffy empire.

Twenty-One
O CHINA-DA

The mid-year exam period meant a rush. It was a mere two weeks after the New Year's long weekend, and everyone was tired. Exams had to be made, printed, given, and marked. Invigilation schedules had to be organized, assigned, and carried out. Cheating, rampant at the school in a variety of ways, was a real battleground for a culture that operated with such a strong the concept of face. Report cards with their dreary comments, work habits, and grades had to be entered on the computer, and inevitably the system would crash as the server could not handle all the people and all the data at one time. The lack of a break made the Canadians weary. They were used to a holiday at Christmas time. Add in the celebrations of Christmas and New Year's Eve–a vacation was needed by all.

Hudson trudged up to Mr. Xu's kingdom to pick up some copying for the exam period. A student stopped him and pulled a dried leaf out of his toque. "Where did that come from? Thanks," he said. The snow had been on the ground here for two weeks now, which was unusual as the powerful winds traditionally swept it away. Smiling at another student who had called out a hello, he continued up the wet, slushy stairs. Inside Mr. Xu's realm, while he was looking for his copying amongst the pigeonholes, Hudson noticed his office colleagues' tests and handouts were done. Being the scholar and gentlemen that he was, he decided to take them back along with his papers to save Simon and Song the nine flights of stairs.

Down the stairs into the main lobby with a stack of papers stretching from his waist to his chin, Hudson Smith moved with the masses. Boys ranging from 4'6" to 6'9" from every part of China, and a few other nations besides, moved like blood cells taking the path of least resistance to their next class. Korean, Russian, Japanese, and English blended with the Mandarin that ruled within the frigid corridors. The main lobby itself could accommodate three hundred boys at one time, and frequently it hosted four hundred.

The library was located in the wing off of the lobby, and two years ago had been split into a Chinese library and an English one. The systems were so different that despite the goal of one school with two cultures, they were pragmatically separated. Hudson, looking over the exams, raised his eyebrow in greeting to Dickens who was just coming out and heading towards the ATM at the lobby's rear. A large boy moved from in front of him to go to the vending machine. Smith had to lower his chin on to the top of the pile to keep the papers there.

The open doors into the building permitted a breeze to come in, and today the wind was pummelling the boys. Smith balanced the papers at the open entrance to put on his sunglasses. With trepidation, the English teacher entered the outdoor courts. Leo and Kevin were rushing to their next class and called out their hellos as they went up the stone steps. Smith turned to see if it had been them, and by doing so exposed the hundreds of fat English exams to the wind. Maliciously it snatched them away from him as though he was a toddler. Pages by the dozens streamed past his surprised face. "Oh. Oh, oh, oh no," he gasped as the problem crystallized in his mind. Exam pages were now roaming the campus like free-range chickens providing sustenance to the hungry student wolves who would either use them or sell them. He started to pick up the loose sheets that dropped at his feet, and when he looked up, his horror was realized as he saw at least ten students running after the fluttering pages. The papers were pinned against the fence, tumbling down the sidewalk, stuck in a tree, wrapped up against the phone booth and trash can, and plastered against the school wall. "What will I tell Tom and Karen?"

He started towards the students, chin firmly planted on his remaining stack when it dawned on him that the students who had chased down all the papers were bringing them back to him. "Thanks. Thank you, Robert. Thanks, Determination. I'll see you in class. Thanks Auden, Benjamin, Vincent. Thanks David. Thanks again Robert." The deliveries continued as the ten returned the free range exams to their English teacher. The wind taunted the lads by playing with some of the distant papers, but after five minutes, Hudson had them all back. A bit wrinkled, a bit wet as the snow crystals melted, but they were back in the pile. Maybe Tom and Karen wouldn't even notice.

Walking towards his office, David offered his help, "May I carry some of the exams for you, Mr. Smith? I can carry them right to my room." He grinned at his own joke.

"Thanks, but no thanks David."

Another student called out, "Mr. Smith, come play *xiangqi*." It was the champ.

Smith thought of the last time they had played a few weeks ago. The English teacher had seen the reigning grade 12 *xiangqi* champ in his room playing one of his students. "I'm next," he had said as he plopped down in the chair beside the school's best player.

The student smiled smugly as he conquered his friend's red general. "Okay."

"Hey, I thought we were going to shop."

"Yeah, we will. This will be quick. We'll go in a couple of minutes right after I win this game for China."

Smith had played it cool as he allowed his opponent to empty his right side. The champ had been surprised and had felt great superiority towards his Canadian challenger as he had picked off a horse, then a cannon with ease. An elephant and the second horse had succumbed as well. Smith, used his chariots, or carts as some of his students called them, to simply set up a double line and as he had moved the second piece into a quick checkmate, he had watched the boys' eyes fill with recognition that his general was in a hopeless situation.

His patient friend had noticed too, and said, "You have shamed all of China."

Quickly Smith had interjected, "No, he has graciously allowed me to participate in his culture." This had allowed the boy to save face, but his pride had been skewered like a squid on a stick. His head had been down. He reached out his hand to shake, as any good sport in the West would do, and ever since Smith had heard the requests for a rematch.

"I'm sorry, champ. I'm pretty busy with the exams right now. How about after the Spring Festival Holiday?"

The young man slowly traced his finger around the vanquished general. "Fine."

Smith sensed it wasn't fine.

Twenty-Two
Fireworks

The early morning silence was shattered–again.

Boom! Boom! Boom!

Chinese New Year celebrations lasted over two weeks, Hudson realised. Each morning he was awakened by the sharp bangs, and pops, and booms of one of the five great Chinese inventions–fireworks. The alarm clock said 4:18am. He groaned. He rolled over. Boom! Still the fireworks continued. Who is up at this time? he thought. Last night it had been the same. Boom! The windows trembled as the display continued. Boom! Each sound was accompanied by a flash of white light. Truly it was man-made thunder and lightning.

On the kitchen counter the teaspoons used for afternoon tea tinkled and rattled like the ladies of the Monarchy League were having scones at The Empress Hotel in Victoria, BC. Hudson got up to solve the problem. Removing the teaspoons from the plates, a bright flash reflected on the kitchen window, and he realized he needed to shut the windows as well. As he closed the lever, he saw gunpowder smoke drifting all throughout the compound. Boom! Another went off. The acrid cloud seeped through the bathroom window, and he shut the window to keep out the two offenders: smoke and sound.

Fireworks were used for a variety of events year round, but the Spring Festival was the ultimate time. Weddings (the first bride of the day took the luck with her–so light the fireworks early to prove you were the first), funerals and business grand openings (to scare away evil spirits trying to mislead the recently departed and potential customers), launching boats (for luck), building projects and exams (to scare away the evil spirits), impressing girls (some fireworks could even spell out her name), engagements, birthdays, anniversaries and above all–Chinese New Year–saw the sky lit up.

Most of the year the fireworks were plain-Janes. The small height reached, the simple white flash, the sharp crack was actually boring. No colour. No spray. No tonal differentiation. The frequency ruined the joy. Smith thought, how can I ever enjoy Canada Day?

Now he was up again. The boys in his class had told him that the fireworks would end tomorrow, and for that he was glad. The bags under his eyes were growing each day. This morning he had gingerly got out of bed hoping not to disturb Jo as she slept. Amazingly, she had said, "I can sleep through the fireworks, but your Darth Vader breathing is a problem."

Boom! A car alarm went off and continued to add to the mayhem.

He would check the Internet, and then he would mark. He loved teaching English, but he hated marking essays. They were the bane of his existence. His friend Tony had said, "Don't give so many papers. You're marking all the time. Ease up." Hudson believed that you reaped what you sowed, and if his students didn't write, they wouldn't get better. It took more work, but things of value usually did.

He looked over at the table as he logged in and saw the most recent purchase he had made. Coins, fake coins from the various emperors of the Middle Kingdom, had caught his eye, and he thought about the weekend trip to Shenyang, the capital of Liaoning province where he had bartered for the coins. A former capital of China, Shenyang had one of the three 'Forbidden Cities' in China as it had been the residence of the Emperor. It had been built in the seventeenth century by the original Manchu emperor, Nuerhaci. The politically astute Manchu wanted to lessen old Peking's importance, and the best way to do that was to move all the machinations of government to another city–Shenyang.

The Snow Tigers had gone there this past weekend for a tournament with the hosts, Harbin, Qiqihaer (Chee-chee-har), and Hohhot, Inner Mongolia. A bus was rented for the four-hour trip, and the team had left only thirty minutes after classes finished. The debauchery began immediately.

Relic, Dickens, McMann, Peterson, Bannerman, Best, and Vander Kwaak all brought cases of beer onto the bus. Best dropped a can of Snow beer on the floor, and it started to spray its contents over the equipment piled in the first six rows of the bus.

"Don't waste it Dan!"

Best pulled the tab off the top and he drank the contents quickly while it continued to spray his chest and neck. The team cheered, clapped, and whistled while they watched his performance.

"Finished!" he announced. "Next!" The players roared their approval.

Over twenty were packed into the bus. The first six rows were piled up to the ceiling with hockey bags effectively creating a wall between the players and their Chinese driver. The team consumed twelve cases of canned Snow beer, four cases of Tsingdao beer, and various hard liquors before they were half way there. Smith, who rarely drank beyond a glass of wine, abstained. He wondered at the ability of the team to perform after abusing itself.

Upon arriving, Smith's earlier fears were mislaid. The drunk Canadians played with style and panache as they wove through the weak Shenyang team cruising to an 8-2 victory. It would have been 8-1 if Dickens hadn't played the puck back to McMann in goal. McMann had turned his back on what he thought was a finished play in his end to take a swig from the beer on the back of the net. The team razzed both of them for the rest of the trip.

On the way up the Danda Expressway to Shenyang–easily the emptiest eight-lane toll road he had ever seen–the team watched DVD's of Canada's Men's Hockey team winning Olympic gold in Salt Lake City and in Vancouver. Enduring the four hours of open unashamed nationalism was one of the Tigers' import players from Minnesota–JJ. Each time the Canadians scored, a slow rhythmic chant began: "Jaaaaay-Jaaaaay, Jaaaaaaaay-Jaaaaaaaay." Each time an American player hit a Canadian, curses rained down on him about dirty players. When Chris Chelios hit Ryan Smyth into the net behind Mike Richter, pizza crusts and beer cans were tossed at him. When the USA scored, the howls were furious. For four hours JJ endured the taunts and the torments because he understood that hockey is the one thing Canadians become passionate about.

Smith admired JJ's patience and his skill. He was a smooth skating defenceman who pushed the puck well, and was a great playmaker with soft hands. Obviously the Minnesota high school system was producing quality players. JJ loved playing with the Canadians too. The good-natured teasing was part of being an American in a Canadian ex-pat society. Even the Chinese teased the *Mei Guo ren* by calling him "Jiji" which was a certain male body part. He had been in China for nearly a year. His wife was a US envoy of trade, and he was a stay-at-home dad, and the hockey trips broke his daily routine. China had surprised him, like it did most North Americans, and playing hockey was the best surprise of all.

When they arrived in Shenyang, it was already nearing nine-o'clock. The metropolis of ten million revealed itself to Smith. There were the ubiquitous KFC's and Tesco, but he also saw unique stores like the "Chinese Pub Full of Love." It was another Chinglish translated phrase. Hudson smiled. He wondered why businesses didn't run their name past an editor who was a native speaker. It would save such mockery and gain credibility. Perhaps, though, the name was meant to be the way it was. Smith shuddered at the thought.

The first game was a late one at ten. Saturday, they played two, and on Sunday, they got the early morning time slot. Vander Kwaak had joined the short-handed Qiqihaer boys to play against the tournament's best team from Harbin.

Boom! Another firework went off, waking him from his reflections. The dawn broke through, and he realised that flag would be this morning. He was tired and worse, he was sore.

On the way to school that morning Smith had run into Don Hawk walking along the road. "Are you sore?"

"A bit," he admitted.

"Me too."

He hadn't spoken to Don often as they worked on separate floors in separate departments. Boom! There were fireworks set off in the distance by the marina where the fishing boats moored. Don had been at C.H.I.P.S. for three years, and said, "Every time I hear fireworks they remind me of Susan. Have you ever heard of Susan Po?" Hudson shook his head in response. "She was here for just a few months, but what a temper. She taught ESL, and in just a few days had alienated herself from all the other staff members in her office."

"How?"

"She would ask the same question over and over again. Each week it seemed that she had a new one. Once I remember it was 'Where can I get oatmeal?' I mean if there is one thing that is plentiful in this area, it's oatmeal. Well, there was a day when I passed by the office, and there was Sutherland, our former principal, pushing Madame Po out–pushing her as she was yelling at him."

They began climbing the stairs together while Hawk continued the story. "Students were there; Chinese staff were there. Sutherland locked the door on her, but she kept screaming at him. Then she lit off a single firework right in the main hallway. Crazy, eh?" Smith nodded his head in agreement.

"Later, Sutherland found out she wasn't taking her medication. She was the second one sent home that year for the same reason." Smith wanted to know more, but as they arrived on the third floor landing, Hawk said, "Have a great day. Maybe I'll see you at flag," and left Hudson wondering who the other teacher had been.

Some flags were uneventful, but not others. Today would be one to remember. Though the sky was blue with the first warm breezes of spring's approach, and the sun kissed the boys' faces like they were long lost friends, all was not idyllic. The rats had emerged from their hiding spots to forage openly on the food left in outside trash cans. As the two principals approached the mic for a combined flag speech, a large brown rat, so large that at first Smith thought it was Chairman Meow's mate, ran out of the building behind the flagpoles towards the administrators. Mr. Zhou, used to the rodents from his days on a Dandong potato farm, kicked the beast; unfortunately, his kick was directly towards Miss Chen and Sarah Whippet.

The women were shocked, but McAdams, sensing a time to be chivalrous was near, stepped between the ladies and the rodent, received the tumbling beast as though Zhou had sent him a lovely through-ball into the eighteen-yard box, and kicked it towards the boys. It was a mighty kick.

The boys in the front rows had a dilemma. They could choose to move and break the order expected of them in flag, or they could stand firm like they were supposed to. They chose self-preservation. The lads may have heard of rats, but being from wealthy families had probably never seen one–until now. Chaos erupted. It was like the rat had a force field around it as the boys' lines dissolved in its path. Once it caught its balance, the rat committed to finishing the good race, and made for the open space it saw behind the boys. The students fell back, tripping on each other in a desperate attempt to avoid the fleeing creature. Arms and legs flailed. Bodies were tangled. Curses in two languages filled the air.

The rat had just reached safety when out of the bush emerged Chairman Meow. The old tomcat couldn't believe its hungry eyes, and it sprinted towards his potential meal. This caused the rat to skid, turn about face, and return from where it came. Again boys fell back, again arms and legs flailed, and the shouts were louder, and the curses were stronger because this time Chairman Meow joined the melee.

Eric Peterson couldn't keep a straight face. He was about to address the lads when he was cut off.

Boom! Boom! Boom! More fireworks.

His usual broad smile was even broader as he greeted the boys with his customary, "Good Morning, Gentlemen."

Twenty-Three
Nut Cracking Cold

The door was banging. "What time is it?" Jo muttered.

"Four-thirty," Hudson groaned after looking at the watch on the night table.

"Well?"

"Well what?"

"Aren't you going to answer the door?"

"It's four-thirty. It's cold. He'll go away." A minute later the door knocking hadn't stopped.

"I'll get it."

"No, I'll get it. I'm going. I'm going." Swinging his feet over the edge of the bed, his toes searched for his slippers. Once that mission was accomplished, Hudson grabbed his housecoat from the hook on the wall and groped his way out to the front entry. He looked through the vibrating door's eyehole, and he could see the top of a head. The matted grey hair was shaking from the exertion.

Smith opened the door quickly, and a wrinkly woman pushed past him using both her hands to move him aside. Like the cold wind that accompanied her, she marched into their kitchen without removing her shoes at the door, without so much as a hello, like a revolutionary guard come to take the unorthodox away, and shouted at the sink, "*Lou shui*! *Lou shui*!" Jo was at his side before he knew it, and the woman kept gesturing to the sink.

"What's she saying? What's the matter?" Hudson said as he wiped the sleep from his eyes.

"She's saying there is a water leak."

Jo went to the woman, whom Hudson recognized lived downstairs, and showed her that there was no water leak.

"Jo, maybe she's sleepwalking."

"She could be," Jo admitted, "or maybe she has dementia," and she gently held her neighbour's skinny arm and started to slowly walk their early morning guest to the door and then down to her own flat.

"What next?" Hudson wondered, knowing that as the day progressed there would be more adventures to encounter as he crawled back into his bed to escape the chill of the apartment's air.

The moment the tone sounded the end of the class the loudspeakers outside on the basketball courts broke the relative peace of the Chinese morning with blaring marching music. Someday, Smith thought, I will have to find out what the name of that song is. It's probably some Sousa piece, or maybe a knock-off; after all, the Chinese imitate everything–why not a march?

He left his class with the couple of boys who were lucky enough to have a medical note from their counsellors excusing them from flag ceremony. Dickens was balancing his computer in one hand while trying to put on his Edmonton Eskimo toque with the other. He joined Hudson in the hall filled with the traditional blazers of the all-boys school bearing the C.H.I.P.S. insignia (a beaver gnawing away at a maple leaf tree), and blurted, "It's nut-cracking cold out there Smith. Got two pairs of long johns on? Otherwise, the jewels are gone. Got to be minus 35 with the wind chill," he opined. Smith grunted and thought of the bone-chilling three minutes' walk from his apartment, how the classroom window blinds were swaying with the Siberian wind, how he and every one of his students wore heavy jackets in the class, and how his Cowichan-knit toque still couldn't keep his head warm even though he kept near the radiator heating his class. It was his first winter in China, and the 1950s NFB productions that showed the warm weather in the south as farmers planted their third rice crop of the year were, he realized as he stroked his goatee, a figment of imagination in Dong Bei on the Liaodong Peninsula.

"Yep, it's nut-cracking cold alright."

At the bottom he prepared to squeeze past the giant blanket placed on the inside of the doors which were constantly left open to allow the fresh air in–because it was healthy. The blanket, he felt, was like a giant germ trap with boys coughing and wiping their unwashed hands on it. He had even seen a boy's gob running down the edge. Why were they never washed? he wondered, but he already knew the answer that Relic had given him on his first day in the Middle Kingdom: "Never ask, 'Why?' in China." Pushing through the heavy cloth, he marvelled at how the sub-zero temperatures inside were intensified by the wind's full force. Oh, my...

It was at flag that he had time to think about life, his job, his wife, his kids back home, and the idiosyncrasies of the Chinese and ex-pat Canadians here at C.H.I.P.S.. The twenty minutes flew by and sometimes back in the fall he enjoyed the sun's warmth, but today Solzhenitsyn's description of poor Ivan Denisovich came to mind. The wind probably had crossed the poor faces of those in the gulags before it descended down through the semi-autonomous region of Inner Mongolia and Jilin province, riding the ridges down Liaoning province towards the end of the peninsula where Shanwan was situated. It certainly was punishing. Even for a Canadian this minus forty with wind chill was cold. Well maybe not for Edmontonians, he glibly chuckled to himself with the smugness of a west coaster. An Island boy, he was unused to the cold and even with a brief tour of duty in Northern BC early in his teaching career, he had never before experienced the cold and the wind that combined here to be a deadly natural spear. He thrust his gloved hands into his pockets as he approached the basketball courts where the boys lined up in homerooms for flag. Smith made a cursory trip past his homeroom class smiling his pity on the boys still dressed in their thin blazers, slacks, and dress shirts. Their breath steamed steadily as though they were old trains waiting for water at a station. They moved back and forth trying to protect themselves from the icy forces by hiding behind the boy in front of them. It reminded Smith of the long dune grasses on the west coast. Hudson stood beside Bannerman who was blowing steam out of his mouth and observing it. The steam curled out in little eddies before it disappeared. Smith thought of the verse in the Bible that says man is but a mist or a vapour. How fleeting life is, he considered. He rubbed his frosty nose with the ski glove, and wished he was with the lads back in room 411. Why, even the beaver on the insignia looks cold, Smith thought.

Reverting his gaze back towards the school and the centrepiece three flagpoles, Smith saw the six students wearing white gloves in addition to their thin blazers. One of two boys who came forward took the microphone from Mr. Ge, the Chinese sponsor of the Zhou En Lai class and spoke, "Welcome to the flag ceremony of Canadian Harmonious International Peace School." The steam pouring forth from his mouth reminded Smith of the dragon stories he had read as a kid. Two new boys left the group and brought out the red flag of China. "Raising the flag of People's Republic of China," the host of the ritual shrilled.

Smith winced, "Use the pronoun," he muttered under his breath. The two boys connected the flag to the centre pole, and one of them with a flourish unfurled the red cloth with a sweep of his arm. All did not follow the rehearsal. As the second student started to hoist the patriotic banner, the free corner got stuck in the ring holding the attached corner. As the Chinese national anthem blared, each eye focussed on the flag. It looked like a wounded mallard after a hunter had winged it. The 1,800 teenage boys sang the words, but the wind stole the lyrics before they actually found an ear. The powerful Siberian wind continued its mischief as it curled the flag with the yellow stars and wrapped it once, twice, and then a third time around the pole. No one moved to fix it. Everyone had their hands in their pockets. There was no turning back. To do so would be a dishonour to the boys.

Warmth, heat, hot tea were the thoughts in his mind as he climbed the stairs to his office. "Mr. Smith, your cheeks are very red," Beckham observed.

"Yes, I feel like I am in Edmonton at the U of A," he teased back. He knew that Beckham was going into the engineering program at the northern institution.

"I will be warmer than it is here, right?"

"Probably. There is heat inside the buildings, and no one leaves the doors and windows open there." Smith nodded towards the window at the end of the hall that was wide open and allowing the blast in to the building.

"What about fresh air? It would not be good for our healthy."

"Fresh air is brought in and heated, then distributed. It is very healthy."

"Oh, it sounds good."

"Trust me. It is." The blocks he once called hands fumbled with his keys and eventually he found the lock. Dickens came beside him and watching the attempt said, "I'll bet that's not all that's cold, eh?"

Twenty-Four

Relic's Last Tournament

Flag was cancelled. It was that cold. The minus 25C combined with a steady 70kmh wind made the outside an unbearable minus 45C. Wang decided to cancel flag when his Mercedes Benz wouldn't start, and he had to walk to his office. Those five minutes convinced him not to go out again. The streets were strewn with garbage as many of the cans had blown over and the contents freed and like prisoners escaping, they hid in every nook and cranny in the neighbourhood. Dozens of plastic bags soared in the air. Red and blue, pink and green, they dotted the sky like some pre-school child's painting easel with no rhyme or reason–just random colours on a blue backdrop. The Headmaster sat on his decision through the first period of the day. When Mr. Peterson came to him for his approval to purchase a box of pencils, he asked if the pencils were necessary, and then he informed the Canadian principal flag was cancelled.

A rubber plant leaf fell to the floor as Eric entered his cold office. As he sat down, the plant was still moving as though it too were shivering. Looking at the withering leaves from across the room, Peterson made a note to water. He logged on and sent the cancellation news by CHATTER, and all who read it welcomed the report. The boys, when informed, cheered. An unanimous agreement? That's a first, thought Smith, as he carried his laptop from his class back to his office. He met Dickens at the office door, and as the two men entered the room, he asked about the hockey trip the department head was arranging for the weekend.

"Hudson, this will go down in Tigers' lore. Never before has a Tigers' team travelled so long to get to a game. We would usually fly, but there is no direct flight from Shanwan to Jiamusi." He adjusted his toque as he settled into his chair. "Relic has arranged it all. He knew a guy who knows someone up there."

"Where is it?"

"We're taking a nine hour train ride to Harbin. Then we'll get on a bus and go six hours to Jiamusi. It's only a hundred kilometres from the Russian border."

"I'll be sure to wear my parka as I read *War and Peace.*"

"You'll need more than that to keep warm, my friend."

"Why Jiamusi? Why not Qiqihaer? We could fly there."

"We've been to Qiqihaer. It has to be special. Jiamusi is known as 'The City of Thieves'—charming, eh? I've looked it up, and it would be like a team from Vancouver going to Yellowknife for the weekend. This will be a great adventure."

The train trip saw the usual rambunctiousness of the Canadian team on the road. Beer and *bai jiu,* cards and stories filled the time, and soon the snoring surpassed what any sane person could bear. Early that morning as the train neared Harbin, a policeman came down the narrow passageway. He asked where the loud

Mei Guo ren were, and Relic peeked out from his thin cover, and answered him in perfect Chinese that the loud ones were Canadians–there were no Americans–and what was his problem. As he rubbed the sleepers from his eyes, he realized this was a man of authority. The uniform was pressed neatly. Its golden buttons gleamed. The epaulettes swayed gently with the train's rocking. What have I done? he thought. It turned out there was no problem, but the steward had told him that there was a thirty-six *jin* (approximately forty litres) crock pot of *bai jiu*, and he wondered if he could fill his small flask. After taking off the red cloth stopper and obliging him, Relic found out that he was the police chief of Jiamusi. Relic told his new friend of the trip they were taking to play hockey in his city. The chief was impressed that Canadians would come all the way from Shanwan to play, and he asked Relic to call him when the team reached the city, and he personally would escort them to their hotel. He took a quick swig from his flask, refilled it, and they exchanged phone numbers.

Six hours on the cramped bus was an adventure just as Dickens had promised. A pirated CD of *Star Trek* played, but it was the translation of the subtitles that made the players howl. Spock's famous 'Live long and prosper' became 'I hope that you will have economic efficiencies that increase your longevity.' The countryside reminded Smith of the Cariboo country's rolling hills. He recalled that when he first saw the Cariboo and the Fraser Canyon, he thought he had left BC as the terrain was nothing like the coastal rainforest where he grew up. This trip was expanding his vision of China as well. It wasn't just the landscape. Hudson gained a respect for the people they had met. He continued to meet in every new place happy, accommodating, helpful people. Everyone should travel, he thought. If you don't like to travel, you must be a misanthrope. If you don't like to travel, you must hate the world, or be fearful of it, and maybe that was worse.

They passed by small villages juxtaposed with ultra-modern windmills. The snow obscured how many there were, but the driver told Relic that they went on for many, many hills. When they neared the city, Relic called the chief who told him he was waiting at the crossroads, and true to his word, when the bus loaded with the Canadians turned off the expressway, the sirens and lights turned on, and the police chief led the group to their hotel. Other police cars joined in the impromptu parade, and soon there were cars, sirens blaring, on all four sides of the bus. On the way in, every head turned to see the spectacle. Every car ahead pulled over. It must be a quiet day in 'The City of Thieves,' chuckled Hudson to himself.

They pulled into the Jia Yun Hotel and Relic announced, "Guys, check in fast. Change into your gear. Get your game face on. We're on the ice in forty minutes." Urgency is a great motivator, and the team was on the bus in a half hour.

"Oh, are my legs ever stiff."

"My back won't bend."

"My feet are numb. I forgot my wool socks."

Dickens stood up as the bus started to roll out. "Quit your complaining. Do you think Henderson was whining about the conditions in Moscow in '72? Do you think Gump Worsley cried every time a puck hit him in the face? No! Today, we play the greatest game ever invented. A beautiful game. The coolest game. Remember, today we are Canadians, and this is our game."

Well, thought Hudson, it's not quite the St. Crispin's Day Speech that Henry V gives, but it was rousing.

It was a pity that the sentiment wasn't matched by the skill level of the Snow Tigers. Since he was one of the first on the ice, Hudson was told to play right defence. "Hey, you know I can't skate very well. I can hardly skate forward never mind backward."

"You'll be fine until the other guys get their skates on."

That turned out to be wishful thinking as the Jiamusi team centre dressed in an American university's jerseys won the face-off back to the defence. He promptly passed it to the left winger who was streaking towards the blue line. The winger picked up the crisp pass and gave a slight fake with his head that truly was superfluous. Hudson took a small pivot on his blades and fell flat on his side, flailing his stick at the speedy forward who continued toward the goal. Where is the other defenceman? Hudson pondered as he tried to get up, but he saw Bannerman in the same position. Cheers rose from the Chinese bench, and Randy McMann scooped the puck out of the netting and shot it over the glass. 1-0 at 0:05 of the first period.

"Com' on, guys! Don't let Smith and Bannerman pair up."

"Peterson, never pass up the middle." 2-0.

Dickens skated slowly towards McMann's crease, beer in hand. "It's okay Randy. I've let one in from centre before too. Have a drink." 3-0.

The Jiamusi team played a Russian style which made sense with the border so close, and they looked for the long pass often. McMann made save after save on the breakaways, but the rebounds were tougher to stop. 4-0, 5-0, 6-0.

Halfway through the first period Relic gave the Canucks their first ray of hope. He picked off a pass at the blue line and skated in unimpeded. Sliding the puck to the right, he dropped his shoulder and swung it back to the left. The goalie bought his first move, and he gave Relic the room he needed as he shovelled a backhander past him. 6-1. “I don’t think his lateral movement is very good guys.”

The second period was more even as the travel-weary Tigers found their legs. Tony scored on a hard, quick wrist shot. 6-2. Jiamusi answered with another set-play goal off the centre face-off. 7-2.

The third period was nearly over, but the scoring had continued and the paper score flip cards read 13-2. JJ took the puck coast to coast and rounding the net saw that four Jiamusi Gophers were converging on him. Trailing the play, as always, the self-named ‘Pylon,’ Hudson Smith, was coming into the slot. The skilled American saucered a pass towards him through the forest of legs. The Canadian bench groaned. The Chinese players turned their heads just in time to see Hudson Smith, one-time a slap shot, as he was falling, to the low stick side to score his first ever goal in a hockey game. The Snow Tigers jumped over the boards, McMann skated the length of the rink, and the players on the ice all mobbed the unlikely scorer. 13-3.

Minutes later, after the traditional handshake, the Snow Tigers were in the dressing room. Relic stood up, and yelled out for quiet. “Men, we were outplayed and outscored. However, the executive and I have met, and we have decided, after a call to Toronto, that today’s Tiger of the Game goes to Hudson Smith for an outstanding Bobby Hull-like goal.” He handed Hudson a patch that would be sewn onto his black Tigers’ cardigan.

“Thanks. Although, I’ve paddled canoes, eaten eggs with maple syrup, given the Trudeau salute, and seen the Aurora Borealis, there was something missing in my life as a Canadian. All that is gone. I now feel more like a Canadian because I've scored." Then someone started to sing "O Canada," and the entire room joined in.

The team rushed back to the hotel to shower before the banquet. "This place is pretty good, Relic. It's way better than the dives we usually stay at," Dickens said. "Isn't it out of our budget?"

"Yep. This isn't the place I booked. When I told the police chief where we were staying, he told me, 'No'. We would stay somewhere else. Apparently, both hotels are owned by the same guy, and the chief is constantly looking the other way for him. He's finally cashing in the favours. Apparently, this is 'The City of Thieves'."

Like the splendid entry into Jiamusi, the opposition provided a huge banquet at the best restaurant in the city. The entrance of the Eight-One Hotel, a name that commemorated the establishment of the army of the People's Republic of China, had a golden statue of Chairman Mao. Some of the Canadians leaped over the rope cordoning off The Helmsman to get a photo with the golden communist. When the Baishantan Snow Tigers entered the dining room, the players from Jiamusi stood and applauded. The Canadians spread themselves out, trying to have at least one Canadian-Mandarin speaker at each table to ease communication.

Bai jiu was served from fancy bottles, and Hudson guessed this was the good stuff. The other *bai jiu* he had tried tasted and burned like gasoline, and he toasted his hosts and tossed back the small glass. Yikes, he thought, even the good stuff is bad, and powerful. I can feel the alcohol directly flowing into my veins. Maybe I can avoid drinking more by moving around.

Hudson reached into his pocket and took out a bag of Canadian and British Columbian flag pins. He gave all of the men at his table one of each, and they toasted him back. He indicated that he wanted to distribute the small tokens to everyone else, and left the men. Each new group received the small pins with enthusiasm, but they all wanted him to *gan bei*, or toast him. He obliged, but at the second table he was starting to feel unsteady. Hudson was never much of a drinker. Then he saw Mattie with an English-Mandarin dictionary, and he had an idea. "Mattie, let me borrow that for a sec', will ya." He flipped through pages quickly to get to the word he desired. When the toast was offered, Hudson declined, and he pulled the closest Chinese player to him, and pointed to the word– alcoholic. After a moment, the man told the rest of the table, and they all solemnly nodded, and started to offer him the food at their table. As Hudson progressed through the room, his dictionary confident came along to explain why the Canadian wouldn't *gan bei* with them.

Both teams tried to communicate to each other by mime as there wasn't enough Mandarin speakers to go around as dish after dish came out to the famished men. In a generous sign of respect, the player sitting beside Hudson reached into a sizzling pot of meat and fished around to find the largest piece. Then he placed the prized morsel on Hudson's plate. The man was maybe in his late 50s, and his childhood would have seen the famine that Chairman Mao had brought to this prosperous land. Older people still greeted each other with "have you eaten today?" like Canadians spoke of the weather. The act of love touched Hudson deeply. "*Xie xie*," was all he could say.

Once the meal was nearing the end, Relic stood up and began a speech in Mandarin. Basically he said, "We are Canadians. We love hockey. We love China. We love the Chinese people. We have come from Shanwan to play. We are your brothers because we skate. Thank you for inviting us. This has been a time of peace and harmony. We will cherish our games with you. Someday we hope we can come back. Thank you."

Once Relic was done, the Chinese organizer came to the front and took the microphone. He was not as succinct as the Canadian veteran, and his red cheeks belied his condition as the *bai jiu* took its toll. Generally, he too thanked the Canadians for coming to their small community and playing a game that they loved. He motioned to the front table, and a group of Chinese players came up and started enthusiastically to sing their national anthem, and much to their surprise Relic stayed up front and joined them.

Then all the Canadians came up and sang "O Canada" and then rowdily followed it up with the only other song that most of them knew: Stompin' Tom Conners's "The Hockey Song."

The next day the Snow Tigers played a team of 12–16 year olds from the local hockey boarding school, and were soundly trounced. "It must be the effects of last night," encouraged Bannerman.

The trip back was silent except for the duelling snoring of Dickens and Vander Kwaak. Hudson Smith read a chapter from *China Road*, and was fascinated by how many times the author's observations matched his own.

As the bus pulled into Harbin, Relic stood up and announced, "Men, I wantz ya to be the first to know becaush you are my brothers. Dish is my last hockey trip, and I am going back to Canada in July. Thank you for sharing your lives with me. It will be hard...to go home, but it is home, and as my daughter is about to enter high school, we've decided a Canadian experience would be valuable for her."

There was silence, and Hudson unconsciously touched his Canadian flag pin.

Twenty-Five
The Maple Leaf Forever

Hudson Smith stared out the classroom window looking at the placid Yellow Sea. He started to daydream about the past year. 'The Good-bye to Canada Tour' (as Hudson called it), began with a drive up the Coquihalla Highway into the dry semi-desert of the Okanagan Valley. The Kootenays were next, the doorway to the majesty of Canada's Rocky Mountains. Banff National Park with the turquoise lakes of Lake Louise, Lake Morraine, and Peyto Lake on the highway to Jasper was stunning. He hadn't travelled this way since he was a child when his parents made the exodus to the promised land of BC from Ontario. Kits Beach, Crescent Beach, and Boundary Bay on the coast provided him with memorable sunsets.

Cultural events he attended once he knew he was going to China included: Bard on the Beach, Art in the Park, Theatre Under the Stars, and the Berry Festival in Abbotsford out in the eastern part of the Fraser Valley.

The Grouse Grind provided exercise. Tubing on the Stave River and kayaking on the Harrison River with his son Carson provided enjoyment. They paddled from the iconic Harrison Hot Springs Hotel on Harrison Lake down the river to the confluence of the mighty Fraser. A quick trip to Vancouver Island to see family and to Seattle to see the Mariner's rounded out a hectic July.

Hudson wanted the memories of his home province and country to be strong, so he had bought a new camera early in the spring and set out to record as much as he could.

His first project in that regard was to provide himself with a virtual garden. Every day he went out to his own personal Eden and photographed the minute changes occurring in the flora. When the crocuses he planted in the grass were done, the daffodils, living sunshine, were next. Tulips, a tribute to his Dutch heritage, followed, the apple and pear blossoms, hydrangea, roses, phlox, blue gentians reminding him of Lake Morraine, grape leaves opening, delphiniums, dahlias, irises, jack-in-the-pulpits, peonies, hostas, ferns, and his prized wild chocolate lilies and trilliums were all duly recorded in the budding, flowering, and seeding stages. Finally, the fruit arrived. Sweet Gewurztraminer grapes, blueberries, Gala apples, and Anjou pears gave off delicate scents and delicious flavours. It was too bad that the images could only capture the plump fullness and the dynamic colours with the light blush. These photos kept him from descending into despair as he looked at them whenever the cold and the brown of a Baishantan winter became overwhelming. He kept these pictures as his laptop's screen saver, and frequently found himself staring at them as they scrolled by. Indeed, he had even shown his classes the photos of Canada's natural beauty, and they spent times asking questions about his travels. The boys had loved his black bear photo taken just outside of the Columbian Ice Fields on his way to Jasper. They were awed at the empty spaces, and Canada's beauty also impressed.

Smith had signed on with C.H.I.P.S. in February of the previous year when it was clear that his soon to be ex-wife wasn't interested in reconciliation. When he emerged from the abyss, he needed a change. China would do. His adult children encouraged him in his decision, and were excited about visiting and seeing some of the must-see sights.

Hudson had discovered that a former friend and long-time colleague, Jo Loch, was working in China, and they soon were in contact. Those early professional questions soon became personal, and when Jo returned to Canada in July, their romance quickly grew. Their short engagement led to a tropical wedding during the long five-week winter break. They were married in Thailand on Koh Phi-Phi. Jo was intelligent, attractive, kind. She was a pleasure to be around. Best friends, they laughed, played, cooked, and chatted together. The time spent with her always seemed short. The times apart were long. They were in love. He thought of the term soul mates. When he had read *Anne, of Green Gables*, he had scoffed at the term, but now he realized that the precocious redhead in Lucy Maud Montgomery's tale had got it right. Jo was his soul mate.

Jo and Hudson wanted to return to C.H.I.P.S. the next year, but after that, who knew what may come? Jo, a seven years veteran in China was ready for new adventures. Back home to Canada? Both their parents were getting on in years. Smith's adult children were entering their reproductive years and being Grandparents was appealing. A calling to Haiti? Hudson had friends in Haiti, Abu Dhabi, and Cambodia. All these places had some allure. Good healthcare was also attractive, and Canada's much maligned system was fabulous compared to what he had experienced in China.

Jo told him that a friend of theirs had taken one of their sons in to a doctor about some growths near his genitals. The doctor decided to cut the growths off, and asked the boy's mother to hold him down. Using no anaesthetic, the doctor began, and the boy screamed in agony. The woman stopped the procedure immediately. The doctor told her to have the boy's father bring the crying child back tomorrow, as her husband would be stronger. The woman then looked up her son's ailment on the Internet. She sent pictures to her doctor back home. Her doctor diagnosed a common fungal infection, prescribed a topical cream, and within a week the growths were gone. It took several years for the young lad to lose his fear of the man in the white coat.

* * *

Sarah Whippet, the vice principal, sat down in the steaming hot pool with Jo. "Ah, this is one aspect of this culture that Canada could import." Jo nodded her head in agreement. The pleasure of the hot water was penetrating her marrow. "Did I tell you about my visit to the doctor this week?" Jo silently indicated no. "I went to the hospital in Kai Fa Qu and told the nurse that I had a back ache. I could hardly get up in the morning. Then as I said this the other person in the room punched me in the back. She almost knocked me over. When I turned around, she was smiling. 'What are you doing?' I yelled at her. 'Are you nuts?' Finally, the interpreter came, and I asked to see the doctor. The interpreter told me that the woman who punched me in the back *was* my doctor. I got out of there as quickly as I could. My back is still sore, and now it's also bruised."

* * *

Dickens had told Smith about his wife's third pregnancy in China. Apparently, during the first trimester all was well, but in her monthly examination, one of the key questions was, "Is this your first pregnancy?" Dickens' wife, wanting to let the doctor know that she was experienced in the delivery room, told him that this was her third. From then on, the doctor ordered ultra-sounds, and each time he delivered the bad news: "Your baby is abnormal. You should abort."

"What is the matter with the baby?"

"One leg is too long." The second time they visited it was, "The baby's head is too large. You should abort," and on the third visit for the distraught parents the physician revealed, "He has no arms. You should abort."

"Baloney!" Dickens shouted at him. "You don't want us to have a third child."

"Well, that is correct. There are too many people in China," the doctor matter-of-factly stated. Katie, his wife, and the two kids were on the next plane home to Canada. A healthy baby boy was born six months later. The doctor's first call was not to Socrates, but to the State.

It had greatly surprised Hudson to discover that China had no universal healthcare. Hundreds of millions did not have adequate access and could not afford it if there were a doctor available. Socialist medicine made Canada more communist than China–where people paid doctors and hospitals and insurance was rare. Women were especially vulnerable. So much for Chairman Mao's famous quotation, "Women hold up one half of the sky," thought Smith.

Though women held up half the sky, they were a rare creature at C.H.I.P.S.. The all-boys' school was a vastly different place than any other school Smith had been in either as a student or as a teacher. The aim of uniting the two cultures was a noble one;

however, money is what drove the place. The independent schools that he taught in in British Columbia had faith and good education as their goals. Here the *yuan* ruled.

The idea that students could go from a bare minimum of English knowledge and skills to mastery of the language in three years was preposterous, but that was the expectation. To achieve this, Smith realized that his regular ways of teaching would have to be discarded. A heavy focus on the BC Provincial English Exam became necessary. The test was only a partial selection of the learning outcomes of the curriculum. These outcomes were the ones the school focussed on. Past exams were copied and analysed. Hours were spent dissecting each part of the test. The original composition was discussed, edited on the screen in front of the class, corrected, and written again using a different topic. The narrative style allowed the boys to write a story that showed some type of epiphany, and with a few adaptations could be used with any topic given in any sitting of the exam. Yes, it was contrary to the spirit of the provincial, but Smith felt that it was all really a game, and his students should know how to play. Rich Bannerman always said, "This too shall pass." He was a classic punster, but the problem was that so many of the boys did not pass. Literature was the true joy of English class, and the exam was notorious for its use of sight passages which were obscure. The exam weighed on his mind as he walked to his apartment with early twilight vanishing and darkness swallowing up the hills in the distance. His apartment was a refuge from the pressure of the Headmaster's expectations, and there he could read and transport himself back to his native land.

The teacher apartments were reasonable for singles, but after they were married, Jo and Hudson found the space was too small. Try as they may, however they arranged the bedroom, there was no way they could get out of both sides of the bed. Storage spaces were small. "Don't they know we're Westerners? We have stuff," Jo huffed one day.

They looked at apartments in Baishantan and were delighted when they found cheaper places that were larger and better designed. The apartment they chose to move into was a new spacious two-bedroom unit in a project right across from the school. They had an ocean view, full shower, but no tub. Very few Chinese homes had bathtubs. It would have fit in well in Vancouver's Yaletown. The nine-foot ceilings added an open feeling and the windows gave excellent natural light. Despite having some of the creature comforts of home, Smith missed getting mail. Whether it was bills or flyers, he loved looking in the mailbox and getting a surprise. This illogical pleasure stemmed back to his childhood when his job at the age of eight was to walk a mile to the local post office to open the box and bring home the mail. This daily chore gave him responsibility and exercise, and his mother peace and quiet for nearly an hour. A different era, he thought, but the memory still brought him pleasure. Growing up in small town Canada on Vancouver Island was wonderful.

The next day, standing here amongst students in this foreign land, Smith felt a yearning to return to such an idyllic way of life. Did Camelot exist in everyone's youth? he wondered, or could it be that the best days still lay ahead? The United Nations Index for Liveable Cities had once again ranked Vancouver as the best major city to live in. It massaged the Canadian ego to hear such news. If he was ever called to testify to the fact, Hudson Smith would give a resounding, ever so polite, "Yes."

Smith looked up at the cafeteria building, and a new sign greeted him. This one was larger than the previous sign whose message was already long forgotten. The Chinglish read, “MILLENNIAL GRAND CAUSE DISPLAYS EXCELLENCE.” Who writes these? he wondered, and where are they made? A plastic bag lazily floated past the new sign, and the magpie left its roost. Mocking the participants with its cackling cry, it glided past the poles with a freedom that the boys hadn't felt and that Hudson yearned to feel again. The flag ceremony was over as quickly as it had started, and he couldn't wait to return to his home and native land.

Twenty-Six
The Chinese National Crokinole Championship

"By the way Mom, I've entered the Chinese National Crokinole Championship."

"Really, that's wonderful dear," Smith's mother enthused over the Skype connection. "I am proud of you."

His father cut her off with a reasoned question, "Wait a minute, how many people play crokinole in China?"

There were seventy teachers...about a third of which played the Canadian board game. "Maybe twenty-five," Smith laughed, "I could be a national champion though."

The bus to Shanwan was loaded with rowdy, beer-drinking Canadians. One would become the national champion. Smith marvelled at the joy created here. All of the players had been issued a tacky brightly coloured striped shirt. The colours were bright, like a carnival, and it had a patch sewn on which said in Chinese characters: Chinese National Crokinole Championship. Jokes were flying back and forth, and Bobby Wilson ranked below his office's microwave, fridge, coffee pot, and chair bore the brunt of the ribbing. Manly bravado was displayed as Dickens, McMann,

Bannerman, and Simon crushed cheap aluminum Bang beer cans on their foreheads like they were at a UBC frat house party.

When the bus stopped a block from the restaurant, several Canadians joined a Chinese street food vendor who had parked his cart and was urinating against a brick wall. This was something that Smith could not bring himself to do; yet, it seemed to be common, and it seemed to be accepted. On their way to the restaurant each of the men bought some candied strawberries on a stick, but Don Hawk went for the squid. "It's actually quite good barbequed," he said.

The Chinese National Crokinole Championship was another one of Dickens's grand schemes. Six years before he had commissioned a local woodcraftsman to build a crokinole board and discs with the specifications he provided, and then he brought it into the office. The game relieved the tedium of marking, and entertained the six men and one woman in the office. Dickens created a ladder, and the following year a league. More boards were ordered and soon it became a standard feature of the C.H.I.P.S. staff rooms located on each floor. The C.H.I.P.S. CHATTER kept everyone apprised of the latest match results.

The inaugural Chinese National Crokinole Championship was held in a downtown Shanwan hotel–The Kempinski. This five star hotel had hosted the event for the first four years; yet, the tourney seemed out of place in the classy place. Dickens created a huge banner which said: Chinese National Crokinole Championship in the gold lettering favoured by all events. He invited local television and the press to cover the results. Surprisingly, the media continued to come, but perhaps that spoke to the excellent foreign beer and the lack of news in the tightly controlled society. Last year the tournament had moved to The Cold Dragon restaurant, and had its first participants from Beijing and Shanghai. They were former C.H.I.P.S. teachers who jumped at the chance to visit their colleagues and friends.

Like Samuel de Champlain and his Society of Good Friends who made life in New France tolerable for the early French colonists, Dickens tried his best to bring the community together. Past events included the Winter Carnival which featured barrel jumping on the ice, a baseball team that had the dubious record of 0-48 over two seasons in a Japanese, Korean, and American circuit, a ball hockey tournament that became a focal point of the late spring at the school, an outside curling bonspiel, and a fashion show that was a tip of his hat to his wife.

A German immigrant in the small town of Tavistock, Ontario invented crokinole. It consisted of a large round board with eight metal pegs covered in rubber surrounding an inner circle worth fifteen points, a hole in the centre of the inner circle was worth twenty points, and two outer circles worth ten and five. Small wooden discs were shot by a player's finger, and like the sport of curling, hit other player's discs off while trying to protect one's own to score points. Crokinole had developed a cult following in Ontario, but really became a national game when the Eaton's Christmas catalogue added it to their pages in the 1920s. A documentary movie had been filmed a decade earlier at the world championships in Tavistock, and it chronicled some of the foibles of small town Canada and the characters of the game. Dickens had written the World Championship tournament organizers informing them of the Chinese event, and he had received word that they would give a lifetime entry to the winner of the Chinese National Crokinole Championship.

The Championship this year was the largest ever. Twenty-four teachers had signed up. They invaded The Cold Dragon, a restaurant run by one of the Baishantan Snow Tigers' Chinese players, Yu. Ten boards were brought in, and Dickens took out a large plastic board that had the tournament draw on it. Players were asked to gather around the bar, and the rules were explained. This was redundant as no one was here who had never played the game before.

Smith slid into a chair that was still warm from its previous occupant, and he nodded yes to the waitress who signalled him about re-filling his ice tea. He reached his hand across the smooth granite table to scoop up the salted peanuts, and he tossed in the whole lot, but they weren't peanuts. The fire in his mouth told him these were wasabi peas. Yikes, he thought, I need some cool tea now. The waitress also brought him some chips. He put one in his mouth, and immediately wished he had not–squid flavour.

The draw for the first time went beyond a round robin with a single board, and like many curling bonspiels, had four flights. Every player would be guaranteed two games, but after that the single elimination rounds began. The top eight players as determined by last year's results received byes. Thus all rookies had to play into the tournament, and the veterans could scout them out. Yu was happy because this meant that more of the players would stick around and consume more of the golden amber that he imported for this event.

Smoke drifted casually in the room lit by large round chandeliers that looked like props from a medieval film. They illuminated the wall that looked like a busload of grannies had been quilting up a storm. Upon closer inspection it was apparent the collection of colours and designs were hockey jerseys from around China. There was a prized national team jersey, a Beijing Dragons uniform from the 1970s when hockey first was played by the new influx of foreigners, a nifty green one from Harbin, and even a Soviet jersey that Yu told Hudson he had traded a former Red Army player for in Harbin at a tournament. There were other curios as well. The strong, wiry Yu had a few strands of distinguished grey hair above his ears and was the proud owner of the establishment that he ran as a hobby after having made a fortune in the Chinese stock market in mobile phones. The stock had been purchased at the ground floor initial offering, and had gone from two cents a share to sixteen dollars a share in the last fifteen years, and it was still climbing. Yu was wealthy. However, when you are forty-five, you are not ready to retire, so Yu opened the restaurant to enjoy himself.

"Yu, you know about the ball hockey rink that Relic and Dickens rent out, right?"

"Yes, I've played there many times."

"Well, there may be a problem with the landlord."

"Really? A problem? I know him. We will have tea."

A beautiful waitress came over to the two middle-aged men with new drinks for each. "Smith, I'd like you for to meet my niece. I think she is best paid waitress in all of China," Yu beamed as his niece winked at her uncle.

The bar gleamed, the next round was purchased as part of the entry fee covered four beverages, and Dickens continued. "So remember, the seat rule means that your seat must remain in contact with the seat at all times." He took a large swig from his stein and continued, "Once you are done, report your score to Yu. He will write your name in so all can see who the next match will be." Dickens stood fully erect, saluted and barked out, "Now I declare the Sixth Annual Chinese National Crokinole Championship has begun!"

His parody was greeted with roars of laughter, and old Rich Bannerman led a spontaneous rendition of "O Canada" that caused the six other couples in the restaurant to look on with bemusement.

Smith had to wait his turn as only ten games could be played at one time. Across the restaurant in a booth sat Nathan Johnson. He was a younger teacher who had taught in Korea and in Taiwan the last two years and there were rumours that he was looking for another placement next year. Nibbling at the squid legs and peanuts, Johnson quickly drank the tall green bottle.

Hudson thought of his own long career and how at the start he moved from the North to places closer and closer to what he would call civilisation, but he only did so after two years in a place. Two years in a spot gave him a chance to get to know people and to fall into the rhythms of life. He knew one couple in their early seventies who moved every eighteen months, and he wondered what they were running from. When he was younger, Smith thought that he wanted to teach back home, but he realised that home was wherever he was and this change of attitude had made him more comfortable wherever he was. Life was best lived in the present. Chasing rainbows would lead one to be tired and restless like the Ancient Mariner in Coleridge's literary ballad. He noticed old Bannerman bringing a Harbin beer to Dickens, and thought the old-timer could be cast as the Mariner if there was a movie made of the poem.

Johnson kept tossing back peanuts, but didn't acknowledge Smith's nod of the head. Then Smith noticed the ear buds. Johnson was listening to his own music in the restaurant. He couldn't converse. He was in his own world. Hudson decided to walk across the room and join him.

His hands are huge, Smith realised when he sat down. Johnson beat him to the punch. "I didn't think anyone would join me tonight," he said pulling out the ear buds.

"Maybe they needed an invite."

"I don't invite many. It's too dangerous, or ridiculous."

"Okay, I'll bite. Why?"

"Dangerous, because if you really want to get to know someone, you have to be open and honest. Actually, you have to give part of yourself away. Ridiculous, because small talk chit-chat is utterly pointless." Yu's niece came over and placed down another Tsingdao for Johnson, and cleared away Smith's ice tea.

Hudson looked Nathan in his hard, blue eyes. They had seen much over the years, and those things were bricks that built a wall that kept Nathan safe and protected. Smith wondered when the wall was first started. What had begun the personal bricks and mortar to be used? What had raised the wall? Before Hudson could continue to explore this train of thought his name was called. "I'll talk to you later."

Smith was paired off against Bobby Wilson. Bobby was not here for the game; he was here to drink. In Room 210, his own office, Wilson had remained on the bottom of the ladder that tracked the prowess of each player. Once in a C.H.I.P.S. CHATTER his good friend, Ali Javaherian, posted a score that said "Bobby

Wilson 45 Microwave 100." This became a running joke, and the CHATTER had received updates on the ongoing battle between man and machine. Wilson good-naturedly posted one the week before the Chinese Championships which said, "I beat the microwave, but I lost to the fridge, and now the toaster is trash-talking me." The day before the big event when Smith went into the office to speak to McMann, he noticed that all three appliances were now ranked ahead of poor Bobby–competition was fierce in room 210.

Smith got to the requisite one hundred points before Bobby got on the board. Now he was in the tournament proper–the sweet sixteen–and Bobby could go to the D Flight where players interested in drinking could do so unimpeded by turns and games.

As a child Smith had frequently played the game at home after supper on those dark rainy winter nights in the Comox Valley. It was a time to talk, but also a time to work on the unconscious geometry skills that he used in high school, and that his father had used as he built the standard box homes so common in BC. Talcum powder kept the board smooth and fast as the Smith family fired discs. Competition was fierce back then as his mother served snacks, but never popcorn as she insisted the butter would slow the board.

Hudson's next opponent was Tom Simon, his office colleague. They had played each other dozens of times, and though Tom made more 'dougies' which is what putting your disc in the centre twenty hole was called, he frequently made mistakes. Simon's Buddhist faith was a calming factor, he insisted, and he felt victory would occur because he had already conquered his inner man. The faith may have been calming, but the alcohol was not as Smith's steady fingers dispatched his second opponent with relative ease 100-45.

Now he was in the elite eight.

On the other side of the draw Relic, the three time defending champion, was progressing nicely as he made short work of Eric Peterson, who had only played once in his entire life. The principal had won his first match against a drunk Don Hawk who usually was a good player. Hawk didn't care about the championship other than to have a good time hoisting the suds. The boss had kidded Relic about a good evaluation report being on the line, and Relic had responded with three dougies in a row. Then Relic eked out a 100-90 win over Tom Simon's son who was homeschooled, and whose PE classes lately had been mastering the game with a regiment of a thousand shots a day at the circle. Relic kept calling him a 'cheeky bugger' when the boy kept making tough shot after tough shot. Ultimately, the lad's dream would have to wait for another year.

Smith now had the tournament's number two seed in Randy McMann. Dickens, the brainchild of so many C.H.I.P.S. events, was still playing and his march to the finals took him to Dan Best's board. It would be the two department heads representing Math and English clashing for a semi-final berth. Dickens dominated Best allowing the math head only a pair of dougies while Dickens hit the century mark before his beer was warm. Smith's hope of knocking off one of the best was erased as McMann edged the newcomer in three by a combined differential of ten.

The top side of the draw brought the curious as Ali Javaherian blew past Mattie Peterson, shot down Tony Vander Kwaak, and schooled Nathan Johnson to meet the champ in the semis. It was a close match, but the sober Ali was cool in knocking off Relic in three games, winning two by five points, and losing one by the same margin. Relic was stunned. He hadn't lost in three years, and to lose to the kid fresh out of SFU was hard to take. He excused himself to go to the washroom after shaking Ali's hand. Relic still was in the tourney though as it was a true double knockout.

The restaurant was loud with the laughter, jeering, and taunts of those eliminated.

Bobby bumped into Hudson and said, "I love this place. I can get cold beer. Do you know how rare that is Hudson?"

It was an unqualified success. The boisterous atmosphere around the kitchen table at home was nearly replicated. All Smith needed was his mom serving some snacks, and his dad's thick fingers showing him how to use angles to not only send opponent's discs out, but to move his own disc into a better, higher scoring position. Smith noticed that Nathan Johnson was gone from the booth. "Anyone see Johnson?"

"Yeah, I saw him leave with the cute waitress."

"Me too. It's the first time I've seen him smile."

The evening dragged on, and Smith, too tired to stay for the finals, left with Vander Kwaak and the two Simons in a black cab.

It was Monday morning at flag when Smith heard that Relic had returned the favour to the tired Iranian-Canadian math teacher in two straight matches, and kept his crown. The old man would go back to Canada with an undisputed six-year reign, but Ali looked to be the next champ in waiting. Across the basketball court as the sun was reflecting off the backboards, Smith waited for the ceremony to begin. The wind had cleared the sky so that the azure blue was so brilliant it almost hurt. The mountains were so sharply outlined they looked like a cardboard cut-out. He noticed Nathan Johnson making his way through the hordes with a smile on his face.

Flag was all about respecting the elderly as they had wisdom to teach the youth of the nation. The banner unfurled and proclaimed: THE ANCIENT FORREST NORISHES YONG TREES.

Twenty-Seven
Wang Has His Day

Each morning in April the thaw became more real, more pronounced, as the Earth's axis tilted the north towards Sol's life-giving warmth. The wind was no longer a knife, but it was not a tender caressing hand yet either. The skies, still azure, did not remind him of arctic ice. Instead the blue promised warmth, growth, and lazy summer days. As Eric Peterson stepped into the All-School-Committee-for-the-Greater-Good, he realized that in here at least the permafrost was still in full force. Wang sat up front on his elevated platform scanning some papers with Miss Chen standing by his side. The computer projector unit was on, and it gave the walls a strange bluish tinge as the remainder of the administration staff trickled in.

Once everyone had entered Wang stood up and said, "Good morning. This is most auspicious day for C.H.I.P.S.. Today we bring forth strategies to make us the best profitable school in China. Today measures we take will change the way we optimize the future of C.H.I.P.S.. Students will benefit. Teachers will benefit. Society will benefit and all will be harmonious. Miss Chen will explain the details." Wang sat down and stared at each person on the Canadian side of the table. He knew the Chinese side would accept the new direction, but he felt the Canadians would be less accommodating.

"Good morning," Chen breathed as she licked her lips. "C.H.I.P.S. needs to take new directions to optimize future. We will strive for the goal, and we will be successful. The five-year plan will touch on students, teachers, and administrators. We will change, and change will benefit."

"The students will now be able to use their cell phones on campus for a small monthly fee." Eric sat up. This was an intrusion into his territory.

"Modern society uses cell phones to communicate, and this represents new and rich area to mine. Students will pay twenty yuan per month to be allowed to call from inside the cafeteria at lunch. Projected value two hundred thousand yuan." There was a gasp from the Chinese side of the table over the huge number. "Since students are in cafeteria, we estimate that food services profits will also rise by one hundred thousand yuan. Student uniforms will be expanded so shoes will become standard, hats for winter will become standard, and C.H.I.P.S. socks and underwear will be standard after three-year phase in period. New clothing revenues: one hundred thousand yuan." She paused to take a drink from the C.H.I.P.S. brand of bottled water, and replacing the bottle on the table, she licked a drop from her lower lip.

Oh great, more things to police, Eric thought. When will I ever be able to focus on leading my staff to become better teachers? Since when did uniforms ever teach what mattered? It's all about appearances, the superficial. What really matters is deep inside people...

Eric felt alive as he made a transformative discovery. He decided his future as Miss Chen droned on about more changes, and though he was depressed about the directions, he was delighted that he knew his own direction for the first time in this land where he was an illiterate.

"C.H.I.P.S. will provide new services such as TV in the dorms and bedding which will also increase revenues projected to be half million *yuan*. This changes will improve student life and optimize C.H.I.P.S. future."

"Teachers will be given more control over their own pension funds as C.H.I.P.S. will no longer invest for them. This two million saving will benefit C.H.I.P.S. so that new projects may be undertaken."

The Canadian admin team looked at each other, trying to read what the others were thinking. Did she mean that the pension money was now to be controlled by Canadians, or was it being eliminated? If the latter, this was a bombshell.

"There will no longer be a free bus service to Kai Fa Qu for teachers, but they may ride with Chinese staff for a monthly fee of fifty *yuan*. We will gain an estimated fifteen thousand *yuan* per year. The health benefits package has seen rates increase by more than Chinese GDP's growth, and by eliminating this program C.H.I.P.S. will be giving Canadian teachers more choice where they spend their medical dollars. C.H.I.P.S. will save over a million *yuan*. Canadian administration will be reduced to one principal. C.H.I.P.S. will save another million *yuan*." John McAdams adjusted his tie with his right hand, and Sarah Whippet reached out for his left.

"BC Program teachers will not be hired at the same replacement rate, and we will optimize class sizes this next year to create better learning conditions. English teachers will no longer teach a double block of students. Math and Science teachers produce results with our students and English teachers had better improve results, or they will be fired. Savings will be five million *yuan*."

Oh, that is rich, thought Eric. He knew studies showed that language acquisition took at least five years before fluency was attained. Saddened by the scapegoating of the English teachers who were often blamed for student inadequacy, he slowly shook his head back and forth. Wang noticed the movement and clenched a pen until his knuckles and forearm were shaking. He turned away from Peterson to focus on what Miss Chen was saying.

"Each Chinese teacher must recruit a new student or face a pay deduction of twenty-five percent. Recruitment successes will be published, and bonuses will be given staff who recruit more than one. New enrolment will benefit all. Estimated gain of five million *yuan*." She reached for her water bottle, and misjudging the distance knocked it over. A worker appeared from nowhere, wiped up the spill, replaced the water, and was back against the wall before Miss Chen delivered her last statement.

This initiative was sure to cause more hardship with the Chinese staff as they were academics, and they travelled in a different social sphere than the well-to-do businessmen who could afford to send their sons to C.H.I.P.S.. The teachers wouldn't have the *guanxi* (connections) to be able to recruit more students. With the one child policy, there were no family ties to draw on anymore. Peterson, Whippet, and McAdams looked across the table and saw the furrowing brows of their Chinese colleagues. Their heads were down, but their minds were working desperately to understand how this would impact them and the rest of the Chinese employees.

"Plan will result in a fifteen million *yuan* increase to the C.H.I.P.S. financial benefit." Wang smiled approvingly and applauded her. As if on cue the Chinese staff joined in while the Canadians did not. The applause died away quickly, but Wang noticed. No eye contact was made by the Canadian contingent with the Headmaster. Indignant, they removed their earphones, placed them on the mahogany table, and left quickly each wondering how this would impact their staff, but also considering their own future with a school that cared more for profit than for student success.

The blue skies were radiant. The wind had picked up. As the trio made their way back to Eric's office, their footsteps echoed down the hall as though they were walking down San Quentin's death row. In the room with the door shut, the trio of administrators sat down in their accustomed chairs and looked at each other silently, and then Eric with a growing smile spoke. "Congratulations to both of you."

"What?" replied Sarah.

"Congratulations. One of you two will be the new principal of C.H.I.P.S., and the other will become the principal of the new Malaysian school."

"What do you mean? asked McAdams. He took a quick side glance at Sarah. Did she know?

Peterson leaned back and raised his arms. He interlocked his fingers behind his head and let out a satisfied sigh. "First we need to figure out what the best way is to tell teachers about the changes to staffing, workloads, pension and benefits, and we need to tell them soon." Contentment poured over him as he discussed his decision, and as he did so, he realized that a weight, an oppressive weight, had been lifted from him.

At the same time Wang was speaking to Miss Chen. "Congratulations. The presentation was masterful. Our Chinese workers are in full support for the reforms you have proposed. Our Canadians seemed reluctant, except for Eric, as he had a large smile on his face."

"I noticed he did not applaud."

"Yes. I, too, noticed that they all did not applaud. This is a problem. I will speak with him privately later in the day about the need and desire for full support. He could become our ally."

"Do you think so?"

"Of course, all men have a price." Wang leaned back in his chair, and with a quick swipe of his finger, cleaned the dust off the mahogany.

Outside, the physical education classes were playing Ultimate with the flying discs soaring and criss-crossing the basketball courts that served as the playing surface. Old Chairman Meow was busy chasing one of the discs that a student had failed to catch. His tail was almost flat out as he pursued the errant disc while a boy was yelling at him to go away. The cat and student arrived at the disc's resting spot at the same time, and the boy grabbed Chairman Meow's tail, and the cat spurted away, leaving the boy with a handful of thick hair. Above, on its perch, the magpie was preening and removing the heavy winter feathers–oblivious to the commotions below. The feathers were stored on the side of the old building for later when the nest would need some soft, comfortable padding.

As Hudson moved outside of the building he felt the warmth of the sun on his face, and he undid his jacket before he went any further. On the opposite building two workers rolled out what might have been the smallest banner he had seen. Its laconic message was CHEERYFULNESS SPRING.

Twenty-Eight
The Lion-Hearted

April had warmed up some, and C.H.I.P.S. had decided it was time to paint.

"Hudson," Jo said, "how would you like that job?"

Shielding his eyes from the rising sun, he saw bravery in action. High above him on the C.H.I.P.S. building looking like spiders dangling from a web were the painters. "My word. They must be fifty feet up," he marvelled.

Buildings in China are often six stories, as any higher structures require an elevator. Still six stories are a great deal to climb day after day, and Smith felt glad that his class wasn't on the top floor. However, when he saw the painters with their single skinny rope hanging off the edge of the roof, he was just glad to be inside. These daredevils tied their rope to a huge sandbag on the south end of the building, fed it outside through a window and up over the roof to allow them to hang off the north side. A partner lowered them off the edge so there would be no sudden jerk in a drop that could remove the tenuous support. There was a small wooden seat attached to the dead centre of the rope. The C.H.I.P.S.'s eaves were extended quite far beyond the walls and the painters could not possibly reach the wall with their short brushes. The solution was for the painters to swing themselves towards the wall. This led to ridiculous results as certain areas were hard to get to. Other attempts were foiled as the painter suddenly found himself facing away from the wall. Winds changed the painters' directions quickly, and some gusts threatened to pull the poor souls off their perches. No fear of heights was allowed. All the painters proved to be brave men bent on doing their job. It was inefficient, but eventually the entire building was painted, and other tasks were found for these courageous warriors of paint.

They are already at it, Smith mused the next morning from his Dayun 125 motorcycle as he watched a pair of the fearless painters dabbing away at the exterior at 6:45am. As Smith waited at the traffic light to go to the school, he contemplated the variety of vehicles streaming by him. Three wheeled trucks and cars, motorcycles, large blue flat-deck trucks moved by as they carried scarf wearing women, or seaweed–kelp–to be exact, and stacks of green-glass floats used by the local fisherman. While considering the menagerie, Smith did not notice the police car at the intersection; however, he soon would as the compact car turned left and pulled up to an abrupt stop right in front of him.

Out popped the policeman. Big bellied, red faced he was speaking quickly in the local slurring dialect. Hudson had trouble following his words, but not his intentions. The passenger, a thin man wearing a red t-shirt with Chinglish stating, "I amm the Kinge of the Wrld," joined him.

Stay calm. Stay calm, Smith reminded himself. This can't be good, he thought. He had been warned of other Canadians being taken to the police station in shakedowns by unscrupulous cops wanting to pad their pockets with bribe money. One had had his motorcycle confiscated, and it had either been sold or given to a friend. There had been no recourse or recovery.

The chunky policeman came right up to Smith and demanded something, but Hudson decided to be polite and to say, "*Ting bu dong*" (I hear you, but I don't understand.), to everything that was said.

Walking around the small bike, the policeman pulled out his driver's license and said, "*Zhege*"–this–to Smith while pointing at his motorcycle.

"*Ting bu dong*." The persistent cop went to his car and brought back what Smith surmised was a registration permit. He pointed at the bike, and Smith responded, "*Ting bu dong*." His eyes scanned the area, and then the cop pointed a beefy hand at Smith, then at the car, and then at the motorcycle key, and then at his unofficial looking companion indicating that this man would drive Smith's bike–presumably back to the station. "*Ting bu dong*."

By this time a large crowd of some twenty people had gathered. The cop's car had blocked one of the lanes, and drivers were frustrated by the delay. One driver started to yell at the cop, a dump truck driver hit the horn, while a nimble taxi tried to skirt the knot by driving on the sidewalk, and some of the crowd started to laugh at the exasperated uniformed man. This seemed to incense the policeman as he combed his thick crew cut as he once again showed Smith his Chinese driver's license, and spoke not to Smith, but directed his comments to the growing number of gawkers. Smith pulled out his own BC license, and he showed it to the perplexed officer. Clutching his ID as the officer pushed his nose on it to examine it, Hudson smiled at the man. The officer obviously could not read the foreign license, and when he came up from scrutinizing the license, he tried to press two boys from C.H.I.P.S. into translating it for him. They did not break stride as they laughed in his face. Their bravado ignited the now fifty plus witnesses who began to shout at the officer. Laughter punctuated the situation, and when Smith calmly stated, "*Ting bu dong*" to yet another request to get off the bike and get in the police car, the crowd aped him. Even the cop's passenger laughed. The man was losing face in a big way, Smith thought, and either I'm safe with the crowd, or he's going to punish me severely for the abuse he's taking.

Finally, the officer wiped his forehead, looked at his feet, said something incomprehensible and marched back to his car a defeated man. Courtesy had triumphed, thought Smith. He looked at the crowd, "*Xie xie*," and drove across the intersection on the green light.

Later that morning walking back from flag, Smith considered his next class. Impromptu public speaking was the unit he was marking. The types of assessments given were a huge debate topic in the English Department this year. Dickens was doing a great job as Department Head, but Sarah Whippet as vice principal in charge of language development, and Jill Redbourne, an English Coordinator hired for her experience in the examinations branch, desired change to increase the boys' scores so that more of them would go to university. The reason? Each had bonuses tied to their contracts and any percentage increase on the provincial exam scores would lead to a corresponding bonus of a thousand dollars. This continued to a maximum of twenty percent. What was the school's reason? For each C.H.I.P.S. student who was accepted for university admission, that university kicked back a certain percentage of tuition fees. Higher exam results meant that more students would be accepted into post-secondary schools. "Good grief, this feels like a business," Smith groaned as Dickens filled him in on what really motivated these administrators. Dickens rolled his eyes at the naive veteran.

"Hey, once I'm done with these debacles, I'll play you *xiangqi*," he said as he continued his marking. *Xiangqi* was Chinese Chess, and it was now a passion with the two English teachers. Smith had learned it first, and Dickens, ever the gamesman, worked with students to catch up to his colleague. Smith had been taught well, and being a chess player at home helped him to look at moves five or six steps ahead. Although Smith had won every game thus far, Dickens was improving, and it would only be a matter of time until Smith would be trapped in a fatal move.

Outside the fourth floor office Hudson realized that today was Leo's day to speak. Leo was a good writer. Unlike most of his peers he knew how to use the gender specific pronouns, and he never missed a subject verb agreement. True, he had some issues with article usage, but what Asian student didn't. Leo's weakness was in his mouth. He was a stutterer.

His classmates were kind and courteous, save for Robert, but Robert was the centre of the universe so that was expected. Whenever Leo spoke, he would get three or four words deep into what he was saying and then the letters and the sounds would jumble together like a salad being tossed. Smith felt pity for Leo after the first week, and asked him if he would want a warning that a question or reading passage was coming his way. Leo thought about it and then said, "No, I think that th-th-th-tha-ttt would gi-gi-gi-gi me time to be sc-sc-sca-scar-afraid." The contortions he went through were heart wrenching, and Smith had offered him to do written assignments instead of oral ones. "No, I mu-mus-mu-have to con-con-conq-beat this." This boy chose a good name for himself, Smith thought.

"All right," Smith agreed.

Once Michael was finished his impromptu speech on rivers, it was Leo's turn. He selected number two. Now Smith had a huge list of one word topics from one to five hundred. Leo could have selected money, soccer, or music, but he did not. He could have selected school, food, or Chinese New Year, but he did not. He selected love. When Smith read the choice off, some of the guys snickered. What would Leo know of love? He had never had a girlfriend. Love? Leo? The topic was enough to make a confident speaker stammer. But Leo? Why this might be the end of his year. Smith sensed this too. Was it a mistake to let this fine young man attempt a topic that he may be embarrassed about? Could this devastate him? Why can't I remember if this has ever happened before? pondered Hudson. The three minutes Smith gave for preparing were flying past. Was he making Leo walk the plank? As he sat in the back of the room, he noticed Leo's fountain pen scratching away. Such pens were favoured by the boys in this elite school, so much so that he wondered if at the school's inception, fountain pens had been mandatory and no one since had questioned their use. As the pen moved across the surface of the paper staining it with his ideas, would he, Hudson Smith, be permanently staining Leo's mind and soul? If there were parent complaints, how would he respond? What would Solomon, that renowned wise king of a united Israel, do?

After Smith scored Michael's speech, he said, "Leo, it's time. Are you ready?"

"Give me a min-min-min-second."

Leo moved up to the podium. The Chinese and Canadian

flags stood behind him as though he was in Beijing at a press conference. He put his paper down on the wooden podium. Leo looked at his classmates. His peers looked back. The tension was great, and Smith said, “Leo, you have three minutes. You may begin.”

“I-ah, I-ah, I-ah...”

Oh, my. It’s going to be worse than I thought.

“...wanta to-a discuss-a...”

Reverting back to the Chinese problem of adding ‘ah’ to the end of every word in English was another signal that this wasn’t going to go well.

“...the greatest thing-ah in-ah the world-ah...”

Come on Leo, you can do it.

“It is-ah, a-a-a-a-a-a-a-a-a-a-a-a mmmmmm-o-th-th-th-er-er-er-er-er-er-er’s lllllllllllllllllllll-o-ah, o-ah, o-ah, ovvvvvvvvvvvvvvvvvv-“

Should I rescue him? Yes. Save him, Smith. “Leo, may I interrupt? Would you like to try again tomorrow, or would you like a fresh start today?” Good job, Hudson.

“I-ah, I-ah would-ah like to-ah start-ah agggggggain, Misst-Missssssstttttt-er Smith-ah.”

Oh...“Yes, Leo. I think the rest of the class wouldn’t mind if you began again. Whenever you are ready, please feel free to begin.”

“Mr. Smith.”

That's better Leo.

"Thank you for not-ah making me go to-to-to-to-morr-ow."

Leo continued his speech, and it was difficult to listen to, but nobody laughed. Nobody made any noise whatsoever. He spoke of his mother's care and concern for him as a boy when his father died. The two-minute mark came and passed. It was morgue-like until Leo neared the end.

"My st-st-st-st-stepppppppp-ah fa-fa-fa-ther would be-be-be-be-be-be-be-bbbbbbbbb-eat me up when he was-ah drunk-ah. My mmmmm-oooo-th-th-ther would-ah step-ah in-ah bbbbbbbbbbbb-eeeeeeeeeee-t-t-t-ween-ah us, bbbbbbbbbbbbbb-uuuuuuuuuuuu-t-tt-t-t-ah he would-ah not-ah stop-ah."

Leo wept openly. No Chinese male teenager wept openly. More than one taboo was being broken this morning.

"She wwww-as-ah hhhh-ur-ur-ur-t-ah so-ah baddah one t-t-t-t-time-ah th-th-th-th-th-th a-a-a-a-a-a-a-a-a-a t-t-t-t that her arm-ah bbbbbbb-rooooo ke-ah." Sobbing he was joined by others who quietly fought back tears, and many of the young men who had kept similar issues under the surface could not stop the tears. "She-she-she-ah hu-hu-hu-hu-rt-ah saving me-ah. Tha-tha-that-that-th-th-that-issah-isah-is what-ah-ah-ah love issah."

Everyone had tears in their eyes. Everyone was shocked. No one knew. Leo picked up his paper and moved to his desk. The tears were streaming down his face. Mr. Smith got up from his chair and walked down the aisle. He placed a loving, compassionate hand on Leo's shoulder, leaned in and whispered, "Leo, if you would like to go to the washroom to clean-up, you may."

"Thank you."

After Leo left, Smith went to the podium. He surveyed the quiet room. The fluorescent lights buzzed away. Down below on the road a truck driver blared his horn as he approached the intersection. "Gentlemen, what you have just seen may be the bravest, most courageous thing that I have ever seen in my class." There were nods around the room. "In twenty-five years, I have not been so touched by a student's words. I would like to know what you are thinking."

A hand shot up immediately. It was Robert. Okay, here we go. "Mr. Smith, I–I think Leo knows what love is, and perhaps we don't." There were nods all around. Tears filled his eyes, and then Smith excused himself and went to see if Leo was feeling better. In the dim hallway, Dickens passed by and asked him about a *xiangqi* game later.

As he continued down the hallway with the paint peeling from the walls, he read the school banner: CHINA'S BEST EDUCCATION–C.H.I.P.S.. He realised that curriculum didn't really matter in education. To become a man, to become lion-hearted wasn't about learning outcomes. It was about our responses to others. He smiled, as he knew that two more boys had become men that day.

Twenty-Nine
The Dong Bei Grail Draft

C.H.I.P.S. female staff in the past considered playing ice hockey with the men, but they decided to play ball hockey instead. This meant an abbreviated season as the outdoor surface was only suitable from September to October and from March to June, but the highlight of the year was in April, coinciding with the start of the NHL playoffs back in North America. The Dong Bei Grail was the symbol of women's ball hockey supremacy in China. Two teams of seven competed for the Grail. A draft was held at the Kangaroo Pouch Bar in early April, and the rigorous training was begun–one of the teams led by Kaitlin Coyote even held a practice. The best of three series was advertised all over the school, and students turned out to watch the Canadian women play the elegant game with their borrowed sticks.

Jo Smith had been a university field hockey player, and her skill set transferred over to ball hockey where both sides of the stick could be used. This new concept allowed her to become a scoring machine.

Dong Bei Grail fever struck the campus and the women wanted to hoist the cup and drink from it as they claimed champion status. T-shirts were ordered; names and numbers were printed on the back.

A local farmer and his donkey cart decorated as though it had come from Mardi Gras were employed as the Dong Bei Grail was paraded around the school's track with the iconic Hockey Night in Canada theme that heralded the Saturday night game on the Canadian Broadcasting Corporation blaring out. On the cart was a player selected as a Grand Marshall of the Parade. Dressed in a long superman cape, the Grand Marshall held the silver Grail in one hand while she held her nose with the other as the stinky donkey made the lap. The farmer, wearing a C.H.I.P.S. coat he had found last year, was thinking about how he could spend his hundred *kuai* without his wife finding out.

This year the captain of Team Coyote, Kaitlin Coyote, had been selected for the prestigious position. In July Kaitlin and her family would be leaving China to return to Canada after seven years at C.H.I.P.S. and two at a school in Hong Kong. Behind the cart trooped all the women involved in the play-off series. Each was wearing her colourful team shirt and carried her hockey stick. When it was time to stop, they formed a colour guard and raised their sticks as the Grand Marshall got off the cart and brought the Grail with her to a table located near the centre of the court outside the fence. Ritual. The event had all the trappings of a strange religion, and isn't that what hockey had become to so many Canadians, Smith thought. The school's PA system, Randy McMann at the controls, described the events for all the spectators.

The fluorescent pink of Team Coyote and the canary yellow of Team Hawk stood at their respective blue lines while McMann sang the Canadian national anthem before the first game of the series. One year a Chinese student was asked to do this, and had bungled the words badly. Since then McMann did it. The teams then walked out to centre to shake hands as the last vestige of courtesy before the competition started in earnest. Dozens of dorm apartment windows were filled with students watching like patrons in the balcony at the opera. Students stood all around the enclosed area cheering their favourite teachers, wearing their teams colours, and waving flags. “This would never happen in Canada, eh Smith?” Relic said as he pointed at the pink and yellow clad students.

“No, no...it wouldn’t,” he agreed as he continued to survey the bleachers and the pastel pink apartment block opposite. In Canada, one might see such student enthusiasm in an elementary school for teachers playing teachers, but not in a high school.

“Let’s go, Jo!”

Jo Smith wore yellow. Her line mates, June Peterson and Janie Brown, were rookie teachers and rookie players; however, they were younger and quicker. The second yellow line was Heather LeRoy, Karen Song, and Cathy Friesen. In goal was Connie Hawk.

The fluorescent pink shirts, Katie Dickens had joked, could be seen from the International Space Station as it orbited. “It hurts my eyes,” Jasminder Gill, another former provincial field hockey goalie, had said. Coyote had picked her team with concern over the friendships on staff so she selected Gerri Lemaire, and Suzie McMann, who also taught physical education, as her line mates, and the second line, which she nick-named the atoms, were three science teachers: Debbie Vander Kwaak a chemistry 11 teacher, Amanda Johnson, a biology 12 teacher, and Terri Patrick (a great-great-granddaughter of the famous hockey player and innovator, Lester Patrick), who was in charge of the AP Physics classes. With Gill, Coyote thought their chances were good to hoist the cup.

On draft day, two weeks previous, the ladies decided to paint the town. Reserving a bar in Kai Fa Qu, the women dressed as though they were going to a formal ballroom dance, and in some senses they were. A microphone was employed as Suzie's husband, Randy, announced the festivities, and acted as general commentator on players, their histories, their love-life, and analysed the reasons for their selection. This mock-u-mentary style would have made *Spinal Tap* and *The Ruttles* producers proud. Beside McMann and in front of six Canadian flags stood the wily Dickens with a starched collar of some six inches in length. Craig Dickens would opine on the selections and satirize the iconic Coach of the CBC segment. He even brought a Chow puppy he had borrowed from a neighbour that he named Yellow.

"Silence!" barked McMann. "Bring out the Grail!" The treasured cup entered the room. Hidden behind the gleaming silver mug, the bearer paused for effect then made his way across the front and went behind the bar. There the tuxedo and white gloves lowered the cup slowly onto the counter top like a priest at Easter Communion handles the chalice at the altar. John McAdams turned and bowed to the crowd. His appearance was a significant gesture as no administrator had ever attended the draft before. When the commotion settled, McMann announced, "I now declare the Canadian Harmonious International Peace School Dong Bei Grail Draft open. Smith?" There was a burst of laughter at the parody of flag ceremony as Smith moved to the stage.

Hudson Smith, a first-timer, had considered not going, but decided at the last second he should, and despite the cold surroundings (was anything heated and warm in Dong Bei? in the bar, he was glad to have made the decision to join the crowd. He had been asked to hold the bag with the Scrabble tiles that would determine which captain selected first. This ritual lottery was like the short story by

Shirley Jackson as it was decided by the captain who picked the blank. Whoever selected the vacant tile went first, and everyone in the room knew that meant she would select Jo. The next two players would go to the unlucky captain who kept choosing letters.

The DJ cranked up the volume of the stereo as Gary Glitter pumped through the woofers, and Kaitlin Coyote accompanied by howls from every man in the room made her way up to the front to pick her first tile. Every conversation's volume rose in response to "Rock and Roll, Part 2," the classic sports' rock anthem and Glitter's cries of, "Hey-Hey!" Kaitlin caught her high heel in a crack in the floor, and Suzie and Gerri both helped her out of the predicament. Hudson Smith held the bag aloft, and Kaitlin reached into the velvet.

"Silence!" demanded McCann, and Coyote banged the letter onto the bar. McMann announced the result: "Like my students' marks," he shouted: "E!"

Laughter and cat calls began as Connie Hawk squealed with delight and adjusted herself before she headed towards the front. Blowing kisses and posing for photos as she passed tables in her little black mini-skirt, she made it as far as her husband Don, who then grabbed her and dipped her dramatically as he planted a big kiss. Grinning, she completed the gauntlet, gave Smith a Middle Eastern cheek-to-cheek kiss, and gingerly moved her long fingers into the bag. With eager anticipation, she pulled out a tile, and placed it on the counter top.

McMann, looked at it. "There are one hundred tiles in the bag, and the odds of pulling the blank are one in fifty. There is only a one percent chance of pulling the X. Connie, go buy that lottery ticket! You picked the one in a hundred." Everyone laughed, and the drama continued.

Coyote pulled an O, Hawk a Z. Coyote's theme of vowels continued with the third selection an A, but then Hawk pulled an S. The beer was flowing. The frosty mugs were raised. The music paused every time a selection was announced. Coyote yanked the bag from Smith's hand and looked in. The jeering began immediately, but of course she gave it back to Hudson who stirred it up before continuing the process. Dickens gave his opinion that the barkeep had kept out both the blank tiles to keep the sales going on well into the night. Kaitlin's pick was a P. Then Hawk took a swig from her stein. "Thatta girl," Dickens encouraged. "Sustain yourself with the golden amber." Hawk picked a letter, but then as she went to pound it into the bar, a server bumped her and she ended up tossing the tile behind the bar where it rattled off of the draft spigot, sailed off the whisky bottles, and lodged itself between the draft glasses.

Dickens cried, "Foul, foul!"

McMann shouted, "Black Hawk Down!"

"Oh crap."

"Sorry, Connie. I couldn't resist."

"Find it. Find it," the crowd chanted.

The barkeep, sensing a tip, looked through the glasses and retrieved the tile as though he had found a treasure. Connie's outstretched hand took the offered wooden square, and her grin told the story. She grabbed the microphone from McMann. "Team Hawk uses the first selection of this year's Dong Bei Grail Draft to take Jo Loch. I mean Jo Smith."

There was a roar of laughter at the mistake over the newlywed's name, and then the mob mindlessly chanted "Number one! Number one! Number one!"

Smith came forward as Hawk reached back for the yellow t-shirt, and she lifted her arms as Connie pulled the shirt down on the number one pick. With her selections, Coyote picked Gerri LeMaire and Suzie McMann. Randy said, "Number three overall, but number one in my heart." This continued through the evening until all the participating women were chosen. The revelry was in high pitch. The dancing was wild, and thus nobody noticed when Sarah Whippet and John McAdams went out the door marked "Entkance."

Now two weeks later the moment had arrived. "Let the games begin," McMann announced, and the ball was dropped for the opening face-off.

Thirty
The New Staff Member

Stephanie announced to her English colleagues after the Winter Holiday that she was pregnant, and that she would be moving to Kuala Lumpur to get married and raise her family at the third term's end. "The world is certainly more global than ever," Tom Simon said as he tallied how this Canadian woman met her Belgian fiancé in Thailand, conceived in China, would marry in Singapore, and live in Malaysia. The others in the office–Dickens, Karen, and Hudson–joined Tom as he congratulated her. The joy the news brought was soon displaced by curiosity. Who would replace Stephanie and join their peaceful enclave?

Mid-year is never the best time for a teacher change, but life happens. Deaths, disease, incompetency, illegal activities, mental breakdowns, pregnancies, and spousal transfers were all reasons that Hudson had seen which caused teachers to leave mid-year, and it was always awkward for the four parties involved. The school was left in a quandary. How could they replace a staff member on short notice? The talent pool was shallow mid-year. Few teachers were available, and fewer still would be willing to relocate. For the teacher leaving it often meant hardship as they disconnected from their peers, students they had grown to love, and a job which provided them with meaning and purpose, not to mention a paycheque. For the students it meant turmoil. Students are often far more conservative towards change than adults Smith had found; although, he wondered whether it was the institutionalization of schooling that had formed the pupils that way. A new style, new expectations, new humour, new routines had to be learned, and the old discarded–right when they had become as comfortable as an old pair of Levis. Finally, for the teacher parachuting into the class, there was mistrust from students, and a new stamp of authority to be established. Nobody won.

The good-bye party for Stephanie seemed to arrive in a blink of time. Eric Peterson came up that Friday afternoon, and after giving Stephanie a hug, told the room that Mr. Wang had hired a new teacher, Katie Richardson, from Hornby Island, BC upon the recommendation of a former C.H.I.P.S. teacher. Eric hadn't interviewed her, nor had he seen her resume. "Wang did this all on his own. He wants a more direct say on hiring which means that he has taken it over." Katie remained a mystery. "Please help her with any questions she may have, Dickens."

Hudson's head snapped quickly as Hornby Island had long had a reputation as a place where time had stopped in 1969. "Hornby is 'The Living Hippy Museum.' People live there in suspended animation," his childhood friend Gord had once told him. Keeping his mouth shut, Hudson's mind quavered between telling what he knew and keeping quiet. The latter seemed the best choice, and Hudson charitably decided to let Katie enter the strange world of C.H.I.P.S. with no bias from him.

Monday was a bright, sunny morning and despite the four flights of stairs, Hudson felt great as he entered the office room. The sight that met him was an oxymoronic blend of normalcy and oddness. Katie did not look like a hippy. No flowers in her hair, no long dress, no bead necklaces nor crystals releasing energy. Her skirt was grey wool, and her blouse was formal white. The sliding windows were wide open, and the blinds near the top of the window frames were banging against the stationary window. The dust and horns of the street entered the room as the Siberian wind directed them. In response to his greeting, Katie lifted her head, but her eyes were directed to the wall on his left. She promptly turned her back and started to turn the stately desk around so that she would be facing the wall away from the room's entry and away from her colleagues. The message was obvious as she sat down with a plop–her back to the others.

Monday at lunch the English 12 Department met in Jill Redbourne's office, and Katie came a few minutes late. She entered the English Curriculum Coordinator's spacious room like the Siberian winds were pushing her from behind. The sun illuminated the former main office, and its warmth was vanquished as Katie clickity-clacked to the blinds, pulled them shut, bringing a pall to the room. Smith's memory bank was jostled. I've heard that sound somewhere, he thought. Hudson was distracted from the meeting as he puzzled over the sound of her shoes. The entire department turned their heads as though connected, and she sat down at the foot of the table with a sigh. "Let's get this over with," was her first comment. Dickens shook this off, but the smiles on the other staff members, Hudson, Karen, Tom, couldn't be stifled. As the meeting progressed Richardson yawned loudly. "Can we get on with this? I have a class to teach."

With all the skill of a diplomat negotiating a Mid-East Peace Agreement, Dickens acknowledged Katie with a smile, and said, "Yes. I'll be brief as we try to arrange the exam schedule."

"Harumph," and with her head diving into her crossed arms on the table, Katie dismissed herself while the rest of the department considered their new colleague. After gaining agreement from the department members about the exam schedule, Dickens moved to the next item–new text requests–but Richardson stood up and bowed to the table, pirouetted, and left the room in a gust. She had a schedule to keep.

Tom was the first to speak, "I'll open the blinds."

"I'll speak to her," offered Jill.

Tuesday right after lunch saw Smith chatting with Tom and Karen about which Hamlet movie was their favourite: the Olivier version which won the famous English actor the Oscar, the Zeffirelli version with Mel Gibson which used Freud's theories, and Helena Bonham Carter as a hauntingly disturbed Ophelia, and the full-text Branagh version which had numerous famous actors in it including Kate Winslet as a sexy Ophelia. They all agreed that *Hamlet 2000*, a contemporary version with Ethan Hawke and the gorgeous Julia Stiles as the poor creature, wouldn't last when Katie blew into the room. Without saying a word, she passed through the midst of the trio and stood at her desk looking out at the cranes across the street. Ignoring her colleagues' greetings, she stood as though mummified. Thirty seconds passed, a minute, then she twirled in place and marched through their midst again, stopped at the door where she mumbled something incoherent, opened the door as though she herself was the wind, and slammed it shut as she left. Smith, Tom, and Karen all raised an eyebrow at each other while the clickity-clack of the stylish pumps made their way down the dim hall. Smith considered where he had heard that sound before.

On Wednesday morning Dickens walked into the office while

Smith was checking the playoff hockey scores on his favourite website. "Smith, what do you think of Katie?"

"I don't know. She seems to be her own person."

"I walked past her class just now. The boys were lined up in two lines, arms down, heads high, and they were reciting poetry all at the same time like they were robots. No emotion. Monotone. It was a bit weird."

"Yesterday, when I spoke to her in the hallway, she turned her head away from me, and talked. She was mumbling something about how the boys deserve dignity."

"Dignity? Yeah, she said something about that to me too. She was angry about the state of the washroom. I told her that the school had been asked for all eleven years that Relic has been here to change the way they clean the cans, but nothing is done. It's China. Compared to some places here, it's not too bad."

"Get out. The place reeks of urine."

"Yeah, it does, but I've seen worse. The cleaning women are not given any supplies. How could they clean it? Maybe Katie will have more success in speaking to Wang."

"Good luck to her, I say."

"If she lets it get to her, she won't last long. China can either be an exciting adventure, or it can drive you crazy. It can't be judged by our western standards."

The next period break Katie stormed in. "These boys are like my boy. He is fifteen at St. George's in Vancouver. I hope that someone there is looking after him because no one is looking after these boys."

"What do you mean?" asked Karen.

"No one is making sure they are properly dressed, properly fed, or properly prepared for class."

Dickens took the devil's advocate position, "Why should they? These boys are old enough to do those things themselves."

"You are part of the problem," she said as she clickity-clacked out of the office. Dickens lifted his eyebrow at Smith who rolled his own eyes while Karen and Tom looked at each other suffocating in the awkward attempt to be professional by not criticizing their new colleague.

That afternoon Smith glanced out his classroom door, and was amused to see a class walking in pairs down the hall with a long rope held up by their hands as though they were in kindergarten. There was no doubt who was steaming ahead and leading them as the pumps echoed through the corridor. It's only a matter of time before the boys explode, he thought. Even the stoic Chinese have their limits. The final three captives looked at him and whispered, "Help us please."

The next period Dickens' former student, Chamberlain, was walking down the corridor and Dickens asked him how things were going.

"Not good."

"Why?"

Chamberlain checked both directions of the hallway and stated bluntly, "I have a new teacher."

The limit was reached sooner than Smith had estimated. On Thursday afternoon Hudson was heading over to the photocopier guy with a pile of exams to get ready. Katie was standing on top of her classroom podium looking like a giant eagle on a cliff top while shouting at the boys who sat in perfect stillness. "I know you can talk. Don't just sit there. Answer me. Answer me. ANSWER ME!" As Hudson turned the corner to go down the stairs wondering how she got up onto the top of the podium, he heard the distraught woman's heels clickity-clacking down the hallway away from him. Hudson remembered the sound now of the Esquimalt & Nanaimo railway cars running to the terminus a mere block from his boyhood home in Courtenay. A smile crossed his face as the week-old puzzle was solved. The stairwell's smudged windows gave him a great view of the new self-congratulatory banner: STRENGTHENING MANAGEMENT ABILITY TO RISE EDDUCATIONAL QUALITIES.

Richardson's desk was cleaned off when Hudson got back to the office, and he never saw her again.

Thirty-One
The Dragons of the Orient Cricketeers Club

"Craig, are you serious?" Hudson was reading the C.H.I.P.S. CHATTER, and he queried from in front of the screen, "Cricket?"

"I am deadly serious," Dickens answered. "I can't commit to the Lumberjacks anymore. The baseball schedule is too hectic with the kids growing like they are. Cricket would be casual–fun. I foresee a season of one game. It'll be a long game, but only one."

"Where would you get the equipment?"

I've been planning this for a while. I picked up two bats and a half-dozen balls in Sri Lanka during the winter break. We can make the wickets, and there's got to be some place to buy gloves."

"Do you know how to play?"

"No, but Zahir Khan does; he's originally from Bangladesh. He's agreed to teach us how to play the gentlemen's game."

"Will you provide the scones?"

"No, but there might be some gin."

Thus, The Dragons of the Orient Cricketeers Club of Gentlemen was born. Sixteen curious teachers answered the C.H.I.P.S. CHATTER invite to the first practice. The spring air beckoned them outside, and the novelty for Canadians was like the Siren's song. All had seen the game on the BBC Asia telecasts. Some had read about it to try to understand what the television showed. Most would turn the channel as the games were another reminder of what they had left behind.

Zahir was soft-spoken, and patient with his new countrymen. "It's not pitching. It's called bowling. Keep your arm straight. Go practise with a partner or two." The men frolicked on the astro-turf like newborn lambs. They joked; they teased; they tried to understand the game. Zahir lined them up to protect an ad-libbed wicket made from two by fours. "Each of you take a turn bowling. Then try to hit it. Tony, use the flat side of the bat. That's right." They all cracked up when Randy McMann threw the first ball, and with the unfamiliar motion, it sailed fifty feet wide of the target. "Um, not bad," Zahir intoned.

Craig Dickens, who was playing the wicket keeper, was less generous in his assessment. "You get that shitty throw yourself, Randy."

Don Hawk's turn also cracked up the men. Trying to avoid the fate of McMann, he over-compensated and threw the ball behind Tony Vander Kwaak. Dickens stopped it and threw it back without comment. This spoke volumes as Dickens was never speechless. George O'Brien, who had never been to a single athletic event at C.H.I.P.S., was next. His bowl was perfectly straight, bounced once near the feet of Vander Kwaak and knocked over the hefty wickets. "That's how you do it," Zahir beamed. "I think we found our bowler."

Zahir inscribed a circle on the field and explained the scoring. Knock it straight out and you get six runs, a bounce out and you get four. Batsmen could hit it in any direction and had a choice of whether to run or not. Khan stopped the new players and reminded them to use the flat side of the bat. The group scattered around the oval and each of the men took turns swinging at the hard ball. Finally, Smith moved in front of the giant wicket. Nearly fifty, some of the younger teachers referred to Smith as Mr. Loch behind his back because Jo was such a great athlete, and Smith was obviously past his prime. Josh Baker was one of these. A P. E. teacher, the former Thompson Rivers University varsity basketball player, and an Adonis, bowled next. His six foot seven frame sent the ball hurtling towards the target. Smith stroked at the orb and connected in the sweet spot. The ball sailed high up and seemed to gain momentum as it cleared the oval, the track, and then the flag podium. The cheering echoed off the apartment walls, and with typical understatement, Smith handed the bat to Zahir. "Your turn."

At the end of practice Dickens said, "We are now brothers. Cricketeers of the Orient." Then he abruptly changed the topic, "My hands are killing me. Does anyone know where we can get gloves?"

Relic replied, "I'll get some made by Sweater Lady."

Within a week, perfect cricket gloves were presented to Dickens. "Thanks. My hands still hurt."

A magpie flapped past Smith, Nathan Johnson, Ali Javaherian, and Zahir after practice. The middle-aged man's weary bones seemed to creak beneath him while the Gen-Y teachers moved with grace and power. Despite the slow pace of the game, the occasional bursts of speed required tuckered Smith out. Still, it was fun, he reflected. Being with younger men made him feel young, but his joints told him the truth. When Dickens took measurements for uniforms during practice, Smith had replaced him as the wicket keeper, and the bending, squatting, and quick steps allowed him to be a part of every play that kept him from boredom. His mind could wander quite easily to other ideas when he stood in the circle awaiting a rare hit. Life was often more like the fielding position than the wicket keeper, he considered. Rarely was anyone the centre of attention at all times. The patience developed in the circle was excellent and necessary for a successful life. As he had aged, this patience had also developed in his classroom as he made far more time available for developing relationships with his students than he did when he had first begun. Smith planned three lessons early in the semester just to talk to the class about themselves, and he found that the community built went a long way to creating a positive atmosphere, which in turn lead to a successful year.

White uniforms with The Dragons of the Orient Cricketeers Club of Gentlemen embroidered in an insignia that used a beaver and a dragon as a background were ordered and delivered in time for the first and only test match in the club's history. Dickens had arranged a match with the Shanwan British Empire Club that included ex-pats from England, Scotland, Ireland, Fiji, Australia, and New Zealand to be held at the C.H.I.P.S. soccer pitch. The atmosphere was electric as wives, girlfriends, staff, and students surrounded the field. The teams shook hands and introduced themselves and Zahir had agreed to officiate the match as the ex-pats club needed every one of their players to form a team while the Dragons had spares. The day was warm already at 9:00am, and a refreshment tent was set up on the side. O'Brien, in his stiff starched white shorts, was excited about bowling, and was sipping something tall and cool to prepare for the test match as Smith walked past him to go out onto the field.

Smith marvelled at how Dickens directed the entire enterprise as though it were a play. Perhaps all the world is a stage, and we are merely players, Smith paraphrased to himself. Truly, the organizer had outdone his previous endeavours. Nearly single-handedly Dickens had created this vibrant community. Vision plus drive; vision plus drive. Sadly, it would be difficult for this creative man to get a teaching job in his home province as the militant union there had all but locked up any new teaching openings for substitute teachers. The reasoning went that they had paid their dues metaphorically and literally, and thus deserved the new positions. Ability meant nothing. Experience elsewhere meant nothing. Such a loss. BC students deserved better. There in his home province, unfortunately, Dickens would not be his brother until he paid his dues.

Smith looked back on the proceedings. The opening ceremony included God Save the Queen and the Canadian anthem. Relic and an English businessman with a posh accent made a short speech. Relic welcomed the guests and spoke of how sport united all people, and the Englishman waxed eloquently on the joys of cricket, and how it was good to play the Canadians who notoriously shunned the game. The Union Jack and the Maple Leaf were hung on the fence. After these formalities, a student from Dickens' art class unrolled a large, homemade banner and taped it the fence. Soon the Brits spied it and stopped playing to read its classic Chinglish message: CANADIANS BEAT EMPIRE DOGS. At the end of the banner an old Johnny Canuck comic book figure from the 1940s was beating a bulldog with a cricket bat.

Hudson Smith moved out deep into the field. The morning sunshine continued to increase its intensity while his colleagues sauntered to their positions. George O'Brien chatted to Zahir, and the older man chuckled over something that the Bangledeshi had said to him. Maybe the Empire wasn't such a bad thing, Hudson mused. It has brought us all together.

O'Brien's first bowl was met with a powerful Aussie swing, and Hudson watched the ball sail up into the blazing sun and land well past the circle inscribed on the field. The gentlemen of the Empire Club politely clapped at the six runs, and Dickens said, "That was a good bowl, George, the guy is a former national team player. Keep it up. Stiff upper lip."

Thirty-Two
The Lushun Speech

Directly south of Shanwan at the very tip of the Liaodong Peninsula (which many people say on a map of China is the chicken's gullet), lies the port city of Lushun. Port Arthur, as the Russians called it, was a military city. The Russians, Japanese, Soviets, and finally the rightful owners, the Chinese, had all moored their navy here in the twentieth century, and several major battles had occurred in its waters. Each of the occupiers had left visible architectural evidence of their presence. Smith had decided to take a page from Dickens's book as an organizer of events. He had arranged a tour of the former restricted zone for interested C.H.I.P.S. teachers.

May is when Lushun is ablaze in flower blossoms–Sakura, cherry blossoms, to be exact. The Japanese planted tens of thousands of the flowering tree, and the hills became a sea of pink for two weeks every year. The flowering cherry trees of Vancouver's south side in March were the closest Canadian example Smith could think of to describe it.

The first stop was the reservoir and garden area of Long Wang Tang where a carnival atmosphere surprised the Canadians. A large, blazing white dragon sculpture breathing water instead of fire formed a focal entry point. Dozens of smiling faces surrounded the pool and its long-tailed fountain, and photos were snapped almost as fast as the shiny cars entered the park's gate and drove towards the parking lot. After paying a fifteen *kuai* park entry fee, the group was inundated with hawkers of pinwheels, paintings and purses, vendors of herbs, vegetables and fruit, sellers of cheap shoes, kids' toys, and snacks, women masked and wearing scarves, men alert and sharp, all called out to the wealthy foreigners as dollar signs flashed in their heads. The park became an extension of the marketplace, and this concept, an anathema to the Canadians who believed parks were to be a quiet escape from the loud rush of life, disturbed them.

Hudson and Jo left the rest of the teachers and walked through the crowded area while sellers crooned to them. "Sir, Sir? Watch?"

"Purse for you?"

"Shooooes–ah?"

Hudson and Jo smiled, "*Bu yao*," and Hudson would wave his closest hand to the vendor to reinforce the idea as they made for the reservoir's walkway. The cherry trees were mature along the path. They had been planted by the Japanese occupiers for over forty years as a way to avoid homesickness. Thick trunks in the full orchard birthed pinks and purples, single blossoms and double. The canopy was like a plush pink carpet above them, and the gentle scent of the greenery was like a spring-cleaning of Hudson's sinuses. Life, vibrant life marked an end to the long Dong Bei winter. Lilac trees' strong fragrance added to the aromas of the garden area. A gentle breeze swept up fallen blossoms better than the men with brooms cleaned up the streets in Shanwan. Numerous swallows flitted among the trees adding to the general hub-bub. Jo snapped a photo of a young woman wearing a crown made from a Sakura branch. She looked like a princess stepping out of a Chinese folktale. The Blossom Festival was a big business, and a big natural event. He squeezed Jo's hand. Despite the raucous crowds, this was a spectacular place.

A television news crew from CCTV 9, China's English language station, approached Hudson and Jo. A slender woman wearing an absurdly large hat with an absurdly large sunflower to protect herself from the sun thrust forward an equally absurdly large microphone and asked, "Will you describe our feelings to our viewers please? I mean your feelings."

Jo spoke first, "This is a beautiful place. The trees remind me of home."

"Yes, it does remind us of home. This place is beautiful."

"Where are you from?"

"Canada."

"Oh, Jianada! I thought-ah you were Americans."

"It's a common mistake."

Looking at Hudson she said, "Please share with us a poem to tell us of your feelings."

"A poem?" Wow, this is tough, he thought. "Okay, I don't think I've ever done one impromptu. Let me see. How about a haiku?" As he spoke he used his fingers to keep track of the traditional 5-7-5 moras or syllable count.

"Pink blossoms cause me

to relish bounteously

trees placed by old foes."

The reporter gushed her thanks over the clip, and then asked, "Can we take a shot of you both coming towards us, please?"

"Hudson, that was a great poem."

"Thanks Jo." Enamoured, he checked his watch, "Hey, it's time to get back to the group."

Two days earlier William, one of Smith's strongest students, stood up to make his impromptu speech. Three minutes earlier he had selected number eighty-eight from a list of three hundred, and Smith had given him the topic–racism. This was a touchy subject in the class. Korean students, vastly outnumbered, had been the targets of Chinese rage last year, and there was still tension between the groups. Some Japanese boys clung to each other, and in any group work the boys rarely mixed. Smith had been appalled, and had spoken to the boys about the need to stop discriminating against others as they would be ostracized for such behaviours in Canada. When the boys spoke about the Japanese atrocities in Nanjing and Lushun, Smith had countered with Canadian treatment of the Japanese in World War II, the Chinese Head tax, the failure of Canada to accept Jewish immigrants in the 1930s, and the ways First Nations people had been forcibly assimilated, or, in the case of the Beothuk in Newfoundland, exterminated. Racism had been the catalyst for each and every one of these black marks on Canadian history. Now, Canada's official position policy was that it was a multicultural society. Diversity was accepted. Smith spoke about how Canada was taking a mature and brave path today in accepting immigrants from all nations, confronting the past ills, and trying to resolve them. Prime Minister Harper's apology to the First Nations and to the Chinese community were two such examples.

Unlike the homogenous Chinese society, he discussed how the boys would be a minority in North America, but there was a huge diversity of people in Canada. He recalled a story Dickens had told him about one of his former C.H.I.P.S. students. The young man, studying at the University of Alberta, had seen another Chinese person across the campus, and feeling homesick and excited to speak in Mandarin, the former student rushed across the concourse and said, "*Ni hao*!"

The other student had turned and said, "Hi. I'm Steve. I'm from Calgary." It was a story that both teachers now used to remind their charges that Canada was an ethnically diverse country, and that some Chinese people had been there for over 130 years.

Smith recalled how his own mother spoke of her experiences as an immigrant from the Netherlands. The little Dutch girl had been made fun of because she couldn't make the 'th' sound. Even now some sixty years later this trait differentiated her from native speakers, and still some people in Victoria gave her strange looks as she said, "Dis or dat." He wanted the boys to realise that there was a better way–acceptance.

Now back in Lushun, the group went to the Victory Tower. Built by the Soviet Red Army after the Japanese surrendered to the Americans in 1945 and vacated the Liaodong Peninsula, the tower rose from its pentagon granite base forty-five meters to a gold leafed star. After paying five yuan each to access the tower, Jo pointed to the sign on the white brick interior, "Be polite and careful," was its message. Exiting the tower over thirty meters up a second sign warned, "For your safe please do not climb handrail," and dismissing the obvious, the two greeted the Lushun Harbour. It greeted them back with the sun shining on the water like an urban cowboy's rhinestone coat. A spit from the closest island (which the locals called The Dragon's Tail), split the bay in two. The blue skies contrasted with the green hills, and for a moment the pair thought they were back on BC's coast–the fresh sea air triggered such powerful memories. However, the Chinese naval base lay at their feet, and after ten glorious minutes of perusing the coast, Hudson and Jo returned to the spiralling stairs leading to the ground and the group. The tower's ominous shadow pointed them towards their next stop: the seat of the Japanese Court.

The Imperial Japanese court had been established to administer justice in Liaoning province, but it soon became an oppressive tool. The museum was quite nondescript. Although most of the signs were in Chinese, some were also in Chinglish, Russian, Korean, and Japanese, and they showed a strong nationalistic bias. Several of the preserved offices used exactly the same furniture: desk, chair, telephone, and shelf. Bureaucrats at work, Hudson thought, just like C.H.I.P.S.. It was when Jo and Hudson went upstairs at the tail end of the group that the significance of the place became apparent. The courtroom was left in the same state as it had been nearly a century ago. The display board spoke about a trial for the assassination of a Japanese crown prince in Harbin. In the next room the silence loomed as the group entered a display with hideous torture devices. Hudson felt the tears brimming in his eyes as he pondered the inhumanity of man, and he prayed silently that such things would never happen again. Jo drew closer to him, needing reassurance.

The tour's last stop was a Japanese graveyard on a hill near the town centre.

William began his speech to the boys who were waiting, anticipating his topic. "In the past the Japanese killed many Chinese people when they invaded Dong Bei and attacked the southern city of Nanjing."

Oh-oh, Smith winced, how do I deal with this?

The Japanese cemetery was well-maintained. Two years before the Japanese government had asked for permission to repatriate the sailors and soldiers buried there, but they were refused. "No need to fan tensions," the Chinese ambassador told the Japanese Prime Minister. "Our two countries must not re-open old wounds unless the Japanese are willing to acknowledge the horrors of Nanjing." The Japanese position on Nanjing minimized its culpability, and that the numbers of people killed was far fewer than China's claims of 300,000. To admit that its army had committed such atrocities would be a huge loss of face, and thus the stalemate continued.

"Like many Chinese, I hate the Japanese for what they did in Nanjing and Lushun. Like many Chinese men, if I had a chance to kill a Japanese, I would." There was a raucous cheer. The testosterone was surging.

Good grief, I need to stop this now, thought Smith. He rose to his feet ready to re-establish his authority in the room. "Will–"

"However, I believe I have learned a better way this year through Mr. Smith." There was an instant silence as Will's message continued. The boys looked nervously at each other to see what their reaction should be. "I have thought long about what he suggested. We Chinese should not be looking to past and thinking of revenge. We Chinese should be looking to future. We should be mature enough to consider that we, too, have made foreign policy mistakes, and we should be courageous as we step onto world's stage and gain respect we desire as nation. We need to forgive to forge ahead. If we are to build better world, we must not use past hurts to stop progress. Only if we do these can we be big enough to show that we mean business."

Smith smiled at the idiom that he had taught yesterday. The class silence continued as they pondered the bait and switch they had just heard. Smith's tears slipped down his face as he prayed that William would go into International Studies at university.

Thirty-Three

The Prom

Unlike their North American counterparts, Chinese high schools do not have a prom. Since, according to the Chinese there is no need to celebrate the completion of one phase of school as another begins, Heather LeRoy had an enormous task in front of her in deciding that a new tradition should begin at C.H.I.P.S.. Another problem was that C.H.I.P.S. was a boys' school and where would she find enough girls to make the event a satisfactory one from a dance perspective? Ticket costs, venue, promotion, music, catering all were problems to overcome, but the first item on her agenda was approval from the Head, Mr. Wang.

When Heather finally arranged a meeting with Wang, it was quick and decided before it began. Wang dismissed the idea outright, until LeRoy mentioned that money would be raised for the school. While Wang asked her to leave, hope, that ever-present balm for the soul, was released from prison when Wang said that he would think about it. "How much do you think C.H.I.P.S. could make?"

Two days later Wang Chattered to her.

On Wed 2:24 pm, Mr. Wang said:

If you could guarantee that the school obtains 20,000RMB, I will permit prom. Please optimize our profits by hosting prom off campus. No damage. No clean-up.

On Wed 3:28 pm, Heather LeRoy said:

I think this is entirely possible. I agree. THANK YOU MR. WANG!!!

Heather

"Check number one, now let's get organizing."

Ms. LeRoy spoke to a number of students about her idea. The three American students at the school were immediately sold. Their parents called her to offer assistance that night. LeRoy started to delegate the various tasks. Everyone got busy on their assignments. Dickens helped out by arranging the music, a DJ he had at an Snow Tigers event was available, and he owed Dickens a favour.

Smith was approached by LeRoy at flag to take photos. The warm winds were whipping her hair around, and her hand was in constant motion trying to fend off the lashes. Smith's bald dome had never felt better. "Of course, I'd love to help out. I will post all of the photos to the school's student FTP site so that every student can access the photos of the night."

Sitting in the main office, Xiaoqing Chen brushed the peeling skin from her arm. Once a year she found the air so dry that her skin seemed to flake off for a few weeks. Dry conditions brought about by the air and the sun impacted the entire populace. She had coiled herself comfortably in a beam of sunshine looking at the grade twelve students' abstract paintings that the Canadian art teacher had hung inside the office when the secretary told her that Mr. Wang was ready. Once she slid past the door and was inside, Chen spoke urgently to Wang, "C.H.I.P.S. can optimize its profits by running the event ourselves. Do not allow Miss LeRoy to advertise on campus. Who can dance all night? Music for part of night–cheaper. Photographs should be paid for by graduates, and they will maximize income."

"Tell me more."

Where does one find girls in a society that has 132 male births to every 100 female births? thought LeRoy. She went to Relic about the problem. "Relic, we need girls for the prom. Where can I get girls?"

"Hey, I'm no pimp, but how about using an old strategy like 'Les Filles du Roi?' You know, like the women the French King paid to go to New France. Maybe contact one of the schools in Shanwan, and give them a fee so they'll bring their girls out to the prom."

"Where would you suggest?"

"I'd contact the modelling school. There's about 300 girls there who are between 16-21, and they are mostly farmer's daughters. They would probably like a night out wearing their best and dancing with the new emperors of China."

"Who would I speak to there?"

"I know the guy quite well. He rents me the place where we play ball hockey. Can I talk to him? The kickback he would get may be enough to make him reconsider the new rent hike he wants. It would be a win-win."

"That would be sweet. I can go as high as twenty kuai per boy. That should be enough. Maybe we should just offer him 4,000 *yuan* as a set rate."

The Chinese students were lukewarm to the idea. "I have to pay 300 *yuan*? That is much money? Why so much, Mr. Smith?"

"Boys, it's not that much. The venue must be rented, the food purchased, prepared, the music man paid, the decorations bought. Proms are expensive, but fun. My own children in Canada would have paid more than twice that–you're getting a deal. Think of it as a celebration of your high school being over, and having one last time with your friends before going abroad."

"Mr. Smith," countered Robert, "I do not need to pay to have one last time with my friends."

"True, Robert, but you also wouldn't get to dance with girls."

"Girls? Where would girls come from?" All the boys were suddenly interested. Females were rare in this male bastion.

"Leave that to us," said Smith.

"Ha ha ha. You should leave it to me. I can get girls," the handsome young man chastised the older man. "What do you know about girls?"

"I've had three children." The boys howled their delight as Smith played the trump card.

Relic reported back to LeRoy that the deal had been made. His friend Yin solved the issue. Three hundred girls from the Modelling School would be coming for the prom night. The owner had agreed to the 3,000 *kuai* Relic offered him, and the Modelling

School would provide bussing to and from the event. LeRoy was delighted. It was still a two to one ratio, but it was better than she had ever imagined. "I think the boys will be pleased."

"Yes, I think they will."

When the news got out that the Modelling School girls would be coming, the tickets were sold out within three days. Every boy was coming, save two. LeRoy went to Mr. Wang and paid him his share of the income. "What is this?" he blurted when she laid the envelope on the mahogany desk.

"The 20,000 *yuan* you wanted from the prom, Mr. Wang."

As he took out the substantial cash wad, Wang smiled, and then said, "Ms. LeRoy, you have future here at C.H.I.P.S.."

Three days before the prom Dickens walked into his class and all the boys were gathered around Leo's computer. Leo had never been the centre of attention. However, as Dickens went to look over the shoulders of the preoccupied boys, he realized why. Girls were on the screen. Good looking girls. "Leo, what are you looking at?"

"This is the website for modelling school, Mr. Smith. They are so beautiful." The rest of the boys nodded their agreement, but they didn't take their eyes off the screen. Smith thought, typical boys, typical boys.

"Yes, they appear to be beautiful Leo, but are they kind, nice, or are they egocentric and stuck-up? Can they carry a conversation?"

"Who cares?"

"I think you will."

The sky brushed with pinks, yellows, oranges, and reds provided the kind of backdrop that every event planner dreamed of. A warm breeze came in from the Bo Hai in the west. The moonlight would give the beautiful soft light that lovers enjoy, and the stars were appearing one by one as though each encouraged a friend to open for business. Prom started at seven, so Ms. LeRoy showed up at six to ensure that everything would be ready. A large banner was the backdrop and proclaimed WARMLY CELEBRATE C.H.I.P.S. GRADUATE PROM. The heavy smell of cooking oil prevailed in the Ballroom. Her American students were there soon after to help. She walked to the kitchen to check on the food prep after they set up the decorations. Originally the Prom Committee wanted a Vegas/Casino theme, but LeRoy nixed that. "Gambling is illegal in China. You won't find any of the props you want." They had settled on a deck of cards and some paper dice for each table.

As she approached the kitchen her smile cracked as a kitchen employee made his presence known with a long, loud hork. "Where did that end up?" the horrified organizer shivered. Bursting through the doors, she breathed easy as she saw a prep chef standing in an open door and spitting an oyster-sized phlegm ball into an outside can.

The Godlen Fine Hotel had promised a buffet that would cater to Chinese, Korean, and Western tastes, though LeRoy wondered when they couldn't spell the hotel name right. The manager, Wang Jia met her at the door and told her that all was well. "We nearly have food ready. My team is putting out display right now."

"That's great. It's time to let the students in–what is that?" LeRoy questioned.

"It is centre piece. I got idea from Harbin ice sculpture."

LeRoy rolled her eyes.

Two men carried a large, poorly painted Styrofoam magpie to the banquet table that ran the room's length. The table bisected the room, and the two meter high magpie was hoisted into place atop of what seemed to be a large colourful pyramid of fruit. Ha, thought LeRoy, it will be just like flag. The boys are used to having a magpie watch them. The servers seemed to create a buffet out of thin air as quickly as Ariel takes the banquet away in *The Tempest*. In order plates, desserts, French fries, the fruit, cutlery, then buns, Chinese vegetables, and a small plate of cold-cuts found their places. Girls wearing bright red sashes with gold Chinese lettering stood ready to assist the non-existent crowd.

The DJ walked in wearing tight leather black pants with a blue and white striped T-shirt. "I'm DJ, Relic friend," he said.

"You're Russian."

"Da, bud I know de music." He set up in the far corner, and quickly Michael Jackson's voice was filling the empty room. LeRoy saw Don Hawk, Matt Peterson, and Dickens moonwalk in unison.

"Ms. LeRoy, the teacher chaperones are here. We've started to let in the students. When will the girls arrive?"

"Soon."

The boys came in and scouted out places to sit, staked out their territory with a tenacity rarely seen outside of the animal kingdom, and they made sure there were empty seats at their tables. LeRoy walked to the punch bowl, and Tony Vander Kwaak was getting a drink for his lovely wife, Debbie. Eric Peterson was surveying the room beside him. From behind the two men she overheard

Tony say, "All the boys look like they are in the breeding grounds. They've built a nest, plumage is bright and attractive, and later, they'll attract the girls with the smooth moves on the dance floor. We are more like birds than we want to admit."

LeRoy smiled, punch in hand, nodded to the pair, and moved across to the desk where the boys were checking the tickets. "Any problems, boys?"

"No, Miss King," William said using the Anglo-version of her Quebecois name as she had taught her classes so they didn't have to torture their tongues with the L and R sound. "Everything is fine. Except..."

"Ah, yes, the girls. Don't worry. They'll be here. I called the Modelling School today, and they are coming. It takes time to move three hundred people."

"Yes, but..."

"Don't worry. By the way, good thinking–volunteering to take tickets. You will get to meet every girl first. Are you ready to flirt?"

"Flirt? What does that mean?"

"It means to speak to girls in a playful manner. It shows that you are interested."

"It's a good idea?"

"Yes, tonight it is a good idea," she smiled and turned to scan the room. The boys were either at tables looking out like a loyal dog waiting for its master, or at the buffet where the fruit pyramid was eroding like the ones in Egypt. The teachers who had come to chaperone were standing around the room in groups of threes and fours relaxed. Unlike in Canada there would be no drugs, no booze, and no fights to deal with tonight. More like cultural coaches they would be teaching the boys the nuances of a prom. She strolled by the buffet table, and noticed that all the bananas were gone, and the French fries were nearly finished too. "I'll have to speak to Wang Jia. I'm sure he will bring more," she said in answer to Robert's question.

Fireworks sounded. They were here. Let the party begin. The boys moved like a wave heading towards the beach, slowly, then gathering strength. Some of them started to stand on their tiptoes to see over top of their taller classmates. The girls walked through the double doors holding each others' hands. They had gone all out in dressing up for the American-style prom. LeRoy considered how movies like *High School Musical* can influence foreign cultures. Would this have a happy ending as well? The girls continued to pour in, and the boys continued to invite them to their tables. Tony, a social studies teacher, said, "This is exactly how the women in New France were received. The courtships were usually a mere invitation, and the marriages produced abundant offspring populating the colony."

"Tony, let's hope there are no offspring produced tonight. This is a dance."

"All birds dance before they mate."

"Not tonight," she said as she moved towards the door.

The music began, and Hudson was surprised as no boys took girls out to the floor; however, the floor was populated with girls dancing with girls. Was this a disaster in the making?

"Heather, the girls are all dancing with other girls."

"Think about it, Hudson. The girls know each other. They probably dance to music videos at their school. They are confident. Don't worry. The boys will get the idea."

The lads did get the idea, and soon the dance floor was rocking. Hudson spied Leo on the floor dancing with a cutie. His stuttering had not been an issue. He was brimming with pride as he led her back to the table. Hudson continued to watch as the conversation flowed between the two, and their smiles grew. By the end of the evening there were hundreds of smiles, and the event was a success. The busses arrived on schedule. The music was good. There were no altercations, no drugs, no alcohol, no problems. Clean-up began with a small army of volunteers.

"Miss King, Miss King, Miss King," William droned as he frantically caught up to her while the clean-up began in earnest. "When can we do that again?"

Thirty-Four
Flag at Half Mast

Chinese is an angry sounding language. It is every bit as harsh a language as German, and the volume tends to be cranked up a notch or two from what Westerners are used to hearing. This morning as usual the Physical Education teacher, Mr. Hu, was instructing the boys who were gathered in the lines of their homeroom class before the actual flag ceremony began. Then two spiffy young men came forward. Their waist sizes were probably 26, Hudson thought as the young man closest to Hu reached out with his clean white glove and relieved Mr. Hu of the microphone. The two students waited for Hu to leave the flagpole area and then began the ritual of every C.H.I.P.S. flag ceremony.

"Good Morning Dear Teachers and Fellow Students!"

"We are from grade 12 class 9."

"It is our great pleasure to perform the flag raising ceremony today. My name is Thomas Pang. This is Chichi Li." The mic was passed from the first boy to the second while a powerful beam of sunlight illuminated the platform area.

"We are the hosts, and the flag raisers are starting from my left hand side are the Honesty Wang, Goat Liu, Alex Yu, Delicious Qi, Robert Wu, and Eisenhower Xiao. The conductor is the John Ma. Now I declare C.H.I.P.S. the flag raising ceremony begins." Polite applause. This part had always interested Hudson because the names the boys had chosen or had bestowed on them by a Chinese Middle School teacher often intrigued him. He would speak to Goat and Delicious to encourage them to reconsider their monikers so that universities might take their applications more seriously.

"Raise flag of People Republic of China, and now play the national anthem of China." After wincing over the missing article and the equally truant possessive "s", Hudson smiled as Robert raised the flag. The boy had been a thorn in his flesh, but he had suggested to the young man's counsellor that Robert be given the task of raising the Chinese flag to show that he was trusted, to show that someone believed in him. Last week Robert had come to him during a tutorial block to thank him for the recommendation. Robert had beamed. It was a real honour. Smith thought of how flags were often used to pay tribute to people.

"Raise the flag, and play national anthem of Canada." Though he couldn't remember the fracas over Lester B. Pearson's government changing the flag, he did remember his great-grandmother's stuffy living room where the old maple leaf ensign formed a back drop for his grandfather's army photo. His grandfather had died a scant two months before the war ended in Europe, and his great-grandmother spit fire when she spoke about the old flag that her son had died for not being good enough for Canada anymore. Smith, however, loved its simplicity and its unique design.

"Raise the flag of C.H.I.P.S., and let's sing our school song together." Grey clouds were gathering, and moving inland from the sea. The school flag did not stand out straight, but decided, as though it were a sentient creature, to wrap itself up into a roll. By the time it was half way up it looked like a snake slithering up the pole. No one seemed to notice though as the students continued to mouth the juvenile words booming from the loudspeakers sung by a taped choir of five year olds in all their kindergarten glory. The smooth, azure sky was now textured with grey pillows laden with moisture. The battle in the sky continued as hot and cold air collided.

"Now I call on King Zhou to make a speech." Another name to change, thought Smith. From the far right came a boy moving with purpose. Public speaking provided great adrenalin to get the legs moving. He made his way past each row, and only halted once as Chairman Meow made an appearance chasing down a dragonfly that darted and hovered with a precision that even the best Harrier jets could not possibly accomplish. He received the mic, cleared his throat, and began.

"I want to talk about Sexgiving." A murmur went through the boys who needed no encouragement in this thought pattern.

"Did he just say what I thought he said?" Tony asked Smith.

"Give Sex to strangers," the speech continued to boom through the loudspeakers. The imperative again brought snickering through the boys' ranks, and the Canadian teachers looked at each other with bewilderment.

"I think he means 'thanksgiving' and 'thanks,' at least I hope he does," grinned a mischievous Smith. "He's trying to be thoughtful and kind. It's actually a pretty typical Chinese trait. We should cut him some slack." Dickens, Relic and old Bannerman were cracking jokes with each other behind the boys. Bannerman laughed so hard that he doubled over, but the loudspeaker kept others from noticing. The speech ended and the mic exchanged places once again.

"Now I call on Mr. Peterson and Mr. Zhou to make announcement."

The two principals moved to the poles in tandem. Peterson towered over his Chinese counterpart who couldn't be five feet tall, mused Smith. Their speeches were refreshingly short. Then the mic went back to Thomas Pang.

"Now I declare Canadian Harmonious International Peace School flag raising ceremony closed. Teachers please go first." The boys always moved first, and the flow of young men up the stairwell was like red blood cells circulating through the veins. Teachers, being older and western, were like white blood cells, Hudson thought. Yes, he extended the metaphor in his mind–white blood cells fighting ignorance.

A student stood in front of him. "Mr. Smith, will you please look at my essay at lunch today? It is most important. I need you to fix it for my IELTS test this Saturday."

"'Need you?' 'Would like you,' is far more polite. Remember that requests are not demands. Didn't you write the SAT last weekend in Singapore, Andy?"

"Yes, but it killed me. I need to write the IELTS to get into a good university."

"Can we go inside to do this? The wind is picking up, and it may rain any second."

"Rain? But it is sunny." The papers in his hand moved as though they had come to life, and he looked up. "I think you are right, but maybe can I see you at lunch?"

"Yes, that would be better. I'll be in my office."

He returned a greeting from a student passing by and grinned as he made his way up the artery to his fourth floor class. Old Rich Bannerman, his arm holding a pipe on the wall, was resting on the landing as Hudson trundled past. There was a copious amount of spit on the floor, he noticed with disdain, and a student painting of "The Scream" was askew.

"Only two more flights Rich," Hudson encouraged as he continued to go to the next level.

"Yes, 'The readiness is all,'" was the raspy retort.

Smith decided to take two steps at a time, and turned the corner on the fourth floor when a shout from below reached his ears.

"Help! Help me! Mr. B needs help!"

In an instant Hudson was down the stairs and saw the prone figure on the landing a few feet from where he had passed him. Bannerman.

"Bannerman, Bannerman...can you hear me?"

Smith looked at the student who had called for help. "Go get Mr. Peterson–now!" To another he said, "Go upstairs. Get Mr. Dickens!"

Hudson checked for Bannerman's pulse. He couldn't find it. Easy–easy–stay calm. Stay calm. Check for breathing. Nothing.

Unbelieving, he checked again. Still nothing. He rolled the heavy old man over and started chest compressions.

He stopped, and checked for a pulse again. He began breathing into Bannerman's mouth. Dickens arrived. "How can I help?"

Hudson began the compressions again. "Get rid of the crowd. Do we have defibrillators?"

"No. We're lucky to have a first aid kit. Boys, move to your classrooms."

"Crap."

More breath was blown into Bannerman's lungs. More compressions followed. Nothing was happening.

"We're losing him, Dickens!"

Two more teachers arrived. Karen Song said, "I know CPR. Let me give you a break." Hudson rolled away while Karen started CPR.

Time seemed to be confused as it concurrently stopped and quickened. Smith shivered. The sweat from his exertions was beading on his forehead. Sunlight, unmoved by the proceedings, penetrated the chaos.

Eric Peterson arrived. "I've called the ambulance." A Chinese teacher kept the boys on the third floor back from the activity. Jo pushed her way past him, and paused at the sight before her. She bit her lower lip and began to pray.

Bannerman's lips were becoming blue. His hands were cool.

"You two–give me your coats." Peterson rolled one up and used it as a pillow. With the other he covered Bannerman's legs. Karen continued the compressions.

Tom Simon suggested that they carry him down to the ambulance. Dickens felt they should leave him here and continue CPR. The sun's glare continued, but Hudson knew that five minutes had now passed. Soon, it would be too late.

Where was the ambulance?

"Karen, let me give you a break," Hudson offered, and slipped into place. The compressions, the breathing continued. His hands pushed. The crowd of teachers grew as Don Hawk, Sarah Whippet, Dan Best, and Tony Vander Kwaak came from below, and Heather LeRoy, Relic, and Matt Peterson came from above. Worry carved itself deeper into their faces with each passing second.

Did the universities teach these young people to face death? Hudson pondered as he pressed the chest beneath him. Bannerman would appreciate the irony that he would meet his end on the same stairs that he had complained about at staff meetings. "Where be your jibes now?" He softly quoted Hamlet while keeping time with the compressions.

Jo knelt beside him. "Hudson, it's over. You tried your best. He's gone." Hudson stopped when her hand was on top of his own. Shadows had replaced the sunbeam on the wall, and looking up, he noticed the student painting was still hanging askew over the proceedings as a wry commentary.

The next morning saw the flag at half mast.

Thirty-Five
The Cohort

Adventurers, travellers, risk-takers. The Canadian Harmonious International Peace School staff was eclectic. Most were from British Columbia, most were young, and most were interested in paying off huge student loans and furthering their own education. C.H.I.P.S. would not be a long-term job for them, but it would provide valuable teaching experience to further their careers. They had found that many international schools wanted teachers with master's degrees, International Baccalaureate or AP training and experience. The University of British Columbia–Okanagan saw an opportunity to meet these needs by educating some of the bright up and comers in the field. The unique master's program in teaching and learning saw the university send professors for the three breaks of the Chinese school year. Each intense week- long course would give three credits. The cohort would then take classes back on the beautiful Kelowna, UBC-O campus for two summers. A major project or thesis would cap their studies, and another degree would be earned. Hudson Smith loved learning, and he wanted to become a better teacher. Jo was also in the program, but had joined it a year before. Realizing the benefits, Hudson applied after attending an informational meeting, and received word a couple of weeks later–he was in.

Initially, sixteen others showed up to the meeting, and another ten expressed interest despite being unable to attend. When the first professor was announced for the new cohort, Hudson discovered that the numbers had dwindled to a half dozen, and the program was in jeopardy of shutting down. The previous cohort had twenty-five students and was financially viable. However, UBC-O hoped that some who had considered the program would join in once it started. Optimistically, the institution sent the first prof for the new cohort to the Middle Kingdom. Hudson was joined by Bobby Wilson, Pete Holland, Heather LeRoy, Ali Javaherian, and Jasminder Gill. Doctor Douglas, a granddaughter of the famed founder of the Canadian medi-care system, was to teach during the first week break at the start of the October National Holiday.

Hudson entered the class prepared with a new Mickay Mouse binder and a new pen he had bought in Kai Fa Qu. He looked at his colleagues. They all had their lap tops ready. Hudson's was at home. School had never been hard for him, but he was a nervous, balding middle-aged man in a room of Gen-Y's. Could he survive?

Dr. Douglas opened the week citing a story about a class learning how to pack a parachute. She said that one student started very well at 80%, but never advanced in all three terms beyond 80%. A second student started at 70% moved to 90%, but at the end declined to 80%. A third student started at 50%, and progressed to 70%, but ended at 100%. "In our education system who would have the best grade?" The cohort silently did the calculations while she continued answering her own question. "The real test is this: Who would you want to pack your parachute? This is one of the struggles we have with assessment. Do teachers really reward those who progress, or do we reward those who are initially gifted?"

The class wrestled with the ideas of evaluation practices and verbally sparred with each other over their educational views. Should students be evaluated on what they could do at the end, or should they be given a progressive grade measuring each step of the way? Jasminder opined, "I think that students should only be given a grade for an exam at the end for a final exam. That's how it's done in India and England." At that moment the lights flickered and went out. All in a day's living here, Hudson thought, as no one moved.

"Wait a minute," said Heather from the dimmest side of the room. "What about rewarding a student's effort and motivating that student for their work throughout the term? If there is no incentive, or mark, why bother to do the daily assignments? I know I wouldn't." Pete Holland and Bobby Wilson laughed.

"What you are proposing, Jas–may I call you Jas?–is a summative assessment system, and you, Heather, are proposing a formative method of assessment. What's interesting is that both are used in schools, both have merits, and both have renowned educators who support these assessment styles. Let's explore them and find out why, and you'll discover where you are in terms of use and support, but first, can someone fix the lights?"

Each day the group ordered food from Peter's into the school to save time and energy, and to allow the discussions to continue. The lights went off at 8:30 each morning like clockwork as a cleaning lady wanted to save the school money. Fortunately, by Wednesday Ali had figured out where the electrical control panel was located and restored the power to the class. On Thursday Dr. Douglas discovered why one needs tissue on their person at all times, but Heather came to her rescue. At the week's end, the cohort thanked Dr. Douglas for her patience and gave her a coveted

Shanwan Starbucks travelling mug.

Hudson decided to take his lap top to the class for the final two days, but he never actually used it as the class gave group presentations. He left Mickay at home and joined the twenty-first century.

At the end of the second term in January the cohort met for a week in the frigid Dong Bei climes while their colleagues were basking in the sunshine on the beaches of exotic locales from Bali to Sri Lanka. The course was Teaching for Diversity in Schools. Dr. Karnowski met with the students. Her published works were cutting edge and found favour with many groups. After the first class break, Heather LeRoy asked Dr. Karnowski if the class should order in or eat out in Baishantan. "Hello? This is the diversity class. We need to experience the diversity of this region. We will be eating out–each day–and none of this Western style food either. I want to discover the culinary delights you love."

The multicultural challenge of Canada was lost on some of the teachers who had only practiced their craft in China. "Of all the countries I know, China is the least diverse nation on the earth. It's a sea of black hair out there."

"Come now Heather," responded Jasminder. "There are some fifty ethnic groups in China."

"Yea, I know. It's just that they are all swamped by the Han Chinese majority."

"But so are my people in BC," Ali interjected.

"Yes, but you are visible. Here, we can't tell the Uyghurs from the Han."

"No. No. You're wrong." Ali was passionate. "They are very different. Do you know how many times I have been called Indo-Canadian or Pakistani? You Europeans are lazy in trying to distinguish people."

"I'm not European. I'm, I'm...Canadian."

The discussion continued through lunch, and as the group finished the feast of eight different dishes washed back with tall bottles of Tsingtao beer, Dr. Karnowski leaned back, fully sated, and said, "China may be the least diverse country in terms of people, but what a diverse menu."

Nodding his head, Bobby Wilson smiled and said, "It sure is, and the best part is this will only cost us 110 *kuai*–about $2.40 a person."

"The Toronto School Board has begun to open up schools which are cultural specific. An Afro-centric school and a Portuguese school serve those communities. Vancouver has a public school with a First Nations focus. The rationale is to give those communities control over their own education. What do you think about this trend?" asked Karnowski.

Hudson listened to his colleagues wrestle with the idea. If Canada was a mosaic, this was a logical extension. Schools would help preserve the cultural community language and values. If schools were places to create citizens, then a common curriculum would assist that goal. If parents were to have control over their children's education, then such schools would be designed with their input. But what about the problem of segregation and isolation? Weren't such schools a step backwards? How would students learn to work with others different than themselves? Couldn't independent schools address such needs? Aren't all parents tax-payers? Why should they have to pay a second time for their child's education by placing them in a private setting? The debates lasted a good hour, and the spirited repartee exposed the cohort to many ideas they hadn't considered. Hudson thought of his neighbourhood in Canada: Russians, German Mennonites, South Asians, Philippinos, First Nations, Roman Catholics, Sikhs. How could the school system cater to their diverse needs, or should it?

Karnowski wrapped up the afternoon with an assignment to create a school that would show tolerance to a minority group through its program offerings and mission statement.

Jasminder objected, "I don't want to be tolerated. The word has such connotations. It's like we are a negative element. You know like the old eccentric uncle that nobody really likes, but he's family, so you put up with his antics."

"You have one too?" Bobby Wilson laughed.

The May National Holiday saw the cohort meet for a third time. Dr. Blackstone led the cohort in "Teaching Outside the Walls." Hudson loved the idea of students leaving their desks, taking their laptops and writing in a variety of locations. Boys especially would benefit from the perspective that the best learning happened while doing "real stuff" he thought, and he considered how the course was designed. Each day one of the students would take the class on a field trip and look at how to incorporate what they saw and did into the curriculum. It was genius, he thought. The prof comes to China, and we, as residents, arrange for tours of hard to get to places for the professor. Places, Hudson considered, that most tourists would never find. It would be fun.

Experiential learning was having a renaissance in the educational research literature Hudson discovered as he browsed through a number of online journals preparing for the course, and Dr. Blackstone had written two articles discussing his use of the concept in elementary, secondary, and post-secondary classes. *The Canadian Educator*, a prestigious journal out of Toronto, and *The American Journal of Alternative Education*, a Cal-Berkeley publication, also had articles where Blackstone had collaborated with other renowned researchers in the field. Thinking back to his own field-trip experiences in school, Hudson marvelled at how, once again, something old had become new.

The class had six trips to organize. Bobby Wilson, a renowned space cadet, arranged for the class to go on the rides at Discoveryland (a Disneyland imitation). There he showed how physics could be taught using the rides as a hands-on way to interest students in velocity, load limits, angular momentum and gravity. At the end of the field trip even Hudson had picked up new knowledge and appreciation for the world of physics.

Pete Holland took the class to the Shanwan Central Planning Committee where the Development Zone in Kai Fa Qu had a large to scale 3D map to show what was coming. Urban geography had always interested Hudson Smith. As a child he had read about how Washington, DC was planned. At one time he had considered going into urban planning as a career. Though the Mandarin translator was slow, the projections for growth, the rationales given for the project, and the enormity of the task were fascinating to Smith. In twenty years ten million people would call this home.

The diminutive Heather LeRoy chose to take the class to the local rifle range where the pacifist, Smith, felt uncomfortable holding the shotgun, but he thrilled at the power it possessed as he blasted at the skeets. LeRoy discussed how the biology of the eyes worked in picking up the moving targets and how the nervous system worked in receiving the signal to pull the trigger finger. Jasminder discovered that she was a great shooter, and signed up for further coaching before she left the facility in the van. Hudson had his faith affirmed in how wonderfully God had created the human body with all its subtlety. How can anyone discount design? he wondered as his ears were ringing.

A trip to the local market provided Ali Javaherian to teach comparative shopping to students and to work on their math skills. The clever Iranian-Canadian gave the students a ratio assignment. They were each given five kuai and told to buy the greatest amount of food in twenty minutes. "By volume or by weight?" Pete asked.

"Both," was the reply.

While the mornings had been dedicated to the trips, the lunches each day were boisterous as the cohort discussed what they had learned. Each agreed that the outings were valuable learning experiences, but the effort it took to arrange them was far greater than planning a class in a schoolroom.

"Is that a good reason to abandon field trips?" asked Professor Blackstone.

"You can't argue that the classes have not been engaging. We've had a blast, and we've learned a tonne."

"Back home, though, a course like this would be the work of one teacher, not six."

A thoughtful pause ensued. "What if the teacher organized a team of parents to help design the trips and handle the details of booking busses and sites, collecting money, and dealing with permission forms?"

"That's a great idea. Then the lesson could be the planning focus for the teacher."

"The trouble is you would have to train a new group of parents each year."

"That wouldn't be so bad, but perhaps a retired parent or teacher could volunteer to assist."

"Who pays?"

"Pays for what?"

"The transportation, the entry fees, the lunches on longer trips."

Hudson thought of the fund-raisers he had been a part of over the years. There had been a carnival hosted by a socials class so they could go to Victoria and the legislature, a calendar to raise cash for a basketball trip, delivery of fliers for the city, flower sales and deliveries near Christmas, Valentine's, and Mother's Day for athletics uniforms, manure sales for equipment, baked goods for international trips, entertainment books, apple pies, candy, ice cream and hot dogs–even coupons for a major grocery chain were all sources of income for school events and trips. There was always a way. "Money should never stop your dreams," he quipped.

Jasminder Gill arranged for a visit to the local wax museum where current events were discussed. The wax figures, a holdover from Victorian England where Madame Toussauds created life-like images of the famous people, allowed Jasminder to explore the rise of the cult of celebrity and discuss the ramifications for today's media that specialized in infotainment.

On the final day Smith's contribution was to explore the old Baishantan area behind the newer blocks of apartments. The cohort spoke to local people pulling their water from a well that had obviously been sealed and re-opened.

"Is the well water safe?"

The translator listened to a farmer's response to his question and told them it was. What about the obvious manure run-off from the field? Hudson considered.

There was a gentrification occurring, and all the small plot farmers had been bought out, but they remained on their land until the developers actually came and started to build the classic grey six-storey apartment blocks that littered the landscape. Buying out the farmers was an interesting concept since in Communist China no one owned the land–it was all government property. Thus with some government *guanxi* relationship, farmers were forced to sell and vacate by those with power.

The group walked past the graveyard on the hill behind the new buildings and discussed land use. "Why should someone buy a plot of land and then be able to use it forever?" Jasminder asked. Though there was a Chinese law banning burial, a fresh mound of earth demonstrated that the law was openly flouted. The simple grave markers and more elaborate granite headstones were silent witnesses to the land use policies. As they walked back down the hillside Hudson realized that the new rectangular, six-storey buildings in their neat rows were themselves larger versions of the headstones commemorating an old way of life.

Dr. Blackstone received his Starbucks China mug with delight. "The dragon looks like he's going places–so it's perfect. I would like to invite you all to a barbecue during the summer session. You've shown me such hospitality. It's the least I can do. By the way, I will be teaching the methods course in July. See you all then." Hudson powered off his lap top.

Thirty-Six
Killing the Chicken

May is lovely in Dong Bei. Sunshine without humidity. Persimmons are in bloom. The grass is as green as the air pollution allows it to get, and for teachers and students at C.H.I.P.S. the end of another school year is in sight. The teachers' anticipation of return to Canada and the senior students' expectation of overseas university admission offers made hope a tangible element. Neither group keenly felt the exam pressure yet.

Student teachers had come and gone, and Tony Vander Kwaak told everyone that the spring migratory peak had come. Smith noticed the magpies busy at their unsightly nests merely building on top of last year's mound until some of the piles of sticks rivalled the Great Blue Heron rookeries he had seen in Victoria's Beacon Hill Park while he studied at UVIC. Some staff made travel plans, some marriage plans, and others career plans. Increasing daylight was a welcome relief to the long, dark Dong Bei winter, and people started to return to the outdoors as though their own chrysalis had opened and released them–new creatures in a fresh, pristine environment.

The Stanley Cup playoffs captured the imagination of the ex-pat Canadians. It became a rallying point for fans and even the indifferent paid some attention as it helped to build community. Despite the growing excitement as the hockey playoff rounds progressed, by late May some teachers also felt the growing pressures of the June exams.

C.H.I.P.S.'s English teachers had resigned themselves to a high failure rate as they undertook the nearly impossible task of preparing students to pass the British Columbia Grade 12 English Exam. Smith knew from his masters' course reading that language acquisition to the point of fluency took five to seven years. What the English department did at C.H.I.P.S. in three years was nothing short of miraculous. However, it was not the passing rate that garnered Headmaster Wang's attention. It was the failure rate. Each year he fumed about the English Provincial Exam results. The fuming turned to outrage, and like a large wok, Wang splattered all who came near him each year with his displeasure.

Wang was behind his cherry desk. The magnolia blossoms nearly filled the entire window space outside his office. Light pink blooms swayed gently with the breeze from the south and the man-made wind of the traffic from Baishantan. The Headmaster's eyes narrowed at the statistics in front of him. Biology, Chemistry, Geography, History, Mandarin, Mathematics, and Physics all had school averages of "A." English had a "D." The grandfather clock in the corner announced that the world hadn't stopped, and its constancy began to grate on Miss Chen as she waited for Wang to speak. A gift to himself, the antique clock used Roman numerals, and though Chen knew what the time was by the positioning of the hands, she could not read the clock's face. Papers were shuffled. Still, Chen waited. Wang perused the sheets like a jeweller deciding where to make his cut. The school results were good in every subject area except for English, but English was the one course the students had to pass. Indeed, some universities actually wanted students to have English scores of 60 or 70%. "Miss Chen, please get Mr. Peterson and the English Department head. I must speak to them about results."

"Yes, Headmaster Wang." Chen left the room knowing that Wang could have summoned the men by using the C.H.I.P.S. CHATTER, but she understood he was now composing his thoughts, weighing his options, planning his actions. Peterson would be easy to get, but Dickens, why, he could be anywhere.

Peterson walked across the secretarial space to knock at Wang's door. Though he could see the Head sitting behind the massive desk, the man made no move at the rapping. A second series of knocks seemed to awaken him, and he beckoned Peterson to enter. "Good afternoon, Mr. Peterson. Please have seat," he said as he reached for the intercom and ordered tea brought.

The Canadian principal hated the low chairs in Wang's office. It forced him to look up to Wang, and therefore, he took his time to look at various items on the walls or shelves before he sat down. Wang said, "That is a picture of school property before I bought it. Oxen used to graze where cafeteria is now. Lower field and dormitories was ocean."

"Yes. There has been substantial change here, hasn't there?"

"A worm must change to become butterfly."

Eric thought about how he used to love teaching about metamorphosis. The miracle of the change had even turned him towards accepting spiritual ideas. How could he ignore the evidence of such miracles? There had to be a God. As he aged, he noticed more and more God's fingerprint on the earth. All things happened for a purpose. He smiled at the Head, and accepted his position by taking a seat.

Tea came in to the room. The door's creaking and the tinkling of the silver ware broke his thoughts. Scents of jasmine and chrysanthemum filled his nostrils. Miss Hu Ying poured the tea.

"*Xie xie*, Miss Hu," said Peterson. He always made his own tea as he wanted the secretarial staff to do their jobs, but he understood that Wang did not share such an egalitarian view of his staff. The two men sipped the tea. After twenty minutes of small talk, Peterson was waiting for Wang to tell him what he really wanted. The Head never got down to business, the Chinese don't as a rule as they prefer to build relationship first, and despite knowing this, Peterson wanted to return to the matters on his own desk.

"I want my school to be butterfly not worm-sa. There must be changes.

"What kind of changes, Mr. Wang?"

"I must kill chicken to scare monkey."

"What?"

"This is old saying. Here comes my chicken."

Miss Chen opened the door, and Craig Dickens walked though. Ice hockey tie, one collar stained, a black knitted sweater with various patches indicating where the Snow Tigers had played, a small tear on his trousers' pocket, and scuffed muddy shoes didn't exude the professionalism that Peterson wanted, but he knew Dickens was competent, trustworthy, and motivated. Peterson would hire him immediately if given another chance. The two men spoke to each other with their eyes, and neither could explain to the other what was happening. Dickens walked over to the Head and offered his hand. It was ignored. "Mr. Chickens..."

"That's Dickens, sir."

"Yes, Dickens. I need to know why English department not work hard. Provincial exam marks are too low. Why?"

"Mr. Wang, I cannot make bricks without straw."

"What?"

"It's an allusion. The boys are not ready for the English test. They need more time to learn English."

"Excuses."

"Mr. Wang, if I try to make a cake, I need the right ingredients. I cannot make angel food cake with mud. I need eggs and flour." Dickens's eyes darted to Peterson. The same puzzled look was on his face.

"Excuses."

"No. No. It's not an excuse. It's reality. Some boys pass because they were ready when they arrived, but you've allowed more and more students in to C.H.I.P.S. who do not have any English. You've eliminated the Communications course which the weaker students took. Of course there will be consequences."

"Excuses. Dickens you are no longer be department head. Please leave."

Peterson stepped in to protect his teacher, "Headmaster Wang, Dickens is the best English teacher we have here. He hasn't done anything to be dismissed from his position."

"You Canadians have sense of privilege. You are right. He hasn't done anything. Exam marks are lowest ever. Mr. Peterson, you should have killed chicken."

Dickens smiled as he knew the proverb. Rising from the chair he considered silently, Wang is a devil and Chen is a serpent, but what will Peterson do? If I am the chicken, then Peterson or maybe the other English teachers are the monkeys. He laughed to himself. Maybe we're all monkeys for working here, he thought. He left the room, nodded to the secretaries, and entered the cold dark hallway pondering his future at C.H.I.P.S.. McAdams passed by, and Dickens said, "Hey you great big ape." McAdams spun around, but the former department head kept walking down the darkened hall. Once outside, he looked up at the flags. The Chinese flag was new. Bright red and five yellow stars shone, but Dickens chuckled as the Canadian flag, tattered and stained, ripped further and wrapped one of its long red fingers around the school flag some five meters away and held it to the pole. Fireworks announcing a new business opening in the village echoed off the school's walls.

"Craig, can I see you in my office?"

"Sure Eric." It had been two days since Dickens had been removed as department head, and the entire English department had been waiting to see what would happen next. Smith, Simon, and Song were all asked to replace him, and all declined. The chimps were scared. Craig entered the office and sat on the long faux leather couch. Eric Peterson started to move from behind his desk, but his phone interrupted him. The room served as the meeting space for Peterson, Whippet, and McAdams. A small round table with plug-ins for computers was a focal point, and along the back wall running the full length was a watercolour painting of the Three Gorges. In the corner nearest his desk, Peterson kept a pot of coffee brewing. If you were special, he would bring out the Tim Horton's can to remind you of Canada. Some teachers tried in vain to visit him frequently for this perk alone. The office door opened quickly, and McAdams, noting Peterson on the phone, asked if Dickens had any toilet paper. A shake of the head sent the vice-principal back to his search. Once again Peterson made to get up and once again the phone interrupted. After a brief conversation, the principal finally made his way to the empty chair across from Dickens.

"Craig," he began, "I would like to ask you to organize the exam session for the English department."

"Eric, I'm no longer department head. I am glad to have this chance to chat to you though. Would you write a reference letter for me?"

Eric adjusted his glasses, and rubbed his chin. Chairman Meow landed on the windowsill outside, and the audacious feline stretched his full length and started to scratch his front claws on the peeling white wood. Whippet opened the door and spoke without looking, "What are you doing for lunch?" When she realized Eric was meeting with Dickens, she meekly said, "Ooopsie," and left.

"It's Grand Central here, eh? Craig, I will write you a letter today. Is there anything you would like me to include? Is it for a particular posting?"

"Thank you. No. There is nothing I would like you to include, and there is no position that I've applied for back home."

"Craig, we will miss your expertise."

"I won't be the last. Expect more resignations soon," he said prophetically.

Peterson turned to the window, and Chairman Meow was no longer there.

Headmaster Wang and Miss Chen were discussing the implementation of Chen's plan that she had developed to save C.H.I.P.S. money. "Miss Chen, I am very pleased with your plan. Can we add other ideas to it? Salaries are too high. We must lower this number one cost. I want to cut all salaries by 20%. Class sizes must be run at maximum level. This is business." He leaned back and celebrated the thought with a sip from his tea cup.

"Will we be able to hire Canadian teachers?"

"Yes, they will come for travel and adventure."

"Will older ones come?" her tongue flicked across her lips quickly while her eyes followed the Head's movements.

"Who cares? Young or old–they do same job. It is decided. Go change teacher recruitment information to reflect new policy."

As Chen left, squeezing past the door and two Canadians gabbing with the secretaries, the Headmaster reached under his desk for his flask. There was a commotion outside his office window, and spinning his chair to the glass he saw Chairman Meow falling off the ledge while a magpie fluttered away with a tail feather bent at an awkward angle. The warm contents of the flask coursed down his throat, as he made his way to the window. More motion caught his attention as a grounds worker finished cutting down a magnolia tree. In the village fireworks shot off.

Thirty-Seven
Squid on a Stick

The magpie, its long, tail feathers kite-like and the body showing a bluish-green tinge was circling the basketball court enjoying the early thermals of late-spring while Hudson scanned the skies looking for anything that might interrupt his children's arrival today in Shanwan. The taxi had been arranged for an immediate departure after school as he and Jo would meet Carson, his second son, and Lillian, his daughter and the baby of the family. Now that university had finished in Canada the two were going to visit and meet Jo as their dad's new wife. The traffic through Kai Fa Qu was as snarled as anything Hudson had ever seen on the Port Mann Bridge, and add in drivers who turned left in front of on-coming traffic and who made six lanes appear where there were lines for three–it was an adventure.

An hour and a half later the Smiths hopped out at the Shanwan Airport where the grey Stalinist structure had to be the grimmest greeting for international travellers anywhere, and they entered the gloomy edifice. Rectangles, grey, low ceilings, and grime ruled here. The carved granite brought no cheer. Flickering fluorescent lights were losing the battle against the darkness. The cheap Chinese cigarette smoke dimmed the room even further as Jo checked the arrival board. “On time,” she announced.

“They should be coming through any second then.”

“Yes. That carousel is the flight from Beijing.”

“I don’t see them.”

“They’re coming.”

“Where?”

“Not that I can see them, silly, but they’re coming.”

“It’s been since August. I can hardly wait to hug them, to introduce you as my wife. They’re going to love you.”

“I hope so...”

“They will. You’ll love them too. You’ll see.”

Seeing the two Canadians should have been an easy task. Carson played volleyball at Camosun College and was a long and lean six foot six–an Adonis. His sister, a twenty-year old nursing student, would fit in with the Chinese population as she barely hit five feet. Carson, fair skinned with blond curls, was a character foil for Lillian as her dark complexion complimented the frizzy chestnut brown locks. He was quiet, but she spoke frequently and loudly. Truly, she was the life of the party. They had met Jo briefly last summer, but since then Hudson had proposed in the fall, and they had been married in January on an idyllic island in Thailand.

All the Beijing passengers had picked up their luggage, and the carousel looked lonely. Hudson was perplexed. “How do we find them? Have they been detained? Did they miss their Beijing flight?

Their Seattle flight? Have they gotten on the wrong plane?"

"Don't worry. I'll ask at the counter, and we'll find them. You wait here just in case they were detained."

Twenty, thirty, forty-five minutes passed. No children. No Jo. Hudson's belly growled. A Chinese woman standing beside him moved away from him and pushed into her husband to distance herself from the noise. It growled again. She grabbed her husband's arm and pulled him further down the hall. Another flight arrived from Xian and immediately after it was one from Shanghai-Pudong. The arrival area became chaotic in an instant as taxi drivers, family, friends all called out to their loved ones. Hudson could see Jo coming down the escalator with something in each hand. His salivary glands started to anticipate the snack, recalling a kinship with the animal kingdom, but his eyes couldn't make out the shape until Jo was quite close.

"Squid on a stick?"

"It's all they had."

"I dunno."

"Try it. It can't be any worse than the chicken heads you had last week."

"True, but that was a one-time thing. I thought they were chicken pieces."

"Well, they were," Jo snickered, recalling Hudson's horror as he realized that the piece remaining on his stick had a beak.

"Any news?"

"Yes, they missed their connection because the flight from Seattle was delayed. They've just arrived."

Swinging their heads back to the carousel, a large backpack with the maple leaf made its way onto the circular track.

"That's Carson's bag!"

Hudson beamed, and Jo squeezed him tightly. From inside the baggage claim area Carson waved. Then, Lillian started to wave, saw her luggage, and darted through the crowd to retrieve it. After the hugs and kisses were exchanged, they went out of the dingy room and into the thick air of China to find their driver. She was waiting. The two young adults marvelled over the heights of the buildings stretching beyond anything that Vancouver could throw at them. Carson, in the front seat, gasped a number of times as the traffic weaved back and forth in front of him. Huge blue flat decks with meter high side rails carrying people and goods, 125cc motorcycles holding up to five people, old wrinkly men sitting with legs crossing the wagon harness swishing their crop across their donkey's back, a chicken, an escapee from one of the three wheeled rural vehicles, wandering on the shoulder and a black Audi swerving its eight cylinders to avoid it, and pedestrians nonchalantly moving across the six lanes of vehicles like a Frogger video game all contributed to the transportation chaos. Chaos it was, but here it worked. Lillian told them of their flight, the delay in Seattle to replace windshield wipers on the jumbo jet, of the stewardess who slipped Carson her phone number, and the snorer they sat beside who had caused his own turbulence. "Dad, he reminded me of you. At first his breathing was like Darth Vader, then it was a full-out rumble."

Jo giggled and Hudson blushed. "Sounds like some of the

students."

"Dad, I want to meet them."

"I was hoping to bring you to class to speak to them about life in a Canadian university."

They both answered, "Yes, we'd love to."

Suddenly, Carson, too, was snoring, and Lillian yawned and released herself to the hum of the engine as her head dropped onto Jo's shoulder. Jo was pleased by how comfortable her new step-daughter was, but wondered if Lill would feel awkward on waking. There was no question: travelling eighteen hours including layovers and jumping a day ahead was tiring.

They arrived in Baishantan and settled in to the apartment that had been rented for the week. Hudson had a second period spare the next day and promised them he would help them get oriented and show Carson and Lill how to operate the motorcycle. Lill said, "I think Carson has been as excited about riding the bike as he is about visiting you and China."

"It is a blast. The freedom to travel down the road and explore is great. We've seen things that some of the staff will never see because we have a bike. It's been an insight into the real China."

Hudson gave his kids hugs goodnight, and he and Jo left the exhausted travellers.

As they walked back to their apartment, Hudson squeezed Jo's hand, and the two lovebirds entered the building.

The next day as Hudson was showing Carson how to ride, Lill, who wasn't interested, came running back. "Look at these photos.

The birds are crazy looking."

"Wow, these are great shots. Let's look them up in Tony's book. He's one of the teachers–an avid birder–he published a guide book recently. I'll get it."

When he came back, book in hand, Lill was snapping shots from the back of the Dayun 125 as Carson's joyful smile was oozing confidence around the school traffic circle. Stopping the machine he said, "Dad, this is great. Can I take it off the school grounds?"

"If you are comfortable, you bet, but stick to the country roads, okay?"

"What kind of bird is it, Dad?"

"A Common Hoopoe."

"A what?"

"Carson, take a look. It's got black and white stripes on its lower body and wings, and a crown like the Stellar Jays back home." She handed him her camera.

"Cool."

"Let me triple you two so I can get back to school."

The day seemed to fly by as all good times do, and then Lill said, "Tomorrow, we want to come to your classes."

"That would be great. The students know you are coming, and they have questions prepared. You'll like them."

The next day the young Canadians made their way into the gloomy halls of C.H.I.P.S.. "Dad, what's with the no lights?"

"It's a way to save money, Carson."

"Told you Carson."

They entered the classroom after going up the four flights, and Lillian said, "Quaint décor. Early revolution?"

Hudson had been accepting of the lack of decorations in the class. He knew that it would not be like his classroom back home, and accepted the plain white washed walls, the ancient speaker system, the rusting desks that creaked constantly with bolts that stuck out ruining at least two pairs of his pants, the tattered, mildewed blinds with their water stains and mould, and the one whiteboard that had no desire to be erased. He now even looked past the dust buffaloes in the corners and his nose no longer registered the stench of the granite floors that were mopped with the same mops that cleaned the boys' washrooms. No disinfectant or cleaner was used. The cost-conscious custodians would lose their jobs if they implemented such a regiment. Fruit flies danced above the large garbage can in the corner where the bag within was never replaced–only the contents were dumped. Standing back, his daughter showed him these things again. This was life in China, Hudson thought, and he had accepted it. "Thanks Lillian. You are taking the scales from my eyes."

The sonorous musical tone summoned the boys to class. Like migratory birds, they came to the school building from the dorms and the cafeteria. Some, like a snow goose driven off course by a winter storm, came onto the grounds from the community by passing through the gate. The uniforms and black hair made it difficult to distinguish any particular boy from another from Hudson's classroom four floors above. The students rubbed shoulders with the teachers getting out of their cabs from Kai Fa Qu. Three abreast up the stairs they moved. At each landing some broke off from the upwards flow to go to their classrooms which were as crowded and noisy as a penguin's breeding ground.

Carson and Lillian greeted China's future leaders when they entered the room and sat at their desks. The early boys whispered to each other while the flow increased and the room filled to its capacity. Finally, the musical tone began again, announcing the commencement of another instructional day.

"Good morning China! Live from Baishantan it's English class with Mr. Smith–no, today's episode is English class with The Smiths." The boys grinned. They were used to Mr. Smith's odd ways, and appreciated his attempts at humour. "Today's guest stars come to us from the universities of Canada. Give a big round of applause for Mr. Carson Smith and the beautiful Miss Lillian Smith–academic stars of Jianada." An arm flourish and dramatic bow followed the introductory words and the slightly embarrassed pair moved from the side to the centre position behind the podium.

"Hello. I'm Carson Smith, and this is Lillian Smith. Our dad said that you had questions prepared for us. Would you please take those out? We will try to answer everything you want to know about Canada." Hudson beamed. It was so good to see his children's poise. He was proud of them, and his eyes started to brim with joy.

The rustling of paper sounded like a Siberian wind, but one boy raised his hand immediately. "Yes?" Carson asked.

Robert asked Lillian, "Do you have a boyfriend?" This was a question that Hudson also wanted to ask, but he had decided that he wouldn't pry. It would be better for Lillian to reveal this on her own terms.

Lillian gave a quick glance to her father, and answered, "No. I'm much too busy with my nursing studies to even think of boys."

Good answer, Hudson thought. Be patient. No rush. The time will come though, he considered. He looked at his attractive daughter with fatherly pride.

The questions continued, and both Carson and Lillian answered them with humour and genuine warmth. Near the end of the period Eisenhower asked them a question that often had been posed to Hudson before, and despite his reassurances, it was obviously a concern to these young men about to embark to a foreign land with strange customs. "Will other students talk to me? Will I have foreign friends?"

Hudson smiled. He thought of Lillian's friends from her school in Canada. The multicultural society envisioned by Trudeau bore itself out in his daughter's life: Koreans, Japanese, Zimbabwean, Dutch, South Asians, Haitians, and even the rare and exotic American were part of her circle. This United Nations visited for popcorn and movies many nights in their home in Canada. Carson also had friends from several continents. People were still people. They wanted to be secure. They wanted to be included. They wanted love, acceptance, and community.

"Yes. Others will talk to you. Canadians are friendly, but you will need to tell them you are from China, or they will just think you are Canadian too."

At the end of the class the boys milled around the two university students and thanked them before heading off to the next course. The pair repeated the process for all four classes that day, interrupted by lunch where the young Canadians tried the squid on a stick and found it quite palatable. It had been an opportunity for both sides to grow, and Hudson considered that good education usually was. "Dad, that was fun, but I'm tired. How do you do that every class, every day, for the whole year?"

"I can't. That's why reading was invented–to give teachers a rest." They all laughed as Hudson gathered his evening's marking.

As they exited, the magpie chattering overhead landed on the building, and with their eyes drawn heavenward they all noticed this week's banner hanging from the building. It read: TWO HANDS ACROSS THE WATER–ONE HUMANESS.

Thirty-Eight
The Last Staff Meeting

Jo stood at the door adjusting her long silk scarf. She changed it once, twice, then with a quick movement, she went back into the bedroom to get a different one. While she was there she also liberated a knitted hat from the closet, and beamed with delight as she surveyed the effect in the hall mirror. She looked like she had just stepped out of a fashion magazine, thought Hudson with pride and stirring desire. The scarf was one that he had purchased for her at the Korean Market in Shanwan for a surprise earlier that spring. Though it was early June, the winds today were substantial. Hudson, on opening the curtains, had seen three plastic bags tumbling along caressing trees and electric lines as they went. The new leaves, light green though already tainted by the coal dust, had hidden the magpies' nests. Jo decided, on hearing her husband's report, to put away the toques and gloves later. "There's change a'comin' from down dere," she said in her best hillbilly accent.

Hudson laughed, "That might not be the only change. There's a staff meeting after school today."

"Yeah, I had forgotten. Isn't it funny how we call it school when it is our work?"

"Hey, it's not work. It's a calling, and I learn something every day. So it is school for me."

"If you are lucky, you may learn some things from me tonight," she winked as he held the door open for her.

"Really?"

"Really."

The school day went by in a blur. Hudson's students explored the idea of death from Robert Browning's "Prospice" where the speaker wants to fully experience life's end–to "taste the whole of it," and not pass away in a drug-induced stupor. The discussion of euthanasia, palliative treatment, and hospices was lively. China had no comparative concept when it came to hospices, but the boys had thought about palliative treatment and euthanasia.

"There are too many people in China," stated Robert. "There should be euthanasia." Hudson had heard this common belief before, but this time he was ready. Robert went on, "Older people should be replaced. They are cogs of business, and every machine part wears out."

"Your dogma has some problems, Robert."

"What is dogma, Mr. Smith?" Nero asked.

"A belief. Any other students want to comment."

Allan said, "First, who are the 'too many'? Are you one of them? Is your grandmother?"

Steven wisely piped in, "People aren't cogs. Isn't everyone important?"

Livingston, a keen AP Economics student, named after the seagull said, "Did you know British economist Malthus said the same thing about people several hundred years ago?" He parroted his textbook, "His assumption was that mankind would run out of resources. He forgot to factor in that we create more food each year."

"We cannot keep adding people. Deng Xiao Ping said that we would never be able to feed ourselves if our population continued to expand," King defended his friend Robert.

Adolph chipped in, "Who decides who the 'too many' are? The government? Those with *guanxi*?" How would the 'too many' be dealt with? What is the upper limit? What is ideal? Is there an age limit? What about the handicapped, aged, insane?" The hands went up across the room, and the discussion lasted the entire period. Hudson loved seeing the students' newfound critical thinking in action.

Dickens came into the office at the end of the day and plopped down into his chair. Hudson noticed the pile of essays the department head was holding and he looked gloomily at his own pile. "I suppose the good news is that the year is almost over, and the paper drivel will cease."

"Yeah, but this paper mountain says we still have some work to do."

"Sure, and part of that work begins now–staff meeting starts in a couple of minutes."

"Don't you wish that Eric would send most of the info by CHATTER? Staff meetings were useful when there were no instant communication systems, but now? It wastes so many man hours." Hudson laughed as he looked at the wasted man hours in front of him in the form of essays. Essays he would mark. Essays which wouldn't be read again.

Changing the subject, Dickens looked out the window as a pink plastic bag pirouetted like a ballerina then continued. "The wind hasn't let up all day. It's like a harbinger of the meeting. You know–lots of hot air." Dickens smiled an impish grin.

The two men gathered up their marking and opened the door. "Mr. Smith, can you please help me with college essay?" pleaded Johnson, one of his lesser lights.

"Of course, Johnson. I'll see you at the meeting in a few minutes, Craig."

"I'll save you a spot."

"Great. Come into the office Johnson. Ah, good, you have it with you. Let's take a look."

A half hour later Hudson Smith entered the auditorium sheepishly as the meeting was in full swing. Only a few heads bobbed up to acknowledge his presence. True to his word, Dickens had saved him a spot in the back row. The teachers were all reading a three page double-sided handout. The paper turning sounded like the Thailand shores that he and Jo had been married on in January–steady and rhythmic, but a tsunami lurked offshore.

"What's up, Craig?"

"I think we are the chickens."

"What?"

"You know the proverb. 'Kill the chicken to scare the monkey.' The changes laid out here are huge. Wang is sacrificing us all. Here, take a look."

After a few moments of his perusal, Hudson knew it was bad for the teachers. Immediate reduction in salary, no increments for experience, no pension, no medical benefits, flight paid for to China but not back, the class sizes would increase, admin would decrease–all spoke of cost-savings. Hudson was surprised by how extensive the cuts were. The present contract was being torn up, and the teachers were being asked to sign a new amended one today. From the corner of his eye, he saw Relic stand up.

"Eric, Mr. Wang's plan as laid out here will not help the school. The quality of teaching will suffer, and the experience we have will diminish. Have you spoken to him about this?"

"This document was given to me five minutes before the meeting. As you are aware the administrators here at C.H.I.P.S. are often messengers. I overheard someone say, 'We need to vote about this,' and I can assure you, this is not a democracy. There will be no vote, no discussion, no teacher-suggested amendments. Mr. Wang is the headmaster, and he has decided this is the new direction at C.H.I.P.S.."

Relic, still standing, looking regal and strong, turned to his colleagues and addressed them directly. "Friends, what Eric says is true. This is not a democracy, but there is still a way to vote. Use your feet to speak for you. It's easy for me to say this as I am already leaving, and I know some of you now consider China home as you've married local spouses and had your children here, but there seems to be no other way to speak to Mr. Wang."

The buzz of discussion rivalled any hive, but the sound continued to increase as though a grizzly bear had stuck his nose right in looking for honey.

"I can't just leave. My wife and her family are from here."

"We have mortgage payments back home."

"I love my job."

"Wang can't do this to us."

"Let's strike."

"Can we speak to him?"

"He's acting like an emperor."

Some of the responses were filled with blue language while some teachers' tones eloquently spoke for them. Anger, passion, despair, rage, shock, confusion, disbelief. Hudson recognized them as feelings he had suffered; although, he had experienced the emotions over time, and he had friends who had shared his burden. Here they were all released at once like Pandora had opened her mythical box in their midst, and each person was experiencing the announcement without the benefit of time to consider and prepare. The pot was starting to boil over like a forgotten chilli, and like every stove top, the results were going to be messy.

Dickens stood up and gave a shrill two fingered whistle which silenced the mob. "I have been here for a while now. I love China. I love the people of China. I love my students. I want what is best for them. It's ironic that in a communist country we capitalist Canadians are speaking about workers' rights and striking. Wang has every right to do this, and we either accept his terms, or as

Relic said, we show our disapproval by leaving here. I made my decision recently, but the school will go on without us. New teachers will be hired. The turnover rate has always been high, fluctuating between 20-66%. We are merely cogs in the wheel. This is a business first–a school second."

The idealistic bubble burst for many of the staff. A tsunami of ideas were changing their lives, and they weren't ready. Were they really just part of a business? Was this just a job or was it a calling–something holy, something important?

Eric Peterson, who had been patiently observing the reaction and considering where he as a leader should be leading his staff, spoke. "I know that this is sudden and late in the year, but Mr. Wang has asked that you sign the new contracts today. I will tell him that you need at least two days to consider such dramatic changes. If you intend to stay, please have the new contracts back to my office by Friday. I, for one, will not be staying next year. I cannot work with a person who does not respect contracts. The meeting is adjourned." Eric stepped down from the stage and a dozen teachers surrounded him immediately.

Eric, Dickens and Relic's announcements took most by surprise. Who would replace Eric? Who would replace the experienced staff who were the heart and soul, the true leaders of C.H.I.P.S.? Some of the staff left the auditorium resigned to their fate. They were the 'lifers'. They had made China their country. Their spouses, in-laws, and children called "the good earth" home. Others only needed the push to realize that they wanted to leave, that other schools and other classrooms were waiting for them. The majority slowly made their way out the auditorium's doors, mulling over the future. To go back to Canada and a sentence of being a teacher-on-call after being master of their own classroom was uninviting. The uncertainty of working, the knowledge that they would be merely a plug, a temporary measure without the opportunity to build rapport or relationship, was unappealing to most. To continue teaching on the international circuit meant it would be increasingly difficult to go home.

Hudson heard Nathan Johnson speaking to Bobby Wilson. "The money is less than Canada, but so is the cost of living. I'll pay off my student loans if I stay another year."

"Can you trust Wang? Do you want to work for him? I don't, and I won't," said Bobby. Hudson continued to walk towards Jo who was waiting at the door.

The tempestuous thoughts in most minds were like a riptide pulling two ways at once. "So that was quite the meeting, eh?" he asked in the most Canadian of ways. Hudson gave Jo a hug.

"That's quite a frown, Mr. Smith," she teased. "Remember this morning when I said, 'There's change a comin' from down dere'?"

"Yes. You are quite a prophetess."

"No. I was wrong. There's change a comin' from above too. I have decided though, Hudson. With my mom's health deteriorating, and now this, it's time to leave." Hudson squeezed her hand and held her close while Jo's decision said aloud finalized her thoughts. Stating it made it real. He knew she had wrestled with the idea for some time, but he did not want to weigh in.

"I'm glad that we both feel the same way. I've been weighing the options too. When I read the papers today, I knew I was finished here."

They were content. The newlyweds walked out the door arm in arm, while the fresh warm air from the south brought promises of new beginnings to the Liaodong Peninsula.

Jo started to laugh, and Hudson raised his left eyebrow as he swivelled his head left and then up, following her gaze. "Hudson, there is more than one change a comin' from above."

Hudson laughed too. The audacity. The chutzpah. The courage. The UBC engineering students, so well known for their pranks, would be proud. What would Wang say? What would the nationalistic Chinese students do? Jo and Hudson's eyes had rested on the flag poles, and the change was dramatic. Now flying high in the smoky azure sky alongside the red flags of the People's Republic and the True-North-Strong-and-Free was the blue and red yin and yang circle of South Korea. The Korean students had replaced the school flag with their own.

Thirty-Nine
Final Flag

Hudson walked into Peter's restaurant and ordered two breakfasts to go. It was the final Monday of classes and he wanted to treat Jo. The final flag of the year, and the final flag ever for many of the teachers.

Inside the swinging glass doors was a backpacker. He must be from New Zealand, Hudson deduced from the stranger's silver fern shirt and kiwi hat. "Brilliant," the young traveller said when told the bagger would be ready in five minutes. Hudson was curious about where the young man was from as he had travelled extensively in the island nation.

"Welcome to Baishantan. What city are you from, my kiwi friend?"

"Actually, I'm from the UK. Nottinghamshire. You know, where Robin Hood lurked in the forest."

"Oh, sorry about that. It's hard to distinguish between the English, Kiwi and Aussie accents. I thought your shirt and hat were the clues I needed."

"I've been travelling round the world, and I'm heading back by the Trans-Siberian railway. I'll catch it at Vladivostok. By the way, I loved America. A dazzling place, really."

"I like to visit it too."

"What? You are American aren't you? Your accent is American."

Hudson winced. "Would you call a Scot Irish? Would you mistake a Welshman for a Cockney?" His mock indignation continued. "I, too, have Elizabeth on the back of my coins. I'm part of the Commonwealth."

The English youth stood with a puzzled look while he tried to solve the enigma standing in front of him, and Hudson seeing his bewilderment helped him out. "I'm Canadian."

"Your accent is American."

"Be careful. Many Canadians wouldn't like to be identified as such. I suppose to the untrained ear, we do sound similar. It's safer to guess that we are Canadian. Canadians will be pleased that you recognize us, while Americans are pleased because Canadians are reputed to be polite."

The traveller laughed. "I'll remember. My mate's waiting and so is Russia. Cheerio."

When Hudson entered the apartment, Jo was just getting out of the shower. "Breakfast in bed, sweetie?"

"No, thanks. We'll just make a mess."

"Okay, I'll set the table."

"Hey, this is a surprise. Thank you. I love Peter's baggers."

"I thought I'd surprise you since this is the last flag for us."

"It is, isn't it? I have been to over two hundred flags. I wonder if this one will be memorable."

"Aren't they all?" Hudson laughed.

When Eric walked into his office that Monday morning, there were five more teachers there with resignation letters in hand. That brings the total to fifty-seven, he thought. The staff was decimated. Probably there were more resignations to come. He considered how grateful he was to not be coming back, but he envied his successor who would hand pick a staff. Then again, fifty-seven staff looked desperate. There were bound to be some poor teachers, and there were bound to be some kooks. He took the new letters and went to Mr. Wang's office to deliver them.

At the same time, Xiaoqing Chen, dressed in high leather shiny, black boots, opened her office door. Things were busy for her. Wang had asked her to reorganize the way new teachers from Canada were integrated into C.H.I.P.S.. There were so many ways to save money. Who needed a welcome party, or a welcome banquet? New supplies? Teachers should supply their own. Xiaoqing shut the door, and placed her short handled Armani purse on the shelf at eye level where anyone entering her office would see it. Its diamond pattern shone in the sun. The room was always sunny in the mornings. It was the cosiest, warmest place in the entire school. When she turned from the shelf, she screamed a hideous scream as she saw a large snake rising from her leather chair to her desktop. The diamond pattern–orange and black–was glossy in the morning sun, and the triangular head warned of its poisonous power. The snake, a good two meters long, was alarmed by the sudden movements, and retreated to a place beneath the desk where it coiled in defence, but Miss Chen assumed that it was heading to the door to attack her, and she screamed again louder and more desperate than before. Several people ran to her aid as she reverted to her village's dialect in her panic so nobody knew what she was saying. John McAdams, who reached the room first, tried to guide Chen to her desk, and the thin woman recoiled and screeched louder than before as she resisted the gentle arm pulling her along. McAdams cooed soothingly, but Chen, who weighed a mere forty kilos, grabbed her purse and swung it like a cricket bat right between McAdams's legs. John's eyes were saucers, and he dropped to the floor where he could see under Chen's desk. It was like he had hit a trampoline, and agonizing pain in his nether regions aside, he burst from the room yelling, "SNAKE! SNAKE! SNAKE!" Chen and the others followed him and slammed the door on the reptile.

Mr. Wang made Mr. Peterson wait outside his door while he slowly inhaled the steam from his green tea and reviewed the financial department report and its projections for the next school year. It forecast the largest profit in C.H.I.P.S.'s history. He placed his tea cup down. Peterson and his concern over an experienced staff for next year wasn't important. Profits mattered, and profits were growing. Almost all the experienced teachers were leaving, and Wang could simply hire new ones at a lower salary. The savings were immense. Slowly his smile grew. He sipped his drink, savouring the flavour. The school bell signalled the end of the first period. "Miss Hu, please send in Mr. Peterson."

Upstairs Hudson Smith dismissed his class, but three of them came to him as he packed up his laptop. "Mr. Smith. We have invited you to become a Facebook friend," William, the Lushun speech giver, stated.

"Thank you men. I won't accept your invitation until school is finished at the end of the month, but then I would be honoured. It's my policy. I trust you understand."

"Yes, we do. In China a lao shi is always a lao shi, and the relationship always has a gap," Nero explained.

Michael added, "We think that Canadian teachers are different. We think that the gap disappears as we learn together."

Leo summed up, "We wa-wa-wa-want you t-t-t-tto-to-to bbbbeeee our friend."

"Leo, Michael, Nero, William," Hudson said looking at each of the fine young men before him in turn, "I already am. I look forward to hearing about your adventures in Canada, and your studies. Send me pictures, and know that you would always be welcome to visit my home in Canada. Hustle to class before the bell goes. One more class until your final flag at C.H.I.P.S.."

"Bye," they chorused as they slipped through the door not realizing the gift they had just given to their English teacher–their *lao shi*.

Flag ceremony began. Ritual, thought Hudson, is such a human trait. The repetition of actions and words, of clothing and song, of objects and location was a powerful reminder to all the participants that they belonged to a unique group, and that the group had a special purpose or cause. Didn't every human being want to belong to a greater purpose?

The clouds were hurrying by when the final flag ceremony began. "Good Morning, Dear Teachers and Fellow Students.

We are from grade 12 class 9.

It is our great pleasure to perform the flag raising ceremony today."

"Hey, he used the article," Hudson murmured to Tony.

Tony, whose eyes were scanning the sky for Harriers or Swifts sailing the strong currents, said, "What?"

"My name is Orange Lu. This is Robert Wang." The mic was passed from the first boy to the second who was rubbing dust from his right eye.

"We are the hosts," he squinted. "And the flag raisers are starting from my left hand side are Paul Xi, Charlie Wu, Leo Cai, John Li, Benedict Zhong, and Gregory Zhou."

"They are all using the names of popes," observed Tony. Hudson smiled at the irony.

"The conductor is Luca Sun." A plastic bag tumbled in the air behind the podium, whirled up in a spiral and continued its way to the Yellow Sea.

"Now I declare C.H.I.P.S. the flag raising ceremony begins." Polite applause came from the grade ten section.

"Raise the flag of People Republic of China, and now play the national anthem of China." Paul and Charlie fulfilled their part of the ritual as the white gloved duo flung open the flag and pulled the rope, sending the banner to its position. As the flag rose, some of the boys jostled each other, but most sang with pride as their nation now contributed more and more to the international scene. Luca, the conductor, swung his arms vigorously, though no one paid him any attention.

"Raise the flag, and play the national anthem of Canada." Leo and John stepped forward in unison and repeated the actions with the red and white flag that Lester B. Pearson had brought to the country and the world. Few Canadian teachers sang. Content to listen, their thoughts drifted home to where they would be in a couple of weeks after the gruelling exam period was done.

Finally, Benedict and Gregory moved to the podium. Following Orange's instructions of "Raise the flag of C.H.I.P.S., and let's sing our school song together," they flung the flag into the wind and the music began on cue, but unlike the previous two flags, the C.H.I.P.S. flag kept sailing. It had not been properly attached to the rope, thus, Benedict's sweeping arm sent the flag into the breeze and, like a kite, it kept sailing up in the strong wind. It sailed up, up, up and the beaver gnawing on the tree soon grew to be a speck as it soared right up over the boys' dormitory building and headed towards the sea. The flag raisers' eyes followed the flag and hoped they could still write the exams after such a mistake. They turned as if on cue, and went back to the line-up behind the podium while the music continued to play.

"Now I call on Mr. Peterson and Mr. Zhou to make announcement."

Peterson moved to the mic. It was the last time he would speak to all of the school at once, and his face smiled. "Today marks the end of our year together. Men, teachers, the exams are coming. You have run a race all year and I ask you to finish well. Mr. Zhou?"

Zhou took the mic, and he said, "Zhou En Lai would say, 'Study hard and bring glory to China.'" He handed the mic back to Eric.

"Mr. McAdams, would like to say something to you all." Mr. Zhou moved back with the Canadian principal while McAdams took the microphone.

"I have the pleasure of announcing that Ms. Sarah Whippet accepted my marriage proposal last night." The boys cheered and the teachers started chatting to each other at the back of the homeroom lines. "I know that some of you are curious about our future. We will move back to Canada to begin our life together with administration positions in Surrey near Simon Fraser University. Please come and visit us." McAdams stepped back and gave the mic to Orange.

"I now declare flag ceremony is over. Teachers, please go first." It was over. It had been eventful. Smith walked alongside Dickens, Vander Kwaak, and Relic while the workers unfurled the large red and gold lettered banner. It implored the boys to: STUDDY HAARD FOR EARTHS FUTRE! Smith saw the magpie looking down from his perch. Maybe, he thought, animals have rituals too.

The campus rhythms changed during the exams. Bells ceased. Students moved in hushed tones. The basketball courts were silent. The teachers held garage sales on the CHATTER, and those staying had bargains galore. It was a buyers' market. Soon one could see the ayis wearing new to them clothing and carrying pots, woks, and flatware back to Baishantan.

By the end of the week, the atmosphere had changed dramatically. Teaching was over. Studying was over. The exams were over. The packing was done. The good-byes were all said, but the learning continued.

It was Hudson and Jo's final day in China. While waiting for the taxi to take them to the Shanwan airport and then on to Canada, Jo looked out of the restaurant window across the road and saw a group of graduating students at the school's fence on one side and a group of poorly dressed Baishantan *ren*–local farmers and fishers–on the other. "Hudson, look at this." The two Canadians were watching love in action. The boys, no longer needing the school blazer or pants, were giving them to the locals. The farmers and fishers, eager to wear their new threads, started changing into the garments either to test the fit or to transform their status.

Hudson stepped outside and asked one of his students, Robert, why they were doing this. Robert said, "Mr. Smith, we are following your class rule. 'Treat others the way you want to be treated.' These people need the clothes and we don't."

Hudson's eyes started to moisten and to hide the fact gave an arm pump, and went back inside. When he told Jo, they both began to tear up. Success wasn't about teaching grammar or how to write a story or even how to logically debate a position. Success was about impacting people for life so that they were better after having met you.

The pair took their backpacks and suitcases with them across the road to meet their cab ride to the airport. An old man, wrinkled beyond belief and wearing military eye goggles, was riding Hudson's recently sold Dayun 125 down the boulevard doubling his wife clad in a neon pink scarf while each proudly wore a C.H.I.P.S. blazer with the beaver insignia. He just missed Hudson and Jo, and the old cyclist's wife, her hair trying to free itself from the restraining scarf, let out what was either a reprimand or a squeal of delight as they raced towards the White Mountain Beach. Jo laughed at the near miss, at the crisp new uniforms, and at the eye goggles' new owners. Ah, China, she thought.

Entering the cab, Hudson and Jo looked back at the school. It had been Jo's professional home for five years, and Hudson's for one.

The community had brought new growth to each of them. Friends were made and lost. Love grew here–love for China, love for their students and colleagues, love for each other. They had taught the future leaders of China, and they too had been educated. What a privilege. What an opportunity to influence the largest population on earth.

A magpie floated by, riding the thermals of the hazy, blue sky. It sailed past the gates, avoided a black plastic bag also riding the currents between the buildings, and rested just above the library's entry with its larger-than-life poster of the Chinese and Canadian administration teams. It was a poster soon to be replaced. Shimmering in the filtered sunbeams, the three flags acted as sentinels. They were the focal point of every Monday morning. They symbolized the bridging of the two cultures, but they had been so much more Hudson thought. One spoke of revolution and repression. One showed the future way to intellectual freedom to the ambitious youth of the Middle Kingdom. The third, newly replaced, would remind them of their youth and their adventures. The three flags unfurled, were flying high above the courtyard, declaring a peaceful, harmonious society at C.H.I.P.S. in China.

Acknowledgements

A community raises a child, and really this novel is my child, and I gratefully acknowledge the community that has helped me raise it. Carrie Jo Williams, my wife and best friend, was also my primary reader, editor, Queen of the Comma, encourager and critic. Every word was read aloud to her, every word was read by her–sometimes many times. She is the best. I love you C-Girl.

Craig, Steve, and Trent also helped out with editing. You have helped to shape my thoughts and ideas. This all takes time–the most precious thing we have–and I appreciate it. Craig also arranged for the Chinese artist, Hu Si Lun, whose painting adorns the cover.

Adrian (aka Rudy Kong), meticulous editor, helped me with publishing as the founder of Bing Long Books. his skills made this work infinitely better. Thanks, Adrian. Tom, my best man, helped with the printing process and was the definitive resource when I had questions of an avian nature. Also, thank you Michelle for your insight into prom and Darren for your historical perspective. Blake, thanks for your photography of the cover.

The expats of the People's Republic of China provided insights, stories, and encouragement. The Canadian teachers were wonderful colleagues during my time in China. They were a community that shared resources, ideas, travel, meals, laughter, worship, and love. To them I am grateful.

Dr. Greg Wetterstrand at the University of British Columbia–Okanagan was my faculty advisor during the master's project. His favourable reception to the idea of a novel as my project blessed me, and his comments on the work were insightful and invaluable.

The people of the People's Republic, but especially Kang Wen, Bella, Wang Ping, Ding lao shi, Liu lao shi, Lulu Mao and Elaine, who showed their patriotism, friendship, kindness, and love to me during my stay–thank you. You welcomed this foreigner, put up with his bad pronunciations, and assisted him in so many ways.

Thanks to Peter who helped me with arranging for a translator, David, and he also translated some difficult concepts for me.

The students I have had the pleasure of teaching and learning from in China, to you I say, "*Xie xie*–thank you." Gentlemen, you are the future leaders of your nation–make a difference, be fully alive, and remember our one classroom rule.

C.H.I.P.S. IN CHINA: Sources

"76. Fog. Carl Sandburg. Modern American Poetry." *Bartleby.com: Great Books Online -- Quotes, Poems, Novels, Classics and hundreds more.* N.p., n.d. Web. 21 Apr. 2010. <http://www.bartleby.com/104/76.html>.

Beeke, Tom. *The Birds of Dalian.* Vancouver: Bing Long Books, 2010. Print.

Chang, Jung, and Jon Halliday. *Mao: The Unknown Story.* London: Vintage, 2006. Print.

Chen, Xuejian. *Travel Around China.* Hong Kong: Harper Collins, 2008. Print.

Dai, Sijie. *Balzac and the Little Chinese Seamstress.* New York: Anchor, 2002. Print.

Gifford, Rob. *China Road: A Journey into the Future of a Rising Power.* New York: Random House, 2008. Print.

Giskin, Howard. *Chinese Folktales.* Dalian: N/A, 2001. Print.

Hessler, Peter. *River Town.* London: John Murray, 2002. Print.

Hucker, Charles O.. *China to 1850: A Short History.* Stanford: Stanford University Press, 1978. Print.

Kong, Rudy. *Dragons, Donkeys, and Dust.* Vancouver: Bing Long Books, 2010. Print.

Li, Cunxin. *Mao's Last Dancer.* Toronto: Berkeley, 2005. Print.

Liu, Po-chen, and Lewis Robinson. *Ancient China's Poets.* Hong Kong: Commercial Press, 1981. Print.

Orwell, George. *1984.* Toronto: Penguin, 1984. Print.

Roberts, David . "WILFRED OWEN - DULCE ET DECORUM EST, Text of poem and notes." *WAR POEMS AND POETS OF TODAY AND THE FIRST WORLD WAR.* N.p., n.d. Web. 23 Apr. 2010. <http://www.warpoetry.co.uk/owen1.html>.

Snow, Don. *Sheng cun Han yu.* Di 1 ban. ed. Beijing: Shang wu yin shu guan, 2002. Print.

Sun, Tzu. *The Art of War.* London: Oxford University Press, 1963. Print.

Thompson, Hugh, and Kathryn Lane. *Eyewitness Travel: China.* London: Dorling Kindersley, 2008. Print.

Traveler's guide to Dalian. S.l.: China Tourism Publishing House, 2007. Print.

Wang, Gang. *English.* Toronto: Penguin, 2009. Print.

Winchester, Simon. *The Man Who Loved China.* New York: Harper Collins, 2008. Print.

Wong, Jan. *Beijing Confidential: A Tale of Comrades Lost and Found.* Toronto: Doubleday, 2007. Print.

Wu, Yuan. *An Idiom a Day: Illustrated Stories of Chinese Sayings.* Singapore: Marshall Cavendish, 2005. Print.

Ye, Ting-Xing. *A Leaf in the Bitter Wind: A Memoir.* Toronto: Doubleday, 1998. Print.

Yuan, Boping, and Church Sally K.. *Oxford Chinese Beginner's Dictionary.* Toronto: Oxford University Press, 2006. Print.

About the author

An English teacher, runner, hiker, coach, sports nut, avid reader, film fan, crossword lover and gardener–Jim Williams is married to Carrie and has three adult children. Jim grew up on Vancouver Island, in British Columbia, Canada where he learned that only one rule is necessary in the class and in life. He has taught at every grade level (except kindergarten), for a quarter century in both independent and public schools in British Columbia, Canada, and in The People's Republic of China. Faith in Jesus guides his life journey. He loves to travel, and he thinks it is truly the best metaphor for our existence. *C.H.I.P.S. in China* is his first novel.

Bing Long Books is an independent Canadian publisher of important literary and other work by, and of interest to, the Canadian expatriate community. China and Asia are of particular interest to many of our authors.

Visit us at **www.binglongbooks.com**

For comments, suggestions, questions, or orders email:

info@binglongbooks.com

Contemporary titles from Bing Long Books:

Dragons, donkeys, and dust: Memoirs from a decade in China, by Rudy Kong

The Birds of Dalian, by Tom Beeke

Titles from the Marco Polo Series:

Among the Tibetans, by Isabella Bird

A Wayfarer in China, by Elizabeth Kendall

Peking Dust, by Ellen LaMotte

Titles from Bing Long Kids:

Crazy Colours, by Brandy Lovell

Normal Am I, by Rudy Kong